A Date
You Can't
Refuse

A Date
You Can't
Refuse

HARLEY JANE KOZAK

BROADWAY BOOKS
NEW YORK

Copyright © 2009 by Harley Jane Kozak

All Rights Reserved

Published in the United States by Broadway Books, an imprint of
The Doubleday Publishing Group, a division of Random House, Inc., New York.
www.broadwaybooks.com

BROADWAY BOOKS and its logo, a letter B bisected on the diagonal,
are trademarks of Random House, Inc.

Book design by Caroline Cunningham

Library of Congress Cataloging-in-Publication Data
Kozak, Harley Jane, 1957–
A date you can't refuse / Harley Jane Kozak. — 1st ed.
   p. cm.
1. Shelley, Wollie (Fictitious character)—Fiction. 2. Women artists—Fiction.
3. Commercial artists—Fiction. 4. Greeting cards industry—Fiction. 5. Dating
(Social customs)—Fiction. 6. Los Angeles (Calif.)—Fiction. I. Title.
PS3611.O75D34 2009
813'.6—dc22
2008028888

ISBN 978-0-7679-2422-1

PRINTED IN THE UNITED STATES OF AMERICA

10 9 8 7 6 5 4 3 2 1

First Edition

For Mary Kozak Coen

Big sister, tough cookie, pilgrim soul

". . . you must be generous to double agents."

—Sun Tzu, *The Art of War*

ONE

"Members of the jury, have you reached a verdict?"

When Judge Roberto Cohen spoke, the fate of Western civilization hung in the balance. Or so it seemed. Judge Cohen had a voice like Moses must've had, resonant with significance and authority. He pushed his bifocals up his nose and stared at us.

In the back row of the jury box, Mimi, the foreperson, stood and spoke in little more than a whisper. "We have, Your Highness." She stopped, stricken. "Your *Honor*, I mean."

To my left, Jeremy, juror number eight, snorted.

I laughed. The last thing I wanted was to incur the wrath of Moses of Santa Monica, but I have no defenses against snorts. I struggled with my laughter, trapped it in my nose, and by some physiological fortuity turned it into a sneeze. That got Jeremy snorting again. To my right, Romaine, juror number six, handed me a Kleenex.

Across the room, the defendant smiled at me.

Pretty confident, I thought, smiling at a moment like this. I looked away from him, back toward the judge.

Judge Cohen's stare was fixed on me, his eyebrows going up and down as he played with his hearing aid. I'd seen a lot of eyebrow displeasure from him, but had never before provoked it. I clapped a hand over my nose and mouth as if fending off an allergy attack.

Judge Cohen motioned to the bailiff. The bailiff brought him the verdict.

At the plaintiff's table, Miss Lemon was breathing too fast, her substantial chest heaving precipitously. She should've brought a paper bag to breathe into, I thought. Her lawyer should've brought her one, knowing Miss Lemon's propensity for drama, but he was oblivious, making notes on a yellow legal pad.

Judge Cohen handed the verdict back to the bailiff. His face gave away nothing.

At the defense table, the lawyer kept his eyes on Judge Cohen.

The defendant kept his eyes on me.

Why? I wasn't the prettiest woman on the jury—that would be Taylor—nor the best dressed (Louise), or the youngest (Taylor again). I was the tallest, and I took the most entertaining notes, filling my court-issued steno pad with cartoons, but that was my claim to juror fame. So why had the defendant, Mr. Milos, taken to staring at me the last few days? His family, too, in the row behind him? It wasn't just unnerving, it was embarrassing, and more than one juror had teased me about it during deliberations.

"Madam Foreperson," Judge Cohen said, "you may read the verdict. Loudly."

Mimi cleared her throat. "In the matter of *Lucille Lemon versus MediasRex Enterprises* and Yuri Milos, we find in favor of the defendant."

Mr. Milos reached over and smothered his lawyer in a bear hug. He did the same for his lawyer's flustered associate. Then he turned to his family and raised his fist in a victory salute. When told by the judge to contain himself, he sat and flashed a "drinks are on me" grin at the jury box.

"Mr. Berkita, do you wish to poll the jury?" the judge asked.

The plaintiff's lawyer rose, weary with defeat. "Yes, Your Honor."

"Jurors will answer yes or no to the following question," the judge said. "Did you find that the defendant, Mr. Milos, or his organization, MediasRex Enterprises, was substantially responsible for the injuries suffered by Miss Lemon on February fourteenth of last year. Juror number one?"

"No."

"Juror number two?"

"Yes."

The final count was ten to two in favor of the defendant, more than enough in a civil case. Once the polling was over, Judge Cohen took off his glasses and relaxed.

"I'd like to commend both sides," he said, "for conducting themselves in a civilized manner. The jury, too, behaved laudably, once we ironed out the cell phone problems. Juror number eight, my clerk will return yours now. I expect the battery is dead." He motioned to a motherly-looking woman to his right, who rummaged around in a desk drawer. "Members of the jury, I now lift my admonition. You may talk about this case with anyone you wish. You are also welcome to flee the building and erase the trial from your memory. That's it. Until your next jury summons, the State of California thanks you for your service and this matter is now concluded."

We stood and filed out like a class of third graders on the last day of school. I glanced over to see Jeremy being handed his cell phone, which prompted me to turn on my own, which distracted me enough that I didn't notice who was holding the swinging door for me until I was brushing against him.

"Juror number seven," a husky voice said. "Thank you."

I looked into the face of the defendant. "No problem," I said. His eyes, up close, were the color of sage. "Uh . . . congratulations."

"May I have a word with you?" he asked.

"Well, okay, but I actually have to—"

"Please." He took my arm, leading me out to the hallway, and whispered into my ear. "You see, I have a rather big crush on you. And an offer I think you'll like."

TWO

The thing about Yuri Milos was that he was very attractive. He wasn't particularly handsome, but he dripped confidence, as though total baldness, medium height, and a cleft chin were the most desirable attributes a man could have. I found him sexy. I'd found him sexy from fifteen feet away, the distance from the jury box to the defense table, but now I was up close, face-to-face with him and my own discomfort.

I didn't want to find him sexy. For one thing, he was too wealthy. His cuffs were monogrammed and he wore a huge gold watch and drove a black Porsche—I'd seen it in the parking lot. Secondly, he was too virile. I pictured him chopping firewood bare-chested or shoeing horses or one of those Middle Ages activities—he'd look at home in another century, wielding a scimitar. Also, he was a little old, old enough to be my father if he'd started young, and I imagined he had. He had eyes that crinkled at the edges, eyes filled with innuendo, eyes that saw it all and found most of it amusing. He'd even looked at Miss Lemon with warmth, all through the trial, as though she'd been wooing him rather than suing him.

"So will you talk to me, juror number seven?" he asked, his hand on my arm.

"Mr. Milos, I'm, uh—at the moment—" I tripped over my words, which annoyed me.

"Married?"

"No, headed for the bathroom, actually, but—"

"You're not married?"

"No, but I'm—in a relationship. Of sorts."

"What sort?" There was that smile again. Good teeth. Good skin. Tan, but not cancerously so. Even his bald pate was golden, suggesting yachting.

A woman pulled him into an embrace. She was his age, fifties or sixties, I guessed, but so well preserved it was hard to be sure. She was also quite beautiful. "Yuri, good job." She turned to me and held out a hand. "Hello, I'm Yuri's second wife. Donatella Milos."

"Juror number seven," I said, shaking her hand. "Wollie Shelley."

"Very impressive. How many centimeters are you?"

"Centimeters?" The metric system, I'm sorry to say, eludes me. "No idea," I said.

"What size shoe?"

As I pondered why a complete stranger was interested in my admittedly large feet, my phone rang. I was glad for the interruption, until I answered it.

"Miss Shelley? Mrs. Winterbottom at Haven Lane, in Santa Barb—"

"What's P.B. done?" I said quickly. "Is he taking his meds?"

"Of course. We insist on that. But your brother pays no mind to curfew, and last night he stayed out the whole night. This is a halfway house, not the Marriott, Miss Shelley. I'm afraid I'm going to have to report him to the Board of—"

"No! Please, not the Board of—"

"—Directors. Yes. I keep telling P.B. we have a long waiting list for his room, from service recipients who are far, far—"

"—wealthier, I know, and—"

"—more *appreciative* of Haven Lane, I was going to say, and your brother—"

"Mrs. Winterbottom, if I had it, I would pay you suitcases full of money—my brother really likes living there, which, for him—"

"Well, we can't simply—just a moment, please—I'm sorry, I see one of the service recipients has neglected to wear her shirt this morning. Your brother isn't the only mischief-maker. Miss Shelley, I must go." And with that, Mrs. Winterbottom hung up.

I hung up too and closed my eyes, offering a silent prayer to the patron saint of mental illness, if there was one. I opened my eyes and dialed my brother's room at Haven Lane. Voice mail picked up.

Mr. Milos, I saw, was returning the embrace of a much younger woman. She was beautiful, with long, blond, Barbie-straight hair. A daughter, I'd guessed, when I'd seen her in the courtroom watching the trial. I ended my call and began to sidle down the hall toward the exit, but Yuri saw me and flagged me down like I was a taxi.

"Miss Shelley," he said, pulling me back into the family circle, "this is Kimberly."

"Yuri's third wife," Donatella said.

"Oh," I said. "How many of you are there?"

"Just one of me," Kimberly said, shaking my hand. "I'm the current wife."

"The first one died," Donatella added. "Yuri, when do we start?"

"I haven't had a chance to ask her," Yuri said. "If you'll give us a few minutes alone, you'll both get your turn."

But Yuri was then taken aside by his lawyer just as Jeremy pulled me over to join the jurors who were exchanging phone numbers. Half of us wanted to stay in touch, bonded by three weeks of a common experience and the injunction not to discuss it. And Jeremy, attracted to the doodles I'd done on my juror's steno pad, was bugging me to illustrate a comic book he was writing. I was resisting, on the grounds that I had no interest in superheroines, and that I needed to actually get paid for my work. After handing out seven business cards to fellow jurors, I headed to the ladies' room. When I came out, Yuri Milos was waiting.

"Come, please," he said, and opened a door to a storage room.

"Mr. Milos," I said. "I'm guessing you want to offer me some kind of—"

"We are not in trial anymore," he said, standing in the doorway with me, "so you must not call me Mr. Milos, but Yuri, and I will not call you juror number seven but Miss Shelley. Agreed?"

I sighed. "Oh heck, call me Wollie."

His smile grew. Point scored. "Wollie. Such a distinctive name. A diminutive of Wollstonecraft."

"How did you know that?"

"I was in the courtroom for jury selection."

"Oh. Right." Since he wasn't a criminal defendant, he'd been able to come and go as he pleased during the trial. Mostly he'd been there.

"You are a graphic artist by profession," he said. "You live in the Valley, and you have no biases that would interfere with rendering an impartial verdict, as far as you know. You are single. You did not mention a significant other to the judge, which was one of the jury questions, but you allude to one now." He looked at me pointedly.

I returned his look. "Mr. Mil—Yuri. What is it you want from me?"

"I want your talents. Your very specific qualifications."

"Which ones?"

"I have a business."

"I know. I was in the courtroom too. I know more about you than you do about me."

"I doubt it." He looked at me appraisingly, but I didn't rise to the bait.

"I have no talents," I said, "that could be used by your company, unless you want me to redesign the MediasRex logo or paint you a sign. Or I could do a mural. Maybe all the celebrities you've represented, holding hands. Standing on a globe. But what I really do is greeting cards. Do you need greeting cards?"

"What I need is you. Do you always undervalue yourself like this?"

"I don't know what you mean."

"You starred in a show called *SoapDirt*, yes? Also *Biological Clock*."

"I wouldn't say 'starred in,' but yes, I did a few episodes of a cheesy reality show and an equally cheesy talk show, which—"

"*SoapDirt* is a large hit in Belarus."

"You're kidding."

"I'm not. Belarus, Moldova, and Slovakia. And Ukraine." He smiled at what must have been a look of horror on my face. "Your soap operas are quite popular in that part of the world. To my friends, you are a celebrity. More interesting to me is your facility for dating."

"I have no facility for dating. What I've had is a series of odd jobs that involved dating, none of which I was particularly good at. What I am good at, apparently, is being single and needing the extra money that these odd jobs—"

"If money is what inspires you, let us begin with salary."

"Money does not inspire me. But landlords require it, as do grocery stores, so—"

"Yes, your living situation is not ideal. I am prepared to take care of that too."

I didn't ask how he knew about my living situation. Addresses weren't hard to come by and mine said it all. The Oakwood Garden Apartments was a complex that rented furnished or unfurnished units by the month, handy for people in transition, like actors during pilot season and men in the throes of divorce. This made for interesting, intense neighbors.

"Yuri, my living situation's fine, I'm not desperate for money, I'm not the person you're looking for, so . . ." I waited for him to cut me off and argue the point, but he was just looking calmly at me. "So," I continued, "nice meeting you."

"Do I scare you?" he asked.

"Why would you scare me?"

"Simple curiosity would dictate hearing my offer. Unless curiosity is overridden by fear."

Who likes to be called chicken? "Okay," I said. "Shoot."

He took two chairs, one in each hand, and set them facing one another. Closer than I'd have set them. He gestured to one. I sat.

"So," he said, sitting too. "Tell me your impression of my organization."

"MediasRex. Media training. You take people who are suddenly famous and unprepared for it and you teach them how not to make a fool out of themselves on *Oprah*."

He smiled. "I would describe it a little differently."

"How would you describe it?"

He turned his chair so he was straddling it, then leaned in. His shirt was black and purple, striped, with a blue tie. It was a color combination that should not have worked, but did. "I change the world," he said, "six or seven people at a time. Most from Europe. In three months they are comfortable with American culture and its media machine. They come as a baseball phenomenon from Madrid or a diplomat's daughter from Macedonia, and they leave as players, with an impact beyond their profession or the borders of their country. My business is transformation. You spoke flippantly, but consider: what would it take to get a shy person on *Oprah*?"

For me, it would take a miracle. "Okay. But I'm not in the transformation business."

He smiled. "I can change that."

"So you'd teach me to transform people? Or you'd transform me?"

"Both. You cannot teach what you don't know. And is your life so perfect? Nothing you wouldn't alter?"

"No," I said. "I mean, I'd like thicker hair. And it would be nice if a few personal relationships were less . . . complicated, but I don't ever want to be on TV again, and—"

"You won't be. I want you on my staff. We are not the celebrities. We are the power behind the celebrities."

I looked at my watch. "I've heard your offer. But I'm not what you're looking for. I mean, I don't know what you're looking for, exactly, but I'm not it. Thanks, Yuri. If you could show me how to widen the market for my greeting cards, that's something I'd go for."

"Too easy. With fifty thousand dollars you can figure that out for yourself."

"Fifty thousand dollars?" I asked.

"For three months' work. Not a fortune, but we'll take care of living expenses."

"You want to pay me fifty grand?"

He nodded.

I gulped. He was right—fifty thousand wasn't a fortune, not in L.A., but to me it was close enough. Still, I shook my head. "This isn't what I do or aspire to do, so . . . thanks, but I think I'll just get on with my life."

Yuri continued to study me. "Anything you truly aspire to, I can help you achieve."

Marriage? Motherhood? Doubtful. I stood. "I can't imagine how I'd explain to my boyfriend that I'm . . ."

"That you're . . . ?" He stayed seated, gazing up at me.

"Okay, what is it you're asking me to do?"

"Join my team. You will be what we call a social coach. A dating surrogate."

"An escort."

He laughed. He had an appealing laugh, one that made you feel special for having evoked it. "An escort is something else, I think. No. Neither are you any kind of sex therapist. You are a native Angeleno, born in Burbank, and so you will show them L.A., be Virgil to their Dante, as you teach them the American way of dating."

"Only the men?"

"For the women we have your counterpart, the male social coach."

"But I wouldn't be expected to sleep with these men?"

He smiled. "Emphatically not. That should reassure your boyfriend."

I doubted this. My boyfriend was a guy who would find nothing reassuring about Yuri Milos. Like Yuri, Simon Alexander was an alpha male.

Simon was also an FBI agent. At the moment, he was working a case that precluded our seeing each other openly. I wasn't able to know exactly why we couldn't see each other openly, only that it had to do with a mink-wearing woman that he was dating. Forced to date, I liked to think of it. I wondered if Simon had ever asked anyone at the FBI a question like I'd just asked, whether he'd be expected to sleep with this woman. I tried to imagine his supervisor saying, "Emphatically not." I failed.

"Yuri, this is all most intriguing—if weird—but I'm still saying no."

He stood abruptly. "And I'm giving you my card. Go home. Look at your life. See what is missing. Whatever it is, I can provide it or help you attain it or show you how to live well without it. This is my promise to you. You come and work for me, you become my family, and that is something I take seriously."

"I kind of like my life," I said, and he cocked an eyebrow. *Wrong answer,* it said. I should have cried, "My life is magnificent! Overflowing with miracles!" but oh, well. He opened the door for me and I squeezed by, aware of the magnetic field around him.

I nearly collided with a woman coming out of the ladies' room. Miss Lemon. I maneuvered myself so that I could hold the door for her, out of the way of her crutches. She thanked me, then recognized me. "You! You're one of the ones that didn't vote for me."

"You're right, I didn't. I'm sorry, I—"

"And you!" She'd caught sight of Yuri behind me. "You . . . creep. We're gonna appeal. We're gonna get a better jury. You can't do that in America, run over people. Why don't you all go back to Czechoslovakia, you and all those clients?"

"Slovakia, Miss Lemon," he said. "Or the Czech Republic. There is no Czechoslovakia, not since 1992. In any case, I come from Belarus."

I eased my way around Miss Lemon and left them to their geopolitical discussion. In the third-floor jury room I turned in my juror ID, donated my fifteen bucks a day to some charity that needed the money even more than I did, then returned to the first floor and phoned my brother again. This time, he answered.

"P.B., what'd you do last night?" I asked. "Mrs. Winterbottom said—"

"I went to the beach," he said. "I slept in the sand."

"Why?"

"I'm doing research," he said.

"What kind of research?"

"String theory."

I was now walking past the metal detector, stepping outside to the kind of fabulous spring day that Santa Monica has pretty much year-round. "P.B., that's fine, but you have to adapt your research methods to the house rules. Factor in curfew. Mrs. Winterbottom will kick you out if you don't. I'm serious. Then what will we do?"

"Nothing. It won't happen," he said. "This is my home. I have to nap now."

He hung up and I dropped my phone into my purse, feeling sick. P.B. was two stops away from homelessness. If he got kicked out of Haven Lane, he wouldn't bother taking his medication, which would bring on delusional behavior and then he'd be sleeping on the sand out of necessity. This was my most-recurring nightmare.

"Wollie. Wollie Shelley."

I turned to see a conservatively dressed man at the end of the sidewalk. There was something mildly familiar about him. "Hello—do I know you?"

"Bennett," he said, and shook my hand. "Graham. We met once before. I'm with the Federal Bureau of Investigation."

THREE

My first thought was that Simon was in some kind of trouble, but then I realized that if he were, the FBI would hardly come and tell me about it.

And then I recognized the guy.

It had been six months since I'd met him, for a few minutes one autumn night. He was aggressively normal looking, middle-aged, average height, medium brown hair. The only memorable thing about him was his authoritative air; he was a man accustomed to command. He outranked Simon. I remembered that too, because he and Simon had argued that autumn night, and Simon had lost. That didn't happen often.

"Let me walk you to your car," he said. He set the pace, neither slow nor fast, but without hesitation, as if he knew exactly where I was parked. In fact, I hadn't planned on going to my car. I was headed on foot to meet two friends for lunch at the Santa Monica farmers' market, but I didn't feel a need to mention this to—

"I'm sorry." I said. "What did you say your name was?"

"Graham," he said. "Bennett."

Did that mean Graham Bennett or Graham, comma, Bennett? I was about to ask, but he spoke first. "You reached a verdict in your case."

"Yes, we found in favor of the defendant."

He nodded, as if this didn't come as news. "We've been waiting ten days. We didn't want to contact you until the case was over."

"The FBI has an interest in *Lemon v. Milos*?" I said.

"Not in Lemon. Milos. Wait." He stopped. I did too. I looked around, wondering what the problem was, then saw, far ahead of us, a black Porsche pulling away from the exit gate to make a right on Civic Center Way. When it disappeared from view, he motioned for me to continue walking. "Yuri Milos is going to offer you a job."

This was old news, I could've told him. "How do you know?"

"That's not relevant to this conversation."

"What are you doing, tapping his phones?"

Silence. Yes, I decided, they're tapping his phones. A motorcycle approached and Graham/Bennett put up a hand, claiming the right-of-way for us. "We've been watching Milos in recent weeks, but he's cautious. His people are either well-trained or in the dark about his activities."

"Which are what?" I asked.

"Nothing that need concern you at the moment."

"Why should any of it concern me?"

He looked at me. "I need you."

He was not speaking romantically. I couldn't imagine Graham/Bennett speaking romantically even in the dark, stark naked, after a bottle of wine. "For . . . ?"

"I need you to work for Yuri Milos."

This time I stopped, alongside an SUV covered in Lakers bumper stickers. "I can't."

"Yes, you can. The job description isn't particularly onerous."

"I don't mean work for Yuri Milos, I mean work for you. That's what you're asking, isn't it?"

He nodded toward the east end of the parking lot, getting us moving again. "We haven't been able to get a break in this case. But over time, people get careless, or we get lucky. This time it was luck. Recently, we heard Milos mention you. His son recognized you in the courtroom. One of my people remembered that you'd done us a favor last year. I believe we called you Kermit."

"Not to my face," I said. "Look, that was a sort of misunderstanding. I wasn't actually working for the FBI, I just thought I was and then it turned out—"

"It turned out well. I was there."

"It was the worst night of my life," I said. "Or at least in the top five."

It was clear from his look that Graham Bennett or Bennett Graham had limited interest in what constituted a bad night for Wollie Shelley. "I've been trying to place one of my people on Milos's staff," he said. "Unsuccessfully. He's a micromanager; even the domestics are known to him personally, down to the crew putting in a new pool. This is the first opening and he thinks you're a perfect fit. Would I prefer you to be an agent? Yes. But I'm not likely to get this kind of opportunity again."

"Yes, I appreciate that this is a great opportunity for you, Mr.—"

"And for you too. There are advantages to working with us."

This stopped me. "What advantages?"

"Is that a yes?"

"No."

"Why not?"

I stopped again by another parked car, this one a Ford pickup covered with American flag bumper stickers. "I would naturally love to serve my country, but I'm more of a jury duty type. Or Get Out the Vote type. Working the phone banks at telethons, knitting socks for soldiers. I'm not an action-adventure sort of person—"

"That's not my understanding."

"Excuse me?"

"Aren't you illustrating an action hero comic book?"

I stared. Jeremy's proposed project. "No, I—how do you know about that?"

He looked at me blandly. "It would save us time if you could avoid asking that question repeatedly. I'm in the business of information. These aren't parlor tricks."

"Okay, but—"

"Since you don't yet have a contract for this comic book project, it's not income-producing. Nor is your greeting card business giving you a living wage."

"Yes, thank you for pointing that out."

"You need a job. Have you any other prospects?"

"No. Work for some Belarusian entrepreneur with three wives and become a secret agent for you. That's it."

"Cooperating witness."

"Yes. CW," I said. "That's right. It's all coming back to me now. Look, I'd rather sling hash or work retail for minimum wage and here's why: I have no physical courage. I'm not athletic, I can't lie well or keep secrets, I'm not especially curious, I don't even slow down to watch traffic accidents. And I wasn't a Girl Scout, so I can't change a tire or do Morse code. I have none of the traits you look for in your spies—"

"Cooperating witness. Your duties for us would require little risk or ingenuity. You would simply overhear conversations. Note family dynamics. Look around the property. You may not have an appetite for this work, Miss Shelley, but you do have a brother."

That got my attention. "Yeah? So?"

"Living in a facility that's subsidized by federal funds. I don't imagine it's easy, coming up with the monthly fees that keep Percy at the facility."

His use of my brother's name startled me. Then chilled me. "No, it's not," I said. And I was nearly the sole support of my brother. Our Uncle Theo helped too, but aging wallpaperers aren't rolling in money.

"Milos is generous to his employees. Your salary would be substantial."

"That's a reason to work for Milos," I said, "but not to work for you."

His eyes narrowed. Graham/Bennett wasn't a man who liked insubordination, even from nonsubordinates. "Then I'll give you a better one. Your brother can be unpredictable and intractable."

"Many paranoid schizophrenics—"

"He's been arrested."

"But he's never been convicted of anything. He has bad karma with police, and—"

"Haven Lane has very high standards of acceptable behavior, and I doubt your brother can toe the line over the long haul. It would be useful, wouldn't it, to have a friend on the Santa Barbara City Council? Or to know a local judge? A word from someone like that would carry weight with the board of directors at Haven Lane. Have you friends like those?"

No, Uncle Theo and I had no influential friends. Ours were normal friends, the kind who would invite you over for beer or donate a kidney, but not the kind who could fix a parking ticket or an election. "So you're saying that P.B. would get to stay at Haven Lane, that you'd pull strings to make that happen."

"It's possible," he said.

"No. I want certainty. I need your word."

His eyes narrowed.

"And also," I said, plunging onward, "assuming you promise to help my brother, it can't be contingent on me doing a bang-up job for you, because as I mentioned, I haven't any aptitude for this stuff."

"That's not what I heard from Simon Alexander."

I did a double take. "This was Simon's idea?"

He gave me a searching look. "No one outside the case knows I'm asking you to work for us. Agent Alexander in particular could have a negative response."

This was a massive understatement.

"Given your history," he added. Simon and I had met when I'd inadvertently waltzed into the middle of an investigation, and it hadn't been pretty. "I understand that you and Alexander became—enmeshed—some months ago."

"Enmeshed. Is that the federal government's term for . . . dating?" I asked.

"It's what can happen when an agent recruits a cooperating witness, exposes them to danger, and feels a heightened sense of responsibility for their well-being."

As opposed to True Love, which is what I liked to think was going on with Simon and me. Either way, Bennett/Graham seemed to think of this in the past tense. "And you don't want him getting re-enmeshed."

"There's no policy on it."

Maybe not, but I was right. My romance with Simon didn't have company endorsement. Its covert nature had allowed me to get on *Lemon v. Milos* in the first place. Number eleven on the juror questionnaire was,

Do you know anyone in law enforcement? I'd told the judge I knew some cops and had once dated an FBI agent. When the judge asked if I was still dating him, I said no. Which was technically correct. Simon and I hadn't dated for some time, if by "dating" one meant dinner and a movie or even holding hands at Costco. Simon and I did have sex, but Judge Cohen hadn't asked me about that.

"Let's go back to my brother," I said. "If I decline the opportunity to work for you, will that jeopardize his future at Haven Lane?"

"I'm not a fortune-teller, Miss Shelley."

This wasn't the unequivocal no I was looking for.

"However," he continued, "I can tell you that it's better to have me and the resources of my agency working on your brother's behalf than to have us . . . indifferent to his future."

I looked into his expressionless eyes. "That sounds . . . threatening."

He said nothing.

I made a decision, one I would probably regret. "Okay, I'm in. But, Mr. Bennett—"

"Graham."

"Okay, Graham. How do I—"

"Mr. Graham."

"Oh." No first-name basis for us, then.

"I'll initiate our contacts at the beginning," he said. "You'll be given a number to call if problems arise, but for now, we simply wait for Milos to approach you."

"That just happened. A half hour ago."

He looked surprised, then stern. "You didn't mention this at the outset because . . . ?"

"Because I wasn't working for you then. I'm trying to be less self-disclosing with strangers."

"Is there now anything else you'd like to set the record straight on?"

Like the fact that I'm sleeping with one of your colleagues? I thought. "No."

"Good. Let's clarify something. No one is to know that you're working for me. This can't be overstated. No one. Not your uncle, not your brother, not your dog, if you have one."

"I don't."

"I know. Any deviation from rule number one jeopardizes your safety and my case."

"I understand. Can you clarify how much danger I'm in?"

He didn't skip a beat. "As long as you follow instructions to the letter, none at all."

The thing was, I didn't believe him.

FOUR

The Santa Monica farmers' market was a cultural crossroads, hip couture meets country overalls, the appeal of produce bringing together people who had no other reason to rub elbows. I was reminded of how rural California was; it was easy to forget in the heart of L.A.

I found my friend Fredreeq picking out French green beans from a Bakersfield vendor. Fredreeq, who dresses for occasions, wore a yellow gingham dirndl skirt, a halter top, and a matching scarf, looking like Heidi might have looked on a warm day in the Swiss Alps, if Heidi had been sexy, and black, and a soccer mom.

"Hey! You're late," she said. "Don't you have to be back in half an hour?"

I hugged her. "I don't ever have to be back. We reached a verdict."

"Hallelujah. Watch it; don't bruise the apricots. So did you fry the guy?"

"It's rare to impose the death sentence for slip-and-fall cases."

"You spent three weeks of your life in a courtroom because someone slipped?"

"Well, the victim did dislocate her hip, requiring multiple surgeries and ongoing physical therapy for injuries sustained while exiting a vehicle in order to fend off the sexual advances of a Hungarian soccer player who was driving without a California license, here under the auspices of a media training company. A complex and compelling case."

"Ridiculous. Come on. Joey's over there."

Joey Rafferty stood out in a crowd because of her masses of wavy red hair. In baggy jeans and a flannel shirt, she looked like a farmer, albeit a wraithlike one.

"Rafferty!" Fredreeq called. We made our way over to a stand of spring greens. "Forget this rabbit food. You look peaked. Let's get you something fattening. There are good-looking nuts on Fourth Street."

"Hey, Wollie," Joey said, giving me a peck on the cheek. "You're late. We thought you'd been sequestered or something."

"No, trial's over. Sent him away for life without parole."

"Really?"

"No," I said. "But did you believe me, just for a minute?"

Joey shook her head. "Nope."

"This way," Fredreeq said, taking the lead. "Nuts ahead."

"Hey, let me ask you guys," I said. "Could I get better at lying? Is it something you're born with, or are there tricks that anyone can learn?"

"Anyone but you," Fredreeq said.

"No, there are tricks. You'll never pass a polygraph, but you could improve with practice." Joey produced a raw carrot from her purse, brushed dirt from it, and took a bite.

"Is that a Prada?" Fredreeq asked Joey. "Are you transporting root vegetables in a Prada?"

"No."

"Good."

"See what I did there?" Joey asked. "A simple, decisive 'no.' I didn't go into unnecessary details. I didn't say, 'No, this bag is not a Prada, it's a knockoff' or 'No, a carrot's not a root vegetable,' because either one is going to provoke further questions."

"So that was a lie?" I asked.

"Of course. But Fredreeq bought it. Not because it was plausible, but because my delivery was pretty good."

"You're right, I should've caught that. Low blood sugar." Fredreeq pulled an apricot from her plastic bag and took a bite. She offered me one. I shook my head.

"No pausing either. You can't stop to think," Joey said. "People who stop to think are usually inventing the answer."

"Wollie's not up to this," Fredreeq said. "She doesn't have the gene."

"Another thing," Joey said, "is don't second-guess yourself. Tell the lie, move on. People who tell the truth aren't critiquing in their head what they just said."

"I do," I said. "Sometimes."

"Then be someone else. You have to adopt the mind-set of, in this case, someone who is not transporting root vegetables in a Prada handbag. Change the subject if it's appropriate, but it can't look like you're changing the subject. It's gotta look like other things are more interesting." She stopped in her tracks. "Is that Maria Shriver?"

"Where?" I said.

She pointed. "By the baby bok choy."

I looked around. Fredreeq too. Then Fredreeq punched Joey's arm. "You're lying."

"Yes. Ouch."

"I've discovered that if something's technically true, even if misleading, I can say it," I said. "As in, did I eat the whole cheesecake by myself? No. I left two crumbs."

"Excellent," Joey said. "So, Wollie, how come you need to get better at lying?"

"Oh. You know. No, um, reason."

They just looked at me. Waiting. I could feel my face turn red. Not a promising start. My phone rang, saving me from further disgrace. "Hello?" I said.

"Wollie? Donatella Milos."

"Oh. Hello. How'd you get this number?"

"Juror number eight." Her accent was enchanting. "I told him I had a job to offer you. So, Wollie. Yuri tells me you have qualms about joining us. Tell me these qualms."

"You know what, Donatella? I've had a—an epiphany. I think I would like to come work for you."

"Excellent. Yuri will be pleased. You will start Monday. Come to the compound."

"Compound?"

"In Calabasas. I will give you the address. Have you a pencil and paper?"

As I rummaged around in my own purse—Payless rather than Prada—I realized Joey and Fredreeq were still staring. And listening. I was not going to get out of the farmers' market without spilling some beans.

Ten minutes later we were sitting at a café on the Third Street Promenade, eating our nuts. Donatella Milos, it turned out, was a woman of some renown. "The former Donatella Timmalini," Joey said. "From Italy, obviously, but studied at the Sorbonne. She came to the U.S. as a nobody, then settled in D.C., slept with a bunch of senators or congressmen, then moved to L.A. and married this guy Milos. What's his first name?"

"Yuri," I said.

"Yeah. She left him but kept his name, even after marrying Bernard Schluntz."

"The chef?" Fredreeq asked.

Joey nodded. "She redesigned his two restaurants and pushed him into marketing his Wiener schnitzel and getting it into Whole Foods."

"So, Wollie," Fredreeq said. "What's your part in this operation?"

"I'm on the media training team."

My friends stopped chewing and stared at me. Again.

"What?" I said. "What's wrong with that?"

"What kind of training will you do?" Joey asked.

"I assume I'm a behind-the-scenes person. I take the celebrities around L.A., show them—"

"Target?" Fredreeq said. "The car wash?"

"I don't know the details. They'll fill me in on Monday. The thing is, you guys, I do need a job. And it's quite a lot of money. For me."

Fredreeq cracked a pistachio shell with her teeth. "He's Eastern European?"

"Milos? Yes. Belarus. Bulgaria? One of those."

She nodded. "Get the money up front. In cash."

Joey was still looking at me with curiosity. "So, Joey," I said. "How come you know all this stuff about Donatella Milos?"

"She was on the political scene. She dated the state comptroller when she first got to town, and we were on fund-raising committees together. I didn't know her well, just to say hello."

"Nice job of changing the subject, Wollie," Fredreeq said. "Why don't you just tell us what the deal is, since we're going to find out anyway?"

"Because I can't."

"Does it have to do with Simon?" Joey asked.

"Um . . . mm . . . n-no."

"You're stuttering," Fredreeq said. "I think it has to do with Simon."

I shook my head, thought about it, then shook it again.

"Indirectly, at least," Joey said. "Is it connected to his work?"

"The FBI? Oh, please," Fredreeq said. "What would the feds want with Wollie?"

I choked on some cappuccino foam.

"I'll take that as a yes," Joey said.

"You might be right about this," Fredreeq said. "The last time she had to keep a secret, she was doing favors for the feds. Look, she's blushing." She pointed at me. "Tell me you're not doing some fed thing again, Wollie."

"Does Simon know about this?" Joey asked. "Because if he does, I have to seriously question his judgment."

Fredreeq nodded. "If he doesn't know about it now, he will soon enough. Look at her. She couldn't fool a parsnip. What are these government people thinking? They may as well recruit from a high school marching band."

I wanted to weep. Any hope I might pull off this operation, whatever it was, died on the vine. "Okay, I quit. I haven't even begun and already I know I can't do it. I can't tell you a thing about it, but I can tell you this: I'm going to fail."

"Damn, Fredreeq," Joey said. "Way to undermine her confidence."

"Okay, you're an actress," Fredreeq said. "Teach her to act her way through it."

Joey raised her eyebrows. "I don't know if I can take artistic theory and squeeze it into an infomercial."

"Try," I said.

"Okay." Joey pried open a pistachio nut. "If we had time, we'd go with Stanislavsky, who liked working from the inside out, as in 'how would I feel in Lady Macbeth's shoes?' and analyzing what Lady Macbeth wants, scene by scene, but that requires rehearsal and it's not what's needed here, is it? Here, you're writing Lady Macbeth's lines as you go, and—"

"Could we use an example other than Lady Macbeth?" I asked.

"Fine. For you, let's work from the outside in. Construct a character, okay? Give her a name. Dress like her, talk like her, act like her and as she sinks into your skin—"

"Like self-tanning moisturizers," Fredreeq said.

"—you'll find that you're feeling more like her and less like you. The longer you live in her costume, the more comfortable you get. It's more clown school than method acting. Put on a clown costume, you feel like a clown."

"Like you're possessed," Fredreeq said.

"For moments," Joey conceded. "Not all the time. That's called psychosis."

"Great," I said. "My life as a horror movie."

"No, as a graphic novel," Joey said. "Since you're a graphic artist. Yeah, that's the ticket. You need to create a superheroine, not a clown. A tough cookie."

I shook my head. "Everyone's into superheroines all of a sudden, but I have no affinity for them. I don't want an adventure. I don't think I can do this, you guys."

"You *can* do this," Fredreeq said. "The question is, should you? I vote no. It's Mercury retrograde, which is no time to sign contracts, and I do not like the sound of this job. Or these Russians. I'm old-school."

"Fredreeq," Joey said, "it's not like they'll use her for black ops, or wet work."

"What's wet work?" Fredreeq asked.

"What's black ops?" I asked.

"Covert operations. Wet work is killing people in a particularly bloody manner. I don't see you doing that. Anyway, whatever this is, given your qualms, you must have a good reason for taking it on."

I did. And it actually helped having a plan of sorts and two people who knew what I was up to, even though they really didn't. The comfort didn't last. It may have been an ocean breeze wandering a few blocks inland, but I was cold suddenly, and I found myself looking around, feeling as if someone was watching me.

FIVE

Calabasas is in the San Fernando Valley just off the 101 free-way. I passed it every week on my way to see my brother in Santa Barbara, but I'd never stopped there. It was, as far as I knew, a place where people lived, shopped, and sent their kids to school. Well-to-do people, for the most part. Unless you were one of them, or knew one of them, there was no reason to be in their neighborhood.

I took the Valley Circle exit, got lost, ended up at the Motion Picture & Television Country House and Hospital, where old movie people go to die, got directions, found Mulholland Highway, and kept driving, checking the roadside addresses, which were few and far between. It was like the Old West here, dusty and dry, brown earth, blue sky. The weather was hot, even for mid-May.

Until I reached Palomino Hills, a gated community. Brown gave way to green, with sprinklers going full blast. A high stone fence flanked a guardhouse. I pulled into the Visitors lane as a sparkling white Lincoln Continental whipped past me in the Residents lane.

What was I doing here? Gated communities made me anxious. If there was a gate or a fence or a velvet rope dividing people into groups, Insiders versus the Great Unwashed Masses, I knew which category I fell into.

"I'm visiting Donatella Milos," I said to the uniformed guard once he'd given a brisk wave to the Lincoln Continental. His expression, when he turned back to me, was studied neutrality. He was large and pasty-complected, and I glimpsed a holstered gun. It wasn't the kind of thing I had ever noticed in my life before Simon, but now I looked for things like that. Guns. Short haircuts. Serious demeanors. The guard asked my name, checked his clipboard, made a phone call, gave me directions, and raised the gate. I drove through.

I passed a picturesque bridge that traversed a small creek and streets with whimsical names and more walls made of stone—an architectural theme, apparently—and even a wishing well. The houses looked like they'd all been built in the same year by the same architect with the same materials. All were large.

I came to a street called Tumbleweed Circle, consisting of four color-coordinated mini-mansions. I drove to the far left one and parked.

I hadn't seen any humans in Palomino Hills, except for the guard. Nor had I seen any palominos. Somewhere in the canyons, a dog barked. I walked up the pathway to the front door. A gecko scurried over my sandal, making me jump. And squeak. I collected myself and rang the bell.

A thought came and went: I hadn't told anyone where I was going. No one in my life knew I was here.

The door opened and a lovely face smiled at me. "You're Wollie, yes? I'm Parashie."

Parashie was an adolescent with the poise of a flight attendant, and she had an accent, slight but charming. I followed her across a foyer to a winding staircase. We walked side by side up the stairs, our footsteps muffled by Persian rugs. We could have added another six people and still walked side by side. The house was done in Mediterranean style, all gem tones and mahogany, and so air-conditioned I could almost see my breath. I shivered. Parashie had bare arms and legs and wore a sporty little outfit paired with pink hiking boots, but showed no signs of being cold. She chatted about the Dodgers as we walked.

Upstairs, we traveled down a long hallway toward an open door.

"Donatella?" Parashie called, pausing at the threshold. "I've brought Wollie."

"In the closet!" a voice called in response.

We walked through a spacious bedroom to a bathroom featuring a sunken square tub and a shower the size of a freight elevator. Then we entered the closet.

The closet of Donatella Milos was nearly as big as my studio apartment at the Oakwood Gardens. It had textured taupe wallpaper, recessed lighting, more Persian carpets, and an antique desk. A soprano aria issued forth from speakers suspended from the ceiling. Donatella sat at the desk, focused on a computer screen.

"One moment . . ." She was dressed in purple velour pants and a velvet tunic. With a click of her fingernails, the computer screen went black, and she turned. "Wollie! My love, it is you at last." She stood and planted kisses on both cheeks. "You have met Parashie?"

"Yes, I—"

"Good. Good. Parashie, bring in the clothes. And send Grusha with refreshments." Donatella indicated a tufted ottoman, which I perched upon, feeling like Little Miss Muffet. She returned to her high-backed chair, and I found myself looking up at her, an acolyte awaiting instruction.

"So." She filled a water goblet from a crystal carafe and took a sip. "We begin. Yuri sends you first to me, as I am the stylist. It all begins with visual presentation, yes?"

"What begins with visual presentation?"

"Life. I am the genius of the dress, the suit, the hair, the walk, the shoes, naturally the shoes, the visage—you have a dermatologist or surgeon that you work with?"

"Uh, no."

"I bring you to mine."

My hand found its way to my face. "What? What do I need a dermatologist or surgeon for?"

Donatella reached out and touched my fingers. "Do not clog the pores, please. Perhaps Botox. There is no time for anything else, to be realistic."

Thank God. And if there were time? A nose job? Chin reconstruction? The only kind of cosmetic surgery that appealed to me was a breast reduction, but I doubted that's what Donatella had in mind. Simon wouldn't be wild about it either.

"You have circles." She frowned. "Under the eyes. How much water do you drink?"

I shrugged. "It varies. On a hot day, I'd say about—"

She held up a hand. "Already I do not like this answer. You must hydrate with consciousness. I do not ask you to carry a bottle; water bottles as accessory bore me. I am not from California."

"I had guessed that."

"But five liters each day, minimum. On this I am insistent."

"Five liters." I was vague on what that was in terms of ounces or quarts, but it sounded like a lot. "Does iced tea count?"

"No. Water. With gas, if you must, but no sweeteners, no caffeine. No and no."

"Gas maybe, sweeteners no." I nodded. That didn't seem too much to ask.

A woman entered the closet. She was shaped like a dumpling, attired in what could only be called a housedress. Where did one shop for housedresses in this day and age? And why hadn't Donatella worked on this woman's visual presentation? The woman set her tray on an antique end table and held up two bottles. "Gas?" she asked. "Or no gas?"

"Gas," I said. Live a little.

She poured water from a Pellegrino bottle into a goblet that matched Donatella's. "Lime or no lime?" she asked.

"Lime," I said.

She set the goblet on the tray and painstakingly peeled a lime, breathing audibly. Her hands were rough and calloused. I bet she didn't use rubber gloves while scrubbing.

Donatella, meanwhile, had returned to her computer, her fingers clicking away at eighty words per minute, minimum. "*Grusha, abbiamo minestrone?*"

"Yes."

"*Va bene.*"

Grusha looked toward me. "Is she staying?"

"For lunch? Of course. She is on the team now." Donatella turned to me. "Wollie, this is Grusha. Tell her your food preferences and allergies, so we do not poison you."

"Hello, Grusha," I said. "I'm easy. No allergies, and I eat pretty much anything. Except beets. And I don't like sauerkraut. Or anything pickled. Oh, and liver. Not crazy about sausage either, for that matter. I had an unpleasant sausage experience once. I saw someone make it."

Grusha shook her head, perhaps not wanting such intimate biographical details on a first meeting. Or maybe beets and liver and sauerkraut were staple items for her, boiling away in a pot at this very moment. After a small "hmmph," she left.

I remembered that I was here in an information-gathering capacity. "Donatella," I said. "Yuri wasn't specific about my duties as part of the, uh, team. I'm curious to know—"

"Yuri will do orientation, but in the nutshell, you are accountable for whereabouts."

"Whose?"

"The male clients. I, the stylist, am accountable for the look. Everyone's look, even Yuri. Some are harder to work with than others. Some are stubborn. You will not be stubborn." She pressed a button on a wall-mounted keypad. "Parashie. We haven't all day."

Parashie's disembodied voice responded. "I only can find the wool pants and the Rykiel and Ungaro jackets."

"Yes? What is the problem?"

"You mean you want those?"

"Yes, of course. What else?"

"But they're Chai's."

"Yes. Bring them, please."

"So," I said, "can you expand on the idea of 'whereabouts'?"

"Stand, please, and walk in circles for me."

I walked and Donatella talked. "Many trainees," she said, "come from countries with no infrastructure, so our freeways present a challenge. We haven't time for driving lessons. Those that do drive present a different challenge."

"The Miss Lemon factor?"

"Precisely. When Miss Lemon first sued us, Yuri created the position of social coach, to teach the proper dating rituals of the United States and to eliminate the need for the trainees to drive. Also, the insurance agent now insists upon it."

"Okay, but I'm not quite clear—what does dating have to do with driving?"

"Nothing. Nevertheless, your job is to date them and also to drive them."

"Where?"

"Wherever they wish to go. But we keep them very busy. You may stop walking, thank you." She turned to her computer and typed.

"How's my walk?" I said.

"We will work on it." She glanced at me, squinted, then turned and typed some more. "Tall, small head, big feet, and large breasts. Nice ears."

"Thank you." No one had ever complimented my ears.

"With you, the challenge is the breasts. With breasts, sexy is easy. Here, we project class. That, not so easy."

"That sounds good," I said. "Class."

"It will be done, but it will not be cheap. And Yuri needs you up to speed tomorrow."

"What's tomorrow?"

"DOA. Day of arrival. The first of the trainees arrive at LAX. The last ones come in the following day. Instantly, we begin the training. This is an intensive course, for you as well, so you must stay hydrated. Kimberly will work with you, so you will be in good shape, which is also important. Not as important as Americans believe, but some exercise is okay."

"I'm expected to . . . exercise?" I said.

Donatella nodded. "Kimberly is the finest personal trainer in L.A."

"Wow. That's like saying someone's the finest chef in Paris."

"*Los Angeles* magazine put her in the 'Best of L.A.' issue five years in a row."

I was feeling less qualified by the minute. "I should tell you that my car's pretty ratty, if I'm to be driving people around."

"Oh, we give you a car to drive. When do you move in? Tonight?"

"Move in?"

"Did Yuri not tell you? Bad Yuri. You will live in the house with the trainees."

"I'm supposed to live . . . on campus? So to speak?"

"Exactly." Donatella looked pleased. "House of Blue, Alik has named it. He also lives there. You have not met Alik, I think. He is Yuri's son."

"But I have an apartment, and my stuff is—"

"You are not to worry, Yuri will work it all out. You must live here, or you will never sleep. Already you will need to be in three places at once most of the time. You will see. We will forward your mail and even your telephone number, if you wish."

This new wrinkle was disturbing. If I lived here and worked here, what would become of the rest of my life? What would Bennett Graham think? And Simon?

Parashie came in, arms filled with clothes, which she hung on ornamental hooks.

"The Sonia Rykiel is good," Donatella said, inspecting a suit. "Where is the Ungaro?"

"With the exaggerated lapels?" Parashie asked.

"Yes."

Parashie looked surprised. "But—it's been worn. Remember? She wore it to the HELP Foundation lunch."

"So? Only one time. Did she spill consommé on it?"

"No, but—" Parashie glanced at me, then away. "Is that . . . okay? I mean—"

"What is the problem? Does it need dry-cleaning?"

"The clothes belong to someone else?" I asked.

"Yes and no," Donatella said. "They were purchased only last month for Chai, who was on the team for the last two training groups. Most have not been to the tailor yet. Parashie, do not be silly. We have a sixteen-hundred-dollar pearl-gray Ungaro that will look better on this woman than it did on Chai. Bring it, please."

Parashie threw another look at me, then left the room.

"Teenage girls," Donatella said, "do not fully appreciate money. Or couture. You do not have a problem to wear this jacket, do you? I promise you it is gorgeous."

"I'm sure it will be fine. It's not like someone died in it, after all."

"No, not in the Ungaro. I believe she was wearing Commes des Garçons."

"Who?" I asked.

"Chai."

"When?"

"When she died," Donatella said. "Come, let us try these pants on you."

SIX

Why should I object to wearing a dead person's clothes, I asked myself while trying on trousers. Especially the ones still sporting price tags? How many things in our lives—antiques, for example—belonged to dead people? It's not like I was being asked to wear used dentures. Not that someone with Chai's wardrobe owned dentures.

But for reasons I couldn't identify, it disturbed me. As Joey had put it, wear a clown costume, you feel like a clown. Wear a dead woman's clothes and—or was she a dead girl? "How old was Chai?" I asked.

"Twenty-one," Donatella said. "Turn, please. Let's see the pants hang."

No dentures, then. "How did Chai die?"

"She drove off a cliff. At night, on Old Topanga. In a classic Corvette. Very unfortunate. No clients were with her at the time, happily."

Happily for them, anyway. "What was her job on the team?"

"Hold your tummy in, please. I need these pleats to fall straight."

"I am holding my tummy in."

"We must have the seamstress in. Chai had good shoulders, but your waist is bigger."

"We could surgically remove some of my ribs," I said.

"There is no time. With luck, the seam allowance is generous."

"So, Chai's job?" I asked again. "What was it she did?"

"The same as you will do. Social coach."

Now I felt almost ill. Same job, same clothes. "A twenty-one-year-old was squiring men around town?"

Donatella nodded. "Precisely. An error in judgment on our part. I was blinded by her beauty. Yuri also. Chai knew the social scene, but not human nature. She was fantastic at presentation, however. Good for attracting business. She was on *America's Next Top Model*."

"Excuse me?"

"It was some seasons ago. And only the seventh runner-up. But to some men, even to date an *America's Next Top Model* loser is appealing."

I was struck by how poor dead Chai's value as a meaningless celebrity so outshone mine. "Donatella," I said, "I have to say, I feel a little inadequate, following in the footsteps—not to mention wearing the shoes— of *America's Next Top Model*."

"Seventh runner-up. Also, did I not say that Chai was a mistake? You, we have vetted. Also, you were demanded by Vlad, our partner in Belarus. Yuri is an intuitive, you see. We have high expectations for you."

That explained the scrutiny I'd felt in the courtroom.

"You are more suited to the job," Donatella continued. "You have a nearly perfect driving record, you are born in Burbank, and you are a mature woman."

"Well, let's not overstate it," I said. "But I am older than twenty-one."

"So you have life experience. And you are fully American, which is vital, as this is an immersion course. Also, you have warmth. Yuri has commented upon this. Chai made a good impression initially, but Chai cared only for Chai."

I turned to see Parashie standing in the doorway, listening. She looked at me with an expression I couldn't read, then said to Donatella, "Here. The Ungaro."

Donatella took the blazer from her. "One good thing," she said. "Chai was skinny, but she had her breasts enlarged, so at least her clothes will fit you around the chest."

That was good news. I wondered how much of my job I owed to a skeletal resemblance to a dead *America's Next Top Model* reject.

I was hoping to avoid Grusha's lunch, because after trying on Chai's clothes, it was clear I'd be better off weighing less. Fifteen pounds, minimum. Fortunately, none of Chai's new pants had yet been to the tailor; if they had, the waists wouldn't have fit a normal human being. In their unaltered state, they were almost big enough for me. If I gave up exhaling.

I was not allowed to skip lunch, however. Donatella would prefer to see me with three or four kilos of body fat less, she said, but not at the expense of lunch. "A meal is more than calories," she said. "In Europe we do not eat standing up or in the car and we do not drink powdered substances or bars of protein and call this a food."

"Okay," I said, "but aren't we introducing the trainees to America?"

"Introduce, yes. Turn them loose, no. Europeans come here and gain ten kilos. Too many choices. Kimberly takes care of that. We cannot send piglets on a press tour."

"I thought food was Grusha's department."

"Grusha cooks what Kimberly tells her. You will see how we work, as one great organism. Now, at lunch we make the first impression, so you wear these pants and the Roberto Cavalli top. With the Chanel loafers. How lucky Chai also had feet the size of skis."

When I was dressed, Parashie led me outside and over a flagstone path that connected Donatella's house to the other three. We passed a gardener wielding a leaf blower, the body of which was attached to his back like a baby koala. Its noise was considerable, and Parashie and I suspended conversation until we were past him. A dozen other men ate lunch on the grass, in the shade of the adjoining house. This was one heck of a gardening crew.

"And where do you live, Parashie?" I asked. "Here on campus or somewhere else?"

She laughed. "That's funny. 'Campus.' We all live on the campus. I live in the house I take you to now, with Yuri and Kimberly. Grusha too. Alik lives in House of Blue. That is where the trainees live. You have a nice room there. It was Chai's."

Naturally. "And the other house?"

"Green House. That is for the workers. They build a pool. Yuri lets them sleep there. That house, it is not finished inside."

I hesitated, not wanting to seem too inquisitive. "Were you friends with Chai? She wasn't that much older than you, was she?"

"Of course we were friends. We are all friends, all of us on the team." She seemed a little less perky, though, so I searched for a safer topic.

"What's your job title, Parashie?"

"Production assistant. Like the movies. Alik gave me this title, like a joke. Yuri thought it was clever."

"That must be interesting, living in the same house as the boss."

"Well, Yuri's not just my boss. He's my father."

"Oh." This surprised me. "So is Donatella your mother?"

"No, my stepmother. Like Kimberly."

Was she from Yuri's first marriage? Before I could figure out how to ask gracefully, we were inside Yuri's house, and Yuri was coming down a black marble staircase toward us.

I was taken in a powerful embrace and kissed on both cheeks, for the second time that day, then Yuri held me at arm's length and positively beamed at me. He turned to his daughter. "Well, Parashie? How do you like her? Is she not exactly right?"

"I like her."

"Good. Good. You look splendid, Wollie. I see Donatella's been working on you."

"They're Chai's clothes," Parashie told him.

He looked at me and raised an eyebrow. "Yes? Good of you to fit into them."

"My pleasure." I was annoyed at myself for feeling so pleased with Yuri's compliments. I was a sucker for charisma. Even as my mind whispered, *He's just saying that to win you over,* I found myself basking in the light of his attention. It's a quality that's fine when you're in primary school, but fairly pathetic when you're all grown up and six feet tall.

"Come into the great room, let's get you a drink. Sweetheart, see if you can find Alik for us." Parashie ran off, and Yuri led me through a formal dining room into a large, light-filled space dominated by a long conference table. The table was modern, made of some alloy and topped with translucent mint-green glass. It was set for seven, but could probably seat twenty. Yuri gestured to a well-stocked bar and asked what I liked to drink.

"Water," I said. "With or without gas."

"Good girl." He smiled and reached for a goblet.

"Was that a test?" I asked. "What if I'd said double vodka, straight up?"

"Then we would have a problem. And yes. Everything is a test. Now tell me," he said. "What was it that made you change your mind and come work for me?"

My heart stopped. I felt my face growing warm and my breath quicken. "Oh, you know. You're a persuasive man."

He turned and handed me the goblet, making eye contact. "But you're not easily persuaded. What was it?"

My whole body was heating up. Could this be a hot flash, a decade or two early? I felt sweat gathering on my forehead. "I have a brother," I said. "He lives in a kind of halfway house in Santa Barbara. It's expensive."

"Go on." Yuri, I got the impression, already knew about P.B.

"And you're paying me a very nice salary. Oh, by the way: Donatella tells me I'm to move in here. That's a little tricky."

"Why?"

"For one thing, I visit my brother every week."

"But you're closer to Santa Barbara here than you are from your apartment."

"Yes, but my Uncle Theo always comes with me. I pick him up in Glendale."

Yuri continued to study me. I continued to sweat. I thought I'd done an okay job of changing the subject, but maybe not. "It can be worked out," he said finally. "Kimberly, my wife, deals with scheduling. Today, go home, pack what you'd need for a long weekend, and lock up your apartment. I want you here tomorrow. Have you any pets?"

"No, and you don't have to pay my rent—"

Yuri held up a hand. "I promised you, no expenses."

But money wasn't what bothered me. Living here made this whole thing less a job than a relocation, like boarding school. Or boot camp.

A telephone rang. Yuri answered it and moved through sliding doors out onto a deck.

I looked out after him, taking in a spectacular view of the Santa Monica Mountains, a vast expanse of wilderness and canyons that seemed incredible, existing so close to Los Angeles. Beyond the mountains was Malibu.

I turned back to the huge room. His house appeared to be structurally identical to Donatella's, but done in pastel desert tones with black accents, a combination that, like Yuri's wardrobe, shouldn't have worked, but did. The black surface of the grand piano was covered in silver-framed family photos, including several of a yellow dog.

The sliding glass opened, and Yuri came back in. "Sorry for the interruption. Ah, here's your male counterpart. This is Alik. My son." He gestured behind me, and I turned.

"Delighted to have you on the team," Alik said, shaking my hand. I recognized him from Yuri's trial. The whole jury had noticed him, but especially the women. Alik Milos had his father's vitality and a lot more hair. He wore glasses, which made him look intelligent, in a dashing sort of way. I guessed him to be twenty-five, a decade or so older than Parashie, who was coming into the room now too. Did they have the same mother?

"I'm happy to be here," I said. "How many Milos children are there, by the way?"

Yuri answered. "Only two. So far."

"That we know of," Alik added, under his breath.

"Unless you count Olive Oyl," Kimberly said, entering the room and heading for the deck. "Hello, Wollie. Let's eat outside."

"My father should've been a Mormon," Alik said, taking my arm and escorting me onto the deck. "Hundreds of children, dozens of wives. That would've made him happy."

"I am happy," Yuri said.

"Wollie, Alik's field is psychology," Kimberly said. "He can't help himself, he psychoanalyzes everything that moves. Damn, there goes my visor." She leaned over the deck, watching her red visor ride the breeze down into the canyon. She wore a sporty dress, tight and sleeveless, showing off a flat stomach and muscular arms.

Parashie looked through a telescope, into the canyon. "I see it, the hat."

Donatella joined us, giving Alik a kiss. "Hello, *ragazzo.* Kimberly, it is too breezy to eat outside. We shall be covered in soup." And back into the house she went, with all of us following. What was it like for her, watching her ex-husband live out his life with his trophy wife? And Kimberly? How was it for her to live and work with her husband's previous wife and a knockout stepson her own age?

"I don't psychoanalyze, by the way," Alik said to me. "I'm not an analyst. But I want to do a Myers-Briggs on you, Wollie. After lunch. The short version. It'll be fun."

"You and your Myers-Briggs," Kimberly said. "Wollie, it's the standard psychology student pickup technique. I'd lie if I were you."

"What is a pickup technique?" Parashie asked.

"American girls," Dontalla said, "do they fall for this silliness?"

"Stepmother," Alik replied, "you would be shocked."

"Come, come," Yuri said. "Wollie has just met us. Wollie, you're family now, and *en famille,* informality rules. When the trainees arrive, we become more discreet."

"We try," Alik said.

"Respect," Yuri said, "for cultural and religious backgrounds is imperative. We resist sexual innuendo and avoid the careless use of the name of God."

"So I guess Pope jokes are out," I said.

Alik put an arm around my shoulder. "Not to me. I love Pope jokes."

"Stop flirting with her, Alik," Kimberly said. "She might not like you."

"She doesn't know me well enough to dislike me, Stepmother."

"Shut up," Kimberly said.

"This must be my orientation," I said.

"In fact," Yuri said, "I planned to do a proper orientation this afternoon, but Zagreb just called. I fly to New York tonight. Kimberly, make that happen, will you, my love?"

Kimberly walked over to a keypad on the wall and pressed a button. "Grusha, are you there? Pack up Yuri again. He's going to New York."

"Lunch first," Grusha's voice barked back.

We seated ourselves at the conference table, joined by a middle-aged woman who introduced herself as Nell and avoided eye contact. No one explained who she was.

Grusha came through an archway with pot of soup. Alik went to take it from her and was told to sit and not treat her like a weakling.

"Yes, Grandma," Alik said, and he winked at me.

I turned to Yuri. "Grusha is . . . your mother?"

"My mother-in-law," Yuri said. "From my first marriage."

So Yuri's household was composed of a wife, an ex-wife, the mother of a dead wife, the son of the dead wife, the daughter of an as-yet-unidentified mother, and Nell, sitting next to me.

And me, of course, taking over a dead woman's job.

"You," Grusha said to me, ladling soup into Wedgwood bowls. "No beets, no sauerkraut, no liver. So. Now you eat."

I looked across the table to see Alik smiling at me.

"Welcome to *la famiglia*," he said.

Lunch conversation centered around cars. The Porsche I'd seen Yuri driving to court turned out to be Alik's, and was the automotive black sheep of the family. "The Audi's out of the shop this week," Kimberly said, munching on celery, "so we can take the Porsche in."

"To do what?" Alik asked.

"To convert it to biofuel."

"Dream on," Alik said. "Can't be done. First, it's not diesel—"

"Stanislas says he'll be able to—"

"Kimberly, you're not feeding bacon grease to my Porsche. Forget it."

"Honest to God, Alik, how can you morally justify that car?" Kimberly asked.

"It is no better than the Corvette," Donatella said. "Bourgeois in the extreme."

Yuri broke off a piece of crusted bread, then said, "I am not convinced biofuel is the Holy Green Grail. I want to see agricultural impact numbers before we do more conversions."

"You miss the point," Donatella said. "It is hypocritical to teach trainees that each action is scrutinized by the media while Alik drives his gas-guzzler. There is a photo of him in the Porsche in the current issue of *Statement*. If you have no restraint, Alik, at least cultivate discretion. Think how that plays in Budo-Koshelyovo district."

"Do you really think *Statement*'s circulation extends to Belarus?" Alik asked.

The blare of an alarm, loud and insistent, assaulted our ears. From inside the house.

Everyone stood. Uncertain, I stood too. Yuri took a gadget from his pocket and pressed buttons. Alik moved to the wall and picked up a phone, covering his other ear to talk.

"What is it?" Kimberly asked Yuri. Grusha entered from the kitchen, wiping her hands on her apron, asking the same thing.

Yuri shook his head, still on his keypad. "Deer. Coyote. Or system malfunction."

Donatella went out onto the deck and looked through the telescope.

"Donatella!" Yuri said in a voice so sharp that I jumped. "In here. Now."

Donatella turned and frowned, but she came inside, sliding the glass door behind her.

As she did so there was a sharp crack.

I flinched.

Grusha cried out in Russian and pulled Parashie away from the table as if she were a rag doll. Nell, my mouselike dining companion, looked at me with wide eyes.

There was a second of silence and then Kimberly left the room. I stared at the sliding doors, looking for the mark of the impact, but there was nothing obvious. Alik, still on the phone, took my arm and pulled me back from the table to where Grusha stood with Parashie.

Everyone stared out at the mountains.

Alik handed his phone to his father. Yuri listened, then said, "What's the range it can pick up? . . . Yes, southwest of the main house. . . . All right. Let me know." He hung up and addressed Donatella. "What were you thinking, going out there like that?"

"You said it was a coyote," she replied.

"I was wrong."

The blaring ended as abruptly as it had begun.

Yuri returned to the table and sat. We all followed. Kimberly came in, accompanied by a dog of uncertain breed, big, yellow, and overweight. "Olive Oyl, down," she said and took her seat. Olive Oyl put one paw on Kimberly's shoe, collapsed, and prepared to nap.

"At least the system is fixed," Parashie said. "The last time someone shot at—"

"Parashie."

The single word from Yuri stopped her. She dropped her eyes to her soup.

I watched Yuri. He stared at his daughter, then turned to me and smiled.

"Now, then," he said. "Where were we?"

SEVEN

Once lunch was over, people took off in all directions, Yuri to catch a plane, Donatella and Kimberly to shop, Grusha to cook, and Parashie to study. "Nell tutors me," she explained, walking me to the foyer. "Yuri wants me to catch up to American kids and go next year to school, to tenth grade. But I like it at home."

"Wollie," Alik said, phone in hand. "I have an errand to run, but I still need an hour with you. Can you meet me at five in the Valley? We'll have drinks."

"Alik, you are just meeting Wollie and already you date her?" Parashie said.

"Shut up, brat," he said, and put her in a choke hold, a staple of big brothers everywhere, that made her scream with laughter and engage in a counterattack.

The minute I was in my car, I tried to call my Uncle Theo, who was waiting to hear about my new job, but there was no cell signal. How inconvenient. Hadn't anyone in the Milos family used cell phones that day? No; they'd all been landlines.

I felt a chill of isolation that dissipated only when I was outside the gates of Palomino Hills. This was a problem. For as long as I was at the compound, I'd be cut off. I could make calls from the Milos phones, but those could conceivably be overheard by anyone in the household. And, of course, by the FBI, if they were indeed wiretapping them.

I told myself that this was a minor logistical problem, but it added to my growing sense of unease. Chai, my predecessor, was dead. There was no reason to think her death had sinister overtones, but I did. I considered Joey's advice, that I construct a character who'd be unfazed by this. The tough cookie. *Big deal,* she'd say. *So the last social coach drove off a cliff. You'll stay on the road.*

Two miles later my phone churned out a Mozart sonata, announcing a return to cell signals and one missed call. I hit my voice-mail button.

"Miss Shelley?" a familiar voice said. "It's Ulf. At Costco on Canoga. I've got your special order in. You can pick it up anytime after six."

I smiled, my anxiety lifted. *Ulf?*

I glanced at my watch, then dialed a number and spoke to voice mail. "I'll be in around six-thirty to pick up my special order. Oh, wait." I did a quick calculation of traffic, geography, and my date with Alik. "Make that seven-thirty. And Ulf? Glad to hear the package is in. I'm dying to open it." That, I figured, would get a return smile.

Only when I ended the call did I consider what kind of questions "Ulf" would be asking tonight. My smile faded.

Club Red Square had a grungy facade that was nonetheless dramatic, a one-story turreted affair on Ventura Boulevard between an abandoned building and a storefront psychic, due east of a Jack in the Box. The exterior was a bold red and black, hinting at exotic pleasures within for those bewitched by the color red painted, curtained, wallpapered, and upholstered onto every available surface.

Alik and I sat on a red leather sofa in the lounge area of the club. Happy hour was in progress, pounding music played, and while Alik processed the results of my Myers-Briggs personality test, I focused on the cocktail napkin on which I doodled, rather than the red and black plaid carpet, which I found nausea-inducing. Or Alik's high-cheekboned face, which I found pleasure-inducing—but only because graphic artists are drawn to beautiful angles, I told myself. This wasn't sexual attraction. Unless the hookah smoke lingering in the air was exerting an aphrodisiacal effect. I had little experience of bars that offered hookahs.

My big dilemma had been whether to answer the Myers-Briggs personality test questions as me, Wollie, or as my tough-cookie character, whose face was even now coming to life on my cocktail napkin. Yes or No: You like to be engaged in an active and fast-paced job. Yes or No: You often think about humankind and its destiny. Yes or No: It's difficult to get you excited.

I decided to go with me, since this action-adventure girl was still evolving. As I drew her, for instance, I noticed dilated pupils and a hookah coming out of her mouth.

"Wollie, you're an INFP," Alik said, reading his laptop screen.

"Is that good?" I asked.

"There's no good or bad. But welcome to the team. We need another introvert."

"So I'm guessing that's me and Nell and Grusha against the rest of you."

Alik laughed and made notes on a legal pad.

"What was Chai?" I asked.

"A bitch," Alik said. "And a mistake. My bad. You, I'll take credit for."

"What was Chai's problem?"

He looked up from his writing. "What makes you ask?"

"Just curiosity about someone who died so young and so suddenly. And I'd like to not make the same mistakes on the job, if I can help it."

"You won't."

"You can predict that"—I nodded to his computer—"from the Myers-Briggs test?"

"No. I can predict that from attachment theory."

"Which is what?"

"It describes the way infants, six months to two years, relate to a primary adult. With a negative or indifferent caregiver, bonding doesn't occur, producing serious, usually lifelong problems. Chai's mother was a narcissist with a substance abuse problem, so Chai had issues. I'm sure you have issues too, but not those issues."

"How can you tell?"

He leaned in. "I've watched you all day. I'm willing to bet your mother loved babies." He was very sexy at close range. Other girls were eyeing him, and eyeing me because I was with him. And they all knew his name. Everyone here knew his name.

"She does love babies," I said. "It's everyone else she has trouble with."

Alik's smile was infectious and I smiled back. There was something troubling about what he'd just said, but I couldn't put my finger on it. So I went with what was more troubling. "Alik, this afternoon when someone shot at the deck—"

"What makes you think that it was a shot?"

I blinked. "I wasn't the only one to think so. Grusha was yelling."

"Oh, I see. You picked up on Grusha's reaction."

"I'd have to be deaf not to. Do you mean she hears gunshots where none exist?"

Alik reached for his wineglass. "My grandmother was a child in Brest in 1944 when the Red Army came through, 'liberating' it from the Germans. Her daughter, my mother, was shot and killed fifty years later during a trip to Budennovsk. Parashie's mother died in Minsk, while a guest of the secret police. So now when a car backfires in Calabasas or a squirrel drops an acorn on the roof, yes, my family takes cover."

"Oh."

He smiled. "Don't look so stricken. It all happened a long time ago. Life goes on. Anyway, welcome. Now you need to go home and pack." He stretched out his hand, palm up. "Hand over the valet ticket. I'll walk you to your car."

He paid for my parking and threw in an extra five, which endeared him to the parking guy. And me.

It wasn't until I was driving down Ventura Boulevard that I figured it out, what had bothered me. How could Alik have been watching me all day, as he put it? Unless he was exaggerating? Because I'd known him a total of two hours.

At 7:48 p.m. I parked at Costco, a big-box store on the corner of Canoga and Roscoe, in the Valley. Costco closed at eight-thirty on weeknights, so it was still hopping, but I had the northeast end of the parking lot all to myself. I turned off my headlights and left the engine running, playing the radio for company, then switched on the map light and picked up my sketchpad. The day's events had inspired a greeting card, as often happened with me. My cards were alternative, but this one was too alternative, a Happy Moving Day card that turned into condolences once you opened it. Maybe because the only place I wanted to move to was back to Simon's. It wasn't that I loved his penthouse in Westwood. I just loved him.

My stomach growled. I reached into my glove box for a protein bar, kept there for the homeless who panhandled on busy intersections. And for Simon. I hadn't eaten anything since Grusha's soup, before the lunchtime incident had put me off my feed. Should I just dismiss the possibility that someone had shot at Donatella? There was no evidence, only a quick succession of events: the alarm, the sharp cracking sound, and the reactions of a few shell-shocked people, which Alik had explained quite reasonably. But they, unlike me, had recovered and gone back to eating the soup.

If I didn't know the FBI was investigating these people, wouldn't I be able to let it go? Maybe. There was the ill-fated Chai, whose clothes I was wearing even now as I sat in my car. I wondered what clothes she'd been wearing during her last moments, as she sat in her car. Okay, I better rein in my imagination and act like a normal person, not one sent by the feds. A normal person abandoning her life overnight in order to spend three months doing some odd job that involved transporting foreign nationals to nightclubs and 7-Elevens while dressed like a dead girl. A normal person who—

My car door opened. As I was leaning against it, I began falling toward the Costco asphalt. A pair of strong hands grabbed my shoulders and steadied me.

"Lady," a low-pitched voice said. "This is private property. No loitering." The man holding my shoulders helped me out of the car, then retrieved my sketchpad.

I looked around. The closest humans were nearly a block away, moving bulk items from shopping carts to trunks. "And I suppose solicitation is frowned on too. *Ulf,*" I added, but my assailant was already climbing into my car, taking over the driver's seat. Then he pulled me in, onto his lap.

I looked into his face. It was a tough one, with a fair number of lines on it, all of which I was familiar with, some of which I'd put there. "Is this a carjacking?" I asked.

"No. Kidnapping," he said and kissed me.

Ulf, aka Simon Alexander, was a very good kisser, which was fortunate, as kissing is one of the few physical activities possible in an old Acura Integra. It's a small car by L.A. standards. As I'm a tall woman by nearly any standard and Simon is five inches taller than that, practicing our skills of seduction in my car was a circus act. Not that that stopped us.

I spent a couple of minutes appeasing my body hunger, untucking his shirt so I could get my hands under it, then sliding my arms around him, touching skin, feeling the muscles of his back. It wasn't until a cramp set in and I felt him wince as I changed position that we got around to talking. Simon leaned back, brushed hair from my face, and studied me in the dim light. "You look tired. Jury duty still going on?"

"Nope." I told him the details of the case without mentioning the name Milos.

"Good. Now that you've done your civic duty, can you stay up late tomorrow?"

"What's tomorrow?"

"I thought we'd meet at a hotel."

I gasped. "And spend a whole night together?"

"And well into the morning. There are one or two things I want to do to you that require a mattress and room service."

Damn. This was something I'd been dreaming of for weeks. But I doubted if "the team" would want me to disappear for twelve or fourteen hours my first day on the job. "Will you still be Ulf when you check in?" I asked, stalling for time.

"No. I'll be Daniel Lavosh."

"That's not the batting order. What about *W*?" I was used to Simon changing names with each communication, progressing through the alphabet two letters at a time.

"Daniel Lavosh has a credit card and photo ID," he said. "I'll check in and you'll come an hour later. I'll park in the hotel garage and leave the key card hidden under my car, the driver's side front tire."

"Lucrezia's giving you the night off?" I asked.

"You don't give up, do you?"

Simon was working undercover, on a case that had occupied him for as long as I'd been in love with him. Or longer. I wasn't sure. All I knew was that it involved a woman named Lucrezia who was well coiffed and favored fur coats. At least, she'd favored them back in December, the two times I'd seen her. Since it was now May, there was a good chance she'd moved on to cloth coats. Or dispensed with clothes altogether. Simon wasn't saying and I didn't ask. Much. The prudent thing would've been to take a sabbatical from our relationship until the case was wrapped up, but Simon, although professional, was not always prudent. As for me, there were many things I'd do for my country, but abandoning this man to a woman in a French twist was not one of them.

"How's it going with Lucrezia, anyway?" I asked.

"Never mind Lucrezia," he said. "How about it?"

So much for stalling. "There's a slight hitch. I may have a . . . thing."

"What thing?" His voice was wary.

"A job thing."

"You don't have a job."

"I do too have a job. What do you mean?"

"I misspoke. I meant apart from your cards. Obviously."

"Just because one is self-employed," I said, "doesn't mean there are no professional commitments that require one's—"

"What? There's a greeting card convention? An interview with Hallmark?"

"I don't aspire to work for Hallmark."

Simon's hand moved toward the map light, but I grabbed it and held on.

"Do you find my work Hallmarky?" I asked.

"No. You're the Vincent van Gogh of greeting cards. What's this job thing?"

"Simon, tell me something. All these security measures we do—the cryptic phone messages, the code names—are we hiding from the bad guys or the good guys?"

"Why are you asking?"

"I mean, I assume Lucrezia can't know about me, but now I wonder, are you keeping me from your boss—you know, the FBI—too?"

"And why do you wonder this now?"

"It . . . I don't know, it occurred to me."

Simon reached up with his other hand and the map light went on. His eyes, when he turned to me, were so ice blue they startled me. They always did. They were also bloodshot. "My God," I said. "Talk about tired-looking. When was your last good night's sleep?"

"Let's stay with you," he said. "What's going on, Wollie?"

"What do—"

"And don't say 'What do you mean?' You're flitting from subject to subject, a diversionary tactic that could work on someone who doesn't know you and love you, provided that person was also stupid, but I'm not that person, so let's cut to the chase."

"Okay," I said. "Here's the deal. I have a new job. And it starts tomorrow. So I can't meet you at the hotel, and I'm sick with disappointment over it."

"What's the job?"

I turned off the map light. "I'm working for a company that does media training and I'll be working odd hours."

"How odd?"

"Tomorrow there are clients arriving at the airport and I think I'm picking them up. A lot of my duties involve transportation. At any rate, I have to be available to them."

"What hours?"

"I'm not sure, but I get the impression . . . twenty-four/seven." I mumbled this.

He switched on the map light. There were those eyes again, blue, blue, blue, with laserlike intensity. "You're a chauffeur?"

"Among other things. Why?"

"Because you dislike driving, and you're not particularly good at it. What other things?"

"Showing them around L.A. Whatever. Playing cribbage with them in their off-hours. I'll find out more tomorrow."

"Right after you learn cribbage. How did you find this job?"

"They more or less found me. It came about through jury duty, in a circuitous way, and the pay's good, and it's just temporary."

"How temporary?"

"Three months."

"Three months?"

"Okay, okay," I said, cringing. "I'm not hard of hearing."

"You're spending the summer babysitting a bunch of—what? Who are these people?"

"Simon, I don't know all the details, but I'm more than a glorified bus driver. These are international celebrities. It's a prestigious firm, I'm well-treated, it's not menial labor—"

"What's the name of this firm?"

I hesitated, then turned off the map light. "MediasRex."

He switched the light back on. "What aren't you telling me?"

"I'm not—nothing. It's just that—see, I knew you wouldn't be crazy about—not that I blame you—the idea of seeing less of you than I already do depresses me, and—"

"I thought you wanted to focus on your art," he said. "And your marketing efforts."

"Well, yeah, but—"

"So why are you doing this? It's not a career move, it's a temp job."

"I told you, it's—"

"—money. What are they paying?"

I looked out the window. "Five minutes ago that moon looked so romantic."

"Salary?"

"Fifty grand. For three months. Not bad for a babysitter."

That quieted him. I took advantage of this by turning off the map light one last time. Then I took his face in my hands and moved toward it. When he showed no signs of resistance, I closed the gap, put my mouth on his, and switched to nonverbal communication. We'd been working on these skills a lot over the last six months and were getting good at it. I had to block out a vision of Alik Milos that jumped in un-invited, but Simon didn't seem to notice and I thought I was home free, until his mouth moved to my ear.

"I'm curious to know," he said softly, "what else these people are pay-ing for."

I was too. But I kept that to myself.

EIGHT

While not exactly a fight, the evening's tryst had been downgraded to a logistics discussion. We talked about the "where" and "how"—possible venues for our next rendezvous and the cryptic phone calls that would precede it—but not the "when." Which was all I cared about. It was cold comfort that my schedule was now as unpredictable as his.

I did not tell Simon that my new job required me to live on campus, as it were, and in a section of Calabasas without cell phone reception. There was only so much wrath I could take in one night from a man with whom there would be no makeup sex in the near future. Makeup sex had seen Simon and me through some rough moments; now I'd have to find other coping mechanisms. Relationship self-help books, if there were any that gave advice on living with a secret agent. Perhaps there was a Significant Others of Spies support group, but I didn't know how that would work, everyone sitting around sharing only aliases and cover stories. Simon's had to do with the textiles business.

The good news was that Simon didn't suspect that I too was working for the FBI. Also, I'd kept the name Yuri Milos out of the conversation, although Simon would undoubtedly check up on MediasRex the minute he got to a computer.

It was in this cheerless frame of mind that I walked up the sidewalk at the Oakwood Garden Apartments. Of all my recent domiciles, this was the one I'd miss the least. Fredreeq and Joey would be popping champagne when they heard I was leaving; Joey felt that proximity to so many divorcés was psychologically unhealthy, while Fredreeq was concerned with the spirit world. She claimed that the apartment complex, so near Forest Lawn cemetery, was in fact built on ancient Native American burial grounds, meaning at best it had bad feng shui and at worst was haunted. Tonight I believed her. It seemed the trees themselves were whispering my name.

"Wollie."

That was no tree. I stopped, scared silly. It was late. And dark. The walkway was lined with lights, half of them burned out. A good place to get mugged.

But muggers didn't usually call one's name.

"What?" I said.

A man emerged from the shadows, and I took a step back. "It's me," he said.

I peered at him. Bennett Graham. "Oh," I said. "Hello. What are you doing here?"

"Let's take a walk," he said.

"Let's go inside," I said.

"I prefer the outdoors."

I did not. While nearly summer, it was still chilly, and Chai's clothes were thin. But Bennett Graham was the boss. I would have to get into the habit of taking sweaters everywhere if this guy was going to keep popping up alfresco.

"Do you think my apartment's bugged?" I asked, moving along the pathway.

"Not necessarily. Let's just say I have a worst-case-scenario mind-set. You'll develop one too."

"How delightful."

We walked toward the pool, which was empty. Beyond the pool, the hot tub held three people who in turn held beer bottles.

"You met with Milos today," Bennett Graham said, walking slowly around the pool. "How did that go?"

It reassured me that he knew I'd been there. I filled him in on my day, focusing on the alarm incident and my impression that a bullet had hit the glass doors. "But I didn't get close enough to see any cracks in the glass, just the sound. And everyone calmed down pretty fast after the initial noise. I mean, they were concerned. But calm. So I may have been mistaken."

"Were the doors exceptionally heavy?" he asked.

"The glass, you mean? How would I know that?"

"You didn't open or close them yourself?"

I shook my head.

"Was anyone armed?" he asked.

"Armed?" I said, alarmed. "Why would they be armed?"

"I'm not saying they were. I'm asking if they were."

"Not that I noticed, but I wasn't encouraged to frisk them. The guard at the gate had a gun. He looked the type, too. A real Gloomy Gus."

Bennett Graham raised an eyebrow.

"Gloomy Gus. It's a technical term," I said.

"Describe to me the rest of the house," he said. "The layout. The dining room table, for example. Was there a chandelier hanging above it?"

"I didn't notice a lot except for colors and decor. I'm into art, not geography. But I'm moving in there tomorrow, so—oh. Another problem. I can't get cell phone reception at the house. I guess that's normal for the canyon, but I don't suppose you want me calling you from a landline, right? Having your office number show up on the family phone bill."

He'd stopped and was staring at me. "You're moving in?"

"Oh, great! You didn't know that was part of the job?"

"Why did you agree to that?"

"What do you mean?" I squeaked. "I assumed I was to go along with the program."

He glanced across the pool to the hot-tubbers. "Keep your voice down, please."

"That's it. I'm staying here. I'll commute. They'll just have to deal with it."

Bennett Graham shook his head. "No. This is good. Your access to the house increases exponentially if you're there round the clock."

"But it's riskier, right? And how do I connect with you? Since it seems I'm on call round the clock too, driving people all over."

"They'll have to give you time off. When they do, get to where there's a cell signal." He pulled out a business card and jotted down a number. "In an emergency, call this number. It's a yogurt place. Ask them to save you a quart of Very Vanilla. Give your name."

I stared at him. This was not my idea of a fail-safe mechanism. "What if they don't have Very Vanilla?"

"They always have Very Vanilla."

"What if they run out?"

"It doesn't matter if they run out," he said patiently. "A quart of Very Vanilla for Wollie is their signal that you need to make contact."

"Oh. Okay, I see. Listen, wouldn't it be easier to beef up the cell signals in the canyon? Surely the FBI is capable of that."

"Thank you for the tactical advice. A quart of Very Vanilla. Then tell them what time you'll be in to pick it up."

"What if it's the middle of the night?"

"You'll get voice mail. Leave a message. It will be forwarded. Then drive there. Here." He handed me the business card. "From the Milos house, go north along Mulholland Highway for five or six miles. You'll see a Gelson's on your left, in a small shopping center. The yogurt store is in the far corner. I can have someone there in forty minutes, if necessary."

"What if you need to reach me?" I asked.

"Check your cell phone when you can. If something comes up on our end, you'll get a message from a woman named Rebecca, telling you what to do."

"Rebecca." I nodded. My stomach was doing little somersaults. "I want to know what it is that Milos is involved in."

"It might be nothing at all."

"That's hard to believe," I said.

"Why? It happens all the time." Bennett Graham glanced at the hot-tub party, then did a slow survey of the pool area while adjusting the cuffs of his shirt. "We get tips, we go on fishing expeditions, and sometimes we come up with nothing. You do just as much a service exonerating the innocent as you do finding proof of wrongdoing."

I wasn't sure if I believed Bennett Graham, but here was the interesting thing: I wanted to believe him. I wanted to believe it was a mistake and that Yuri Milos was a man of integrity, guilty of nothing but being European and wealthy and having an unorthodox family. "Okay, I'll buy that. So what's the wrongdoing that Yuri Milos might not be doing?"

"It's not necessary for you to know."

"That's stupid. How could I be more useful as an ignorant person than an informed one?"

"I don't have time to give you a lesson on how intelligence operations are run and why certain practices increase efficiency."

"Maybe it works for you," I said, "but I'm putting myself in some degree of danger here. I want to know how much."

"You're better off focusing on your job and—"

"Ignorance can't be good self-defense, so telling me 'don't worry your pretty little head' is just—"

"It has nothing to do with attractiveness."

On the other side of the pool, a shout of laughter was followed by excessive splashing. We both turned to it. Then I turned back to face Bennett Graham. "I'm thinking seriously of quitting. I can't tell you what a bad feeling I have." And it was true, I couldn't explain how spooked I felt, replacing the departed Chai. Not to this guy.

"First of all," he said, and his tone softened, "you've taken the hardest step today. Don't throw that away. These doubts are normal. By tomorrow night, you'll have a different outlook. Secondly, Milos values you. And you're safer living there than you are here in this place"—he nodded toward my building—"with its lax security measures. Milos probably has alarms and movement sensors around the periphery of the house. Cameras too."

"Where will these cameras be?"

"I have no idea. In general, assume that surveillance is ongoing anywhere that power is present."

"What's that, the J. Edgar Hoover dictum?"

"James Bond. Finally, remind yourself of the reasons you said yes to this job."

P.B. At least Bennett Graham had the good taste not to mention him outright.

"Your brother," he said, quashing that fleeting good impression. "Do you really see him living here with you at the Oakwood Gardens in your small apartment? I don't imagine it's easy to keep him on his medication."

For me, it was impossible. And I couldn't leave him alone, even on meds.

I took a deep breath. "Well, give me a clue, then, would you? Spell it out for me what I'm supposed to be doing in all my ignorance."

"Note anything irregular on the premises."

"Like what? Meth lab in the basement? A cache of explosives?"

"Those would certainly qualify. As would large sums of money. I'm also interested in any animosity among family members. As to the particulars, I'd like you to find out the names of the old woman, the housekeeper, and the young girl."

"Grusha. She's Yuri's former mother-in-law. Parashie's his daughter."

His eyebrow went up again. "You see, you're good at this already."

I blushed at the compliment, even knowing he was probably humoring me.

"Engage these people in conversation," he said. "See if they have criminal histories."

"Do people generally volunteer that?"

"Do your best. For the incoming trainees, I want names and countries of origin. Passport numbers. Write things down, but keep your notes well hidden. Also, look for a room that has film or recording equipment, or shipping materials, especially to and from Europe. And take note of any regular visitors that have nothing to do with MediasRex."

"Wait. Go back to the room. Do you mean like a media center? A screening room?"

"No," he said, beginning to walk, forcing me to walk with him. "It may be a basement or even apart from the house. It won't be included in any tour. There might be editing equipment. Duplicating machines. The room will probably be kept locked."

"Then how am I supposed to get into it?"

"Listen. Observe. When your eyes are open, opportunities present themselves."

"'Observe what's vivid. Notice what you notice. Catch yourself thinking.'"

"What?"

"Allen Ginsberg," I explained, but he only looked at me blankly. "So what is it that's being edited or duplicated in this room?"

"That's what we'd like to know."

"It all sounds very Bluebeardian." I shivered. The night air was getting to me now, seeping into my bones along with thoughts of the fairy tale that used to haunt my childhood. Talk about an unhappy ending. Like half of Yuri's lovers. "So did you know," I asked, "that my predecessor died? In a car accident?"

His eyebrows drew together in a frown, too quickly. "When?"

"Oh, great. So you didn't know about it?"

"When did it happen?"

"I don't know. Recently. Her name was Chai."

"No last name?"

"She was on *America's Next Top Model*. A few seasons ago. The seventh runner-up. There can't be too many of those walking around."

"I'll look into it. Anything else?"

"Only that I bet Yuri Milos valued her too, yet she came to a bad end. So there goes half the argument you just made a minute ago."

"One-third of my argument," he said, correcting me.

I looked right at him. "So you didn't know her?"

He turned to me, but it was too dark to read his expression. "I just said I didn't."

"It occurred to me that she might have worked for you."

"I told you we were unable to place anyone inside the household. Anything else?"

I shook my head. I wanted him to pooh-pooh my fears, but he wasn't a pooh-pooh kind of guy, he was a worst-case-scenario guy. So I sucked it up and shook his hand and he left me at the pool, in full possession of my anxiety. After a moment I waved to the hot-tubbers and walked back down the path for a last night in my own bed.

NINE

I was on the road to Calabasas by seven-thirty a.m., which gave me something in common with half of Los Angeles, slogging along on the 101 North. The other half, from what I could see, was on the 101 South. "Get used to it," I told myself. "Traffic is now your life."

Yes, there'd been bad feng shui at the Oakwood Garden Apartments, but as I'd packed in the predawn hours, listening to the drone of a television through an open window, I was stricken by nostalgia. Whatever heartache or loneliness the residents might feel, whatever restless spirits inhabited that earth, not one bore the combination of secrets weighing me down like a bunch of sandbags. Only one person was in on my clandestine life, and my only connection to him was a frozen yogurt place on Mulholland Highway.

And I had my doubts about him.

Coming to a dead stop just before the 405, I used my time calling everyone who needed my change of address. With the exception of Simon; even if I wanted to tell him, contacting him required a series of steps so complex that I hadn't yet tried them. Now that I'd heard Bennett Graham's yogurt arrangements, I wondered if such security measures were second nature to these people, taught in FBI 101.

My other loved ones had mixed reactions to my move.

"Ah, Calabasas," Fredreeq said. "You let me know if you come across any black people there. We'll alert the news media."

"A gated community and no cell phones?" Joey asked. "Sounds like rehab."

"Calabasas!" my Uncle Theo said. "The word means 'pumpkin,' you know. I'm not familiar with Palomino Hills. Your mother once lived in Calabasas, in a treehouse. Before she met your father and me. She was studying Wiccan. I doubt the coven is there anymore."

I tried to imagine Palomino Hills rolling out the welcome mat for Wiccans. No.

Only my brother was indifferent to Calabasas. "I'll be needing more books," he said. "I'm almost done with *Cutting Through String Theory*. Do you have bookstores there?"

"Yes, P.B. I'm still in America."

I'd used up half my cell phone battery before the 101 North disgorged me onto Valley Circle. At 8:55 I left a message on the MediasRex voice mail, saying I was fifteen minutes away, relieved to confess to a machine and not a person that I was late for my first day of work, thus letting down the team. Also, I was in moving-day clothes. Bad call.

The guard at the gate of Palomino Hills was even less affable today, unable to choke out so much as a hello. I decided to make it my goal to win him over. With a smile, I nodded to the backseat. "I'm moving in. Hence the suitcases. My name's Wollie, by the way."

He didn't acknowledge me, but did show interest in my car, writing its license number on his clipboard before waving me through. Wordlessly. He could've worked for Bennett Graham.

Grusha stood outside Yuri's house, looking grim. She wore an apron over her housedress, reinforcing the impression of hard manual labor. I imagined her getting up in the morning with the cows and accomplishing by noon more than most of us achieve by midnight. She ignored my apologies and grabbed a bag from my hand.

"Late is bad. You give me car keys. I take things to your room. I park your car. You go inside now. Everyone is in library. They wait for you."

"Yes, sorry, but—where are you taking my stuff?"

"House of Blue. You go inside now, the Big House."

Federal prison? No, she must mean Yuri's place. Odd, since all the houses appeared, from the outside, to be the same size.

"Quickly," Grusha said. "Everyone waits for you. In library."

It took me a few minutes to find the library, and they were indeed waiting, all eyes turning to me as I entered the large room. I grew conscious of my painter's pants and Nebraska Cornhuskers sweatshirt, since the Milos wives, Donatella and Kimberly, and the Milos children, Alik and Parashie, were dressed for a Fortune 500 meeting. With them was a man I didn't know.

"Sorry, everyone," I said. "Sorry I'm late."

"Wollie, meet our first arrival," Donatella said, adding, sotto voce, "Change clothes."

The strange man stood. He was over six feet and gave the impression of having football gear under his skin, because his upper body was all muscle, straining to break through the seams of a polyester shirt. His nose was bulging. Even his ears appeared to bulge. He was dressed at least as badly as I, in huge, ill-fitting corduroy pants of some indeterminate earth color. I judged him to be around thirty, maybe younger.

"Wollie, this is Zbigniew," Donatella said. "Zbigniew is just now come to America for the first time and he is one full day early." This seemed to irritate her. "He is from Moldova. Zbigniew, you will no doubt recognize Wollie."

While I wondered why Zbigniew would recognize me, my hand was taken in one the size of an oven mitt and squeezed rather than shaken. His lips parted in something resembling a smile, revealing crooked teeth. "Sop deert," he said.

"Oh. *SoapDirt*. Yes," I said, recalling that this show had made me some kind of celebrity in—Moldova? "Nice to meet you, Zbig—Zb—"

"Zbigniew!" Donatella supplied. "All right, this name, it is impossible. Zbigniew, in America you will be Zbiggo."

Zbiggo was fine with that. Or perhaps he didn't hear. "You will date me?" he asked.

Uh-oh. "No. Well, not"—I glanced at the others, then back to Zbiggo—"exactly. I'm your social coach. We'll be spending time together, certainly, and—"

"She will date me?" he said to the others.

His use of the word "date" suggested more than dinner and a movie.

"Yes, of course, date," Donatella said. "Wollie will certainly date you, Zbiggo."

"Yes," I said, "But let's just clarify—"

"Let's sit." Alik put an arm around Zbiggo, which was a stretch. "Wollie, on the sofa next to Kimberly. Zbiggo, over here by me. Wollie, I was just explaining to Zbiggo that it's your first day so we're late getting up and running. Due to an Air Moldova snafu, Zbiggo was forced to take an earlier flight, or else be delayed three days. Zbiggo, good choice."

"What is it you do, Zbiggo?" I asked.

"Box," he said.

"How . . . nice," I said.

"Heavyweight."

"Yes. I can see that."

He smiled at me then, a wide, happy grin of a smile. "I fight Vegas in December."

"Wonderful," I said, wondering if he meant Vegas the city or Vegas a fellow boxer. I'd never seen a boxing match in my life. Not even on television. I confused boxing with wrestling, in fact.

Kimberly, wearing a tight black suit, said, "Zbiggo's trainer was delayed due to a passport problem. When he gets here, Zbiggo's training schedule will be synchronized with our seminar schedule, and it will be your responsibility, Wollie, to make sure he gets where he needs to go and still makes his sleep quota."

Zbiggo continued to smile. I smiled back. "How much sleep do you need?" I asked.

"Again?"

"Sleep," I said, enunciating carefully. "How many hours each night?"

"With who I am sleep with?" he asked.

I turned to Alik, my smile frozen in place.

Alik nodded at me and hopped up from the sofa. "How about a snack?" He went to an intercom on the wall of the library and pressed a button. "Grusha, let's get Zbiggo something to eat, please."

"Protein," Kimberly said.

"Protein," Alik repeated. "Sausage, or—"

Grusha's disembodied voice cried, "I know, I know. Am I stupid?"

Alik turned to his younger sister. "Parashie, will you show Zbiggo to the kitchen?"

I worried about the diminutive Parashie being alone with leering Zbiggo all the way to the kitchen, but no one else appeared concerned. Certainly not Parashie.

"Come on, Zbiggo," she said and headed out, with Zbiggo shambling after her.

"This is an annoyance," Donatella said, closing the door after them. "He could not warn us he was coming early? And you, Wollie. You must always, always be on time. It is fortunate that Yuri was not here, as he is mad for punctuality. We will not tell him."

"Cut her some slack," Kimberly said. "Her day's going to be All Zbiggo, All the Time. Wollie, it can't be helped, but we'll make it up to you. We've got nothing scheduled for him till tomorrow, so today he's all yours. Good luck."

"What about jet lag?" I asked. "Might he not like to rest up?"

"One can hope," Donatella said.

"He looks pretty wired to me," Kimberly said. "Keep him on a short leash."

Grusha's disembodied voice squawked at us. "A man is at the guard gate. Bob."

"To see whom?" Donatella called.

"The new one."

"Wollie, do you mean?" Donatella turned to me. "Do you know a Bob?"

"Everybody knows a Bob," I said. "Bob who?"

"She doesn't know him well enough. Send him away," Donatella called to Grusha.

As I wondered about Bob, Alik stood. "I'll get you tomorrow's schedule." He crossed the room and opened double doors, revealing an office. Nell was inside, working at a computer. Kimberly explained that Nell was the English tutor as well as Parashie's homeschool teacher, and did record keeping besides. Alik came out of the office with a file and spreadsheets, one of which had "Zbiggo Shpek" written at the top.

"The week's schedule," Alik said. "Zbiggo starts tomorrow morning with two hours of language skills, along with four other trainees whose English needs work; that will be here in the library with Nell. Then lunch, then a group hike in the afternoon. Today, you're in charge. Here's five hundred dollars for incidentals," he said, handing me an envelope. "Keep receipts. You'll have a MediasRex credit card by next week, but let me know when you run out of money. Here." He peeled off another bunch of twenties from a money-clipped wad and handed them to me. "Just in case. Whatever it takes to get Zbiggo through the day."

"What does that mean, exactly?" I asked, but the phone rang and Alik grabbed it.

"Okay, I'm outta here," Kimberly said. "Gotta pick up hiking gear before the airport run. Wollie, what size shoe do you wear?"

"Oh, don't worry about me, I'm not much of a—"

"She is an eleven," Donatella answered. "Wollie? Yuri expected us to have a team meeting this morning but you were late, so that is that. Alik? Are you finished on the phone? Can you give Wollie the tour?"

"No time. I've got to deal with customs," he said. "Athletic equipment. Then Long Beach Airport for Nadja, then back to LAX for Zeferina—Wollie, later. Good luck."

"Here, Wollie," Donatella said, putting keys in my hands. "Keys to the car that you will drive. It is in the garage. The big one. And for God's sake, change clothes. This sweatshirt gives one nightmares. And logos? Never. And no jeans, please."

"Yes, okay, but can you tell me what exactly I'm supposed to do with Zbiggo?"

"This is completely up to you. As Yuri likes to say, keep them out of jail, out of the newspapers, and off the streets."

Any hopes I had that Zbiggo might be sleepy were dashed the moment I found my way into the kitchen, a big state-of-the-art affair with the usual granite counters, center island, Sub-Zero refrigerator, and industrial-sized oven that was so common to upper-crust Los Angeles houses, whether or not anyone actually cooked.

Zbiggo stood at the center island, chowing down on what looked to be raw meat.

"He drinks a lot of coffee," Parashie whispered in my ear. "And he is restless. Maybe you could take him out for a run or something."

Like a dog. Or a Clydesdale. "Can you come too?" I whispered back.

"No, I have a ginormous shopping list. Grusha runs me ragged."

"Parashie, come." Grusha clapped her hands at the girl, then removed her apron. "I drop you at Ralphs, I go to farmers' market." She then pointed to Zbiggo and me. "You. And you. Dinner is seven o'clock. Not sooner, not later. Now, you go. Out of my kitchen."

"Grusha, where will I find my bags?" I asked.

"In your room. House of Blue."

Zbiggo and I followed Grusha and Parashie outside. They hopped into a cute little Honda parked in front of the house and zoomed away. I led Zbiggo to the house I'd not yet been in, the House of Blue, only to find the front door locked. Great. I led Zbiggo back into Big House, and called out, but no one answered. I led him next door, to Donatella's house, but that too was locked. We returned to Big House.

We appeared to be alone in the complex. What a good time to do spying, I thought. But what to do with Zbiggo?

"Hey, I've got an idea," I said. "How about we hang out here for a while?"

"What is that?"

"Hang out? You know, lie around, watch TV, or sit in the library and read. Great opportunity to improve your English, unless they've got some books in Moladovian. Which they might. Anyhow, want to?"

"No. I come to see L.A."

So much for that. "Okay, one problem is that I'm not dressed very . . . elegantly."

"What is this means?"

"Elegance? It's . . . the point is, I look like a bum."

"What is bum?"

The best description of bum would be Zbiggo himself, but it hardly seemed kind to point that out. "Never mind," I said. "You want to see L.A., let's go."

En route to the garage, Zbiggo attempted to hold hands, so I explained in stringent tones that this was not customary in America between people who'd just met, unless they were under the age of six. This could get tricky. Zbiggo was not remotely my type. I have nothing against large people—Simon himself was six foot five—but there was something ungainly about him, and uncivilized. Too much testosterone. Not a wolf, more like a moose. An oversexed moose. I would just have to find something likable about him.

The garage, not surprisingly, was huge. One car resided there, with room for at least seven more, by my estimate.

"And this must be ours," I said. "My, it's big, isn't it? Good. I'd hate to have you squeeze into a Mini Cooper. For instance. This is a—what is this, anyway?"

"Zuhboodbun."

"Pardon me? Oh, of course," I said as Zbiggo pointed to letters on the back of the vehicle. "A Suburban. Great." Another first. I'd never driven a sports utility vehicle. I avoid sports, period. I tried the doors. Locked.

"You drive me?" Zbiggo asked.

"Yes, that's the plan."

This seemed to fill him with glee. "You drive me. You date me."

"You and two others. That's the gig. But I am not a standard date, I am a social coach, and there's a distinction." I pressed buttons on the key until I heard a click, then tried the door again. It opened with difficulty. When I pulled on it, I nearly dislocated my shoulder. "Good God, it's like it's made of concrete," I said.

Zbiggo stepped in and took the door from me, swinging it wide. I brushed against his massive torso, which was rock hard, and then he made a move toward me and I imagined him tossing me up and into the Suburban the way you'd throw someone onto a horse. To preempt this, I launched myself into the driver's seat, avoiding full physical contact. His hand did connect with my derriere, but there was a slight chance he was just trying to be helpful. I pushed him away with a firm "Thank you."

He got in the passenger seat but rejected the seat belt. "I don't like."

"Click it or ticket, Zbiggo." I folded my arms, prepared to spend the next eighteen hours in the garage. After an aggrieved sigh, he stretched the safety harness across his broad expanse of chest and buckled it.

The engine started up with a roar that would make an airplane proud, and I backed the SUV down the driveway with something akin to terror. It felt like I was driving a house.

"What this? TV?" he asked, pointing to the small screen on the ceiling behind us.

"Probably a DVD player."

"How it work?" he asked, pressing buttons on the dashboard in a random manner, causing windshield wipers to wipe and the radio to blast forth static. Zbiggo kept himself happy for several minutes, finding music stations. I pulled out of Palomino Hills and noticed a grungy red car parked on the shoulder of the road just outside the gates on Mulholland Highway. It started up and, with a squeal of spinning tires, jumped onto the road behind me.

Zbiggo settled on hip-hop.

"Well, then," I said with a glance in the rearview mirror. "Now that you're in America, how would you like to spend your first day?"

"Meet girls," he said. "Beverly Hills. Hollywood. Disneyland."

"I can do two out of four," I said.

The drive through the Santa Monica Mountains was long and tortured, and the red car, a Ford Escort, stayed behind us the whole time. Part of the torture was moving this whalelike vehicle through the winding Las Virgenes Canyon roads—not the best route, I discovered—then down Pacific Coast Highway at a reasonable speed while staying in one lane; the rest was Zbiggo's fractured speech. The hip-hop station disappeared into static, and Zbiggo felt a need to talk. After twenty minutes or so, his accent began to yield up its secrets and I could hear letter substitutions that were consistent, the d's that were actually rolled r's and a clipped quality on certain vowel sounds. We kept at it and began to experience something approaching conversation. Zbiggo, when not focused on sex, was a lot more bearable, although I found myself glancing at the Sub-urban's dashboard clock, wondering how many waking hours he had in him.

". . . the car Chai drive?" he said, interrupting my mental calculations.

"What?"

"Is this car also for Chai?" he asked.

I glanced over at him. "You knew Chai?"

"Da."

"When?"

"In my country."

I was confused. "Chai visited . . . Moldova?"

"April, she is come to Ukraine, to Kyiv. With Yuri. I come to Kyiv also. To meet. MediasRex."

Interesting. Why would Yuri take Chai to Ukraine, if her job, like mine, was transporting the clients around Los Angeles? I glanced in the rearview mirror as PCH turned into the 10 East. The red car was still with me. "Zbiggo, you know that Chai's dead?"

"Da. In Kyiv, she is sick."

"Chai was sick in Kyiv?"

"She is stay in hotel. Sick. Throw out."

"They threw her out? Of the hotel? For being sick?"

He shook his head, then made retching noises. "Throw out?"

"Oh. You mean throw up. Well, that's a shame. But Chai didn't die from being sick. She drove off a cliff."

Zbiggo grunted.

"So, Zbiggo," I asked, "was Kimberly also in Kyiv? Or Alik? Or—"

"No. Yuri. Chai. Only these."

I found this disquieting, that Chai had traveled alone with Yuri. And what exactly was Chai's job there? Not driving, probably. And was this something I'd be expected to do too?

Speaking of jobs, I was working for Uncle Sam now too, in addition to MediasRex. "Hey, Zbiggo," I said, "can I see your passport?"

"What for you want it?"

"Well, it's a hobby of mine. A new hobby." So new, in fact, I'd just that moment started it. "I love to see passports from other countries, check out what they look like. Every country's different. It's always fun to see how other people do it."

"Do it?" He looked at me and grinned. "Do it?"

"Yes. Do . . . passports. Design them."

"You like to see people do it?"

"We're talking about passports, right? Yes. I would find that interesting." How had this become sexual?

Zbiggo grinned bigger, showing me the full glory of his teeth. No state-subsidized dental care in his country, apparently. "You want see my passport?" he asked, spreading his hands, palms up, in a "be my guest" gesture. "Come. Look for it. You find it, you can have."

"Okay, never mind," I said. "In America, we keep our hands at ten and two on the steering wheel while driving."

Some of us did, anyway. Me and one or two frightened student drivers. But this shut down conversation for a moment, giving me time to reflect once more on my dead predecessor and wonder how she'd handled the clients. And wonder again why the FBI seemed not to have heard of her, let alone express concern. And wonder why that damn red car was still behind me.

I got off the Santa Monica Freeway without signaling, and lost the Escort.

The Four Seasons Beverly Hills was an imposingly high white building guarded by palm trees. I led Zbiggo through the lobby, telling myself that no one was looking at us. There were employees and guests dressed impeccably, even gorgeously, and many dressed casually as well, but no one was dressed like Zbiggo and me. Perhaps if the Teamsters were holding a union meeting in one of the ballrooms, Zbiggo wouldn't appear so out of place. As for me in my Cornhuskers sweatshirt, I just looked like a very tall, aging college coed.

One problem was Zbiggo's gawk factor. I tried to keep him moving, but he moseyed along, stopping to turn in circles and admire the hotel lobby. At one point, he plopped onto a sofa and expressed a wish to "haf drink."

"Water, definitely," I said. "Alcohol, no."

"Vodka, yes?"

"In America, we consider vodka alcohol. Come."

"Why I not drink vodka?"

Good question. If he was drinking, he might grow sleepy, which could make my life easier. Unless he turned mean. Or danced with lampshades on his head. Yuri would probably not like that. "Later, Zbiggo," I said. "I promise."

I got him through the lobby and onto an escalator, where he continued to ogle not just women but also men, artwork, the ceiling, flowers, shops, and the escalator itself. "Are you from a small town, Zbiggo?" I asked.

"Vulcanesti."

"Ah." No Four Seasons there, probably.

On the lower level, I found Spa Services. Inside, the strong scent of lavender greeted us. Ambient music permeated the room, the kind that always seems to accompany expensive massage. A sign on the desk requested that we abstain from cell phone use, to preserve the spa experience of our fellow guests. I took a moment to turn off mine.

"May I help you?" whispered the woman behind the desk.

"I'm here to see Fredreeq Munson," I whispered back.

"Are you the Fruit and Pumpkin?"

"Excuse me?"

"You're her eleven o'clock? Mrs. Van Breughel? Fruit and Pumpkin Enzyme Peel?"

"No, Ms. Shelley. Friend."

She frowned, a tinge less subservient. Then she saw Zbiggo, and visibly stiffened.

"And he's . . . with me," I said.

"You give massage?" Zbiggo asked her, not whispering at all.

"Me personally? No." She matched his volume. "I can schedule one for you."

"No," I said. "He doesn't need a—wait. How much are they?"

"Swedish? Deep tissue? Shiatsu?"

"Any. All."

The treatments began at one hundred twenty-five and went up to over a thousand for the all-day plan. As I looked over the price list, Fredreeq came out from the back room.

"Wollie, what are you doing here?"

"Got a minute?" I asked.

Fredreeq looked at Zbiggo and then at the receptionist, who frowned at her.

"What?" Fredreeq asked. "Hey, no need to give me the evil eye. When Mrs. Van Breughel comes, they'll go."

I looked at Zbiggo. "You like massage, right?"

"I get woman?"

"A masseur would be far better." I turned to the receptionist. "Is that possible?"

"I'll see who's available. Which type of massage would you like?"

"Shiatsu."

"When?"

"The sooner the better."

She looked at her book. "For how long?"

I handed her Alik's envelope full of cash. "As much as this will buy."

Fredreeq, as I suspected, knew quite a bit about *America's Next Top Model*.

"I seem to remember a Chai," she said, closing her eyes momentarily. "Yes. It was the season that Yolanda 'Yolie' Yvonne ended up winning. Chai, yes. Tall? Blond?"

"Aren't they all?"

"No, they like to get some ethnic variety going, stir up racial tension. What do you want with Chai?"

"Nothing directly. I just need to know how she died."

"Chai *died*?"

I told Fredreeq what I knew and explained my sense of disquiet that was approaching obsession. "So anyhow," I said, "I'm wondering what the official word was on Chai."

Fredreeq picked up the phone. "Shaz will know. She's a shut-in. TV is her life."

Fredreeq put her cousin, who lived in Mar Vista, on the speaker-phone. "Sure I remember Chai. Brown hair, not blond. They tried to make her cut it, but she wouldn't. They kicked her off for not having enough range, but also, the child had a bad runway walk."

"Did you know she's dead?" Fredreeq asked.

"Dead? No."

"Yes."

"No. Hold on. I'm googling her."

Fredreeq turned to me, raising her eyebrows. Within sixty seconds, Shaz was back on the line. "Well, would you look at that?"

"What?"

"She's dead all right. Sad little obit in the *Oxnard Star*."

"Shaz, this is Wollie," I said to the phone. "How come the *Oxnard Star*?"

"Her hometown," Shaz said. "Nothing in *TV Guide*, or the *L.A. Times*. Not even *Variety*. That is just plain wrong. She was one of our own. Show some respect."

"Do you have the obituary there?" I asked. "How's it say she died?"

"Now that's another thing." She tsked into the phone. "'Cause of death was not reported.' Is that really the best they can do? Be glad you don't come from Oxnard."

An intercom on the wall announced the arrival of Mrs. Van Breughel.

"I don't like it," Fredreeq said, walking me out. "No media attention for that girl? I'm not saying she was A-list, but she was young and beautiful and that should get you a paragraph in *The Hollywood Reporter*. You'd think *Top Model* would get some press out of it, maybe an *ET* segment. Thank God Chai isn't around to see it. Not to sound cold."

It did sound cold, but it was true. And I found it sad.

"I'm going to tell you something else," Fredreeq said. "I'm having a bad feeling about this. And my bad feelings are never wrong."

Which wasn't what I wanted to hear. Because I was having the same feeling.

TEN

Zbiggo's all-day shiatsu was not a success.

All masseurs having been unavailable, he'd been given a masseuse, and had then done something unspeakable to her—no one told me what—that made her walk away. But the Four Seasons had a powerful the-customer-is-always-right policy and offered him instead a detoxifying moor mud wrap with manicure and pedicure, on the theory that three women working on him at once would lessen their chances of suffering whatever indignity Miss Shiatsu had undergone. They also served him three Bloody Marys.

I discovered this only after Donatella called me. I was at the Four Seasons bar, a lovely place called Windows, sketching a greeting card that featured a superheroine ("Good luck on saving the world!") and hydrating. I had gone through an entire bottle of Evian, had been to the bathroom twice, and was on my way there again when my cell phone rang.

"What are you wearing?" Donatella asked.

"Uh—what I had on this morning," I said, looking down at myself. "A Nebraska Cornhuskers sweatshirt—"

"I knew it! There is an outfit hanging on your closet door. Why are you not in it?"

"I never made it to my room, Donatella. Everyone ran off, doors were locked—"

"Yes, never mind. Where are you?"

"The Four Seasons. Beverly Hills."

This produced an anguished scream. "Are you mad? Wearing that Cornsuckers shirt? And Zbiggo without a shower for seventy-two hours? Do you not see that you represent MediasRex? You *are* Medias-Rex. Yuri would remove my head if he were to see you."

"I'm sorry to hear that, but—"

"Come home. At once. You must go to LAX and fetch Stasik. But now you must first change clothes, so now we are in a huge hurry. Huge. Drive like the wind. You cannot be late, ever, for an airport pickup."

"Okay, but Zbiggo is having an all-day shiatsu, so could I—"

"Cancel it. You cannot leave him there." And then Donatella hung up before explaining anything else, like who Stasik was. My next date, presumably.

I rushed to the spa and explained that I needed to collect Zbiggo, which was when the receptionist explained the shiatsu snafu. "I'm very sorry," I said. "He's new to our ways."

"So I heard. He's informed us that in his country, he's a professional killer."

"Excuse me?"

"A hit man."

"I'm sure he miscommunicated. He's a boxer. His English is—a work in progress."

She sniffed. If she weren't so refined, she would've snorted. "This way," she said, and she led me to a room where three women were working on Zbiggo. They appeared unmolested. He appeared asleep. Naked but for a towel over his private parts and covered in mud.

"Zbiggo." I prodded a bicep or tricep, but he didn't move. I had no idea how three Bloody Marys could do this to someone his size, but Zbiggo had hit the wall. I addressed the women. "Please, I must get him out of here. Fast. Preferably clothed. Family emergency."

The quartet gazed at me with interest, but no one cried, "Allow me to help!"

I handed out twenties and promised to write a letter of commendation to the president of the hotel, at which point the four seasons, as I began to think of them, rose to the occasion. They got Zbiggo dressed with great dexterity and no squeamishness, and with the help of two bellhops and a luggage cart, got him into the Suburban and buckled up. Small pieces of moor mud were caking off all over the upholstery, but this was the least of my worries. The operation had set me back forty minutes. I headed west with Zbiggo next to me sawing logs, his body sprawled across the seat, held in place by the shoulder belt.

Traffic was nightmarish. I called the compound to report my whereabouts and ETA, but there was no answer. I left Donatella a message. There was a time when I considered it dangerous to talk on the phone while driving, even with my hands-free unit, but progress on the 10 West was so slow, I could've crocheted sweaters along the way.

My cell phone, now fully awake, chose to inform me of two messages that had come in earlier in the morning, something it did only sporadically. P.B. had called requesting a book on quantum physics, and Simon had called, wanting to see me. "No kidding," he said. "And ASAP. I'll be in touch. Meanwhile, be careful. Very."

What? This was bad. I glanced quickly in the rearview mirror, out the windows, and then at the snoring, heaving hulk beside me. That "be careful, very" would not be idle chitchat. Simon didn't indulge in casual messages, especially since he couldn't call me from his cell. But if you have to troll for public pay phones that actually work, why not say something specific? And must it all be warnings and negativity? An occasional "You're a wonderful human being," for instance, would not go amiss.

At least there was no red car behind me, I thought, checking the rearview mirror again.

Another spylike thought occurred to me. This was a golden opportunity to find Zbiggo's passport. I glanced at him. Still out cold. I didn't understand it, but I couldn't overlook a gift like this, my big chance to get in his pants.

I waited for the next halt in traffic, then went for the pocket nearest me. It was a long reach across the Suburban, but I have long arms. I was able to get two fingers into his pocket before the traffic moved, then steered with my left hand while my right did a search. His snores and grunts reassured me. Eventually I unearthed a plane ticket from Chişinău, wherever that was, to Istanbul. There was also a bottle of pills. Prescription, probably. I couldn't read the label, but on it was a tiny martini glass with a diagonal line through it. Aha. That could explain Zbiggo's comatose state. I returned these items to his front pocket and turned my attention to his rear.

I couldn't search the back pockets with Zbiggo's seat belt on, so at the next traffic stop, I made the sign of the cross and unhooked him. Instantly he started to list toward me, a two-hundred-something-pound husk of a man. I pushed him back into an upright position. After putting my right hand in places my hand did not want to be, I found the passport. It belonged to Zbigniew Alexeyevich Shpek, born May 7, 1980, in Vulcanesti, Moldova. I wrote the passport number on a gum wrapper in my purse, looking up from this task just in time to slam on my brakes and avoid rear-ending a Honda Odyssey. This sent Zbiggo careening forward, his head banging into the dashboard, but neither this nor my "Aaagghh!" awakened him. I pushed him back into his seat. So much for writing while driving. I decided to commit the other vital statistics to memory, and thus strengthen my memorization muscles. "Shpek, Vulcanesti, 1980," I mumbled repeatedly, returning the passport to the pocket.

I was trying to rebuckle Zbiggo when my phone rang, nearly sending me through the roof. It was Kimberly. "What's your location and how's it going with Zbiggo?" she asked.

"I'm on the 10 West, nearing PCH," I said. "And Zbiggo—is calmer."

"PCH? Heading to Calabasas? No! You've gotta be at LAX. You're picking up Stasik, because I'm caught on the Antelope Valley Freeway, there's a four-car collision ahead of me and nobody's moved an inch in days. Didn't Donatella tell you—"

"Yes, yes, Kimberly, I *am* going to LAX, but Donatella said to change clothes, so—"

"Babe. Listen to me. Does that make an iota of sense to you? I don't care what you look like, I need you to be on time to pick up this guy. Rule number one. On-time pickup. Yuri's a freak about that. Get off the freeway and turn around."

"Okay, but—"

"I'll take care of Donatella, you just get to the airport. Stasik Miroj-nik, international terminal, a flight coming in from Heathrow, I'll call you back with the flight number. Bye."

"Goodbye," I mumbled and hit the turn signal, getting the Suburban off the freeway before being pulled into the vortex of Pacific Coast Highway, from which there would be no escape. I'd only just achieved this feat, with lots of self-congratulation, when the phone rang.

"Wollie, it's Donatella. Where are you?"

"I just exited the 10 West, and now I'm trying to get back on the 10 East, and—"

"No! No! Turn around. You are to come to Calabasas instantly."

"Yes, but Kimberly just called me—"

"Is she your boss? No. I am accountable for your look and I will not have you running about in those clothes. Also Zbiggo looked like a train wreck. I gave you instructions—"

"What? Zbiggo was supposed to change clothes too?"

"We will settle for you. You cannot represent MediasRex looking as you do. Come now. If you hurry, there is just enough time. You should not have gotten off the freeway."

"Okay," I said, "but isn't it more important to be on time to—"

"That is minimalist thinking! That is not how we do things! I will not hear excuses from you because Yuri will not hear excuses from me. Do you hear? Do you love this job?"

Zbiggo began to slump toward me. I stuck out an arm to prop him up, and this caused my hands-free earpiece to slip, but I trapped it between my ear and shoulder, at an angle that precluded good driving. "At the moment, Donatella," I managed to say, "I am not in love with—"

"If you value it at all, you will get back here at once. At once. I will hang up now."

I hung up too and made my way back to the 10 West. I had no idea who was top dog in Yuri's absence, his current wife or his former wife, but I knew who scared me more. Also, if I drove fast and prayed hard—not that I'm any prayer expert—then I might be able to make both women happy. Or, if not happy, at least not viciously unhappy.

This became my mantra, to reach Calabasas as fast as this automotive elephant could get me there. This meant not stopping to rebuckle Zbiggo, because stopping meant pulling over and once out of the flow of traffic, I was doubtful about my ability to jump back in. Precious minutes would be lost. My determination to pull this off got me to wondering about Donatella's last question. I did not love this job. Who could? I needed it, though. And they'd hired me in good faith, so I had to give it my best shot.

Which included not killing Zbiggo. He was being awfully quiet. Was he even breathing? I reached out and grabbed his wrist. I couldn't find his pulse. I started to panic, then grabbed his throat. No pulse there either, but suddenly he erupted into a kind of extended groan, frightening yet comforting.

By the time I reached the Calabasas highlands, I was exhausted, and I'd only been on the job for six hours. I parked in the driveway of Big House. My charge was still in the Land of Nod, so I left him there and ran inside.

"Wollie, thank God," Donatella cried, meeting me in the foyer, arms filled with clothes. "You have only forty minutes now to get to LAX and pick up Stasik. We must pray his plane is delayed. Where is Zbiggo?"

"In the driveway. Asleep."

"Alone?"

"Do you think someone will steal him?" I asked.

"Never mind. Dress, now. There is the bathroom. Is that clay on your face?"

"Yes, I—"

"Don't explain. Here—" Donatella handed me a folder. "The flight itinerary and a photo of Stasik and a sign for you to hold so he will know it is you. He will carry a banjo case. Hurry. Hurry. And water! Take water for him. Their hydration is your responsibility."

I glanced out to the driveway. "And Zbiggo?"

"You will have to take him, of course."

Of course. It was either that or dump him in the driveway, since I could see him still sleeping, his mouth wide open. I changed into the suit, grabbed three bottles of water from the kitchen, and headed outside. I couldn't help but notice a dozen or so men on the far side of the property. Couldn't one of them be pulled off the gardening detail and temporarily reassigned to transportation?

Once again, I nearly dislocated my shoulder opening the door to the Suburban. Was it made of iron? Closing it took three tries. None of which woke my passenger.

Los Angeles International Airport is not where most people would choose to be on a Tuesday at rush hour, and many were grumpy, as evidenced by excessive honking of horns and cutting off of other people when lanes merged. Approaching the international terminal, I tried to wake Zbiggo. In fact, I'd tried to wake him since Calabasas, because I couldn't get his seat belt on him. He was sitting on the buckle part and no amount of pushing could budge him. I'd wasted five full minutes in the driveway working on it before deciding that risking his life in slow traffic was less dangerous than letting Donatella see him covered in moor mud.

His continued unconsciousness presented a problem, because I couldn't just park the Suburban and leave Zbiggo alone in it. I could write him a note, explaining where he was and that I'd be right back, but I had no guarantee he was literate in English and my Russian—was that what he spoke?—was limited to "nyet" and "borscht." So I placed on the dashboard the sign saying STASIK MIROJNIK and kept driving. With luck, Stasik would find his own way through immigration, baggage claim, and customs and out to the sidewalk. I tried to call the cell phone listed on his fact sheet, but it wasn't accepting messages.

Curbside parking at LAX is a crime for which you can be shot on sight, so I was forced to circle the terminal, which meant circling the whole airport, an exercise in stress. I kept one eye on the collection of buses, limousines, and other drivers determined to keep me away from the curb lane, and one eye on the passengers, looking for Stasik. His photo didn't help. There were thousands of people waiting for rides at the international terminal, seven hundred of whom could conceivably be Stasik Mirojnik, all of them wearing the patina of travel exhaustion, their will to live having been sucked out of them by untold hours spent sitting elbow to elbow with their fellow man. Happily, very few carried banjo cases.

And then I saw him. At least, I saw the banjo case, which was enough. I honked, he raised a hand in greeting, and the Suburban muscled its way through the crowd and over to the curb, nearly annihilating a PT Cruiser in the process. As I was looking for the button to roll down the window, after realizing they were all tinted, Stasik opened the passenger-side door. Zbiggo began to slide out, but Stasik had good reflexes. He crammed Zbiggo back in and slammed the door shut—on the first try, too, meaning he was stronger than he looked. A second later he opened the back door and threw in his luggage, then hopped in after it.

"Who's he?" he said, nodding at the front seat.

"This is Zbiggo . . . Shpek."

"Dead?"

"Dead? No, he's not dead. He's jet-lagged."

He paused. Then, "Where's he from?"

"From—" What was the name of his country? My memory faltered. "He's a Vulcan. Or something. And a Taurus."

"What's on his face?"

"Moor mud. You're Stasik, I hope?"

"Yes."

"Good. I'm Wollie."

"You're late." He spoke in such clipped tones, it was hard to be sure, but he sounded British. He was twenty-four, according to his fact sheet, and from what I could see under a scrunched-up Greek fisherman's cap, both good-looking and bad-humored.

"I am late," I said. "You're right. I'm very sorry. On behalf of Medias-Rex Enterprises, welcome to America."

"You can skip the spiel," he said. "What's your part in this?"

"I'm your social coach."

He leaned back in his seat and pulled his cap down over his eyes. "Meaning what?"

"You may well ask." At least his English was excellent. "I believe I'm a combination chauffeur, concierge, companion, translator, and tour guide. And date."

"You believe?"

"It's my first day."

"It was Chai's job."

"You knew her too?"

"Obviously. So now she's dead and they've got you. Are you a model?"

"Do I look like one?"

"Not from here."

I resisted an urge to check my face in the rearview mirror. "Where'd you meet Chai?"

"Bratislava. With Yuri."

"Do you know how she died?"

He didn't answer at first. Then, "What do you mean?"

"The newspapers here didn't mention how she died," I said.

"The American media is stupid."

Hard to argue with that. "How was the flight, by the way?"

"I lived. Let's lose the pleasantries."

"Okay." I glanced in the rearview mirror. "Your English is amazing."

"Given that I went to Oxford, not all that amazing."

That was it. British with a touch of Eastern Europe.

"So how did Chai die?" I asked again, but he didn't answer. I looked in the rearview mirror and saw he was on his cell phone. I was left alone with my thoughts.

Had he really thought Zbiggo was dead? It must've been some kind of Euro-witticism, because who but an undertaker would jump to that conclusion, seeing a sleeping body?

And what was the deal with Chai?

My own phone rang.

"Wollie! It's Uncle Theo. My dear, did you say you're in Palomino

Hills? Wonderful news: Apollo has a Caltech professor whose mother lives there, and tomorrow—"

The call-waiting beep sounded. "Uncle Theo, so sorry, I gotta take this call, I'm actually working right now." I hit the talk button. "Hello?"

"Wollie, it's Alik. Where are you?"

"Sepulveda, going north," I said. "I just picked up Stasik and—"

"Good. Listen, can you meet me? I need to give you my passengers. I have an emergency situation that needs to be dealt with."

"Sure," I said, glancing at snoring Zbiggo. "The more the merrier."

"There's a Hamburger Hamlet on Sepulveda. I can be there in five minutes."

"I'll be there in ten," I said.

"What's going on?" Stasik asked, interrupting his own conversation.

"We're meeting Alik Milos, picking up more passengers."

"*Govno.*"

"What's *govno* mean?" I said.

"Take a guess."

I came to a sudden stop and Zbiggo once again hit his head on the dashboard. "Shit," I mumbled.

"That's it," Stasik said. "Very good."

Emboldened by something approaching a kind word, I asked Stasik to help with Zbiggo's seat belt. He was able to simultaneously buckle up Zbiggo and teach me more Russian phrases. By the time we reached Hamburger Hamlet, I knew *govno, yobe tvoyu mat,* and *zhopa,* none of them suitable for polite company.

ELEVEN

Alik stood outside Hamburger Hamlet, surrounded by luggage. His back was to me. I pulled up in front of a fire hydrant just as he turned, revealing a cell phone at his ear.

"—know my *father's* lawyers, yeah. What, you suggest I call *them*?" he said, implying he'd sooner stand naked on Hollywood and Vine. Then he saw me and ended his call.

"You made good time." He opened the driver's-side door and hit a button, popping the hatch. "Hey, Stasik," he said, then switched to Russian. Obviously, they were well acquainted, and they launched into a spirited, irritable discussion as Alik converted the huge cargo space into a third row of passenger seating.

"That's a whole lotta luggage," I said, climbing out of the Suburban and grabbing a suitcase. "Will it all fit?"

"It'll fit," Alik said. "Let's get the trainees in."

"Where are they?" I asked, breathing heavily.

Alik nodded toward the restaurant. "Inside, checking out our American culinary institution." He threw the last of the bags into the back and slammed it shut. Then he turned to me. "Wollie, you're saving my life here. Yuri won't like it if he learns I dropped this in your lap, but I know you can handle it." His pointed look made it clear what he was asking.

"Yuri doesn't need to know about it," I said. "I mean, he won't hear it from me."

Alik kissed me on both cheeks. "You're a sweetheart." With that, he dashed inside Hamburger Hamlet, leaving me standing there, smiling in response. He came out a moment later with four people trailing him. His cell phone rang and he answered it, turning away.

I stepped forward to greet two women and two men. They were a motley crew, making me wonder why Alik and I had to be so dressed up to transport them. "I'm Wollie."

"*Mucho gusto*," said a motherly woman, shaking my hand. "Zeferina Maria Catalina Hidalgo de Abragon, but just call me Zeferina Maria Catalina."

The man next to her stepped forward. He wore a dreadful Hawaiian shirt, but he himself was pleasant-looking, with red hair and freckles. "I am enchanted I am meeting you," he said, beaming, then pulled me into an embrace. "My name is Felix. What a wonderful opportunity to be here in United States."

"Welcome to Los Angeles, Felix," I said, letting myself be hugged. When he released me, I turned to the third passenger, a thin, pale girl. "Hi. My name is Wollie."

"Nadja," she said, crushing my hand in a surprising grip.

"Ivan," the other man said, nodding at me. He had at least three days' worth of beard going on and red-rimmed eyes. "I am the uncle of Nadja. Call me Vanya."

I smiled. "Uncle Vanya. Like Chekhov." No one smiled in response.

"What? Now?" Alik said into his phone. "Don't do a thing. I'm on my way. Wollie," he said, turning to me. "Gotta fly. Get them home and hand 'em over to Grusha." Without waiting for an answer, he got into the Voyager double-parked in front of me.

"Alik!" screamed Nadja. "My bicycle! Where it is?"

"In the back of my van," Alik called to her. "It's safe. I'll be home later tonight."

"No! I don't go nowhere without! Also my tings!"

"Nadja, I don't have time now to—" Alik said.

"Then I come with!" Nadja ran toward the Voyager, nearing hysterics. "I don't go without I have my bicycle!"

"Damn it." Alik hopped out of his van, raced to the back, and began to pull items out of the trunk. Among Nadja's "tings" were a bicycle enclosed in bubble wrap, wheels, a helmet, and miscellaneous sporting gear. Nadja and her uncle took the items from Alik, and then I went to help, with Zeferina Whatever-the-rest-of-her-names-were and Felix right behind me. The stuff kept on coming, until all of us were loaded up with various bags and oversized items. I carried a bicycle pump and swimmer's fins.

"There. That's everything," Alik said to Nadja as he closed the hatch. "You've got some trust issues we're going to address, but I don't have time now. This isn't the third world and no one's going to steal your bicycle. Okay?"

"Okay, it is only that—"

"It's fine, just go with Wollie and get some sleep."

And with that, he was gone. Leaving us on the corner of Sepulveda with way too much stuff even for a Suburban. I knew this because when I opened the rear, the things Alik had just crammed in started spilling out. A garment bag slid onto my foot.

"The ceiling," Zeferina Etcetera said, pointing to the top of the car. "In my country, we put things on ceiling."

"The roof?" I said. Sure enough, on top of the Suburban there was a luggage rack, but how to reach it without a ladder?

"But not my bicycle. My bicycle, she sit with me." Nadja clutched her bubble wrap.

"Also the wheels," Uncle Vanya said, holding them up.

"You can put my suitcase up there," Felix said, hoisting a duffel big enough to hold a body. "I have no trust issue."

"Okay, good." I climbed onto the back bumper and checked out the luggage rack. "I've never operated one of these. Anyone know how they work?"

No one did. Nadja's uncle hoisted me up on his shoulders for a better look. It was a simple metal apparatus, like a big dish rack, with no way to hold anything in place. In my own car I carried bungee cords, but the Suburban, under all the luggage, held only tools, the kind I figured were for changing tires. Not that I'd ever done that. "Anyone have a belt?" I asked. "How about a rope? The sash of a bathrobe? Extra-long shoelaces, that's all I ask."

"I have suspenders." Felix set to work opening his bag. "I find them now for you."

Stasik emerged from the Suburban. "What's the bloody holdup?"

"Just getting luggage squared away," I said, throwing bags back into the trunk. "Got a bungee cord on you?"

Stasik stared at me, appalled. "I realize this is your first day," he said, "but if it's any indication of how thing are run here, I've made a big mistake."

"Stasik, it's not an indication of anything except—me. I'm underprepared. It's not MediasRex. MediasRex is a well-oiled machine." Why I felt so protective of Yuri's organization was anyone's guess. "Look, suspenders!" I took them from Felix gratefully. "Have you all met? Go ahead and introduce yourselves."

Felix and I hoisted his suitcase/body bag up onto the Suburban. I trussed it as well as I could, thinking about what Joey had said to me, that I had only to summon up my tough-cookie character and inhabit her in order to pull off this operation. The problem was, she'd need superpowers just to get me through the job part of the job, never mind the spying part.

The sudden *whoop! whoop!* of a police siren interrupted my operation, and I turned to see a squad car pull up behind me.

"Got a problem there, ma'am?" the cop called through his open window.

"No—yes—no," I said. "Just securing a bag, Officer. I'm not parked. I know this isn't a parking space. I know it's a fire hydrant. Sorry. Very sorry. Be gone in a second."

"Right now," the cop said. "Or I'll have to cite you."

Okay, that wouldn't be good, getting a parking ticket on the first day. Under any circumstances, encounters with cops gave me a fluttery stomach. Not happy butterfly flutters, either. More like a bucket of worms. I worked feverishly and managed to get the suspenders tied around Felix's oversized bag. "No problem," I said, climbing down the rear bumper.

Which was when I saw that there was no sign of Stasik, Felix, Zeferina Whatsername, Nadja, or Uncle Vanya. Or the excess luggage. I opened the driver's door to the Suburban and stuck my head in. There was Zbiggo, snoring softly, but no one else. I looked around the street.

"Ma'am? This is your last warning."

"Yes, I'm going." I got in the car, started the engine, and rolled down the window. I pulled forward slowly, fighting back panic. How could I misplace five of the six people I was in charge of? I glanced in the rearview mirror. The squad car was there, tailing me, making sure I was leaving. I'd have to circle the block and come back. Please God, I thought, let someone commit a real crime in the meantime, so this cop has someone else to pick on.

It seemed like an eternity before I got to Exposition Boulevard, my first opportunity to turn left, at which point the cop peeled off, seeking bigger lawbreakers. I got back to National Boulevard without getting sucked onto the 405 freeway, but it was ten minutes before I made it to Hamburger Hamlet again. There, thank God, were my trainees, complete with the bubble-wrapped bicycle, waiting on the sidewalk.

"What was that all about?" I asked as they piled in.

"Did you lose him?" Stasik asked.

"The police? Yes," I said. "But why'd you all disappear?"

"I don't like police," Nadja said, apparently speaking for all of them.

"In America," I said, "they don't throw you randomly in jail. Not even for parking in front of a fire hydrant." I felt like some kind of tour bus operator. Or docent.

No one responded to that. They simply arranged themselves in the two rows of seats, moving bags and bike gear around them as best they could. Next to me, Zbiggo snored on.

"Can we go now?" Stasik asked.

"Absolutely," I said. "Everyone buckle up. Cops do take that seriously."

Everyone complied without further ado. *Things are looking up,* I said to myself.

And they were, until I glanced in the rearview mirror and saw through the back window Felix's bag bouncing onto Sepulveda Boulevard.

TWELVE

If you've never caused a traffic jam by dropping a large object onto a six-lane boulevard, I can tell you that it's an experience that generates terror, noise, embarrassment, and a large amount of bad will and bad language. In our case there was also underwear.

Felix was gracious about it, considering that it was his underwear, and socks, shirts, and pants strewn across Sepulveda. I pulled over as soon as I could, around the corner on Exposition, and then I hopped out, along with Felix, Zeferina, Nadja, and Stasik. Uncle Vanya stayed in the Suburban, presumably to guard the bicycle and perhaps Zbiggo.

Stasik ran into the street, dodging traffic to rescue the soft-sided suitcase, an act of heroism that completely surprised me. The rest of us grabbed clothes and sundry items liberated from the suitcase due to a zipper that must've given up the ghost midair. There were also books littering the landscape, mostly foreign, but three in English. I'm always intrigued by what people read and even now noted the titles: *Don't Put the Lord on Hold* and *Big Dreams, Big Results* and *Alternative Energy Sources for the 21st Century.*

Felix, chasing a shirt, called to us to let everything go, assuring us that he had nothing worth risking our lives over, but this was a strangely determined group and only when all visible items were gathered did they call off the search.

We piled back in the car, rearranging bodies and luggage and the former contents of Felix's suitcase. Every passenger held something on his or her lap. The ice was broken now, and conversation flourished. Felix overflowed with gratitude at the communal rescue effort.

"I think your suspenders are history, though," I said. "Sorry. This was all my fault."

"My suspenders, they now recycle. Someone will find who will have need of them."

I tried to think if I'd ever seen a homeless person in L.A. in suspenders. A greeting card image popped into my head: CNN's Larry King pushing a shopping cart. I discarded it. "What is it you do, Felix?" I asked.

"I spread the good word."

"Which good word is that?" I asked.

"Two hundred thirty-seven pounds have left my body."

"What? How have you done this?" Zeferina asked.

"I have not done it. Jesus has done it. 'By myself I can do nothing.' John, chapter five, verse thirty. I have written a book on my adventure. It is called *Jesus Made Me Skinny*."

Nadja let out a scream. "You wrote *Jesus Made Me Skinny*?"

"Yes. Have you read it?"

"No. At World Triathlon Cup, the German girl, she reads it. She tells of it. I want to buy for my sister, my sister is fat, but she does not read in German."

"I can send her my book in Dutch, Japanese, Serbian, Slovak, or, of course, Russian," Felix said. "And in August my book is in English."

"Yes. She will love," Nadja said. "Tell me, Jesus can give bigger quadriceps?"

"Jesus can do that," Felix said.

"Oh, Christ," Stasik said.

"So that's why you're here, Felix?" I asked. "To promote your book?"

"Yes, Yuri will help me to say my message for the American audience. Also I will remove some skin."

"Skin?" Zeferina asked.

"From when I lose my weight. I have so much skin now."

"Jesus cannot remove this skin?" Nadja asked.

"Jesus will guide the hand of the plastic surgeon. You cannot imagine all this skin. Under my clothes I am very, very baggy."

Conversation ebbed for a moment, as we pondered that. A minute or two later I said, "You're a triathlete, Nadja?"

"Yes, number sixteen best in the whole world. I go to Olympics."

I glanced in the rearview mirror. No extra skin on Nadja. "So you're here to—?"

"I come to meet Oatees."

"Who is Oatees?" Zeferina asked.

"Is like Wheaties, only not so famous," Nadja said. "Is possible for number sixteen to be on Oatees box. Wheaties, no. What is the word, Vanya?"

"Endorsement," Vanya said.

"Endorsement. I learn to look happy and promote my sport and country."

"That's great," I said. "Zeferina—uh, Maria—"

"Zeferina Maria Catalina."

"Yes, sorry. What about you?" I asked. "What do you do?"

"My husband, in my country, has now the important government job. I come to speak better English and not so fat, so I am here."

"Wow, interesting," I said. "How about you, Stasik?"

"I sing country music."

I craned my neck around to look at him, surprised.

"What country?" Nadja asked.

"The country I'm from," Stasik said, "is Belarus. The music I sing is American country and western."

"You're kidding," I said.

"Why do you think I'm kidding?"

I hesitated. "You don't seem the type."

"What's the type?" Stasik asked, a note of challenge in his voice.

"Never mind. Stereotypical thinking on my part," I said. Why not a bitter, sarcastic Belarusian country and western singer?

"You have a CD, Stasik?" Nadja said. "I can hear you on radio?"

"I can give you a CD. I'm on the radio, but in Europe, not here. Yet."

There was a subtle camaraderie among the trainees that intrigued me. I looked in the rearview mirror. "Do you all know each other? I mean, before today—have you all met?"

There was silence, and then three or four people said no all at once. This was followed by more silence.

"The snoring bloke," Stasik asked after a minute. "Zbiggo. What's he do?"

"Zbiggo's a boxer."

No one took issue with that. After a while, travel fatigue set in and my passengers drifted off to sleep or to commune with their own thoughts. I tried to sort out my own, making mental notes about what I planned to discuss with Bennett Graham (everything, with the possible exception of Felix's underwear) and Yuri (much less, if I wasn't to rat out Alik) and Simon (next to nothing). By the time I left Pacific Coast Highway, turning up Topanga Canyon Boulevard, I thought I was the only one awake. But when I looked in the rearview mirror, I saw Stasik leaning over the seat, talking to Felix. Their voices were low, so I couldn't hear a word, but it was interesting to see them halfway to friendship.

Then I saw Stasik hand something over the seat to Felix. It was a quick movement and the sun was setting over the ocean behind us, so the light was fading, but I saw a glint of metal. What passed between them looked very much like a knife.

THIRTEEN

*T*hunk. *Thunk.*

The sounds entered my dream, in which I was driving a forty-foot truck, and then pulled me into consciousness. I opened my eyes.

I held my breath in the darkness, not knowing where I was. It took time to remember being escorted to House of Blue the night before, shown to my room, and falling into bed, into a deep sleep. Now I was wide awake, half curious and three-quarters scared. *Thunk.*

Someone was throwing rocks at my balcony.

I fumbled for the bedside lamp. The room lit up. The rock throwing stopped. I turned off the light.

Thunk.

I turned on the lamp again, got out of bed, and moved to the sliding glass doors that led to the second-story deck. It had to be Simon. It was such a *Romeo and Juliet* thing to do, finding my bedroom. I was too groggy to figure out how he did it. I just wanted to be with him. Wrap my arms around him. My legs too.

"Simon?" I whispered, leaning over the balcony. He was a dark blob beneath me.

"Catch," he whispered back. "Climb down."

Something hit my arm and I grabbed it. It was a heavy rope, knotted on one end. I reeled it in; on the other end was a rope ladder. The ladder had big hooks I was able to attach to the railing, and I set about climbing down, the moon lighting up the night sky just enough to help. The things I do for this guy, I thought, and stumbled on the last step. He took my arm to steady me. I turned and stifled a gasp.

I was face-to-face with a total stranger.

"Sssh." He was tall, very skinny, and young, and had some gadget on his forehead.

"God in heaven, who are you?" I asked, shaking off his arm.

"I gotta talk to you," he whispered. "We gotta be quiet. C'mon. This way."

"Are you nuts? I'm not going anywhere. It's freezing. It's the middle of the night. Who *are* you?"

"Okay, just duck down, then. Here." He took off his hoodie sweatshirt and put it over my shoulders. He readjusted the gadget on his head. It was a flashlight, I saw, like a miner might wear. "Please. If we're standing up, they can see us from the main house. Please."

I sank into a squat. He was too polite to be sinister, and he was trying to grow a beard, with mixed results, which made him look vulnerable. "Tell me who you are," I whispered.

"Crispin Harris," he said. "I tried to see you earlier, but they wouldn't let me in."

"Are you—Bob?"

He nodded. "Then I tried to follow you, but I lost you."

"In the red car? You scared me. Okay, so you found me. What's this about?"

"Chai. Her and I were gonna get married."

"You're Chai's—fiancé?" I pulled his sweatshirt on over my head, glad I was in pajamas, at least. And socks. Calabasas nights were freezing, even in May.

"Well, we sorta broke up, but we would've got back together. You're Wollie Shelley. I found about you from their website. There's a whole thing about you already. They gave you her job." His head whipped around suddenly. "What was that?"

I turned. I couldn't see anything in the darkness, but then I heard a yelp and a series of howls from the canyon side of the property. Not far away, from the sound of it.

"Animals," I said.

"Coyotes. Probably killing a cat. Here—" He pulled a blanket out of a backpack and put it in my lap. "I knew you'd be cold. Chai always was cold."

I spread the blanket around me gratefully. "But why are you here?"

"These MediasRex guys. They did something to Chai. They got rid of her."

I started shivering all over again. "Wh-what do you mean, got rid of her?"

"Murdered her."

I knew it. I'd known it for a day and a half. "Wh-why?"

His eyes narrowed. "You don't have any idea? You don't know about the scam?"

"What scam?"

He looked around, then leaned in. "Okay, that's what I figured. I figured you didn't know. Chai found out about a scam going down. She wouldn't tell me what. A week before she died we talked about it. Me and her met like this a bunch of times."

"She didn't tell the cops about this scam?"

"No." He looked over his shoulder. "I told her to, but she wanted to work it."

"You mean blackmail?"

"Uh-uh. She didn't want money. She wanted to be in movies. These people could do that for her, they got connections. That was gonna be the trade-off. They'd get her into movies and she'd keep her mouth shut about what she'd found out. I thought it was a bad idea. We had a big fight over it."

"So you're saying they murdered her instead?" I asked.

Crispin nodded.

I gulped. "How?"

"See, that's exactly what the cops said. 'How?' Like I'm supposed to figure it all out for them. Hello, that's *their* job."

I took a deep breath. "So you don't actually know for sure that—"

"And her mom, she goes, 'Crispin, don't you think the cops would know if it was a murder?' Everybody's like, yeah, right, Crispin, you watch too much TV. But you know how many murders happen every day in America?"

"No."

"Forty-six. Every single day. Forty-six people get whacked, why not her?"

"Good point," I said. "Okay, back up. So Chai wanted to be an actress, and—"

"Actress and model. She was good, she just didn't have the connections. It's all about connections. It's not what you know, it's who you know. That's how it works in Hollywood."

I knew that wasn't quite how it worked, but I let it go. "Was there any kind of investigation?" I asked. "The cops must've looked into it, at least."

"Yeah, CHP or whatever. Said it was a car accident. There was an autopsy, too, what was left of her. They said it didn't show it was murder. But here's the thing: it didn't show it *wasn't* murder, right? It couldn't prove that, right?"

I felt ill. "How long ago did she die?"

"Three weeks, two days ago. I'd been leaving messages on her cell and she wasn't calling me back and I called her mom and her mom goes, 'Cheryl's dead. She crashed the car that she drove at her work.' And then her mom had her cremated. Can you believe that? Who cremates their kid?"

A lot of people. But I felt his frustration. Cremation. Game over. Case closed. "I'm so sorry," I said, reaching to touch his shoulder. He was shivering. Then he began to cry. I pulled the blanket off me and put it around him.

He grabbed my hand and gripped it. "I just—I saw your name on the website and it said you'd been on TV, so I checked out a clip they had on YouTube, so that's how come I knew I had to come see you. You got connections, right? You know TV people, so you could get on the news, get them to pay attention to this."

"I don't, really. I'm not in that world. Chai was lots more famous than I am."

"Then how come nobody's talking about her?"

Good question. I wanted to tell Crispin that publicity wouldn't ease his grief, it could prolong it, that he had a sweet face and from what I'd heard of Chai, dumping him was the kindest thing she'd done. But he couldn't hear any of that. "Crispin, I'd like to help, but no one's going to listen to me. I wasn't here. I didn't know Chai." Feeling bad vibes while wearing her clothes didn't count.

"You think you're safe, working for these criminals?" he asked. "You're not safe. She said she lost her diary. Yeah, right. They stole it. I guarantee you. People spied on her. If you think you got friends here, you don't. Don't trust any of them."

This was exactly what I didn't need to hear.

A squeal from the shrubbery set my teeth on edge. It sounded like some little creature being tortured. This was followed by the yelps of coyotes. And then, from inside the Big House, a bark. Crispin started.

"Olive Oyl," I whispered.

"She'll come out the dog door. This happened before. I gotta make a run for it."

"How'd you get in past the guard?" I asked.

"I didn't. I came through the canyon." He stood, turning on his head-lamp.

"I thought they had some major security system here."

"The main house, yeah. Not this one, except for the first-floor doors and windows." He was poised to run.

"Wait." I grabbed his arm. "Was it you shooting at the house yester-day?"

He looked over his shoulder and talked fast. "I wish. I'd like to shoot them all. Murderers. Thinking they can just get away with it. They will, too. If you don't say anything, then it's just me, I'm the wacko, I'm just the loser she dumped."

"Crispin—wait." I was feeling desperate. "The thing is, they need evi-dence. Do you have any proof at all? Anything you can point to and—?"

"I got proof." He stopped to look me in the eye. "The newspaper. It came out a week ago, after I'd already been to the cops. I told them, I left messages, they said okay, we'll get back to you, but they never got back to me. To them it's not proof, it's nothing."

"What'd the paper say?"

"That she drove off the road in a Corvette." He gathered up his back-pack and slung it over his shoulder. Olive Oyl, still inside the house, was in a frenzy. "She couldn't've."

"Why not?"

"Chai in a 'Vette? I'm the one taught her to drive, in high school. It took six months. She flunked driver's ed. Chai wouldn't touch a stick shift, not in a million years. At night? Alone? In the dark? Not in a million years."

Just like me.

My heart was pounding, watching him disappear into the night. I was sold. I believed him. His "proof" might look weak to the cops, but not to me. I was certain, right down to my socks, that somewhere on this property, a murderer slept.

I wanted Simon.

I climbed up Crispin's rope ladder to my room. Chai's room. And, still in Crispin's sweatshirt, crawled into Chai's bed. And lay there shivering, alone in the dark.

FOURTEEN

I awoke hours later disoriented. Light poured in my window, brighter than the bedside lamp I'd kept on all night. I sat up.

My brain was on the same loop I'd fallen asleep to: *I gotta get outta here. Chai's dead, and I'm the new Chai. She knew too much and I know too much. I want Simon.*

But now, in sunlight, a new voice entered the mix: *Call Bennett Graham. Get instructions. Do it now.*

I looked at my bedside clock. Nine-fifteen. Why was it so quiet? Of course: I was in House of Blue and the trainees were in an English seminar in Big House.

I got out of bed and went rummaging around in my suitcase for some sweats. Then I did another quick check of the room. Behind the bed was a phone jack, but no phone anywhere. Strange, but no stranger than the bedroom itself, done in strong reds, blues, and purples, a sophisticated look, but not especially restful. It was, in fact, suggestive of nightmares. I could almost believe I'd dreamed Crispin's moonlight visitation, if not for the rope ladder and hoodie sweatshirt draped over an acrylic armchair. I stuffed them in the back of a closet. Had Crispin ever come in this room? I imagined him climbing up that ladder, having frenzied sex with Chai in the fuchsia four-poster, wrapped in sapphire silk sheets under the magenta ceiling. Thinking of sex led back to Simon and the weeks since we'd done it ourselves. It had been even longer since we'd done it in a bed.

Be careful, he'd said in his phone message. Why hadn't he called back? Oh. No cell signal. Right.

Time to find a regular phone.

I stepped out into a hallway that was mind-bogglingly blue—blue tile floor and deep blue walls—and headed to the left, toward the wing I assumed to house the bedrooms.

The first door I came to was wide open. Interesting. My room could be locked from the outside with a key—Grusha had given me one the night before. I'd stuck it in my pocket, thinking, Who locks bedroom doors with keys, outside of *Jane Eyre*? Now a more sinister thought occurred to me: Could someone lock me in? Better hang on to that rope ladder.

I glanced back down the hallway, then entered the room. I couldn't find a phone. *But as long as you're here,* said the voice in my head, *you might as well spy.*

I glanced around. Unmade bed, suitcases on the floor, clothes spilling out. So who was the slob? I went through my mental list of the trainees I'd met last night, with my mnemonic devices: Felix, Formerly Fat. (Until Jesus Made Him Skinny.) Nadja Triathlete. Zbiggo-the-Boxer. Stasik Banjo. Zeferina Maria Someone or Other. Uncle Vanya.

The clothes on the floor were male. I moved around dirty-looking boxer shorts, gently, with my sock-clad toe. The taboo of going through someone else's stuff was strong.

Spies, said the voice in my head, *can't afford taboos.* Okay. I read the luggage tag. Zbigniew Shpek. Since I'd already been through Zbiggo's pockets, this was no big deal. But aside from several pill bottles, I found nothing of interest. I moved on.

The next room was Felix's. I recognized his body-bag suitcase, now empty. Felix had not only unpacked, he'd made his bed and affixed a crucifix above it with a pushpin. I nosed around but didn't find the knife/knifelike object I'd seen Stasik hand to him in the Suburban, or a passport, or anything suspicious. Nor did I find a phone.

But in the next room I found Grusha.

I stopped in the doorway, frozen. Her back was to me. She was hunched over, intent upon something, her arms moving very slightly.

I got curious. I wasn't supposed to be here—but was she? What was she doing? I inched into the room and to my left, for a better view. She was dressed once more in a housedress, this one lavender and gray, covered with a dotted swiss apron. I heard a clicking sound and Grusha turned slightly.

She was loading a gun.

I gasped.

"Aggh!" she screamed, jumping up and rotating midair to face me. It was an astonishing move for someone so old and not in the NBA.

I backed up. My hands flew into the air in a gesture of surrender and then back down again. "Grusha. Hello. Sorry. Didn't mean to scare you. What are you doing?"

"What are *you* doing?" she hissed.

"Looking for a telephone."

"Big House," she said.

"Really? There are no phones in House of Blue?"

"Big House."

I stared at her, and she dropped her gaze, putting the gun in her apron pocket. She then set about making the bed—Stasik's bed, I asssumed, as his banjo was against the wall. "Do you always carry a gun?" I asked.

She said nothing, and I watched her for a moment, wondering how far to push it. If I weren't working for the FBI, if I were a plain, everyday social coach, wouldn't I be interested? Concerned? Alarmed, even?

"Grusha," I repeated. "How come you have a gun?"

She didn't look at me. "You miss breakfast. Every morning, Big House. Seven o'clock. At eight-thirty, finished. You sleep, you starve."

"That's fine," I said. "I don't need breakfast."

She glared at me. "You can have fruit. And water."

"Fruit and water will do fine."

She gathered up an armful of sheets. "You can have coffee."

"Wonderful. Do you always clean house with a loaded gun?"

She grabbed a mop and I jumped back, like she was going to swing at me. Unlikely, of course. Why assault someone with a Swiffer if you're packing heat in your apron?

"One o'clock is lunch," she said, moving toward me. "I don't wait. You come, you eat. If not, no." She brushed past me and out of the room.

I followed her long enough to see that she was really leaving. And she looked back too, maybe to see if I was. But once she hit the stairway, I doubled back to Stasik's room.

Nothing grabbed my attention, aside from a dozen CDs marked "demo." I borrowed one. Okay, I stole it. I couldn't say why, but since I've never been kleptomaniacal, it must have been my inner spy. She was developing nicely, this tough cookie. I, however, unnerved by my own actions, ran back to my room. And locked the door behind me.

I didn't bother to unpack my own clothes, just pulled some designer hand-me-downs from the closet, a pair of brown wool pants and blazer and a champagne silk blouse, and tossed them on the bed. I glanced at the alarm clock. I'd have to hurry if I wanted to leave the compound to make calls on my cell before my workday began. Then I glanced at the clock again, realizing it was also a CD player.

I popped in Stasik's CD. Track one was a festival of dissonance. The lyrics were mostly "baby, baby, baby, baby," with Stasik stretching for notes he had no hope of reaching. This must be the kind of music played at full volume to force people out of buildings in hostage situations. Simon told me ATF agents had done this in Waco, Texas.

Unless it was the latest in country and western and I was simply out of the loop. I needed a second opinion. I put the CD back in its case, but I couldn't find my purse—could I have left it in the car?—so I hid it under my mattress.

But I was curious now, and went to the desk and hit my laptop's on button. If Stasik had fans, I'd find them in cyberspace. I'd google Chai too. Suddenly I wanted to see photos, to know this dead girl, this almost-certainly-murdered girl—

Except that my laptop wasn't working.

The screen stayed dark. I checked the cable, the AC adapter, jiggled the computer, listened to it, knocked on it, spoke to it, and concluded it was on strike.

Now what? I knew next to nothing about computers, only that every little thing that went wrong was expensive to fix. And when would I find time to take it in for repairs? I had my greeting card documents backed up, so that wasn't a problem, but what about e-mail? I wasn't Hallmark, but I did have customers, for God's sake.

Aggravated, I stood, threw off my sweats, and headed for my little scarlet bathroom. I plucked from a rack a fluffy magenta towel and prepared to jump in the shower, when I caught sight of the mirror.

I gasped.

I backed up.

There, along with the reflection of my face, was a message.

It was handwritten, in large letters, in what appeared to be dried blood.

And it was in Russian.

FIFTEEN

My gaze shifted to my own reflection, one hand on my heart, naked, panting.

I wrapped the towel around me and willed myself to calm down. I scanned the bathroom, checked the shower, then backed up into the bedroom and assured myself that I was indeed alone. I looked under the bed, just in case. Then I checked to see if I'd locked the bedroom door. I had. Then I locked myself into the bathroom.

Okay, I told myself. This was not something to freak out over. This was silly, a horror movie staple, people writing on mirrors with—lip pencils. I stepped closer. My own lip pencil. There it was on the counter, its point worn down, my favorite MAC pencil, a color called "Nightmoth." The nerve. The graffiti artist couldn't have brought his or her own supplies? And it's not like MAC is cheap. That pencil had set me back fourteen bucks. There was a Maybelline lip pencil too, in my makeup bag. "Melon Ball," for $5.99. They couldn't use that? No, because a message written in cantaloupe juice isn't as scary as one written in blood.

I grabbed tweezers and plucked the MAC pencil from the counter, then dropped it into a clean glass. I wasn't sure why, but I wanted to follow crime scene protocol, at least as much as I'd gleaned from TV. If there were any fingerprints or DNA on that lip pencil, I would preserve it. For whom, I didn't know. I'd think about that later. I stuffed it into a drawer.

I looked at the message again: Cyrillic letters and the number 31. Maybe it wasn't sinister. Maybe a trainee had mistaken my room for that of a fellow trainee and, in a moment of summer camp–like hijinks, had written, "Come over for cocoa! Room 31!" I grabbed a pen and sketchbook from my suitcase and copied the letters. I would do as Joey had suggested and don my spy persona. She was heroic, even superheroic. Would she be all quivery over a couple of lipstick marks? No. Tough Cookie would laugh—ha, ha!—in the face of this sophomoric communiqué.

But why was it in Russian? I was probably the only person in the whole compound who didn't understand Russian. Well, except for *tvoyu mat* and two other phrases I'd already forgotten. Was the message meant for someone else? And when had it happened? I'd last gone into my bathroom the previous night. Had someone snuck into my room while I slept? Or while I was searching the other rooms? Grusha was a likely suspect.

Except that Grusha had given me the key to my room. Was this why? Were these lipstick messages a recurring problem at House of Blue?

"Wollie?" A disembodied voice sounded from across the room, nearly sending me through the roof. I found an intercom on the wall and pressed a button.

"Hello? Yes?"

"It's Nell. There's a man at the gate that says he's your uncle. Theodore?"

"Uncle Theo, yes, yes. Let him in. I'll be right down."

I threw on my clothes without showering. I still couldn't find my purse. The thought that someone might have taken it from my room further unnerved me. My pants had no pockets, and the blazer pockets were sewn shut, so I ripped one open, enough to hold the folded paper on which I'd written my Russian message. I left the room, locking my door from the outside with the key.

My footsteps were loud, clattering down the blue marble staircase, echoing through the empty house.

"Uncle Theo! Apollo!" I waved to my uncle and our teenage friend, who sat in deck chairs on the porch of Big House. "Is everything okay? Is P.B. okay?"

"Yes, P.B. sent us here!" My uncle wore his usual serape, drawstring hemp pants, and Birkenstocks, his white hair sticking out as though electrified. "Well, not here; Malibu. Pepperdine University, for a guest lecture by Joseph Polchinski. We're on our way there."

"P.B. has sold me on Polchinski," Apollo said. Fifteen years old and scrawny, he wore blue jeans and a Caltech sweatshirt and was eating from a large bag of Sun Chips. "My cousin is coming too. He is driving us." He pointed to a Kia parked in the street, with a burly man in the driver's seat. "Archimedes! Here is Wollie!"

Archimedes waved and honked.

"Okay, yes," I said, waving back, suppressing an urge to hide. Donatella would not approve of our visual presentation. "Is there something you need?"

"Well, dear, we just wanted to see where you work and see if you're well."

"Oh!" I said, touched. "Well, I'm fine. Sort of." I looked at my uncle's kind face and Apollo's eager one and found my professionalism slipping. "Okay, not really. Okay, not at all. Frankly, you guys, I'm freaked out."

I told them about Crispin. And Chai. I explained my illogical but absolute conviction that Crispin was right about Chai. I found myself looking over my shoulder as I talked, just as Crispin had done the night before, which was a little theatrical, given the sunny morning, blue sky, and the sound of leaf blowers in the 'hood. They listened attentively, with one "holy cow" from Apollo. I was about to explain the mirror message when Uncle Theo held up a hand. "So," he said, "because of your own strong aversion to manual transmission cars, you've convinced yourself this unfortunate girl was murdered. Is that correct?"

"Put like that," I said, "it sounds silly."

"It's just so unscientific," Apollo said. "I could teach you to drive a Corvette."

"The question," Uncle Theo said, "is whether the victim could've been taught to drive one. When Wollie puts herself in this girl's shoes, then her theory is—"

"—still ridiculous, I know," I said. "Although I don't have to put myself in her shoes, I'm already in her shoes. Ferragamos."

Uncle Theo looked at my feet. "You're wearing her shoes?"

"I'm wearing all her clothes, except for underwear." I explained about the couture that fit me with minimal alterations.

Uncle Theo frowned. "But this is serious. And now it becomes quite scientific."

"What do you mean?"

"You're caught in this poor girl's vibrational field. If she was undergoing stress prior to her death, that would affect her biochemistry, which would extend beyond her physical body and conceivably seep into the fabric of a shirt or a pair of trousers."

I stared. "You can't be serious. Are you saying little pieces of ourselves, little particles of emotion, get stuck on our clothes? Even after dry-cleaning?"

"Not particles," Uncle Theo said. "That's old-school."

"Strings," Apollo said. "Theo, I don't mean to be disrespectful, but your central thesis assumes several—"

"Yes, I'm not presenting it to Dr. Polchinski," Uncle Theo said. "I'm more philosopher than scientist. I merely suggest that Wollie's sense of dread is a vibration in this web of quantum entanglement, stretching across time rather than space, conducted through fabric. Whatever the ultimate source, this dread is a reliable indicator of something gone powerfully wrong. She can't ignore it. It's instinct, a force as fierce as gravity or electromagnetism. My dear, is this job so important to you?"

"Yes. Don't suggest I quit," I said, backpedaling. "I've got several good reasons to stay, and really, what if this thread theory of yours is mere imagination?"

"*Mere* imagination?" Uncle Theo said. "That's an oxymoron. Imagination, dread, instinct, faith. Don't disparage these. In the immortal words of Kierkegaard, 'There are two ways to be fooled. One is to believe what isn't true; the other is to refuse to believe what is true.'"

And on that encouraging note, Uncle Theo and Apollo took off, leaving me with barely enough optimism to wave goodbye. I turned to go into the house, but not before I saw the window shade fall into place in the library.

From inside the house, someone had been watching me.

In the kitchen of Big House, I found Alik, suppressing a yawn. His black hair was damp, his face freshly shaved, but still, he looked scholarly, like he'd read Proust before breakfast. It was an erotic combination. "Wollie, thanks again for last night," he said. "Coffee?"

"Yes, please."

He handed me the cup he'd just poured, then reached over to give me a kiss on the cheek. I was startled, but pleasantly so, and smiled at him. The smile faded as I realized I couldn't talk to Alik about Crispin. Or the message on my mirror. Or the fact that his grandmother did housework with a loaded gun.

"How was your first day?" he asked. "I heard about Felix's suitcase. And Zbiggo is a piece of work."

"Oh, Zbiggo slept for six straight hours. He woke just as we got home. I handed him off to Grusha, who fed him a side of beef, so it all ended up happily." I noticed Alik's eyes, tired-looking behind his aviator frames. "Your emergency get handled?" I asked.

He glanced at the doorway, then back at me. "Yes, thanks. I had to bail out a friend. Literally, which is why it's better if Yuri doesn't hear about it. He's got a problem with some of my friends. My father's a little on the straight side."

"Yes, but you're"—I hesitated, not wanting to offend him—"not a teenager."

Alik laughed. "No, I'm twenty-eight. Too old to fear parental disapproval. And I don't fear it. But life is simpler when I don't throw it in his face."

"Throw what in his face?"

"Whatever I'm doing that my father would find unacceptable. Things I try to save until I'm off the clock."

I nodded. "It must be tricky, having your father as your boss. And working for your mother too. Stepmother, I mean. Stepmothers. There are just two of them, right?"

He turned to pour himself coffee. "Stepmothers? Yes. Kimberly's my second, Donatella's my first. My own mother was Ludmilla, Yuri's original wife."

"And Parashie's mother? Who was she?"

"One of Yuri's lovers, when he was between wives. They met doing cleanup work after Chernobyl. Yuri didn't know about her death or Parashie's existence until a few years ago. He found Parashie and brought her here. We're quite the blended family. But we share a common purpose. The family business. Nothing unusual about that."

"But the business is unusual," I said. "And you live in a veritable commune."

He smiled. "Multigenerational living is common where my parents come from. You're an L.A. girl, so you'd never live with your family."

"My uncle, maybe. Not my brother. We've tried. I love him a lot, but it's complicated. And I can't imagine anyone living with my mother."

Alik sipped his coffee. "And here there's a stigma about grown children living at home. America places independence above all other values."

"But you're an American, aren't you?" I asked. "Do you feel stigmatized?"

"I was born in America, yes. And I've spent half my life in Europe. And no, I don't feel stigmatized, I feel part of something. But I also have a life outside my work, one I fight to maintain. Which is why I appreciate you pinch-hitting for me yesterday, and I'll return the favor. When you need it, just ask." Behind his glasses, his eyes were sea green, and entrancing. "I like you, Wollie. You know that? I want you to be happy here."

"Thank you." I was about to add *I like you too,* because I realized it was true, realized how lonely I'd been lately with Simon gone so much. But it scared me to like Alik.

Because I wasn't sure I trusted Alik.

He picked up a *Los Angeles Times* and began to read, drinking his coffee. I watched him. I had a strange impulse to reach out and touch a lock of his hair that was drying in the sun coming through the skylight. What would he do? I imagined he'd respond in kind. I wondered how real spies did this, ingratiate themselves, form friendships and all the warm fuzzy feelings that went along with that while maintaining a baseline level of suspicion.

A loud voice coming from the next room got our attention. Alik followed the sound, and I followed Alik.

In the great room, a large—not just large by L.A. standards—woman was facing off with Kimberly. She wore a long, capelike wrap in a tangerine color that complemented her auburn hair, which was fluffed and sprayed. She had on a lot of makeup, including false eyelashes.

"I prefer to be driven in a limousine," she said. "It is what I am used to."

"Naturally, when you're performing, but this is a training. You have no need of your driver here. We'll take care of your transportation needs."

"In a limousine?"

"No, in a modified, fuel-efficient—"

"Ms. Bjöeling." Alik stepped in deftly, and Kimberly moved back a step, toward me. "We heard your beautiful voice from the kitchen. Hello, I'm Alik Milos. We are honored to have you with us."

Ms. Bjöeling, whoever she was, was not immune to the charm and Baltic good looks of Alik Milos. "Yuri's son?" she asked, thawing slightly.

Alik nodded.

"I was expecting Yuri himself to be here on my arrival. It was my understanding that your exorbitant fee guarantees the man himself and not his apprentices. Also, I do not take English classes. My English is excellent."

Alik didn't blink. "Yes, it is. Yuri flew last night to New York on short notice, and returns this afternoon. I apologize on his behalf. And I promise you, Yuri is involved in all aspects of MediasRex. That said, Ms. Bjöeling—"

"You may call me Bronwen."

"Thank you. That said, no staff member here is an apprentice. Kimberly's a world-class personal trainer and a licensed nutritionist. I've got a master's in psychology from Yale. Nell, a renowned linguist—whose seminar you need not take—has coached countless film and stage actors, including two Oscar winners, as I'm sure you read in the résumé section of your packet. Nell's brushing up on her Norwegian, to make you feel welcome."

Bronwen Bjöeling now turned on me. "And who is this?"

"Wollie Shelley," I said, stepping forward and extending my hand. After a moment, she extended her own very white, puffy hand, from which protruded long tangerine nails.

"Wollie," Alik said, "is my opposite number, in charge of transportation, logistics, and the social needs of half our trainees. Wollie, you no doubt recognize Bronwen Bjöeling, renowned lyric soprano."

I didn't, but decided it best not to volunteer that.

"And are you a psychologist?" Bronwen asked me.

"No, I'm a graphic artist," I said.

She looked around the great room, perhaps thinking I'd painted the walls. Before she could ask for my résumé or alma mater, Kimberly caught my eye and said, "Bronwen, I'll—"

"*He* may call me by my first name," the woman said, turning on her. "Not you."

It was so rude, even Kimberly, whom I'd thought completely redoubtable, blanched. I spoke up. "For the rest of us, do you prefer 'Miss' or 'Ms.'?"

"'Miss' will do. I'm no feminist."

I wanted to ask what Bronwen considered herself, what feminism's opposite number was, but Alik was watching me. He winked, then looked at Kimberly and shook his head. Kimberly turned and left the room.

"I'll give you a tour, Bronwen," Alik said. "And do you have your passport handy?"

"Why?"

"We make copies, in case they're lost or stolen. It saves time and headaches."

Bronwen said, "My driver has it."

"Fine. We'll walk that way," Alik answered. I was interested in how he'd smoothed her feathers, and I expected he'd dispense with her limo just as gracefully. "This is the great room, where many of our meetings take place."

Donatella came down the hallway toward us. "Wollie, there is a phone call for you."

"For me?" I asked, startled. "From whom?" Who knew I was here?

"Wendell."

"Wendell who?" I asked.

"You don't know him?" Donatella shrugged and handed me a piece of paper. "Here. He said you are to call him now, as he will be at that number only a few minutes."

I stared at the unfamiliar number. The only Wendell I knew of was Wendell Willkie, who'd run for president against someone like Herbert Hoover or Dwight D. Eisenhower. It probably wasn't him.

"Is there a problem?" Donatella asked.

"No, but—is it okay to get personal calls here?" I asked.

"Not much choice," she said. "Since we don't get cell reception. You didn't get the team logistics sheet? Come to the office. I will find you one as you make your call. Oh, these last days have been chaos."

"Well!" Miss Bjöeling said, overhearing. "That does not inspire one with confidence."

"Creative chaos, Miss Bjöeling," Donatella said, leading me away. "You as an artist will understand that."

I followed Donatella through the library, where Nadja, Zeferina Maria, Zbiggo, and Felix sat in a semicircle, facing the taciturn Nell, conjugating the verb "to be." They looked up and I gave them a little wave, then entered the office. Wendell was probably one of Bennett Graham's people. The frozen yogurt guy, maybe, to get a progress report.

I dialed the number, aware of Donatella beside me, going through a file drawer.

"Hello," I said when a voice answered. "This is—"

"I know who you are," he said, cutting me off. "The question is, where the hell are you?"

Not a frozen yogurt FBI agent at all. Simon.

I took a deep breath.

SIXTEEN

I'd pissed off Simon Alexander often enough—and I don't consider myself a contentious person—that you'd think I'd be used to it. But I wasn't used to it. And my boyfriend was definitely angry. This was apparent from the note of tight control in his voice.

"Yes," I said, "not to worry, Wendell. I'm fine, but I've been working, and it turns out my new job puts me out of range of cell phone communications." Donatella was now looking through paperwork on the desk next to me. *Don't be paranoid, she's not listening,* I told myself. "How did you get this number, by the way?"

"Phone book," Donatella answered, as though this were a three-way conversation. "Or the website or one of twenty-two publications we advertise in."

"Who's there with you?" Simon asked.

"One of my colleagues."

"Which one?"

Which one? He'd done homework. "Donatella Milos," I said.

"Jesus. All right, look. We need to schedule an appointment. I'm worried about your carburetor and I want to get a look under the hood. When's good?"

"I am so anxious to make that happen, you have no idea. Hold on. Donatella?" I said, covering the receiver. "Do I have an actual day off?"

"In theory, yes."

"But in practice?" I asked.

She considered this. "In fact, until Zbiggo's trainer arrives, it is difficult. The first week we are completely crazy, so . . . Why? What is it you need?"

"What did you have in mind?" I said into the phone.

"Tonight."

"Tonight?" I asked Donatella.

"Tonight is impossible," she said.

"Tonight is—" I said.

"I heard." He was working to keep it together, I knew.

I said quickly, "I am, however, eager to know the nature of your concerns. Regarding—my car."

"Let's just say you're parked in a bad neighborhood."

"How bad?"

"Bad. But unless you're well versed in the political upheaval going on in several former Soviet bloc countries, I'd rather—"

"Stop!" I screamed. Next to me, Donatella jumped. It hit me that if the FBI was wiretapping the phones in the house, they would hear this conversation. The word "Soviet" might get their attention, and worse, one of Simon's colleagues could recognize his voice. "I've gotta go, Willkie. I mean Wendell."

"Wait—"

"Work thing. Sorry. Bye." Panicked, I slammed down the receiver, then stood there, stunned, thinking, *I've just hung up on him. The man I most trust, the voice I most love.*

"Wollie," Donatella said. "Did I not just say you could make this call? Any call. Communication is fundamental. It is the thing that matters most in life."

"Yes, okay. I didn't know whether I should tie up the phones. You better give me that rule sheet."

"Team logistics. And here are the fact sheets on the trainees. Also the schedule. You didn't get this either? At orientation?" She handed me a small stack of papers.

"No, I—" I was about to say I'd had no orientation, but realized that this might come in handy at some point, as an excuse. "Uh-uh." I shook my head.

"We have many phone lines," Donatella said, "and Parashie has per-haps already set up a voice mailbox for you, I will ask her, and then you may receive messages. So you did know this man, after all? The Wen-dell?"

"Yes, he's—a guy I'm supposed to meet. I'd forgotten. Car guy. Long story."

"Your boyfriend?"

"No. But—what do you know about my boyfriend?"

Donatella shrugged. "Yuri said you have a boyfriend." She studied me, probably because I was beet red, which happens when I tell a lie. "So you meet with a car mechanic. But why? You do not need your car for three months."

"For work, no, but what about my free time?"

"The Suburban is for your use always. Yuri says you should have no expenses."

Except for lip pencils. "I didn't know that," I said.

"Do you want to call this mechanic and tell him?"

"No, later will be fine. Although—do I have time to run an errand or two?" I was desperate now. I had to talk to Simon on my cell phone.

"My dear," Donatella said, "if you want to make assignations with a car mechanic, or any other man who is not your boyfriend, do so. I will not judge you. I am European, and I find your American morality sti-fling. I can tell you this, however: you are not drinking enough water." She took the paper she'd just handed me, circled something, and handed it back to me.

#14. Southern California is a desert. All team members and trainees should drink 5 liters of water daily.

"Yes. Thanks. Bye," I said, preparing to leave.

"What has happened to your pocket?" she asked, staring at my blazer. "Are those threads? Have you broken a seam?"

"Where? What? No," I said, clamping my hand over my pocket.

She moved my hand aside. "Wollie! You are not putting *things* in your pocket?"

"No, I—well, only a very tiny, flat little thing. A nothing. Paper, that's all."

Donatella's eyes flashed. "Why not just carry a phone book there? That is also paper. You ruin the line of the jacket, you make it droop. It does not want to droop. It does not want to bunch up. You are not a tissue box." She caught sight of something over my shoulder and gasped. "*Yuri, mio.* You startled me. When did you get in?"

I turned to see Yuri Milos standing in the doorway. He looked relaxed, his arms were crossed, and I wondered how much he'd seen or heard.

"Moments ago." He moved in to kiss Donatella on both cheeks, lingering to murmur, "It's happening. I'll meet you in half an hour to fill you in. Now I want to hear from Wollie."

Donatella left and Yuri closed the office door behind her.

"Sit, please," he said.

I sat, feeling a strange combination of jitters. I had to remind myself that Yuri didn't read minds, that my cover wasn't blown, that he couldn't know I'd been talking to Simon, that I wasn't in high school, that this wasn't the principal. "Welcome back," I said.

"Thank you." He smiled, a smile so filled with warmth that it melted my anxiety. His face was both weathered and animated. He looked vital, not like a man who'd taken two transcontinental flights in the last forty-eight hours. "So. Tell me your impression of your first day." He perched on the edge of the desk, his body language inviting confidences.

"It was . . . a full day."

"A baptism of fire, Kimberly tells me."

"Oh, not as bad as that," I said. "I mean, no one drew their guns."

He gave me a quizzical look. "Perhaps you can tell me how it came about that you were driving everyone from the airport last night. Not just your trainees, but Alik's too."

That was intentional, I realized, the disarming smile, the charm, then the direct question. "I guess you heard about the luggage rack."

He looked at me calmly. "Well?"

Wait. What if Yuri knew that I'd been asked to keep Alik's secret? What if this was a test, seeing if I would lie for Alik's sake, bond with a team member, value loyalty over authority? I made myself meet his eyes as a frisson of energy ran through me.

"Are you going to tell me?" he asked.

"About the driving arrangements? It was a question of—logistics. There were travel snafus all day, and everyone was helping everyone else. An improvisational kind of day."

I tried to recall what Joey and Fredreeq had told me about effective lying, but it didn't matter. I couldn't pull it off, not without years of practice, not on a guy like Yuri Milos. He had eyes that sucked the truth out of you. I looked away, but that was probably a bad call. I bet he was as good as Simon at recognizing the techniques liars employ.

Liar. Such an ugly word. But that's what I was, that's what I was here to do.

"Alik probably knows how it all came about," I added, since Yuri wasn't saying anything. "You might ask him."

"I might do a lot of things," he said softly.

I looked at him again, and something in the air between us, highly charged—

"Yuri." Kimberly opened the door enough to pop her head in. "I've got him waiting on line one." Below her, Olive Oyl's head appeared too.

"I'll take the call in the bedroom." Yuri kept on looking at me.

"Babe, he's waiting," Kimberly said.

Yuri stood. He put a hand on my shoulder and briefly squeezed it. "I want to talk to you later." Then he bent down and retrieved something from the floor. My piece of paper. "Yours?" he asked, reading it.

I took a deep breath. What the heck. "Yes."

"What's it say?" Kimberly asked, reading over his shoulder.

"*Poprobuji 31 Aromat, tebe legko budet osmotretsya—Udachi,*" Yuri said.

"*Poprobuji 31 Aromat, tebe legko budet osmotretsya—Udachi*? Damn," she said softly. So Kimberly spoke Russian. Did she write it, too?

"What's it mean?" I asked.

Yuri continued to stare at the paper. "Where did this come from?"

"The words were written on the mirror in my bathroom this morning. In lipstick. I copied it. What's it mean?"

Yuri threw a glance at Kimberly, then looked at me. "It's nothing. Slang."

I held out my hand for it, but Yuri didn't notice.

He was already turned away from me, feeding my note to the paper shredder.

SEVENTEEN

I wanted to pack my bags and get out of Dodge. What did Yuri mean, slang? What slang? "You're toast"? Because he wouldn't shred a note that said "Have a Nice Day."

But I couldn't ask him because he and Kimberly had gone, taking Olive Oyl and leaving me in the office. Alone.

I was of three minds. On one hand, I was taken aback at Yuri, because it was an imperious gesture, even hostile, to destroy my painstakingly written note. On the other hand, I was frightened. On the third hand, Yuri had just handed me the opportunity to actually do what Bennett Graham had hired me to do. Find passports.

I glanced out the door. The coast was clear.

Even scared, I could do this much. I'd said yes to Bennett Graham and the reasons I'd said yes were still good reasons, and maybe I could quit tomorrow or the next day and he'd still keep his promise about P.B. If I gave him something worthwhile. I had to try. Also, I couldn't just flake out two days into the job. Three or four days, okay. But two was pathetic.

But wait! Surveillance cameras. Should I be worried about that? I looked around. Nothing looked like a lens. Which was not to say there wasn't one hidden in the electric pencil sharpener, for instance. But I decided that (a) no one at MediasRex had enough time on their hands to watch camera footage all day long; (b) if some off-site security company was watching, they'd be looking for suspicious activity; so, (c) if I didn't do anything egregiously attention-grabbing, I'd be okay. I just had to look normal, not spylike.

I turned to the desk. A computer flashed its screen saver, the Medias-Rex logo. I tapped the space bar experimentally, and the screen changed to a bunch of documents. They had titles like "Week Log" or "OHP4," nothing as helpful as "Illegal Activities." I clicked on one called "Bio," hoping for some nice biographical dirt on someone, but it was a treatise on converting standard-engine cars to diesel. I tried a few more—I'd look like I was checking my e-mail, right?—but found nothing of interest. And this could use up hours of my life. I scribbled document titles on a scrap of paper, in case Bennett Graham was interested, casually hid the paper in my shoe, and turned back to the desk.

It was neither shipshape nor a complete mess. I found spreadsheets and faxes in various languages, but no passports. I checked the cubbyholes above the desk. No passports. Searching desk drawers and files could take hours and I had only seventy-five minutes to spy, leave the property, phone Simon, and get back to start work.

I scratched my ear and "dropped" my earring, giving me a reason to explore the floor. Aha. Under the desk was a safe. Closed, but not locked. I looked inside.

Passports.

I heard someone behind me. I spun around.

Olive Oyl nosed the door open and ambled in.

"Okay, come," I whispered. "Sit."

The aging mutt obligingly shuffled forward, but her "sit" was a mere transitional moment en route to a slump. Once on the floor, she offered her stomach for my perusal.

"Very lovely," I whispered and got up off the floor, passports held surreptitiously.

They came in different colors, from different countries, but I didn't stop to admire the packaging. I kept them on my lap and wrote furiously on a yellow legal pad, getting name, passport number, and date, country, and city of birth. The scratching of my pen sounded loud, and a drop of sweat actually landed on my writing. From the library I could hear the hum of the English class going on, but couldn't distinguish the words or speakers. *They can't hear you either,* I told myself.

The sound of knocking sent me flying out of my chair, but it was only Olive Oyl's tail thumping on the hardwood floor, in a vertical wag. Her eyes were closed. Dreaming of dog biscuits, maybe.

I had to speed things up. I stuck Stasik's passport in the copy machine and hit the button. The machine shrieked.

Paper jam.

I frantically jiggled the cover and found the offending shreds of paper and cleared them out. Then I saw the paper tray was empty. I opened a drawer, looking for extra paper, and saw instead files, one of which stopped me cold. It said "Wollie Shelley."

I grabbed it. I opened it. I sat.

Page one was the results of my Myers-Briggs test; I was "a moderately expressed intuitive personality and a distinctly expressed feeling personality." *Hmm.* Next was a four-page typed report that detailed my life in terse prose. I skimmed it fast. There were all my addresses for the last ten years, except for the three weeks I'd spent in Simon's penthouse. *Thank God.* Employment history, listing nearly two decades of odd jobs. Brief engagement, preceding year. Brother, paranoid schizophrenic, often institutionalized. Paternal uncle, Theodore, Glendale. Mother living in Ojai, served two weeks in county jail in 1964. *Really?* Father missing since 197—?, presumed deceased.

Presumed?

Tacked onto the last page was a Post-it with sprawling handwriting: "Subj. good candidate, meets criteria re driving record, criminal record, credit rating, health. Marked loyalty to friends, strong ties to brother, uncle. May be turned to asset if required, use appeal to idealism. Pref. to keep ignorant. IQ unavailable."

The door opened. I jumped up, slamming my file shut.

Alik stood there. "Hi."

"Hello!" I stepped in front of the desk. Hands behind my back, I picked up the "Wollie Shelley" file, then fished around for the yellow legal pad with the passport information.

"Okay, not good." Alik moved past me. "Safe wide open, passports everywhere. Kimberly can be really careless. Yuri will throw a fit."

I shuffled away. "Miss Bjöeling, too, seems a little high-strung. What's she in for?"

Alik stretched his leg to kick the office door shut. "She's 'in for' physique transformation, aka diet, exercise, and cosmetic surgery, but the real challenge . . ." He paused, counting passports. One was missing, of course—Stasik's. In the copy machine.

I sidled over to the copier, still facing Alik. My free hand worked to lift the cover of the copier. "So for Bronwen, we're a fat farm?"

Alik counted again. "Don't say the f-word in front of Kimberly. It's 'UFP,' untapped fitness potential." He turned back to the desk. "Where's Stasik's?"

"What?"

"His passport." He turned. "Something you need, by the way?" Probably I appeared to be handcuffed, with my arms tucked behind me, trying to extract the passport from the copier. To make matters worse, Olive Oyl was now sniffing me.

"I'm worried," I said. "Yuri asked me why I was driving all the trainees last night, yours included. I did my best, but I'm not great at—" Olive Oyl was now licking my hands.

"Lying." Alik smiled. It was his father's smile. "I like that. It means you don't do it enough. Forget it. If Yuri asks me, I'll tell him. Anything else on your mind, Wollie?"

Only that Stasik's passport was now clutched in Olive Oyl's teeth. On impulse, I let her have it. I fed her the passport.

A honking horn got Alik's attention. "Gotta go," he said, and tossed the passports into the safe. He shut it, then turned to see Olive Oyl. "Jesus, Olive!" he said. "Aren't you too old for this? Drop it. Drop it. Release. I'm telling Kimberly. You want to be crated up?"

He got the passport, opened the safe, and shoved it in with the others, then locked it. And then he was gone.

I refiled my own file, tore off the yellow legal pages I'd made notes on, and gave Olive Oyl a kiss on my way out. "Good work," I said.

In the driveway, five men were gathered around a black SUV, talking animatedly. In Russian, I realized. I circled back and came up behind Alik, who was under the car's hood.

"Alik, I'm taking off, be back for lunch." I turned to the closest of the strange men and grasped his hand. "Hello, there. I'm Wollie. Social coach."

"Pyotr."

"Pleased to meet you, Pyotr." I moved to the next man. "Hi. Wollie Shelley."

"That's Sergei, and Alyosha, Andrej, and Josip," Alik said, speaking quickly. "Wollie, what do you think of this car? We're thinking of buying it. It's a hybrid."

"Cuter than the Suburban," I said.

"Yeah, 'The Tank.' You don't like it?"

"No, it's just—"

"No one likes it. Yuri bought it in Europe years ago, and it's been refurbished so many times, its own mother wouldn't recognize it."

"Refurbished how?" I asked, my interest piqued.

"Diesel to battery, back to diesel, then biodiesel . . ."

"I guess I should be happy it's automatic."

"It wasn't, for about a month. But the improved mileage was minimal, and no one liked to drive it, so at some point we gave it a new transmission."

No one liked to drive it?

One of the men said something in Russian that evoked a laugh from the others. I continued to the garage, scared by the last thing I'd heard, the one English word among all the Russian ones.

It was "Chai."

EIGHTEEN

My sad little car was in the garage, being worked on by a strange little man who said only, by way of introduction or explanation, "What Yuri tell me do, I do." He then hit the on button of a loud vacuum cleaner, drowning out my cry of "But it's *my* car!"

This wasn't part of the deal, that my car would be—what, rigged? Like the Corvette that Chai had driven to her death? Because surely that's what Crispin suspected. And what about staying in a room I could be locked into? Had Bennett Graham mentioned that when he'd recruited me? Had Yuri? None of this had been in the job description.

I hopped into the Suburban, so eager to be away that at this point I'd drive a horse and buggy. The good news was that my purse was there, on the floor. Stuff had spilled out, but my money and credit cards were safe.

Halfway down the driveway, I swerved to avoid Parashie, who was flagging me down. Behind her came Grusha.

"Where are you going?" Parashie asked when I'd rolled down the window. "Can we come with you? Can you drop us at the store? We have no ride. Yuri and Kimberly have taken the Voyager and Grusha will not drive Alik's Porsche."

How sad. I loved the idea of Grusha in her housedress gunning the engine of a Porsche GT. "Sure. Hop in."

"And Nell too," Parashie said. "She is just coming."

The English instructor rushed toward us, head down, hand in front of her face as if hiding from paparazzi.

"There seems to be a car shortage," I said. "Should I not be driving this—"

"No, we have cars," Parashie said. "Only Kimberly, her Audi has a problem today and goes back to the shop. It is the oil, you see. Vegetable oil. Always it's in the shop."

"Audi, huh? Is it a stick shift?"

"No, it's normal."

"So, Parashie, do you drive a stick?" I asked.

"Yuri says I'm too young to drive. Next year, yes."

"Next year?" Grusha exclaimed. "No. Five years, maybe. Ten years."

"Ten years?" Parashie cried. "I'll be two hundred years old!"

I glanced in the rearview mirror. "Do you drive a stick shift, Grusha?"

"Of course."

"How about you, Nell?"

"Nell doesn't like to drive," Parashie said. "Yuri wants her, but Nell has agoraphobia, so for her it is no fun."

"I was sorry to hear about that, Nell. That must be difficult." Then I added, as casually as I could, "How about Chai? Did she drive a stick?"

"I don't know," Parashie said. "Nell, you can sit here, I will go in the back. Wollie, can you drop us at Gelson's? Or Vons? Any market. Just we need greens for dinner. And then we wait for you. You have to drive home too, yes? For lunch?"

"Gelson's," I said. "Is that in the little mini-mall with the—"

"Veterinarian, UPS shop, karate, card place, photo place, clothes cleaner, hair salon, and nails." Parashie showed impressive mall knowledge, as befitted a teenage girl.

"No frozen yogurt place?" I asked.

"Yes, that also. But it's new."

Parashie kept up a steady stream of talk during the ten-minute ride to Gelson's, punctuated by the occasional *hrmph*s of irritation or contradiction from Grusha. Nell remained silent. I did too, preoccupied as I was by the knowledge that there was no obvious need for anyone in the household to drive a stick shift. The possibility that Chai had learned to drive one out of necessity was dwindling.

I dropped the trio in front of the market, all of them with canvas shopping bags, either an old-school European habit or a New Age California habit. I parked at the south end of the lot, after cruising past the frozen yogurt place, then turned on my cell phone and called Joey.

I described my nocturnal visit from Crispin, and Joey was nearly as concerned as Uncle Theo had been. "He says she was murdered? That must've scared the pajamas off you. Definitely tell your handler."

"My—"

"Your FBI contact that I'm not supposed to know about. The feds won't want anyone interfering with their investigation, so you can't go to the cops. Although it sounds like there's no hard evidence for the cops anyway. But I'll check out Crispin too. Last name Harris, you said? I need a new project. It's either this or Sudoku. Anything else you need?"

"I don't suppose you speak Russian?"

"Not well."

"Okay, never mind. But as long as you're googling people—" I rattled off the names Felix, Stasik, Zbiggo, Nadja, Zeferina Maria, and Bronwen, and then slowed down to spell them. She made little "I'm impressed" noises about Zbiggo, Nadja, and Bronwen. "And here's something else." I gave her a number, asked her to call it from a phone other than her own, speak to a Mr. Wendell, and tell him that the client with the carburetor issue was waiting for him to call her back. Joey agreed to this without further questions. There is much to be said for a friend who embraces subterfuge.

I considered my best approach to the upcoming conversation, should it occur. I'd never contacted Simon this way. I'd been saving it for emergencies, and this was close enough, but the trick would be to get more information out of him than he got out of me. While I waited for him to call, I searched the Suburban for other junk that might have fallen out of my purse, and rescued some coins and a small jade Buddha that Un-

cle Theo had given me. It would have been fabulous to find Chai's missing diary; instead I unearthed, from between the center console and the
passenger seat, a DVD. The title was in Cyrillic, but the plastic cover left
no doubt as to the subject matter. A girl stood in a doorway, holding a
pizza box, wearing nothing but high heels and a beguiling smile.

My phone rang. I shoved the DVD into the glove box and hit talk.

"What the hell," he said, "is going on with you?"

"Can I speak freely?"

"You better."

I decided to overlook his tone of voice. "I didn't mean to hang up on
you, but I can't use the phone from the compound. Anyone could pick
up the extension."

"And hear you talking to your auto mechanic. So?"

"It's complicated to explain."

"Give it a shot."

"Simon, I miss you so badly, it's like a physical malady, I'm getting a—"

"Wollie."

"—skin rash. What?" An SUV drove past me, with a man inside that
looked remarkably like Alik.

"I don't want you working there."

"Simon, why don't you tell me what you've found out about Yuri Milos, so I can make that determination myself?"

"Can't you just trust me on this?"

"Look—" I said.

"No, you look—"

"No, you look," I yelled. "Do I ever give you a hard time about your
career?"

"Constantly."

"Yeah, but I don't tell you to quit. Or that the hours are too long, that
it takes you away from your home, or from me, that it's dangerous—"

"This isn't your career, Wollie. You're a graphic artist."

I looked over my shoulder at the SUV. "The job supports my career.
It beats minimum wage at Wal-Mart. I'm not quitting, Simon. That option's off the table."

There was silence on the other end. I was not handling this well. And now I was distracted, thinking it was Alik in that SUV looking for a parking place. I forced myself to speak more softly. "I'm sorry, I don't want to fight with you, I'm crazy about you. I'm just—not getting enough sleep. Please tell me what you've found out, what the deal is with Yuri that has you so worried."

His tone matched mine: enforced calm. "Yuri Milos made his money in the currency boom in the nineties. His facade of respectability is recently acquired. In the former Soviet bloc countries, in his youth, he was a political refugee, a political dissident, an environmental activist–slash–terrorist as well as a black-market profiteer and a mercenary. And an arms dealer. He's a grab bag of shady occupations and his Christmas card list probably includes half the Russian Mafia."

"But—okay, if he's so bad, then how did he get to be a U.S. citizen?"

"I don't run Immigration," Simon answered. "There are a lot of bad people out walking around, Wollie. The one that concerns me at the moment is the man who's signing your paycheck."

"But what's the FBI's interest in him?" I asked. The SUV had stopped. It was the hybrid Alik had shown me in the driveway, I realized. Alik must be test-driving it.

"What do you mean?" Simon asked.

"What—what do you mean, what do I mean?"

"Why should the FBI have an interest in Milos?"

I hesitated. "Didn't you just say they did?"

"No."

Uh-oh. "Well, I just assumed that you found out all this stuff by, you know, phoning your office. Asking to see his file."

"It doesn't work quite like that."

Yes, it was definitely Alik getting out of the SUV. Walking toward the vet clinic? Or the UPS store? "So what'd you do, google Yuri?" I asked.

"If you'd googled him before going to work for him, like a responsible person, you'd know that very little of what I'm talking about shows up there. He's been laundered."

Alik was going into the UPS store. I turned my attention back to Simon. "I didn't have to google Yuri," I said. "I sat on a jury for weeks hearing about him. If all this is true, why didn't the prosecution mention any of it?"

"Relevance. His past probably didn't figure into a slip-and-fall case. And most personal injury attorneys have no access to classified files."

"But you do."

He said nothing.

"You have a nice Christmas card list of your own, don't you?" I said. "And not just in your own office. Friends in the State Department too? CIA? Immigration?"

"How am I going to sleep nights, knowing you're working for this guy?"

I was starting to notice how many people, when they don't want to answer a question, just ignore it. I'd have to practice that. "Nothing you've just said proves that Yuri's into anything shady now. This isn't the former Soviet Union, it's Calabasas. The burbs."

Silence. He knows more than he's willing to talk about, I thought. "Simon," I said, "whatever he was—and don't we all have checkered pasts?—at present Yuri Milos runs a legitimate media training organization. So maybe he's reformed. Or maybe he hasn't, but there's nothing sinister about what he's hired me for. I just drive people around—"

"That in itself makes me suspicious."

"Hey, my driving record, for the record—"

"And scared. Has he ever been in a car with you?"

"But let's say something problematic does happen," I said, choosing to ignore these childish barbs. "Is there any way I can reach you?"

"Hold on," he said, and clicked into another call.

I looked toward Gelson's, to see if my passengers had reappeared yet, and noticed that Nell was sitting at one of the wrought-iron tables outside the market. She wore a hat and sunglasses, and appeared to be studying the tabletop. Around her, people were eating, reading, talking on phones. Not Nell. Interesting. And now Alik was coming out of the UPS store, a hundred yards away, carrying a box.

He didn't seem to see Nell, nor she him. He pulled out his cell phone, moving to an awning at the veterinary clinic.

Simon came back on the line. "Okay." He gave an audible sigh. "Wollie, I'm about to throw caution to the wind."

"Really?" My heart stopped. Was this a marriage proposal?

"I'm going to give you a number, but you can't call it from your cell phone. Any other phone is okay, just not your own. Ask for Mr. Lavosh. Got that?"

My heart started up again. Okay. No proposal. And anyway, who wants the Big Moment to come over a cell phone in front of the UPS store? For that matter, was I ready for marriage? "Mr. Lavosh," I repeated, copying down the number he rattled off. "Him again. But why are we going out of sequence?" I thought of Ulf and Wendell, the recent aliases, and the every-other-letter code. "Shouldn't you be Mr. Yellow at this point? Or Yam? Yeltzin?"

Silence.

Something occurred to me. "Are you telling me what I think you're telling me? That Mr. Lavosh is your—"

"Cover. Yes. I'm Daniel Lavosh."

I sat there, awed by the secret I'd just been handed. "My God, your cover," I whispered. "I will never tell anyone. You can trust me."

"I know." He let that sink in, and when he spoke again, his tone was brisk. "Now, when you call that number, you're a textiles client. Don't use your own phone or your name. If you call Mr. Lavosh, you're Harriet Spoon."

"Harriet?" As Mr. Lavosh was hanging with a beautiful woman named Lucrezia, why did I have to be Harriet? "I'd prefer a name with more—"

"Harriet Spoon. With Landmark Woolens. And Wollie? I don't need to tell you, do I, the kind of danger I'd be in if you ever, even unintentionally—?"

"No, you don't. I would never—"

"Good." There was a long exhalation. "I know you'll never use it for anything but a dire emergency."

"I won't."

"Although with you, dire emergencies are fairly common. Especially in light of the company you're currently keeping."

Alik was moving again, toward his car, then stopped dead in his tracks. It appeared that he'd spotted Nell. He stuffed the UPS box under his arm, lowered his head, and hurried to his car. Curious.

"Wollie?"

"I'm here," I said into the phone.

"Is there something you're not telling me?" Simon asked.

My heart rate sped up. "Such as . . . ?"

"That's an evasive response," he said.

"Is it?"

"Baby. What kind of trouble are you in?"

"I'm not. I mean—what do you mean?"

"You didn't go home last night."

"No. Were you—how did you—?"

"I'm a spy."

Okay, clearly I was going to have to fork over some information. "I have a room at the compound," I said slowly. "It's a long drive to Calabasas, so it's easier to stay there when I'm working late than to—"

"You're living with Yuri Milos?"

His tone of voice stopped my heart again. Surely this wasn't good, these cardiac stops and starts.

"Not in any romantic sense, of course, but—"

"God almighty, Wollie, you're *living* there?" Now he was yelling.

"It's a perfectly reasonable—"

"Are you listening to me? The man deals in armaments. Guns. He's involved in affairs of state in Eastern Europe—"

"We're not in Eastern—"

"For all you know, he's stockpiling arms for a revolution. You have no idea what you're in the middle of—"

"Then give me an idea—"

"I can't."

"So I'm supposed to accept on faith, when you say 'jump,' it's in my best interest—"

"Yes."

"Well, forget it."

And then there was silence. Simon had hung up on me. Or gotten cut off—that happened a lot, of course, with cell phones, so it was possible. If he'd been on a cell phone.

But it felt like he'd hung up on me.

I pressed "end" on my phone, fighting the impulse to cry. How had we gotten here from there? A minute before, Simon had given me his cover name. As grand gestures go, this was more than a key to his condo or the PIN to his ATM. This was a piece of him that all his experience told him not to trust anyone with. And he'd entrusted it to me.

This wouldn't have meant as much to me even a week earlier. But now I was in the same boat, worried about my own cover and figuring the only way to ensure my safety was to keep my mouth shut and assume that every person taken into my confidence was a person who could betray me, even without meaning to, even with the best will in the world. I'd learned this from Simon. And maybe I wasn't so good at it now, but I would get better.

Except that what was good for spies, I was beginning to see, was hell on long-term relationships.

Four minutes later, I was still waiting for my Gelson's trio. Alik's car hadn't moved. But as I watched, Alik got out of the SUV and headed into the Calabasas vet clinic.

Without giving myself time to think, I jumped out of the Suburban and walked quickly to his car.

It was a black Toyota, a Highlander Hybrid, so new it didn't have plates. I peered in the windows. They were tinted in the back but not the front, so I could make out the UPS box on the passenger seat. It had a fair number of stamps and stickers on it, probably showing tracking numbers, insurance labels, and the like. I couldn't make out the return address, but I guessed, from the stamps and stickers, that it was foreign. That gave me an idea. After a glance toward the vet and another one toward Gelson's, where Nell sat, corpselike, I went into the UPS store.

The place wasn't busy. In fact, there were no customers. There were three men behind the counter, one of them young, one middle-aged, and one elderly.

"Can I help you?" the oldest and the youngest asked in unison.

"Well, I hope so. I've got a new job, and I may already be messing up." This was close enough to the truth to be credible. "One of my bosses, a guy named Alik Milos, has a mailbox here, and—"

"Milos? He was just here," the kid piped up. "Alik Milos."

"Thank goodness." I gave him what I hoped was a pathetic smile. "See, I have a big list of stuff I'm supposed to do, but if he picked up a package already—you're sure he did?"

"Yeah, he signed for it."

"Was it the one from Europe? Wait—let me just consult my notes—" I rummaged through my purse and pulled out my greeting card sketchbook and thumbed through it. "I thought I wrote it down, but—oh, my goodness, I am in trouble if I don't stay on top of this."

The kid picked up a spindle with little receipts skewered onto it. "Don't worry, he only comes once a week or so. Not even." He looked through the receipts like he was going to show me. This was my lucky day.

"Is it the package from—Belarus?" I asked, stepping closer to look.

His elderly colleague moved in on him from behind the desk. "That's not information you're to give out, Brewster."

"Oh." Brewster put down the spindle. "Sorry."

"No, I'm sorry," I said. "I don't want to get you in trouble, I just—anyhow, see you next time. If I've still got my job. Which I hope I have." I smiled my pathetic smile. "Bye."

Walking out, I wondered what this meant. Alik had a mailbox here and picked up packages every week. But why not have them delivered to the house?

"Hey!" The voice behind me made me jump.

I turned to see the elderly man standing in the doorway of the UPS store. "Yes?" I said, walking back toward him.

"Not Belarus. Estonia."

"Excuse me?"

He held up a bunch of slips. "The package he picks up, every two weeks, is from Film Estonia. That's where he sends them, too. Now listen: for pickups, you'll need a letter of authorization from him, and for anything you bring in to send, you fill out these waybills and commercial invoices at home, and it will save you quite a bit of time. And can I give you a bit of advice, young lady? Write things down. Don't depend on your memory. You should go right now and jot down everything I've just told you. You're a professional and you need to act like one. That's the way people keep their jobs."

Alik hauled a gigantic bag of dog food into the back of the Toyota, slammed the door, and took off.

I pulled up to Gelson's in the Suburban and collected my produce-laden passengers. When they were buckled up, I asked, "Hey, if I have a package to mail, should I bring it here to the UPS store? Is that easier than the post office?"

"You don't have to," Parashie said. "We have FedEx; it comes to the house. You just call, and they come."

"So you never use UPS?"

"Never," Grusha and Parashie said in unison, with more vehemence than I thought the subject warranted. I wondered why.

Nell, in the backseat, said nothing. But through her sunglasses I could see her watching me.

NINETEEN

"Did you not read the schedule?" Donatella called, rushing to meet me as I emerged from the garage. "You are to be teaching your class."

"What?"

"Class! Class! Your class on dating!"

"Right now?" I asked, alarmed. "But I thought I was free until—"

"Three minutes ago!" Two bangled-covered arms danced in the air, punctuating her points. "You don't understand English? Is there another language we should talk in?"

"I mean—okay. I didn't realize it was an actual class, I thought I was just—what exactly am I supposed to be covering?"

"Dating!" The bangles shook violently.

"Yes, I know, but what aspect—"

"All of it. You are responsible for their social skills. My God, you are so slow. And I must be off. They wait for you in the library. Now. Go." She brushed past me into the garage, quick yet graceful in a pair of seriously beautiful high-heeled shoes.

I hurried into Big House, straight into the library. Zbiggo, Stasik, and Felix lounged there on the leather furniture, each with a bottle of Pellegrino nearby.

"Hello, boys—uh, guys. Gentlemen."

"Good morning!" Felix, at least, seemed delighted to see me. "And what do we call you? Woman?"

"Wollie's good," I said. "Oh—you mean, people of my gender? 'Women,' if you're talking about us in the third person. But don't address someone as 'woman,' because that's too John Wayne—"

"How about 'dude'?" he asked.

"No. 'Babe,' if you're talking to a bird," Stasik said in his Oxford accent. "Doll. Crumpet."

"Chick," Zbiggo said, and added something in Russian that made Stasik laugh.

"Yes, if you want to alienate half the population. You could always use names. First names. Or," I added, remembering Bronwen, "as a gesture of respect, Ms. Whomever. Oh, if you're hailing a waitress, at dinner, you don't yell 'Waitress!' because that's considered rude. And—" I stopped as the library door opened and Parashie came in, armed with a pen and notebook, and took a seat near the back, giving me a smile and a nod. I returned her smile, wondering what she was doing here. "But let's back up. As this is a small class, I'm happy to tailor it to your specific—"

The door opened again. This time a man, large and florid, entered the room. He looked like he'd just fallen out of bed, despite wearing a suit. "May I help you?" I asked.

"No, no—" He began to cough but waved me off in a "don't mind me, just go about your business" manner.

"So, anyhow," I said, addressing my trio, "I'm here to help you feel at home in the culture of L.A., which is representative of America as a whole." I thought about that. "Well, except for the Americans who consider L.A. the land of fruits and nuts. But many customs, like opening the car door for your date, are universal. In polite society."

Zbiggo asked, "What about sex?"

"Not on the first date." I owed the women of America that much; anyone seeing Zbiggo more than once was on her own.

"Are you saying," Stasik asked, "that a guy who wants to boink you has to shell out twice for your dinner, then?" The florid man stopped coughing and Parashie looked at me with an expression of interest, pen poised to write.

"Charmingly asked, Stasik," I said. "I myself came of age in the era of going dutch, so money isn't the—"

"Three times?" Felix asked.

"What?" I asked.

"Three times dinner, then sex?"

"There are no hard-and-fast rules, Felix."

"And how long must you wait," Felix asked, "until you telephone her after the first dinner, before the second dinner?"

"She is hot, this chick?" Zbiggo asked.

"Make her wait a week," Stasik said. "Supply and demand. Withhold supply to create demand."

"Stasik," I said, "are you sure this is your first time in L.A.?"

"*Govno,*" Zbiggo said. "A week? If she is hot? His balls fall off."

"I ask this," Felix said, "because I am a virgin."

There was a moment of silence, except for the sound of Parashie's pen scribbling, and then Zbiggo said it again. "*Govno.*"

"Felix," I said. "Don't worry about it. Women respond to conversation. Show genuine interest in her, look her in the eye, pay attention when she talks, don't order chateaubriand for two if she just told you she's a vegetarian, be your normal, kind self, and don't even try to hit on her until the second, maybe the third—"

"You have kiss a girl, yes?" Zbiggo asked Felix.

"Yes, I have kissed a girl."

Zbiggo turned to me. "You buy dinner, then you can kiss?"

"Possibly," I said. "However, it depends on—"

"Mouth open?"

"Occasionally," I said. Simon flashed through my mind. "But again, there's no—"

"How about this?" Zbiggo said to Felix, his hands outstretched, palms out, making spasmodic squeezing gestures. "You do this?"

The florid man in the back of the room made a barking noise, less like a dog than some creature from Sea World. Felix turned to me, eyes wide.

"Zbiggo," I said. "Have a seat, please. Felix, there are plenty of women, especially in other parts of the U.S., like Utah, who would consider it a plus, your lack of previous—"

"Or this?" Zbiggo asked, making a circular movement with his forefinger. He was talking to me now.

"I'm not sure what that is," I said.

"I think you do," Zbiggo said, advancing toward me.

In spite of myself, I backed up. "Zbiggo, have a seat, would you?"

But Zbiggo kept coming, finger twirling, mildly menacing in a classclown kind of way.

Stasik stood.

Zbiggo walked past him and I couldn't see what happened then, only that Zbiggo's hand, which had been in front of him, was suddenly behind him. He stopped, uttered something—the Russian equivalent of "ouch," probably—and then he was looking at his fingers. I saw a dot of blood appear on his index finger, which he then stuck in his mouth.

"Sorry," Stasik said, moving nimbly away, out of Zbiggo's reach. His hands were behind his back, slipping something into his pants pocket.

A knife?

Zbiggo threw him a confused look, but let it go. I was confused, too, about what had just happened. Had Stasik really nicked Zbiggo's finger? Did all my trainees carry knives?

At the other end of the library, the florid man was holding up a cell phone, apparently taking photos of me, and Parashie was writing in her notebook, seemingly oblivious. I was about to ask the florid man who he was and if he'd mind not taking photos of me, when he slipped away into the office and closed the door.

I spent the rest of the hour discussing tipping procedures in restaurants and the relative merits of handshakes, hugs, and a kiss on the cheek as goodbye rituals, using Felix for my demonstration model and making Stasik and Zbiggo practice on each other. Parashie complimented me on this, walking me to the dining room after class.

"Also, that was good, about tips," she said. "No one from Europe remembers to tip."

"I know. I used to wait tables, long ago. Were you really taking notes?"

"No, I am doing my homework," Parashie said. "Nell gives me so much. But I like noise while I study, so I sit in the library during the training classes."

I was distracted by the sight, out the window, of a dozen or more men in tactical pants, shirtless, gathered on the north end of the lawn. I asked Parashie who they were and she told me they were putting in the swimming pool. Which was interesting, as the pool was going in behind the Green House, on the other side of the estate. "Did Chai teach the same class I just taught?" I asked.

"Oh!" Parashie brightened. "Yes. Only Chai taught which are the cool clubs to go to in Hollywood and how to dress to get in and what is a cool drink to order, like a sidecar, and what celebrities to see in which club."

"Oh." Insecurity set in. "That's not my area of expertise. I hope Donatella isn't disappointed."

"Donatella goes today to Mogilev for an emergency. Something big is happening there. Vlad comes from Mogilev and Donatella goes to Mogilev. This is not a good trade."

"Vlad—was he the man in the back of the room?"

"Yes, the ugly one," she said, nodding. "Bad Vlad, Kimberly and I call him. Stay away from Bad Vlad. He is a real asshole."

The last thing I wanted to do after lunch was hike. Hiking ranks high on my list of Activities I Don't See the Point Of. It's not like there's a skill involved, other than the ability to slog along, mile after mile, in blinding sun or torrential rain, for no discernible purpose. But Kimberly assembled us all in the great room, everyone in hiking gear, except for two men in tool belts measuring the glass doors leading to the deck. No one else paid attention to them, so I took the opportunity to sidle up to one and say, "Are we getting new doors?"

"One-way glass," he said, his accent Russian. No wonder Bennett Graham had a hard time placing an agent inside the compound. Even the glaziers were Yuri's countrymen.

I thought back to my first lunch. "Maybe it should be bulletproof glass."

"Is already bulletproof. It stop the bullet, yes?" He pointed to a small indentation on the outside of the window.

Jeez Louise. I was right. It had been a bullet. I was living in a place where getting shot at was common enough to warrant bulletproof glass. I looked around at my fellow hikers. Were they all aware of that? And which one had written my mirror message? The bloodred letters had still been there when I'd gone to change into hiking clothes, and I'd copied them again on a scrap of paper, which I planned to carry with me until I found a translation.

Kimberly handed me a shoebox. "Boots. Hey, did you see Olive Oyl throw up?"

"No," I said, startled. "Is she sick?"

"Parashie says she is."

"She is!" Parashie said heatedly, overhearing. "Twice she vomited this morning."

"Dogs do that," Kimberly said. "It's no big deal."

"What if someone poisons her?" Parashie asked. "Zeferina Maria Catalina says—"

"Oh, that reminds me," Kimberly said. "Zeferina Maria Catalina? Your name's great, but too long for Americans. How do you feel about Zeffie?"

Zeferina Maria Catalina looked up from her new boots. In camouflage gear she was more interesting, a cross between Betty Crocker and Che Guevara. "If I must, okay."

Alik approached me with a Swiss Army knife. "Boots fit? Can I clip the tags?"

I held out my foot.

"You were right," he said, snipping the tags. "Someone did shoot at us during lunch the other day." He nodded toward the glaziers. "Not going to scare you off, is it?"

"Heck, no." Two days earlier it had been scary, but now other things were scarier. Like Chai's murder. And Alik's admission reassured me; it showed he was honest. *It's a good tactic,* a voice said, *telling you a truth you already know.*

Was that my inner spy? She certainly was cynical.

"You look good," he said with a final squeeze of my foot. "Grab a pack."

I chose an army green backpack from the mound on the table, but Kimberly took it out of my hands, replacing it with another. Inside was a rubber water container attached to a tube that ran along the outside. Parashie showed me how to flip the plastic switch at the end of the tube and suck, for hands-free hydration. She then tightened the straps on the pack, forcing my shoulders back. For the thousandth time, I wished I were flat-chested. If there's a sport in the world where large breasts give you an advantage, I'd like to know about it.

"All right, team," Kimberly yelled, pulling on her own pack. "Ninety minutes till happy hour, which we'll observe on Eagle Nest Overlook. Sadly, Olive Oyl will not join us, because Parashie is worried about her health."

I was worried about my own health. A three-hour round-trip hike sounded serious.

Nadja raised her hand. "I can bring my iPod?"

"You may not. This is a bonding experience—iPods isolate." Kimberly indicated posters set up on easels around the room. "Watch for red ants, rattlesnakes, poison oak—"

"Rattlesnakes?" Zbiggo said, his deep voice quivering.

Kimberly pointed to the "Poison Reptiles" poster. "Don't freak out. I have serum."

Zeffie said something in Spanish and then Felix and Stasik were talking, until Kimberly called, "Let's bond in English. Listen up: coyotes and bobcats will be too afraid to hurt you. Mountain lions, no, but the chances that we'll see one of those are slim to none."

Zbiggo raised his hand. "The mountain lion, she kill if you jog, yes? In California, yes? I hear in newspaper. *We* are in California."

"Yes," Kimberly said. "We *are* in California, but this is Los Angeles County. The mountain lions who kill joggers are in San Diego County— a very few, anomalous incidents. There's a bad gene pool down there. Los Angeles County has good mountain lions."

"What about bears?" I mumbled. Stasik, overhearing me, uttered a short laugh. I couldn't tell if it was a nice, bonding sort of "I'm with you" laugh or a "you fool" laugh.

"Last thing." Kimberly gestured to the window, where the workmen continued to work. "Out there, we carry the same packs, we drink the same water, we walk in the same boots under the same sky. But your hike is your own, determined by your self-talk. Your experience has nothing to do with circumstances, and everything to do with who you are."

Who was I? A grump. So I was in for a grumpy hike. But was this fair, a philosophy that didn't allow for activity preferences?

"Happy trails, friends," Kimberly said. "Last one to Eagle Nest is . . . the last one."

After Kimberly's inspirational address, the march down the suburban driveway felt anticlimactic. But at the end of Tumbleweed Circle, we turned onto a trail that took us directly into the canyon. One minute, a gated community; the next, the hinterlands. We walked single file along a skinny path. Alik led the way and Kimberly brought up the rear to en-sure that no one bailed and headed for home. Like me. Or Bronwen. We were clearly the weak links in the chain, placed at the end so as not to slow everyone down.

The day was hot. Within minutes I was sweating and panting and, half an hour later, as happy as a member of the Donner Party. Behind me, Bronwen moaned. Ahead, people kept up a good pace and animated conversation, even Zeffie showing more stamina than I'd expected.

"Wollie." Yuri trotted up the hill toward me, with Olive Oyl at his side. He wore the red MediasRex baseball cap we all wore, and with his baldness covered and biceps exposed, he gave an impression of youth and virility. Olive Oyl, in her yellow fur, looked hot.

"Is Olive Oyl okay?" I asked. "Parashie said she wasn't well."

"She's fine. She needs exercise."

"Like me," I panted.

"Transformation." He clapped me on the backpack. "Never comfort-able. So tell me your goals. We will place them on the mountain ahead of us and hike toward them."

"Okay."

He laughed. "But you have to say them aloud. Sound gives them substance."

I considered that. Making up with Simon, that was a goal. Kissing Simon. Sex with Simon. Not what I cared to share with Yuri. "I'd like to know what happened to Chai," I said.

"I'm happy to talk about Chai. But I want to focus on you first."

"Is this part of the job, sharing my innermost desires?"

"Yes. What I ask of my trainees I ask of my trainers." He took my arm. It might have seemed a chivalrous gesture, except for the fact that he was forcing me into a faster pace. "What is your purpose here, Wollie?"

"Purpose?" I flashed on Bennett Graham and felt a stab of paranoia. "In Calabasas?"

"On earth."

"Oh, okay. Well. You'll probably say there are no right or wrong answers, but—"

"No. I won't say that."

I took a deep breath. "I used to think that I was put on earth to keep my little brother out of trouble."

He nodded. "What if you had had no little brother?"

I thought about my friends. And Uncle Theo. "There's always someone to worry about, isn't there? Someone who needs your help."

"Yes, there is. Now widen the circle."

"What circle?"

"The one that describes your life." He looked at the sky. "You travel rarely—due to your brother. You belong to no groups, except Tree People and the Graphic Artists Guild."

"And the Humane Society." It no longer surprised me, the things he knew about me. "I may not travel much, but my greeting cards do. In a manner of speaking."

"Exactly. Your work is seen in distant galaxies, by those who buy them and send them, in turn, to other galaxies." He pointed to the canyon below, vast and stark. "This view makes you feel insignificant, yes? And you are. It is our ties to others that give us power."

"Yuri, can we slow down?"

"No. If you slow, you give Bronwen permission to slow." He glanced over his shoulder. "She wants to sing at the Met. She has the voice, but her reputation is shot. No relationship skills. No one will work with her. We are going to rehabilitate her."

I looked back at the soprano, who was falling farther behind. Just ahead of us, Olive Oyl began barking at something on the side of the trail. Yuri let go of me to investigate.

"No, Olive Oyl," he said, grabbing her collar and handing her to me. "Hold her."

This was easier said than done and it took all my might to restrain the dog, now beside herself with excitement. What was it she'd discovered?

Then I heard it, between Olive Oyl's barks and urgent whines. A rattle. It took longer to see it, the way the snake blended into the brown dirt. To my astonishment, Yuri stepped on it, behind its head, then reached down and grasped it in one hand. His arm wound up like a baseball pitcher's, and the rattlesnake went flying, launched in an arc far into the canyon.

"Jesus, Mary, and Joseph," I said.

"You can let go of the dog. She's not terribly smart, but she won't follow it down there." Indeed, Olive Oyl, when I released her, merely sniffed the ground around Yuri's feet. "A good trick, isn't it?" he asked. "Impresses the girls, especially when it's a big fellow like that one. It's the babies you have to watch. They don't have rattles, but they have venom, and they see threats where none exist. Much more aggressive than the adults."

"Is it dead?"

"Let's say it's relocated. Can't let the dog get bit, or Kimberly would kill me. And Bronwen's not ready to encounter a rattler."

"Me neither."

"You just did." We resumed hiking. "I'm a good judge of people, but I make mistakes. Chai was a mistake. World-class looks, and clever in the ways of the world, an interesting trait in one so young. It fascinated me. I saw her potential, and so I overlooked what I should have seen, what was clear to the rest of the team."

"What was that?"

"She had no heart."

He pronounced it like a medical fact. It unnerved me.

"So what happened to her?" I asked.

"I thought you knew. She had a car accident."

"There was practically no mention of it in the media."

"I can keep people out of the news as well as get them into it. It's my job."

"Why would you?"

"Having a team member die is not good publicity."

"I thought all publicity is good publicity," I said.

"Only if the goal is notoriety. Mere celebrity." He gestured to the climbers higher up the path. "For us, the goal is influence. Each of them desires to reach a wider audience, to make a difference in the world with what talent they possess. Now you are part of that. Do you feel it? The connecting string, running through them, to you, back to Kimberly and Bronwen? Feel its vibration? You affect the course of human events."

And with that, Yuri released my arm and continued up the trail at a run, easily, to catch up with Zeffie. Olive Oyl loped after him.

What was he talking about? Was I Joan of Arc? No, I was Wollie of L.A. I'd be lucky to make it up this hill, never mind affecting the course of human events.

And what about Yuri's own purpose? I thought of the note in my file, that I could be turned into an asset. Was this a recruiting technique? And what was I being recruited for? Arms running, or something higher-minded? It didn't matter. I wanted to save the planet as much as the next person, but I had enough on my plate, taking care of my brother in the face of mental illness and insufficient medical coverage. That was my real purpose here, the sole reason I was hiking and spying for my country.

The trail was really winding now, with frequent switchbacks, causing me to lose sight of Zeffie ahead of me, the only one I could see.

"Wollie, catch up to the others," Kimberly yelled behind me. "I'll stay with Bronwen."

Catch up? Kimberly overestimated me. And I'd underestimated her;

she'd achieved a first-name basis with Bronwen. I upped my pace, which was no fun at all. Yeah, the view was idyllic: pristine wilderness, no houses, and few power lines. But beauty's not everything.

I came to a fork at the foot of a hill, with one path going up and the other around. I chose the one that looked most traveled, but I chose wrong. After a time the trail grew weedy, then stopped. I looked behind me. No Kimberly. No one ahead either. I was alone.

The hair on the back of my neck stood on end.

There was something fierce about all this. I was a child of the suburbs, I didn't belong here, didn't belong to this outfit, in this job. In spite of the heat, I shivered. Then I climbed higher, through the brambles to the top of the ridge, to get my bearings.

In the distance, I saw a person running. I squinted. It was one of our team—the red baseball cap was unmistakable. He or she was tearing through the canyon, off trail. Why? It was harsh going, as I'd just discovered, and with no clear destination . . .

And then I spotted another figure, farther away, the red cap just a spot moving through dense brush, in a different direction from the first hiker. With this one, too, there was speed and determination. These people weren't out gathering wildflowers.

A bark echoed through the canyon, a yowling, yapping, frenzied sound, the canine version of a shriek.

And then came its human equivalent, a scream, high-pitched and hysterical.

TWENTY

scrambled back down the trail faster than I'd come up, with no thought of poison oak or poison snakes, just following the voice that was still screaming in the canyon.

I was pretty sure it was Parashie, but hysteria messes with the voice-recognition factor. I kept hearing the word "dead," but I told myself that Parashie would probably scream in Russian, in which case I wasn't really hearing "dead" at all but "dyed" or "nyet" or "da" or something. Maybe. I wanted it to be true, anyway.

Someone began to blow a whistle, the obnoxious kind favored by football coaches. It was a strange thing to hear in the wild, no doubt giving heart attacks to the little rabbits and fawns. I assumed it meant "Come! Fast!" and so I was coming, as fast as I could. I got to the fork in the trail and took the path I should've taken initially. Within minutes I saw them.

Bronwen and Kimberly were on the trail, both on cell phones, which apparently worked fine up on the mountaintop. Kimberly had the whistle. Twenty yards down the hillside were others, working their way up to the trail, carrying something. Someone.

I closed in, straining for a better look. Stasik had the guy's head, his back obscuring my view. Zbiggo had the torso, gripping the armpits, with Felix at the waist. Nadja had the legs. I couldn't tell who it was.

Following the body-bearers was Parashie, with Zeffie supporting her. Parashie was a wreck, her movements jerky and erratic, her face streaked with tears and dirt. She was quiet at that moment, but then she started in again. "Olive Oyl, stop! Stop the barking!" Her voice was raw, used up with screaming. "Olive Oyl, she is the one. She finds him. She is climbed down to him. His shoe. Is sticking up. Then the face. Dead. He's dead, isn't he? He's dead."

I was close now, standing on the trail directly above the body-bearers. I realized that the body wasn't wearing camouflage gear. He wasn't one of us. He wasn't on the team.

My relief startled me. When had that happened, me feeling like part of the tribe, like what mattered most was that it wasn't one of our own?

Stasik changed his position and I got a glimpse of the man's face, and my relief withered.

His face was bruised. The area around his eyes was mottled, not black-and-blue but red, with dried blood all around his mouth and chin.

His eyes were wide open.

It was Crispin.

TWENTY-ONE

I fought back an urge to scream. This became a need to vomit and I squatted, turning away from the group coming up the hill. My stomach heaved, but nothing came out. After some moments, I said a silent prayer to whatever Being might be presiding over this, and turned to face the nightmare.

They had Crispin up to the trail now. Yuri had just come upon the scene, appearing from around the bend, his face flushed. He said to put Crispin down and they did, lowering him carefully onto the dirt.

Except for Parashie, people seemed calm. Even Olive Oyl had stopped barking, confining herself to heavy panting, and the pallbearers, too, were collectively catching their breath. Kimberly was still on her cell phone, with a trail map in hand. She described landmarks, speaking with the matter-of-factness of a police dispatcher. Bronwen, talking on her phone in Norwegian, was intense but not hysterical.

But I could be hysterical. Panic was closing in on me, the realization that Crispin was dead, and by some unnatural cause. I'm no medical examiner, but I could see that this wasn't snakebite or a heart attack or even falling down the hillside in the dark. Something bad had happened to his face beyond coyotes chewing on him for breakfast. That image made me turn away again, my stomach heaving, determined to lose its lunch. I had to keep it together, but I had no idea how.

Look up, Wollie, a voice said.

I looked up. I saw trees. Grass. Clouds. Dirt. Wildflowers. Rocks. Details to ground me in the face of a world spinning out of control. Something glinted at me, catching a ray of sun and reflecting it back. A beer can, maybe. A prosaic image, stopping my brain from replaying the image of what lay behind me on the trail.

Think, Wollie, the voice said.

I took a deep breath and began to think.

Crispin had left me in the middle of the night, gotten this far, and met whatever bad end he'd met. If it was murder—did it have to be murder? Could it be an accident? A misunderstanding between Crispin and Mother Nature?—if it was murder, then I shared some of the responsibility. Didn't I?

I did.

He'd been at the compound to see me. That's what he'd come there for. And he'd died going back home.

I turned once more to face the team. Parashie and Zeffie had reached the trail. Yuri moved to his daughter and folded her in an embrace, keeping her head buried in his shoulder, not letting her look at the body. Not that it mattered now. If she'd found Crispin, that vision was stamped on her brain. That shoe, sticking up. That face.

"Who is he?" Felix asked finally.

"He looks a child," Zeffie said. "No older than Parashie."

Bronwen stowed her phone in her pocket and said, "Is he local? From this town?"

"He could be anyone," Kimberly said. "Hikers from all over L.A. use these trails."

"What happened to his face?" Zbiggo asked.

"He was stabbed," Zeffie said. She spoke with authority, and if anyone found it odd that a politician's wife knew from stab wounds, they didn't comment on it.

Yuri said, "Kimberly? Did you reach someone?"

"The sheriff's station. They patched me through to the park ranger. They're coming."

Yuri released Parashie, but kept an arm around her. "Does anyone know who he is?"

I opened my mouth to say yes, I know exactly who he is, but my hand crept upward and clamped itself around my mouth. I waited for someone else to speak up, then remembered that Crispin had been jilted by Chai. I didn't know when the breakup had happened, but it was possible Chai never introduced him around the compound. Was I really the only person who knew him?

You don't know him either, the voice said.

This time I actually looked around, as if someone had spoken aloud.

I've never been possessed by spirits, but I had an impression of a woman considerably bigger than me, a disembodied something-or-other, saying, *Keep your knowledge to yourself. Silence is not lying. Silence protects you.*

I stayed silent. Whoever she was, this specter I'd summoned, the tough cookie, she sounded sure of herself. That was enough for me.

Yuri caught my eye.

"Wollie?" he asked. "Do you know him?"

My head, of its own volition, did a quick shake.

And that was that. I kept silent, and kept watch, right up to the moment the park ranger showed up.

TWENTY-TWO

The ranger drove a truck. We saw it coming a mile away, appearing and disappearing from view as it made its way along the winding mountain roads. I put my arms around my shoulders, hugging myself as if to keep the truth from spilling out. I would be of no use to anyone, least of all Crispin, if I didn't keep it together. Well, presumably Crispin didn't care whether I kept it together or not. Unless his soul was hovering around. Fredreeq believes that souls hover, on their way to the Other Side. I looked up. A huge brown hawk flew overhead, so large that, just for an instant, it blocked out the sun. Maybe that was Crispin. It did have an omen-ish quality. But would Crispin be a hawk? A pigeon would be more like him. A duck. A sitting duck.

The ranger arrived in a cloud of dust, bringing his sports utility vehicle to a stop close to us. He hopped out.

He hitched up his pants repeatedly as he approached the body. I had a moment of relief, embuing this man with all the powers of law and order, Man's dominance over Nature, sanity, authority, and the State of California. But he got to the body and said nothing, just kept hitching up his pants over and over. It occurred me that (a) he needed a belt and (b) he would know all about mountain lions and snakebites and the importance of staying hydrated while hiking, but was perhaps of no use when it came to dead bodies. Humans, anyway. Probably he was at home with animal carcasses.

Yuri greeted the ranger with a handshake and shoulder clasp. "Jeff, how are you?"

Ranger Jeff grunted, then squatted, gesturing toward Crispin. "Better than him. What's the story? How'd this happen?"

"I don't know," Yuri said. "He's not one of ours."

"You found him here? On the trail?"

"Down the hillside, fifty yards. My dog discovered him."

Ranger Jeff squinted up at Yuri. "Dogs aren't allowed in the state park, you know."

"Write me a ticket. Olive Oyl saved you a search-and-rescue operation, I think."

"No question there. Where is the dog?"

I looked around and realized that not only was Olive Oyl nowhere in sight, but the rest of the team, with the exception of Kimberly, had disappeared too.

"Just around the bend, in the shade," Yuri said. "With my daughter."

"The heat is getting to them," Kimberly added. "And the stress."

"You three moved the body up to the trail yourselves?" The ranger looked at Kimberly, then at me, raising an eyebrow.

I was about to speak, but Yuri jumped in. "He wasn't heavy," he said. "I have a few clients here too, but I'm keeping them out of the sun. They're not conditioned yet, and some are jet-lagged, just in from Europe."

I stared at Yuri. Lying to a park ranger—a government official!—and so casually, was shocking to me.

"This a new bunch?" Ranger Jeff said, standing.

"Yes," Kimberly chimed in. "You may have heard of them. Nadja Lubashenko, Zbigniew Shpek—"

"The heavyweight?"

"That's the one," Yuri said. "Jeff, you have my phone number and address. If the police have any questions . . ."

The ranger gestured to Crispin. "Why'd you move the body?"

"I'm happy to talk to you at length," Yuri said, "but may I send my team home?"

"What happened to his face?" Ranger Jeff asked. "One hell of a mess, isn't it?"

"Yes," Yuri said. "Look, my daughter is very upset. I'll have a case of heat exhaustion on my hands if I don't get her out of here."

Ranger Jeff hitched up his pants some more. "I don't know that anyone should leave, seeing how this is a crime scene."

"Crime scene?" The words popped out of me. "Was he—killed? The dead man? Are you sure? I mean, of course he was killed, he's dead, but was he . . . you know, murdered?" My voice sounded loud and unnatural.

Ranger Jeff looked at me, then squatted again, peering at Crispin's face. "Never saw an animal do this kind of thing. Wonder how long he's been dead?"

"I'd say a day or so," Yuri said. "Overnight, maybe."

Ranger Jeff looked up. "How would you know something like that?"

"The war," Yuri said.

What war? I wondered.

"Infantry?" the ranger asked.

"Medic," Yuri said.

"Well, you've seen your share of dead. Yeah, send your people home. Except your girl. She's the one who found him?"

"It's my girl I'm worried about. She will talk to the police later today, anytime they like, and meanwhile, I will stay. I can show you where we found the body. You can see the path we took." Yuri pointed to where the earth had been matted and trampled.

"Yeah, you shouldn't have moved the body," Ranger Jeff said. "How come you did that, by the way?"

"I was acting on instinct, wanting to get him up to the road, away from the wild. I wasn't thinking in terms of foul play."

Why was Yuri claiming he'd done this? Did he really need to protect everyone? Foreigners, after all, could hardly be expected to know local crime scene laws. Unless they watched a lot of American TV.

Ranger Jeff stood. "I tell you what, I don't know that the sheriff's going to like that much. I don't know that I should be releasing witnesses either."

"We're not witnesses," Yuri said, "to anything but our dog discovering this poor man. Let my team go and I promise, they'll all be available for questioning, if it's found to be necessary. The sheriff's department knows where I live. Carol and Lee Baca have been to my house for dinner. I am happy to put in a call to Lee, if you like."

I wasn't sure who Carol and Lee Baca were, or if in fact they'd been over for dinner, but this carried some weight with Ranger Jeff. Within minutes, all of us but Yuri were going down the mountainside, heading for home.

Kimberly kept us going at a good pace. Fortunately, it was downhill, so Bronwen and I were able to keep up, planted in the middle of the bunch, which was now in a much tighter hiking formation. Conversation was sporadic and mostly in Russian. Kimberly didn't complain, so I assumed that discovering Crispin's corpse had bonded us sufficiently for the English-only rule to be suspended.

I walked alongside Bronwen until we reached a narrow stretch and then I moved ahead. At one point I stumbled, crashing to one knee before my hands reached out to break my fall. Bronwen, behind me, called out, and Stasik, ahead, was suddenly at my side, hauling me to my feet with surprising gentleness.

"I'm okay," I said, touched by the communal concern, and continued on the path. Moments later I looked down to see blood soaking through my camouflage pants and staining the sock peeking out of my hiking boot. I started to cry. I didn't know why; I wasn't in pain. I tried to suppress my tears, but that made it worse, like trying not to laugh at a funeral, but eventually I got myself under control, relieved that no one had noticed, as we were now starting to spread out. It was a stoic group, except for Parashie, and I was determined to suck it up and fit in. I reached in my pocket for a Kleenex and found, instead, my cell phone.

I turned it on and it sprang to life, pulsing with messages. The first was from my brother. "Wollie," P.B. said. "I need you to buy me *Superstrings and the Search for the Theory of Everything*. And where are you? When are you coming? These people here are bugging me. Mrs. Winterbottom is a witch. Not the good kind."

I considered calling him, longing for familial contact. P.B. wasn't known for his sensitivity, but he could be helpful in times of stress. But while my brother was a man of few words, Mrs. Winterbottom was a woman of hundreds, even thousands of words, and none of them were the sort I'd want to hear right now, and chances were, she'd answer.

The next message was from Uncle Theo, wanting to know when we'd be visiting P.B.

The next message was from Simon.

"I'm frustrated," he said, "about the accessibility issue, the lack of immediate feedback, and the manner in which we concluded our last call. For a variety of reasons, but most are summarized on invoice 27WSGN388. Call me."

There was now a new lump in my throat. Other couples have pet names; Simon and I had invoice 27WSGN388. The numbers meant nothing. The letters stood for "We Should Get Naked."

It took a lot not to call Simon, if only to listen to his outgoing message. But if I heard it I'd be weeping all over the trail, and I couldn't tell him even a fraction of what was going on anyway. I hit "save" and went on to message number four.

"Wollie," Joey said. "I've been talking to Fredreeq about that model who's gone to that great catwalk in the sky. We have an idea about that. I also found out stuff about your new colleagues. And your middle-of-the-night Romeo. Call me."

Could I? Bronwen was far enough behind to be out of earshot, but Felix was in front of me, Stasik having jumped ahead of him. He was holding up well, especially for a self-described Formerly Fat Person. There was a spring in his step. I'd have thought that someone so religious might be more subdued in the face of death, but maybe the opposite was true. Maybe Felix was happy that Crispin was now with Jesus. I would ask him, when the moment was right, how that all worked. Maybe I could pray my way out of the guilt I felt.

I slowed my pace, putting distance between Felix and me, and hit the "return this call" key. Joey answered.

"Joey," I whispered, "the middle-of-the-night Romeo is lying dead on the trail in the Santa Monica Mountains."

"No!" she yelled.

"Yes!" I hissed.

"What happened?"

"I don't know. The dog found him. No one but me seems to know who he is and I feel so responsible for his death and when the cops show up and start questioning us—"

"Whoa. Whoa, whoa, whoa. Say nothing. Tell no one."

I glanced behind me. Bronwen was on her own phone, oblivious to me. "But that's withholding evidence, isn't it? And also, I'd feel better if—I feel so guilty that—"

"Wollie," Joey said. "You're undercover. You don't have the luxury of confession. Five'll get you ten that the cops don't know about the FBI investigation, and you shouldn't be the one to break it to them."

"But what am I supposed to—"

"Take off if you see them. Is there a back way out of this commune you're living in?"

"Not really. It's a gated community. I suppose I could escape on foot and just hide out here. In the canyon. With, you know, the mountain lions."

"Better them than the cops. Until you talk to your fed."

"Simon?"

"No, your other fed. The one I'm not supposed to know about."

"You're not supposed to know about Simon either," I whispered. "Joey, I don't want to do this anymore. I'm scared."

"Of course you are; you'd be nuts if you weren't. But your best bet is to stay on the job and keep quiet. If you leave MediasRex or come clean with the cops, either one, you might need the witness protection program."

"What?!" I squeaked. Felix, ahead of me on the path, turned. I shook my head at him, giving an "oh, never mind me" wave, until he resumed walking.

"I'm only saying," Joey said, "that you can't just quit. You're a spy. You have to come in from the cold. That's a different thing."

Her words shocked me. If she was right, I was trapped. "How do I do that?" I asked.

"Talk to your handler. Meanwhile, there are three basic skills in intelligence work: improvise, adapt, and overcome. You can do the first two easily. The last one—well, in a pinch, walk with your right hand in your purse. People will think you have a gun."

"Really? I'd never think that."

"Not you. Gun people."

"What if I don't have a purse with me?"

"Always carry a purse. A pocket works too, but it's more subtle. Remember: improvise, adapt, overcome. Hand in purse, team player, contact your handler. And keep inhabiting that character you've constructed. Better give her some superpowers."

I hung up and dialed the number I knew by heart, the number for Yogi Yogurt. I gave my name and asked for a quart of Very Vanilla. The voice on the other end told me to drop by at ten o'clock that night to pick it up. "Can you wait that long?" he asked.

Seven hours. "If I must," I said.

Anyone could keep it together for seven hours, right?

TWENTY-THREE

had no appetite for dinner that night, even though others, notably Zbiggo, packed away food like a bear going into hibernation. Grusha grunted approval at him as she cleared plates between courses. At me, she merely grunted.

I described to my nearest dining companions, Zeffie, Felix, and Nadja, the peculiar thing I'd seen on the hike before being distracted by Crispin's corpse—team members crashing through the brush. All three looked at me with the same opaque expression. As this was also the look of people listening to a language other than their own, I couldn't tell if it was a suspicious reaction or not. Nell, across the table, also scrutinized me in silence. She hadn't been on the hike. Nor had Uncle Vanya. In fact, I hadn't seen him since driving him home from Hamburger Hamlet. I asked Nell about him, but the question seemed to distress her, and she simply shook her head. "Gone."

I was curious too to know who was responsible for *Poprobuji 31 Aromat, tebe legko budet osmotretsya—Udachi,* but couldn't figure out how to casually inquire whether anyone had written on my bathroom mirror in lip pencil the color of Grusha's borscht. As I pondered this, the police showed up.

Their arrival was presaged by the doorbell, followed by Grusha entering from the kitchen to whisper to Yuri, who was in the middle of a lecture on dressing for *Good Morning America* as opposed to the *Late Show with David Letterman*.

Yuri stood. "Excuse me. Representatives from the sheriff's office have arrived."

A stream of Russian erupted from Parashie, which Yuri managed to stem by walking behind her chair and putting his hands on her shoulders and massaging. "I will meet with them in the library," he said. "Continue dining. Parashie, they may want to speak with you later, but I'll be there with you. Finish your dinner and start your homework. If we need you, I'll come get you. All right?" Yuri looked at her, waited for her answering nod, and then smiled at us all. He was quite relaxed, a lecturer giving tips on how to handle a sheriff's interview as opposed to a *Tonight Show* interview.

I waited until he'd left the room before I stood up, mindful of Joey's warning to avoid the cops at all costs. "Excuse me," I mumbled to Felix. "I'm just going to—"

Felix stood too. "I am feeling a little tiredness. I will lie down."

There was a general scraping of chairs, suggesting that half the team shared Felix's Sudden Fatigue Syndrome. My big fear was that Grusha would take this as an affront to her cooking, as the entrée had not yet arrived. I would make my escape now, before she discovered the defection.

"Not that way, Wollie," Nadja said as I headed out. "You will run right into them."

I turned to her, startled, and saw Stasik shake his head at her.

"I mean—nothing." She looked confused.

I was confused myself. How had Nadja known I was avoiding the cops?

Oh. Because everyone else was avoiding the cops.

"Thanks," I said to Nadja. "I'm just going to use the ladies' room. I forgot where it is; you're right, it's this way. Bye. I mean, see you in a minute. For dessert. Probably." I was chattering, not wanting her or Stasik to think I noticed anything amiss in her comment.

I was actually grateful for the directional help, being still fuzzy on

how things were laid out in the Big House. I left the great room and
turned right, toward a tiny half bath.

I locked myself in and took stock of the situation. Maybe I was being
paranoid, but it certainly seemed that there was some big secret that
everyone but me was in on, and that Nadja had momentarily forgotten
I was not privy to. And it had to do with avoiding the police. I knew why
I was avoiding the cops, but why were they? They couldn't all be undercover agents, confidential informants for the FBI.

Well, just one more unanswered question to add to my bulging mental file. I might as well hop into the Suburban and go early to Yogi Yogurt.
I had a sudden yearning to be in public, surrounded by normal people.

I opened the door a crack, just in time to hear Nadja's voice in the
hallway, speaking in Russian, until Stasik cut her off. "English," he said.
"It's bloody irritating, but it's what you're here for. And stop freaking.
She's the stupid girl, not you. She didn't notice a thing."

Great. Stasik thought I was stupid.

I shouldn't care, I told myself. I could use it to my advantage, their
underestimation of me. That would actually be smart. But my feelings
were hurt and I felt left out. What power did these people have over me
that I would actually long to be part of the inner circle, to be a valued
member of Team Felony? *Get a grip!* I yelled at myself, and for emphasis actually grabbed onto the pink granite powder room sink. *You're an
undercover agent, damn it. You don't need feelings, you need instincts. And guts.
And maybe some superpowers.*

I splashed cold water on my face for further emphasis, came out of
the bathroom, saw that the coast was clear, and followed the hallway to
its end, a door that led outside.

I'd never been out here before, in the backyard. I was about to head
right, toward the House of Blue, when I heard voices coming from that
direction. I went left. I didn't want to encounter any more team members just now.

A flash of yellow rubbed against me, knocking against my legs with
a wagging tail, then sashayed off. Olive Oyl. I followed her. She was
company, she liked me, and she didn't think I was dumb.

She led me to the next house over, Green House, the one I hadn't yet been in. She went straight to a small door almost below ground level as the hill sloped down. A storage area, I guessed. Olive Oyl scratched at it, wanting in, then turned to whine at me.

"No," I whispered. "I'm not going in there. I'm sure there are mice. Or worse, rats."

Olive Oyl barked again, suggesting that mice and rats were what she had in mind. "Ssh," I said. "It's probably locked."

But it wasn't. The knob turned, and before I could stop her, the dog barreled her way in. I heard a movement in the brush, and after a moment of indecision, I went in too.

There were no visible rats, but I did imagine rat droppings. Too dark to tell, until I found a flashlight hanging on the wall near the door. I turned it on. The room was damp and cool and smelled of dirt. Paradise for a dog, probably, but not me. I suspected snakes, too, and worms, and whatever else lived in dank surroundings. Slugs. Mushrooms. There was a lot of junk stored there, gardening supplies and a lawn mower. Olive Oyl went farther into the room, whining and barking some more until I went to investigate. She then knocked over some kind of weed-whacking equipment, which in turn knocked over a bunch of other stuff, revealing a wall. Olive Oyl, on a mission, barked at it.

It wasn't a solid wall, but a panel set into a wall, one of a series of panels. Olive Oyl didn't care about the others; she liked this one. I began to push experimentally all around the edges and, sure enough, on the bottom right section there was some give and then the panel swung toward me. "Ha," I whispered. "How stupid do I look now, Stasik?"

Olive Oyl went through the hole in the wall.

After a look over my shoulder, I went too.

TWENTY-FOUR

Light.

The overhead fluorescents must've been activated by a motion sensor. If I'd hoped to find the editing room Bennett Graham had told me to look for, this wasn't it. But it was clean, well constructed, and well lit, a far cry from the anteroom that preceded it.

I couldn't figure out the purpose of the room, but it had an industrial look to it, long and skinny with brick walls painted white. The floor was concrete. Black beams traversed the length of the ceiling, some kind of pulley system, reminding me of cable cars. Glass partitions at one end of the room, six of them side by side, split the room into sections, like a bowling alley. Six black boxes were mounted on the ceiling above the partitions, with a green computer screen next to each, just above head height. There were metal clamps attached to the side of the glass partitions like giant paper clips.

At the far end of the room, away from the glass partitions, the wall slanted. I walked over to check it out and found it was made of metal. Above it was some sort of huge filtering system, making a fanlike noise. The noise had started up along with the lights.

There were big storage lockers along one wall, shut with combination locks.

What was this place?

Olive Oyl, now that she was here, wanted to be gone. My guess was that whoever she'd thought would be here wasn't, and that the room itself held no food, mice, or soft doggie bed on the concrete floor and therefore no further interest.

Inside a wastebasket was a single torn sheet of paper. I pulled it out. One side was blank and on the other was a stylized image of a man's head, no more than a black rectangle with the suggestion of ears. He appeared to be wearing a backpack, and the paper was torn at his rib cage. I pulled a pen from my pocket and, sitting on the floor, made a detailed sketch of the room. Olive Oyl nudged me with her cold nose. I wanted to be gone too, I realized. I'm not overly sensitive to ambience, but I found this room cold, hard, and prisonlike.

"Fine with me," I said, taking a last look around. "Let's go."

We retraced our steps, leaving the industrial room, and put the gardening tools back in place in the dirt foyer. I made it back to my bedroom for my keys, purse, and a sketchbook and pens—my artistic emergency kit, in case I got stuck somewhere—and left a note on my bedroom door saying I'd gone for a walk. This was true. The walk was to the garage. My own car was now nowhere in sight, probably getting a new transmission, but the Suburban was there. I started it up and, when no one came running out to stop me, took off.

I couldn't stop thinking about the room and I couldn't shake the feeling that I'd stumbled onto a key piece of evidence—but evidence of what? If Crispin and Chai were any indication, it was dangerous to know too much. It had to be even more dangerous to know and not to know what it was I knew.

I kept looking in the rearview mirror to see if I was being followed, but all I saw was blackness.

TWENTY-FIVE

pulled into the parking lot, turned off the Suburban, and
sat. I was early. The night was gorgeous and the moon was full. I expected to feel liberated, but in fact, I had a strange, untethered feeling. I
wondered what everyone was doing back at MediasRex, and it wasn't
professional secret-agent curiosity, it was personal. Having lived alone so
much of my life, to suddenly have people cook for me, overhear a conversation, maybe notice my absence, held a certain charm. If only I'd
gone to college and lived in a dorm—or even summer camp, a quick
hospital stay, prison—this wouldn't seem so exotic.

But it was more than that. Against my will, and despite their alleged
illegal activities, I was growing attached to these people. Never mind
that one of them was almost certainly a killer. Was this normal? Did it
happen to Simon? Was there any research done on the subject, the emotional drawbacks of spying?

The silence around me broke into my reverie and I sat up. No, it
wasn't my imagination. The mall looked closed. Yogi Yogurt, at the far
end, was definitely dark.

Anxiety clutched at me.

There were a few parked cars, but no real signs of life. What kind of
place was Calabasas, where malls shut down at nine-thirty p.m.? Where

were the teenagers avoiding homework, working on their gang skills, loitering? Where was Starbucks?

It always amazes me how a place that's nonthreatening by day can be so sinister at night. I locked myself into the Suburban and drove across the parking lot. Yes, Yogi Yogurt was closed. Now what? I called Joey both at home and on her cell and left messages, saying where I was and what was going on; in case anything happened to me, I wanted people to worry. And in case nothing happened, I told her where to meet me, if possible, in an hour.

Did I have to get out of the car to make contact? Probably. My instructions had been shockingly vague. Did they expect me to somehow just know how it was done? What if I was being set up? By whom, I couldn't imagine, but I had a free-floating feeling of terror. I reached for my purse, as per Joey's advice. This was the moment to pretend to have a gun.

Okay, I'd get out of the car, but should I leave it running so I could jump back in and take off fast? Or would that encourage some lurker to jump into it himself and drive away? I went with option one, and ran to the door of the yogurt store with my hand in my purse, which was neither efficient, graceful, nor threatening. And yes, on the door were the store hours. Yogi Yogurt closed at nine each night. Probably the whole mall did. I knocked anyway.

"Miss Shelley?"

I whipped around and pulled my hand out of my purse, clutching a tube of hand cream. I stopped just short of aiming it at him. "You scared me."

The man stepped out of the shadows. He wore a sports coat; at the very least, not a gang member. "Let's take your car, okay?"

I put my hand cream away. "Let's see some ID, okay?"

He handed me a leather badge. It was exactly like the one Simon carried. His name was Lendall Mains, and the photo on the card was of a man visually unremarkable in every way except for one distinguishing feature, ears that stuck straight out. I looked at the man in front of me. Yup. Same ears. I handed the card back.

"Okeydokey," I said and held up my keys. "Wanna drive?"

"Better if you do."

Lendall was not a big man, and I had the satisfaction of seeing him open the Suburban's passenger-side door only after a first unsuccessful try. "Whoa," he said.

"Yeah, why are the doors so heavy?" I asked.

"They're reinforced," he said.

"How come?"

"Let's talk in the car," he said.

He directed me back to Mulholland Highway, toward Calabasas High School, and I asked again about the reinforced doors.

"Bulletproofing."

I pulled over to the shoulder, parked, turned off the engine, and faced him. "Look, Lendall—or do I have to call you Mr. Mains?"

"Lendall's fine."

"Good. Lendall, where's Bennett Graham?"

"At this moment? I don't know. But I report to him. He's my supervisor."

"Can you get him on the phone? Because I thought I'd be seeing him tonight, and I need to. "

"May I ask why?"

"I'm living in a bulletproof house and driving in a bulletproof car, and maybe that's the kind of thing that would make you feel safe, but it doesn't make me feel safe, especially in light of the dead people showing up. It's not what I signed on for." I told him about *Poprobuji 31 Aromat, tebe legko budet osmotretsya—Udachi* on my bathroom mirror, about Crispin's insistence that Chai's "accident" was murder, and about Crispin then reappearing twelve hours later as coyote food. Lendall made notes in a spiral notebook, sometimes asking me to stop so he could catch up. This left me time to study his ears and the subtle plaid of his sports coat.

"All very interesting," he said at last, looking up from his notes. "And you think someone in the Milos household killed this person, Miss Shelley?"

"Call me Wollie," I said. "I have no idea who killed him, but I need to know what I'm doing there. I need to know what the big crime is that Yuri Milos is supposedly perpetrating."

"Why?"

"Why? Why, Lendall? Because only an idiot would just go about her business with people around her dropping like flies, rolling down the hillsides of Calabasas like pebbles. I don't want to be next, I don't want to be a rolling stone, I want to live long, gather moss—"

"Miss Shelley—"

"Call me Wollie—"

"Wollie, you need to calm down, because—"

"No, Lendall, what I need to do, and I think you can tell by my anxiety level that I will, is walk away from this whole operation, and maybe tell the sheriff on the way out what I know about Crispin, because I feel responsible for him being dead, unreasonably, perhaps, but I do. So unless you can make a compelling argument for me staying, I'm going."

"Wollie, I can see that you feel frustrated and, yes, scared and perhaps a little emotional, not that we know each other well, but if you'll just trust that—"

"Are you not authorized to tell me anything? Is that it? You're not high enough up in the food chain to decide this?"

He said nothing, but his face took on a mulish look. I glanced away from him and back to the road. "Look," I said, "I didn't mean to hurt your feelings, I've spent my whole life, practically, at entry-level positions. I'm just saying that if you can't talk to me, I can't talk to you either. Nothing personal. Get Bennett Graham on the phone if you need to, but I either get some answers or I'm out of here."

"Okay." Lendall took out his cell phone, then hopped out of the car.

Could I do it, though? What if they called my bluff? Would I really leave tonight? I didn't know where my own car was, so I'd have to commit grand theft auto in order to quit my job. Giving notice scared me, and I had no faith that I could stand up to Yuri's persuasiveness. What I could do was drive to an all-night grocery store and leave the Suburban and call Joey or Fredreeq—

The passenger door opened and Lendall hopped back in and handed me the phone. He looked disgruntled.

"Hello?" I said.

"Wollie, Bennett Graham." His voice was crisp and cold, like the night air. "I understand that you've encountered a peripheral incident.

This will be investigated. You are not to worry about it; your instructions remain intact. Tell Mains what you've discovered."

"Whoa, Nelly," I said. "There was nothing 'peripheral' about it. I got a close-up of this poor kid's face, there was blood in his *eye*balls—"

"You'll get over it. This shouldn't have any impact on what you're there to do."

"Of course it has impact, it's inherently impactive, and I can't do this job unless—"

"Stop. Emotionalism will not help you. I need you to focus on the reasons you came to work for us. Do you remember them?"

P.B.'s face rose up in front of me. "Yes."

"Have those reasons changed? Your brother's situation is still tenuous, I assume?"

"Yes. No, it hasn't changed, but—"

"No. And that's the relevant point. So let's move on. What happened today puts you in no additional danger, so there is no reason—"

"How can you know that?" A motorcycle whizzed by us, engine loud.

"It's my business. If you think that walking away from MediasRex is a real option, I suggest you reconsider. Milos would be suspicions about you and your reasons for leaving and would easily find you. You have no experience at going underground. Trust me on this."

Underground. Apt word. If I were six feet underground, and horizontal, there was a chance Yuri wouldn't find me. Otherwise? "But do you trust me?" I asked. "Because I see another option. I could tell Yuri that you're investigating him and that could buy me enough goodwill for him to let me walk away. P.B.'s interests aren't served by me ending up at the bottom of Malibu Canyon. Who'd take care of him then? You? I don't think so."

I hung up.

My hands shook as I passed the phone back to Lendall Mains, who stared at me openly. I stared back, feeling a coldness run down my spine. The phone rang. Lendall answered it with "Mains," and then passed it back to me without a word.

"Miss Shelley, if you ever make a threat like that again, I will file charges," Bennett Graham said. "Your brother's interests will not be served by you ending up in federal prison. Are we clear on that?"

"Yes."

"Good. Give the phone back to Agent Mains."

"You go first," Lendall Mains said.

I rattled off the names Sergei, Alyosha, Pyotr, Andrej, and Josip, as Lendall wrote them down. "And there are lots more," I said. "Guys hanging out around the compound."

"How about the trainees and staff? Any strange behavior there?"

"Lendall, if these people were any more eccentric, they'd have their own reality show. Zbiggo Shpek, for instance. Heavyweight boxer and hit man, according to him."

"Tell me some examples of irregular activity."

"Alik Milos using the UPS store, back there near Gelson's. To and from Film Estonia, something he does on a regular basis, so I guess it's not irregular at all, but why do that when FedEx is at the house every day?"

"A package *from* Estonia? Really?" He made a note. "Anything else?"

"Today's hike," I said. "People were running up and down hillsides, climbing into the canyon, risking life and limb and poison oak, and for what? I saw this from a distance, but I wasn't supposed to see it at all, because when I asked about it, no one would talk about it."

Lendall perked up at this. "Did they have compasses? Other gear? GPS equipment?"

"Too far away to see. I think we all just had backpacks. Filled with water." I remembered then how Kimberly had stopped me when I'd tried to help myself to a pack. "No, wait—mine had water. I don't know what other people had. Why?"

"Just curious. Go on."

I told him about the room Olive Oyl had taken me to, and showed him the paper on which I'd done my artist's rendering. He studied it, front and back.

"The main thing," I said, "is Chai, my predecessor. Everyone seems to know her, including the trainees who just arrived, but you guys don't seem to find it odd, her death—nobody finds it odd, and that's what I find odd."

He looked up. "How so?"

"Lendall, a sudden death—that's interesting. That's something people discuss. It's human nature. But this happened recently, and everyone's kind of matter-of-fact about it."

"Like they're hiding something?"

"No. They'll talk about it, but they don't say anything. Normally, people will tell you where they were when they heard the news, what time it was, their relationship with the deceased. At least early on. Yuri said he kept it out of the press, but how can he squash people's tendency to talk about it at home? And why would he?"

We were back at the mall and I pulled up to where Lendall Mains directed me, alongside a Honda Civic nearly alone in the parking lot, far from Yogi Yogurt.

"Okay," I said, turning off the engine. "Your turn."

"You must understand," he said, "that nothing I'm about to tell you is true. We're just having a casual conversation. Shooting the breeze. It would be irresponsible for me to divulge information about an ongoing case, as Special Agent Graham explained."

"Of course."

"Okay, then." He talked for maybe ten minutes, after which he gave me a small box with a set of instructions. "And one last thing," he said. "I have something for you. In my car. Wait here."

Uh-oh. Was I about to be issued a gun by the federal government? If so, I thought, it had better come with lessons and a personality transplant.

I peered out the window, toward where Lendall had opened his hatchback. The interior light displayed a cooler. My mind went to body parts. Speaking of transplants. I could use some body parts. A braver heart. A stronger stomach. Bulletproof skin.

Lendall extracted a package from the cooler and brought it over.

"Your alibi," he said. "No charge."

Inside the white bag was a quart of Very Vanilla frozen yogurt.

TWENTY-SIX

did not return to the compound, but waited until Lendall Mains had driven off, then headed farther into Calabasas, to the Sagebrush Cantina. Joey was at a table in the back, drinking Diet Coke. Fredreeq, in a cowboy hat, sat opposite her, sipping a margarita.

"Fredreeq, what are you doing here in the wild?" I asked. "Isn't it your bedtime?"

"Never mind that. Here are the words I want to hear from you: 'Fredreeq, I have quit this ridiculous job, which I took on against the advice of people with common sense.'"

"And I want to hear about the chewed-up body you found," Joey said, pushing a plate of appetizers to me. "Here, have some."

"What are they?"

"Tijuana egg rolls."

I pushed them back. "Okay. I'm going to quit, as soon as I do a tiny favor for—uh—"

"The FBI," Fredreeq said. "What's the favor?"

"Install a bugging device in the dining room at the compound. And one in the office. And in Yuri and Kimberly's bedroom."

Silence.

Joey was the first to speak. "How well do these FBI people know you?"

"Now listen up, Miss RadioShack," Fredreeq said. "You can forget devices. You and I are going to drive tonight to this death trap you're living in and pack up a bag for you and I will explain that I've come to take you away to a family funeral."

"Fredreeq, we're not in the same family," I said. "You're black."

"Nobody cares. The point is, you are not staying another night in that place."

"I'll make a deal," I said. "I tell you what I just found out and in return—" A waitress appeared at my side. "Just hot tea, please. Chamomile or something," I said, then waited till she'd gone. "Look, I'm very close to finishing up. And I know what the investigation's about." I paused meaningfully. "Film piracy."

Joey and Fredreeq looked at me blankly.

"Okay. I admit, it's a little anticlimactic. But that's the beauty of it. First of all, it makes me less scared. These MediasRex people are pirates. Not axe murderers. It's just a crime against technology. Against Hollywood. That doesn't seem so dire. Which is nice, because some of these people are growing on me."

"I don't buy it," Joey said.

"Me neither," Fredreeq said.

"What don't you buy, film piracy? They just told me."

"The feds?" Fredreeq said.

"They're lying," Joey said.

"Why?"

"To keep you on the job," Joey said, and Fredreeq nodded. "Did you seem freaked out to them tonight?"

I thought about having hung up on Bennett Graham. "A bit."

Now they both nodded. It grated on my nerves when they did things in unison. "Wiretaps and bugs," Joey said, "indicate something a little bigger than filched films."

"Actually," I said, "film piracy costs three to six billion dollars annually to an industry that this city values very highly. And because this crime involves customs, interstate transportation, and ITSPs, certain judges appreciate its complexity and fiscal impact and are willing to issue warrants for surveillance. Not that it necessarily happened in this case, of course. I must point that out. But it could have."

"Thank you for the public service message," Joey said. "The feds tell you that?"

"Inspiring, isn't it? And because they have reason to believe the whole operation may be packing up and relocating soon, they need to move in quickly. Which is why I'll be out of there in a day or two. And just today I saw Alik Milos at the UPS store picking up a package from Film Estonia. It all fits."

"No, it doesn't," Joey said. "The piracy thing goes from here to Europe, not vice versa. Californians aren't lining up to see Estonian films."

The waitress came by with my chamomile tea. "And what about the dead bodies?" Fredreeq asked, oblivious to her. "I don't care if your employer is a pirate or a podiatrist, if people are dying over at his house, it's not the right job for you."

"Thanks," I said to the waitress, whose eyebrows were raised. "Waiting tables is no picnic either, huh?"

"Sucks," she said and moved off.

"Okay, yes," I admitted. "There are a few things I can't figure out. Like why Crispin was killed. Also, the trainees all seem to be in on some secret, but they've only been here two days and they've just met. So what's that secret? If it's DVD piracy, why are they in L.A., why aren't they back in their countries selling *Spider-Man 6* on the streets?"

"Why do you think they're all in on something?" Joey asked.

I told them about the hike, about team members going off trail, scrambling through the brush in a big hurry. "What's that got to do with stolen movies?" I asked.

"Not a damn thing," Fredreeq said. "That's geocaching."

"What?" I asked.

"Orienteering. Francis and the kids are all over it. It's a big scavenger hunt in the wild, using GPS and Boy Scout skills and all that woodsy stuff. They search for treasures."

"Have you ever done it?" Joey asked.

"I treasure hunt at the mall," Fredreeq said.

"It sounds very Outward Bound," Joey said. "A party game to get everyone loosened up and connected, the kind of thing they do on corporate retreats."

"But if that's the case," I said, "why not just tell me? I'm part of the team too."

Joey shrugged. "Anything else that's weird?"

I described the room I'd found with Olive Oyl. And *Poprobuji 31 Aromat, tebe legko budet osmotretsya—Udachi.*

"People writing on your bathroom mirror is something I don't hold with," Fredreeq said. "Using your makeup? That is just a violation. Excuse me. I'm going to the bathroom to check my own makeup."

"The thing is," Joey said, toying with her Tijuana egg rolls, "I don't see Zbiggo Shpek being in on some big conspiracy. I watched him on pay-per-view a year ago; he was the undercard and, believe me, the guy's no Einstein. And Nadja Lubashenko? I looked her up and she's ranked number sixteen in the world. That's serious. Where does she find time for a life of crime? Do you know how much training triathletes go through?"

"What about the nonathletes?" I asked. "Did you google them?"

"Well, Bronwen Björeling—she's huge. The idea that she's into stolen DVDs is absurd. My brother wants her autograph, by the way. She's a classic diva."

"She is a diva, but we're doing social rehabilitation. How about Stasik Mirojnik?"

She shook her head. "Came up blank."

I reached into my purse and handed her the CD. "I stole this. Country and western. I meant to give it to the—well, anyhow. I forgot. So can you listen to it? But I need it back."

"You stole something? I'm proud of you."

"It's my character," I told her. "The one you told me to construct for myself. The tough-cookie character. I gave her kleptomania."

"Great. Now, this other woman, Zelda—" Joey dug into her enormous purse.

"Zeferina Maria Catalina Hidalgo de Abragon."

"Yes. Look, I printed out this photo. It's doctors at Chernobyl after the nuclear reactor disaster. A medical aid team from Cuba. There's a Dr. Z. Hidalgo. Is that her?"

I studied the printout. The face was younger. "Possibly. It does look like her, but no one's said that she's a doctor. I assumed she was just a political wife needing glamorization."

"And Felix Seriodkin. That's another ball game." Joey handed me a stack of pages. "He just sold *Jesus Made Me Skinny* to a major publishing house here. Big advance, but is it justified? The book's hot in Europe, but we Americans are picky about our diets, so whether we'll buy a weight-loss technique from someone in the third world is unknown."

"How about religious readers? Won't the title attract them?"

"Maybe. But it could repel the agnostic overeaters. Is the guy telegenic?"

"Excuse me?"

"Attractive. Could he become a televangelist?"

"Um, I don't know enough televangelists to say. Felix is very sweet. I wouldn't call him attractive, but he might have attractiveness potential. He claims to have baggy skin, but he's getting it removed."

"Sounds like a natural for MediasRex. All these people could be legitimate clients." Joey stuck an ice cube in her mouth. "The question is, are they also part of the illegal ops?"

"If it's film piracy, my guess is no. But they're into something strange, because they disappear every time the cops show up. These guys are celebrities, with their visas intact and their passports stamped. Yet they're all police-averse." I told her about Hamburger Hamlet, then hiding from the park ranger, and then again fleeing the dining room table after the borscht course. "And something else strange: the MediasRex staff—there's all this emphasis on communication, but then odd things happen and I ask questions and no one is talking, and I can't stop talking. And I'm the one who's supposed to be closemouthed."

"You can't stop talking," Joey said, "because it's in your nature to talk, and you have no other outlet, no cell phone, no e-mail, your computer's crashed, and you're living in the sticks."

I dumped a bunch of sugar into my tea and stirred vigorously. "Maybe that's why Chai kept a diary. Which, by the way, disappeared."

Joey glanced at Fredreeq, walking back to the table, then at me. "Wollie, did you sign a contract with Milos?"

"Not yet."

"Okay, I'm starting to slide over to Fredreeq's side. I think you should quit."

"She is quitting," Fredreeq said, sitting. "Or I'll quit for her."

"Joey, earlier you told me I couldn't quit without a witness protection program."

"I changed my mind."

"Why?"

"Never mind why. Just tell Milos that you're freaked out, seeing the dead body, you're just not a good fit for the job. He'll buy it. Then walk away."

I shook my head. "He won't buy it. He'll know I'm hiding something. And the feds won't let me. They were very unpleasant when I suggested it. So it's easier now to stay than go, and all I have to do is plant the bugs and the feds will get their evidence, make their case, and get me out of there, and I won't have to tell Yuri anything. My 'handler' says they're very close. And if the bad guys are behind bars, they're not coming after me."

"Yeah, take that to the bank," Fredreeq said. "And if the feds can't make their case?"

"I'm out of there anyway. I just need to plant the bugs. And avoid conversations with Yuri, because I can't lie to him. I think he can read my mind."

"Can you read my mind?" Fredreeq asked. "Because guess what it's saying—"

"Okay," Joey said. "Stay. But give the feds a deadline. Two days and you're out. No extra little errands for them. Because your safety is not anywhere on the FBI priority list. And there's something I don't like about this handler of yours."

"There's something I don't like," Fredreeq said, "about dead supermodels and their stabbed-in-the-eyes boyfriends."

"Anyway, I've got something for you," Joey said. "I don't want to undermine your confidence, but since you're functioning as unofficial law enforcement, at the very least you need what every other cop takes for granted."

"What's that?" I asked.

Joey stuck her hand in her purse. "Backup."

I turned down Joey's offer of a gun, but let her walk me to the Suburban, parked in front of the restaurant. Once I was alone and had started the car, I was bombarded by images of every scary movie I'd ever seen where some murderous maniac sat in the backseat. In the dark. With a knife. Waiting.

I whipped around. No. No one in the backseat. But what about the cargo area?

This wasn't paranoia, I told myself, turning off the ignition and pulling out the key. Simon called it "situational awareness" and was always trying to impress upon me its importance, even for civilians. I hopped out of the Suburban, walked around to the back, and—

"Wollie."

"What?" I screamed.

"Did I scare you?" Alik Milos crossed the street, laughing, and when he'd closed the distance between us, hugged me. "What are you doing out so late?"

"Just hanging with some friends. Girlfriends," I added for some reason.

"Sagebrush Cantina?"

"How'd you know?"

"You're parked twenty feet from it. Come have a drink with me."

"Where? What's open at this hour?"

"Private party. I was leaving, but now I'd rather stay." He took my hand and we crossed the street.

Calitalia was simple and sophisticated, wood and bamboo and neutral colors, a far cry from Club Red Square, but here, as there, Alik seemed to know everyone. The private party was on its last legs, or dregs, and half-empty wineglasses dotted the mostly empty tables.

Alik found us a private corner and brought over two glasses of wine. "Friends of mine bought a Malibu vineyard. We've been celebrating their chardonnay."

"Alik, is there anyone in Southern California you don't know?"

"Yes. You."

"You know me. You Myers-Brigged me. I'm the resident NFLP."

"INFP." He smiled.

"See? You know me better than I know myself. I want to know you."

"Fair enough," he said. "It's our second date, after all."

I hesitated. "This is a date?"

"It doesn't feel like a date?"

"Not exactly."

"How about if I kissed you? Would that feel like a date?"

The room grew hot. Yes, that would do it. I hadn't kissed anyone but Simon for a long time, hadn't wanted to kiss anyone but Simon. But I realized with alarm that I could kiss Alik. That I would like to. "You know I'm older than you."

"Yeah, I know your stats." His hand stretched across the table and the tip of his finger touched my forehead. "And I know this, a little." His fingertip moved to my heart. "It's this that interests me now."

"Why?"

"Why? You're going to make me spell it out?"

No, I didn't want him to spell it out. I shook my head and took a small sip of my wine, and after a moment he asked about my family and I told him about P.B., the little brother who was never far from my thoughts, and Uncle Theo, and Joey and Fredreeq. I talked about my line of greeting cards.

"The Good Golly, Miss Wollie cards," he said, nodding. "And have we inspired any this week?"

I shook my head, not wanting to mention the Good Luck on Maintaining Your Cover card for secret agents. "I should be working on the Valentine's Day cards for next year, but I find myself sketching—other things." I didn't want to talk about the tough cookie. My superheroine. Talking about her could drain her of her superpowers.

"Ah. A mystery. A window into your soul." He reached into his jacket and took out a pen. "Care to demonstrate?"

I shook my head. "Not on a second date."

"Okay. We'll talk." He was good at eliciting information, and I had to stay focused to not mention Simon. I took only one more sip of wine, saying quite truthfully that I was, after all, driving. And I watched how he did it, the listening to my every word, the eye contact, the appreciative smile. Everything I revealed seemed to fascinate him. When the moment was right, I said, "Now you. What's going on inside your head?"

"Funny you should ask. I'm wondering why someone as hot as you is walking around unattached. No strings. Able to move in with us so easily."

"I have strings," I said, a shade defensively.

"You have a family," he said. "And friends. Girlfriends."

"I have a—there's a guy. In my life. But he's not . . . we're not . . ."

"Committed? Sexually exclusive?"

I blinked. "Well . . ."

"Sorry. I'm sounding academic. Do you have keys to each other's place? Keep toothbrushes and sweatpants there?"

"Uh . . ."

"Does he let you drive his car?"

"God, no."

"Well, that's not a great indicator in L.A. I wouldn't either. No offense. I'm sure you're a great driver. Speaking of that, you okay with the biofuel thing?"

"Excuse me?"

"Donatella didn't tell you? Before she left?"

"Tell me what?"

He sat back and laughed. Then he handed me my glass of chardonnay. "Brace yourself. My stepmothers sent your car to have its engine converted to diesel and from there to run on vegetable oil. It'll be ready in two weeks."

I drove down the highway, alone. Alik had shown good instincts in not pressing me for anything more than a goodbye kiss after walking me to the Suburban. He'd moved from my cheek to my lips, lingering for just a moment longer than friendship dictated. I could've gone further. And longer. I was relieved I hadn't.

But he'd planted some seeds of doubt about my affair with Simon. Not seedlings, just seeds. Still, that combined with this flirting we were doing . . . was "flirting" the right word? This was more like playing with a gun that wasn't loaded. Or loaded, but not cocked. Although that too might be the wrong choice of words.

Something occurred to me.

I pulled over on Mulholland Highway, hit the map light, and found the paper on which I'd sketched the hidden room. I picked it up, ignored my drawing, and flipped the paper over.

The stylized rectangle was a man's head and, yes, those were ears. But he wasn't wearing a backpack on his back.

It was a target.

There was a hole in the piece of paper. Someone had been shooting at this guy and had hit him at least once in the head, and who knows how many times in the back where the bottom half of the paper had been torn away. Before they'd tossed away his head, too, in the garbage can in the secret room.

The room was an indoor shooting range.

TWENTY-SEVEN

The next morning I awoke bleary-eyed and scared. I dressed quickly and was on my way into the kitchen when Nell came out, teacup in hand. I said good morning, and she mumbled "hello" and scurried past me, sloshing tea as she went. Did Nell practice shooting? Did she deal in stolen DVDs?

In the kitchen I found Kimberly, and wondered the same about her. Then I wondered if my absence had been noticed. "How'd it go last night with the cops?" I asked.

"Fine. Yuri's friends with those guys. Gives a chunk of change to the Police Foundation every year." Kimberly was mashing leaves and branches in a bowl. She wore bright teal gym clothes and a jaunty ponytail; I imagined her brimming with antioxidants.

"What's the deal with Nell?" I asked. "Parashie says she's agoraphobic?"

"Oh, she's doing really well, now. Two years ago she was nuts. Wouldn't leave her apartment."

"I saw her in the library yesterday, teaching. She sounded normal."

"When she's teaching, she's fine. Passionate about languages. Dialects. You watch. She'll have Zbiggo reciting Shakespeare by next Wednesday."

"That should be fun. Where did Yuri find her?" I asked.

"Nell wrote a book on bilingual children, and during some big immigration debate, the president quoted her. And she hit the best-seller list. A fluke." She was mashing her twigs with a vengeance. "Her publisher wanted to send her on tour, but when they found out what a head case she was, they called in Yuri to fix her."

"And Yuri got her to do *Oprah*?" I asked.

Kimberly shook her head. "Yuri's not God. And her book's not really Oprah. He flew to Kansas City and rented the apartment next to hers and after two weeks managed to get people into her living room to tape a short piece for a *60 Minutes* segment, then got her through a series of live radio shows. A month later she came to L.A.—by bus, mind you—to work for us. Yuri had become her 'safe person.' She lives here, works on her next book, and teaches. She's perfect for Parashie, who's got a problem with schools and institutions, having lived in an orphanage. And Nell keeps getting better. Yuri makes her leave the house once a day and drive herself to Agoura Hills every Thursday night."

"What's in Agoura Hills?" I asked.

"Agoraphobics Anonymous. She'll do anything for Yuri. She worships him."

"But she didn't go on the hike yesterday."

"No, too much open space. We're working on it."

Nell didn't seem a likely candidate to murder Crispin and throw him down the hillside, then. "What's that like for you," I asked, "people worshipping your husband?"

Kimberly poured boiling water over her bowl of herbs. "Normal. That's how I started out, hero worship. When I met him, I was a cheerleader and PE major at USC. I interviewed him for my journalism course and fell for him. I thought he was God."

I sipped my coffee. "Do you still?"

"Well, if your vision of God is a Supreme Being who leaves his underwear on the floor and snores and travels too much and never takes vacations . . ."

"Never?"

"Never. Too many people need him."

I looked around the überkitchen, the view out the window. "Medias-Rex must be doing well, to pay for all this."

"MediasRex breaks even. We can't do enough volume to make big profits, not with the kind of personal attention we give."

"So where's the money come from?"

"Oh, Yuri made his fortune back in the nineties, the currency market—Hey, Grusha," Kimberly said, looking past me. "We're running low on pomegranate juice."

Grusha galumphed across the kitchen to the refrigerator, scowling. I wondered what it would take to make her smile.

"Anyhow—oh!" Kimberly looked at her watch. "Gotta run." She sealed up her bag of branches. "You come too. I'll brief you on the day's activities."

"Is MediasRex Yuri's only business now?" I asked, handing her a twig. "Or is he still into—currencies?"

"Currencies, commodities, commercial real estate—you name it." She poured her twig tea into a mug. "We're loaded."

"What is *this*?" Grusha yelled. I jumped.

"Jesus, Grusha!" Kimberly said. "Give me a heart attack, why don't you? What is what?"

"This in my freezer. Just stuffed in here, to fall out. To crush my vegetable stock."

"Oh!" I said. "That's mine. Frozen yogurt. I'm sorry."

"Frozen yogurt?" Kimberly asked. "Wollie. Are you an addict?"

"Uh—no. I just—"

"I am. It's my dirty little secret. Where'd you get it? What flavor?"

"Very Vanilla," I said. "Help yourself. I had a sudden need last night for—"

"No." Grusha blocked my way, arms akimbo. "You don't put in my freezer without you get my permission. Not my freezer." It was the longest speech I'd heard from her.

"I'm very sorry," I said. "I didn't realize there were freezer rules."

"Chill, Grusha," Kimberly said. "Wollie's not here to—"

"Chai, *she* fill my freezer. Vodka, ice cream, Snickers. I throw it out. Everything."

"Fine," Kimberly said. "No one expected you to keep it. But Wollie's not Chai, so—"

"Never listens, her. I tell her. She listens? No. She laughs."

"Okay, but she's dead now, so let's move on, Gru." Kimberly walked over and placed her hands on the old woman's shoulders and began to massage them. Grusha, to my surprise, endured this for a full minute, even closing her eyes.

"I work now," Grusha said, opening her eyes abruptly. "You go too. You—" She pointed to me.

I grabbed the offending yogurt. "No frozen foods. I don't know what I was thinking."

Kimberly led me out of the kitchen. "Now, Zbiggo's trainer is stuck at Heathrow with visa problems, so I'll be in the gym today with him." She walked fast, and talked faster. "You take Felix to his doctor's appointment in Beverly Hills. Afterwards, stop in Tiffany's to pick up a ring Donatella's having fixed. I'll give you the receipt. Buy Felix lunch, show him how to get the check, that sort of thing. Before he found Jesus, the guy had no social life, so you'll be doing remedial work. Yuri will want a full report when you get back. Write down everything. He loves documentation."

"Okay. What about Vanya, by the way? I haven't seen him since—"

"Oh. Don't worry about Vanya. He's gone."

"Why?"

She turned, startled. "Oh. We—he—had to go back. And don't worry about Stasik for today," she added, picking up the pace again. "He was up at six this morning, tagging along with Nadja on her fifty-mile bike ride."

"Ah, women!" a strange voice said. "Beauties!"

"Shit," Kimberly whispered.

I turned to see Yuri approaching with the florid man from my dating class. Bad Vlad. I felt Kimberly, next to me, stiffen. Up close, I estimated Vlad to be pushing sixty. He had a full head of curly hair, a large, sensuous mouth, and a well-fed appearance. He came toward us with outstretched lips and outstretched arms, as if to capture both of us in an embrace and maybe swallow us whole, but at the last moment, he zeroed in on Kimberly.

"My love," he said. "The little *devochka*. How is the sexy cheerleader?"

"Vlad, always a pleasure," Kimberly said, her voice devoid of expression. Yuri, a step behind his companion, gave his wife a rueful smile.

"And this one!" Vlad cried. He crushed me in a full-body hug worthy of Zbiggo. His stomach met my stomach, mashing my frozen yogurt container between my breasts. The sensation was not pleasant.

"Hello," I said, attempting to extricate myself. "My name is—"

"I know who you are!" he said. "Am I dead? Not yet, I think. Everyone knows Wollie Shelley, the toast of *SoapDirt*, the heroine of *Biological Clock*. Yes, we have television in my country also, and a woman of your attributes could never go unnoticed. We adore you. Who do you suppose got you this job?"

"Did you? Well, thanks. I'm really—"

"I insisted. Yuri, tell her! Once I knew he had seen you, on his jury, *you*, I said to him, 'Yuri, we will have that girl and no other. She is divine. I must have her.'"

"Well, thank you very—"

"Yuri was not so sure. Eh, my partner? He said, 'We know nothing about her, it's not so easy, this job,' but what did I say? What do you think, eh?"

"I don't know," I said. "What did you say?"

"I said, 'Who cares? With a figure like that, my athletes, they will line up to come to America. Everyone will want the media training, to meet the great Wollie Shelley. The men, yes. Also the women! You know these athletes, the women—so often they are, shall we say—" He made a hand gesture that seemed to indicate hitchhiking but, in this context, I had to figure meant lesbianism. "You know what I'm saying, yes? Eh?"

This was painful. I glanced at Kimberly, who looked distressed on my behalf, and then to Yuri, who looked amused. I looked back to Vlad, who was breathing heavily.

"I'm afraid you have the advantage of me, uh, Vlad," I said. "I take it you're Yuri's—business associate?"

"Yuri did not speak of me? Yuri!" He turned to Yuri. "You did not tell her of Vlad, who knows where all the bodies are buried?"

Yuri stepped forward and took my arm, gracefully causing Vlad to release me. "There is no way to prepare one for the force of your personality, Vlad. Wollie, this is Vladimir Rosenovsky. He is the head of the Eastern European League of Athletes, and my old friend. All our athletes—half our trainees—are represented by Vlad. Currently, Nadja and Zbiggo."

"I could have sent you a dozen," Vlad said. "Once I knew you had captured the luscious Wollie Shelley, I could have sent the whole soccer team." Vlad turned to me. "My athletes do not want media training. They think it is school, it steals time from their sport. You are the draw. Chai closed the deal many times for us, eh, Yuri?"

Yuri folded his arms. "Athletes see only the world defined by their sport. Once here, I show them a bigger world. That is *my* sport."

"Sex, for example!" Vlad said. "Sex lures them to Hollywood. This is where we need you, Wollie Shelley."

"Yes, but I'm not having sex with anyone," I pointed out.

"Do they need to know that?" Vlad asked, and laughed heartily. "The suggestion of sex is enough. A whiff of sex!"

"Well, Vlad," Kimberly said, "Wollie has a very full day ahead of her, so this was delightful, but I need to drag her off now. Bye! Wollie, after you."

I walked resolutely into the office and Kimberly followed, closing the door behind us. "My, he's colorful," I said.

"He's a creep. I can't stand the guy. But he's the Soviet Don King, and athletes are important to us. He comes over three or four times a year."

"Does he stay here?"

"No, he prefers hotels, so he can entertain hookers." Kimberly gave me a folder with my day's itinerary, including Felix's medical records, and then began to collect her stuff. "We can store the yogurt in the freezer in the gym," she said. "And I'll try not to eat it all. Come get it when you need it. Bring your own spoon."

I refrained from pointing out that I'd never been given my full orientation and, thus, didn't know where the gym was. In the breast pocket of my blazer, I had three bugging devices given to me by Lendall Mains. One bug was destined for Kimberly and Yuri's room. If I went looking for the gym later today and accidentally found myself in the master bedroom, would that be so odd?

Except—

"Kimberly?" I said, "I have a strange question. I know you guys have a state-of-the-art surveillance system. Is it possible for someone like Vlad to—I don't know, see me eating breakfast? Or . . . ?" I shrugged.

"Hell, no," she said. "You think I'm going to have some bozo watch me floss my teeth? Or walk around in my jammies? Please. Trust me, there are no cameras in this house. Elsewhere on the property, yeah. In here, no."

Okay, that was reassuring. I closed the office door and took from my pocket a tiny plastic bag. I'd been reading the instructions on and off all morning, and now took the bug from the bag. It was a small black metal disk the size of—well, a bug. I peeled off the adhesive backing and stuck the bug on the underside of a cubbyhole shelf above the desk. "Testing, testing," I said quietly. "This is location number one, the office. Please, God, let the adhesive hold." If it didn't hold, if it fell off, the bug would land on the desk. That would be problematic.

I waited a few minutes. The bug stayed where it was. I walked out of the office and through the library. One bug down, two to go.

"Wollie." Nell jumped up from behind one of the oversized armchairs.

"What?" I said, jumping myself.

"Come here." She beckoned me over to a sofa and indicated that I should have a seat, then pressed a button on a sound system built into a wall unit. Sounds of opera pealed forth. "I found it for you," she said loudly, adjusting the volume. "Bronwen as Liù in *Turandot*."

"Thank you," I replied, just as loudly. As I hadn't expressed a desire to hear Bronwen sing, this was naturally interesting. Nell came and sat very close to me.

"Hi," she said, far more quietly. "We haven't talked much."

This was an understatement. I nodded.

"We should talk outside," she continued, nodding toward the window, "but I don't enjoy outside. The problem is this. I'm a little worried about you."

"Why?" I asked.

"I just am. Are you feeling okay?"

"Physically? Why, yes. I think so." I thought about it. "Pretty much. Why?"

"Do you think you could be very careful not to be . . . alone with anyone?"

"I'm alone with you," I pointed out.

"I mean, really alone. When there aren't people within hearing distance."

"You mean alone with—Vlad?"

"Vlad? That goes without saying. Lock your bedroom door when Vlad's here."

"From the inside or the outside?"

"What do you mean, the outside?"

"Grusha gave me a key to lock it."

Nell looked startled. "They gave you Chai's old room? The purple one?"

"Yes. Why?"

Nell looked over the back of the sofa, as if making sure there was no one hiding there. "No reason. The other thing is, could you perhaps not express so much curiosity about what's going on here? Not ask too many questions?"

"You mean, the kind of questions I'm asking you now?"

"Yes. Could you not sound like a cop?"

I felt my jaw drop. "I sound like a cop?"

"Sometimes. I mean, clearly you're not one. But it's like you're doing an impersonation of a cop. Are you familiar with the term 'nosey parker'? It's a British colloquialism. Stasik noticed. He called you a bit of a nosey parker."

I couldn't believe how hurt my feelings were. I'd thought I was being subtle. "But—I mean, no one likes a nosey parker, of course, but I'm just trying to get my bearings and do a good job, and—"

"You're doing fine. Yuri likes you a lot. And Alik. But you'll be around longer if you just stick to your side of the street."

I took a deep breath. "I take it Chai wasn't so good at that."

She looked directly at me. "No one's happy about what happened to Chai, but there wasn't much crying at her funeral." She paused, glancing toward the doorway. "These are good people. They're doing important work that they believe in. When you've lived with them long enough, you'll find that out."

"Except for the ones I'm not supposed to be alone with."

"Look. No system's perfect. Sometimes you have to pick a side and go with it, flaws and all. If you want to be part of something bigger than you." Nell stood and moved to the sound system. "Beautiful, isn't it?" she asked loudly. "Heard enough?"

"Yes." I stood too. Half of what Nell had said was too cryptic to understand and sounded vaguely cultlike. The other half of what she'd said was just scary.

I wanted to plant my bugs and be gone.

There was no one in the great room. I peeked into the kitchen. Empty. Good.

But this bug was tricky. Lendall Mains had been very clear about the need for it to be directly above the dining room table, where it would have the best chance of picking up conversations throughout the great room. The chandelier was modern, gunmetal gray. Wrought iron, with frosted glass around the little round lightbulbs. Not a bad match for the bug; much better than a crystal chandelier would've been. The problem was height. It was suspended from the mile-high ceiling. I reached up and figured I needed to be a yard taller. My heart was pounding.

Shoot. It was obvious what I had to do. I looked around and then thought to hell with it. I had to do it quick, before I lost my nerve. I took off my shoes and climbed onto a chair. This wasn't easy, as today's ensemble was a straight, knee-length skirt that didn't give me any breathing room, let alone climbing room. I had to hitch it up a bit to even get on the chair. I reached up. I couldn't even touch the metal base of the chandelier.

I climbed onto the table. Closer.

I went back down, then climbed back up, this time in my heels. Success.

I'm six foot tall and an okay weight, but I wished I hadn't eaten two baguettes the night before. Was I heavier than place settings for twelve, plus a large soup pot? Would the pale green Plexiglas hold me?

I looked down. Mistake. An unaccustomed sensation overtook me. Vertigo?

I took out my bug, peeled off the adhesive with shaking hands, beads of sweat forming on my forehead, and gently attached it to a piece of the wrought iron that hung vertically. There was no place to hang it so that it faced downward, but this would do, right?

Wrong. It needed to face the other direction, for when people were out on the deck. Shoot. Because now the adhesive was off, and the instructions had been explicit: once the bug had adhered to a surface, it should not be expected to stick elsewhere.

To heck with it. I wasn't climbing Mount Everest twice. I reached up and removed the bug. I was pressing it into place on the opposite side when I heard an intake of breath, then, "What in the name of God do you do?"

I turned too fast and looked down too fast and was already breathing too fast. The room spun. I was still holding the chandelier, but there are things one should not count on for support, light fixtures suspended from ceilings among them. I realized this as both I and the chandelier began to sway. I let go.

And fell off the table.

TWENTY-EIGHT

I looked up to see Grusha looming over me, livid.

"Grusha," I rasped, grabbing onto an overturned chair. "I'm okay, I just—"

"You!" Her voice was a hoarse shriek. "What is this you do?"

"I was just—"

"On my table! My table! You with your shoes!"

I struggled to find a sitting position. No bones seemed to be broken. "I'm—I will—they're actually Chai's shoes, they're— Ouch."

"My chandelier! What do you want with my chandelier? To steal it, maybe?"

I glanced up. The chandelier still swayed, gently. "No, I—"

"Tell! What you are doing?" She spat out the words. "On my table? Horrid girl!"

"It was a stupid thing to do, I admit," I said.

"Horrid!"

"Okay, horrid even. I was just looking for something, and I thought it might be in the chandelier." True enough: I was looking for a place to plant a bug. "Let me just—" I tried to stand. This was tricky, given the high heels and the tight skirt, so I grabbed onto the table.

"Off," she said, squirting her Windex bottle at the table with violence, suggesting that it could be turned on me. "You swing from my chandelier? No. Ha. I tell this to Yuri."

Okay, I had to do better in the plausibility department. Where was my tough-cookie character? "It happens," I said, getting to my feet, "that my Uncle Theo has a birthday. And he is a fan of the Art Deco era, the Bauhaus movement, and if this chandelier is a Rolf Solomon or a Mies van der Rohe, then of course I can't afford it, but if it's a knockoff, from, you know, Pier 1 or Cost Plus World Market . . . so I wanted to find out. Do you know where it's from?"

Grusha was looking at me with lips clamped together. "No," she said finally.

I smoothed down my skirt and made my exit at a sort of dignified trot. Maybe Grusha bought it. It wasn't the worst story in the world. Okay, it wasn't great either. I needed to get to the office fast, or the bathroom, anywhere I could close the door and be alone and decompress. Tough Cookie, her assignment ended, had retreated, leaving me shaken.

I made my way back to the office, where I closed the door and examined myself for bruises. I counted five, in the incipient stages.

"Testing," I said once more, addressing the cubbyhole. I looked underneath it, making sure the bug was still there. "So, I guess you guys heard what happened in the dining room just now. Assuming I planted that bug properly. If I did, then that's the good news. The bad news is, I have no aptitude for espionage. I have a hard time thinking on my feet. In heels. On tables. And if Yuri Milos interrogates me, I don't stand a chance. I'm just saying. Expect no miracles." I picked up the phone and put it to my ear, just in case someone burst into the office and wondered why they'd heard me talking to myself.

This reminded me to call my cell phone voice mail, except that I didn't know how to do that from a remote phone. The best I could do was my home machine. There were two messages. One was from P.B., asking me, once again, to bring him a copy of *Superstrings and the Search for the Theory of Everything*. The second message, like the first, contained no preamble, no "Hello, Wollie." This was simply a name, Yusuf, and a number. I tried Haven Lane first, to talk to my brother, but got no answer. Then I called "Yusuf."

I knew I shouldn't talk to Simon on a phone that was being monitored by his own colleagues, in a bugged room, but the message had come in only forty minutes earlier and who knew how long he'd be at that number?

He was there now. He answered.

"Yusuf," I said. "I can only talk for a second, but I'll call from my cell in an hour."

"Will you be there this afternoon? I need to see you."

"No, I won't be here. I'll be in Beverly Hills, and—"

"Three o'clock. In front of Neiman Marcus."

"I can't promise," I said. "And even if I can get there, I won't be alone, and—"

"Try," he said, and hung up.

I left the office. If I hurried, I could return to House of Blue and retouch my makeup and fix my startled hair, making me more worthy of Beverly Hills, where such things matter. Okay, to heck with Beverly Hills. I wanted to look good for Simon.

I tiptoed so as not to disturb Nell's class now convened in the library, discussing prepositions. I moved so silently, I passed Yuri and Vlad, who had their backs to me, without making a sound. I knew this because I heard Vlad say very softly to Yuri, ". . . much does she know?"

"Nothing," Yuri replied. "Keep it that way. I don't need another Chai on my hands."

There wasn't a doubt in my mind that they were talking about me.

TWENTY-NINE

The only reason I go to Beverly Hills on a regular basis is for the knife sharpener on Little Santa Monica. The cutlery shop is in Old Beverly Hills. I love the craftspeople of Old Beverly Hills, the aging artisans toiling away in rent-controlled buildings from the 1920s, the bookbinder, the engraver, the shoe repair guy. I like the history. Fredreeq goes to Beverly Hills because that's where her hair colorist is. Joey goes there to see her shrink. There are also, of course, those who go to shop, but these are people I have little personal knowledge of, people whose idea of a sale is a purse marked down from four grand to $3,500. The stores that cater to this clientele are minded by salesclerks trained to ignore riffraff like me, shoppers without the watch or shoes that signal excessive income or a face so staggeringly beautiful it has charging privileges on some Old Rich Guy's credit card. I avoid these stores. Life's too short to be snubbed by minimum-wage sales staff.

Felix's cosmetic surgeon was Dr. Eli Rosen, on Brighton Way. It was hell getting there because the Suburban was too big for the streets, and Beverly Hills is the rare L.A. neighborhood overrun by pedestrians. I found street parking, but after stalling traffic on Roxbury trying to squeeze into it and getting honked at by seven or eight cars, three of them Mercedeses, I gave it up and moved on. Relinquishing a parking spot is a huge psychological defeat, but so is the public humiliation of having others, many in luxury cars, witness one's efforts to parallel park the vehicular equivalent of a humpback whale.

"Wollie, don't worry how people think at you," Felix said as we hit the street after pulling into a lot six blocks away. "Jesus too, if He is living today, I believe people will honk at Him. Can He park a big car? Maybe yes, maybe no. Maybe He is thinking of other things."

"Felix, that is comforting," I said, leading him down Beverly Drive, "because if the entrance exam to heaven includes parallel parking, I'm not making the cut." I paused to let a family of seven—tourists, as seen by their matching Birkenstocks and number of children—pass in front of us. "Tell me something. Does Jesus ever condone crime?"

"Yes, maybe," Felix said, ogling a store window. "Which crime?"

I pulled him onward. "Well, stealing. Could He justify stealing? Not like a pizza if a guy's starving to death, but dealing in stolen goods?" Was I being too obvious? "Maybe to raise money for a worthy cause, or something."

"I think this answer is no. 'Render unto Caesar what is Caesar's and unto God what is God's,'" Felix said. "What is this store? It is so beautiful."

"Scandia Down, which we don't have time to explore," I said, pulling him away from the window. "Where, for the price of a down comforter, one could feed a village of hungry children."

I instantly regretted bringing up children, as Felix's eyes filled with tears. "In my country, the orphanage, so many children, no mother, no father."

"Was this because of a war?" I asked.

"The war, yes. Also Chernobyl. Long time ago. Still, people gets sick. Or the children. Because maybe birth defects. I learn this from Zeffie. Chernobyl heart, they call this. This is what I do with my money from my book. I save the children."

His humanitarian zeal impressed me, even though his sadness was short-lived, giving way to a keen interest in Bijan, Yves Saint Laurent, and Pierre Deux. Affluence delighted him. He smiled at people as if the whole neighborhood was made up of old friends. This affability accompanied us into the doctor's office.

Dr. Rosen's office was staffed by two strikingly lovely women in lab coats, who asked eagerly about Donatella, Kimberly, and Yuri. And Chai. When I told them that Chai was dead, their smiles drained off their faces, leaving them curiously expressionless.

I took the clipboard I'd been handed and helped Felix with the paperwork. As I was armed with his medical records, provided by Kimberly, I now felt useful. After this, I perused the brochures in the waiting room, which told me everything about the beautifying procedures available to mankind, except for how much they cost and how much they'd hurt. Felix was there for a "full-body lift" consultation.

On impulse, I hopped up and went to the window shielding the nurses from their clients. "Can I ask, how long will Felix be in with Dr. Rosen?"

"Oh, an hour minimum," one of the nurses assured me.

"Fabulous. Mind if I leave and come back?"

"No problem. We'll take good care of him."

I stepped out of the office and was dialing Daniel Lavosh within sixty seconds. I left a message that Harriet Spoon would be unreachable at three, but was currently on her way to Neiman Marcus and would wait there a full hour on the chance that he might be available. I left the same message on his cell phone.

I was there in five minutes. Twenty-six minutes later, so was he.

The window displays at Neiman Marcus, on the South Roxbury side, used shiny white mannequins that appeared to have landed from Neptune. They were bald and featureless and dressed in squares of iridescent paper. It was not clear to me what they were advertising, beyond existential anxiety. I looked away from them, scanning the faces of the pedestrians, hoping to see the one I loved.

And there he was, crossing Wilshire Boulevard. Coming toward me. He was dressed in a suit but carried the jacket, as the day was hot. When he reached the halfway point in the crosswalk, I started moving too, to meet him, legs shaky with anticipation, feet wobbly in my heels, stride short in the tight skirt.

I reached him. Without a word, he took my hand and led me around the side of Neiman Marcus, to steps leading to rooftop parking.

The roof was populated by cars, but devoid of humans.

Once I'd determined this, I turned to him and untied his tie and opened the top buttons of his shirt. Skin. Chest. The heart beating underneath. I put my hand there, the first move toward satisfying my need for touch. Then I put my forehead on his collarbone and breathed him in. His skin was hot; I tried to remember the last time I'd seen him in sunlight.

He let me do all this to him. We didn't speak. When a car drove up the ramp and passed us, we separated. Simon, his shirt still open, walked away a few feet, studying the parking lot, practicing his "situational awareness." I took in the big picture, Saks Fifth Avenue to the east, Wells Fargo Bank to the north, jacaranda trees all around, blooming madly, advertising the color purple.

The car drove back down the ramp. We were alone again.

Simon came back to me and took my hand, leading me to the southeast wall.

A rectangle was formed by the edge of the stairwell and the corner of the parking structure, maybe four feet wide and six feet long, a tiny bastion of privacy.

Simon threw down his jacket, displacing some leaves and an empty bottle of Vitaminwater. After a glance behind him to the parked cars, he pulled me down, hiding us from view.

We knelt on his jacket. He took my face in both of his hands, looked at me a long moment before his eyes dropped to my mouth, and then he moved in on it and kissed it.

The sun beat down on us.

After a while, he pushed the hem of my tight skirt up to my waist and I undid his belt buckle and unbuttoned his pants and then he grabbed my thighs and I grabbed the back of his neck and he pulled my legs around until they were straddling him and after that I was falling backward in slow motion, with his hands holding the small of my back, until I came to rest on hard concrete, pebbles, and a Milky Way candy wrapper. We were already sweating, and we were about to sweat a lot more.

We didn't talk much.

A half hour later we walked back down the stairwell to the street. We moved languidly. Our clothes were wrinkled and my blouse was dirty. I felt beautiful. We smelled like each other.

"How are you?" he asked.

"Fine, thank you, and you?"

He put an arm around me and kissed the top of my head as we strolled. We reached Wilshire and broke apart, walking side by side. We no longer held hands.

Now that inches separated us, I realized I wasn't all that fine. Crispin was dead, partly because of me, I was in the midst of a conspiracy I didn't understand, in a job where people shot guns and dealt in stolen goods, and no one was telling me the entire truth about anything, including those I was really working for, the Federal Bureau of Investigation.

And I couldn't tell any of this to Simon, and my frustration about it was enough to wipe out the postsexual nostalgia I was feeling.

"I'm thinking of quitting my job at MediasRex," I said.

His head turned. "When?"

I reached over and flicked away a piece of gravel that was stuck to his cheek. It was a gesture more proprietary than romantic and still my insides went wiggly, touching him. "I'm not sure. Soon. A few days. I need to finish up some things before I can back out gracefully."

He stopped. I stopped too, and turned to him. "Closer," he said, and I came closer, but didn't touch him. We were in public now and public displays of affection were to be avoided. This wasn't something we'd ever discussed, it was a tacit understanding.

I hated understanding it. I wanted to renegotiate the whole thing.

"I'm glad you're quitting. I want you to," he said quietly. "I never want to go through this again. Not knowing where you are or if you're safe."

"We want the same thing," I said. "I want all that and I want never to use a code name again. I want to do what we just did and do it in a bed. Not always, but mostly. I want to be able to call you at the office and ask you what time you'll be home for dinner."

He looked away.

"What?" I asked.

He looked back. He'd recovered and was smiling. "Are you going to cook for me?"

"I could cook." I'd planted bugging devices that morning. Could a pot roast be any harder?

He looked away again.

"That's not what you're talking about," I said. "We don't want the same thing. You want me to be home safe, but you want to be out there, doing whatever it is you're doing."

He scratched his head. "It's not a good time to discuss this."

"When's a good time?"

"Things are heating up on the case. We've put in a lot of work toward this end. I need it to succeed. I need this." He turned to me again, with the same intensity he'd had earlier, when we'd been sweating on each other. "When it's over—I don't know. I can't look ahead right now. I'm in the middle of something and I can't question myself the way you want me to. I won't be able to do my job."

"When's a good time to talk about this? When won't you be in the middle of this?"

"Weeks, maybe a month. And Wollie?" He touched my chin with a finger. "Chances are I won't be able to see you again till I've wrapped it up."

To hell with it. I reached out and grabbed his hand. "A month?" I was fighting now to stay calm. "Do you see what you're asking? You want me to endure something that drives you crazy when it's me we're talking about. Being in danger. Being incommunicado. I'm not saying I can't or won't endure it, but look. Do you see what you're asking of me?"

"It's not the same—"

"It is exactly the same."

"I'm trained to do this, I have years of experience in this, while you're doing God knows what for Yuri Milos—"

"It is the same. You don't know what I'm doing, I don't know what you're doing, no one's home for dinner, nobody gets to fall asleep wrapped around each other or wake up together in the morning, it's a long-distance relationship in the same town, it's sex with a married man, except you're married to the FBI and you're never getting a divorce, it's—"

"Why do we have to talk about this now?"

"Because," I said, "it's my best chance of making my case, of making you see what it's like to live with the kind of uncertainty you're putting me through—"

"Not *now*, Wollie." His voice held a note of command that must have slipped out. He didn't usually let himself do that, knowing it set me off.

"No problem," I said, and dropped his hand. "When it's convenient, I'm sure you'll be in touch. June or July? And will we start over at the beginning of the alphabet? With *A* or do we do jump to *B* and do the even-numbered letters this time?"

"Wollie."

"For the record, what's the record? What constitutes a long-term relationship? Three times through the alphabet? What's the longest anyone's lasted with you?"

"Screw this."

"This?" I asked. "Or me?"

"At this moment? Take your pick."

I stared at him, waiting for him to take it back, then saw he wasn't going to.

I turned away. There wasn't a snowball's chance in hell I was letting him see me cry right now. Or ever again, maybe. Ahead of me, the light at Wilshire and Brighton Way turned green. I took it as a sign and hurried toward it.

Simon didn't stop me.

THIRTY

Felix was waiting for me on the street outside Dr. Rosen's office, people-watching, eager to be off to Tiffany's. "So famous!" he said. "I feel like a movie star. I feel like—"

"Audrey Hepburn?" I asked, wanting his mood to infect me. "George Peppard? Whoa—you have to watch the jaywalking in Beverly Hills, Felix." I reached for his arm. "The cops will swoop down on you and—"

"Okay!" Felix jumped back onto the sidewalk with such alacrity, I feared being knocked over.

"Felix, is it my imagination or are you unnaturally frightened of cops?"

"Of cops? No. Frightened? No." He accompanied this with a jolly chuckle that sounded forced. "My goodness, what you have been doing?" he asked, turning his attention to me—a classic diversion technique, I realized. Still, it worked.

"You mean my clothes?" I said, blushing. "A little dirty, aren't they? I—fell. Sort of."

"You must have fallen hard."

"Very hard."

"On your back?" Felix asked.

"Look, the light's changed. Come on."

Tiffany & Co. was at Two Rodeo, a tiny and exclusive piece of real es-

tate designed to look like a tiny and exclusive European street, complete
with cobblestones, fountains, and costumed valet guys. Tiffany's was
the jewel in the crown, although it shared the crown with other lumi-
naries like Valentino and Cartier. It brought to mind a bank vault, built
in matte-finished steel. The main floor featured relatively affordable
baubles, and it was packed, mainly with camera-toting tourists. So packed,
in fact, that I immediately lost Felix.

I looked around for ten minutes, baffled. I asked where the restrooms
were, and went so far as to ask a man in customer service to scout out
the men's room for me. No Felix. I took the beautiful Deco elevators
down to the basement level, where the fine jewelry lived. Here there
were few customers, and none with cameras. No Felix.

I began a pattern of going from floor to floor, convinced that he was simply looking for me at the same time that I was looking for him and we
would have to bump into each other eventually, according to the laws of
physics. I turned on my phone, even knowing that Felix didn't have my
number and didn't have a cell phone himself. I picked up a single message—
from my brother, asking—okay, demanding—that I bring him a copy of *Superstrings and the Search for the Theory of Everything*. Speaking of physics.

After twenty minutes of floor patrol, I was in a panic. On the top
level, near the restrooms, a wall was lined with mahogany cabinets the
size of gym lockers. I had no idea of their function, but I began to wonder if Felix could be dead and his body parts stuffed there.

Finally, I approached a salesperson. I chose one from fine jewelry, in
the basement, because no one on the main floor in affordable baubles
looked like they had time for missing persons. Sharon, on the other
hand, looked both available and gratifyingly human.

"I've lost my friend," I told her. "It's been half an hour. I can't find
him anywhere."

"Is he—a young person?"

"A child, you mean? No, but he is an odd person. A foreign person. He
may have wandered somewhere off the beaten path. There are just the
three floors, right?"

"Yes." She eyed my clothes, then picked up a phone behind the
counter. "Let me check with security."

I felt a stab of fear. Might they arrest Felix? Was he up to something arrest-worthy? Unless Sharon was suspicious of me. She seemed friendly enough, but I did need dry-cleaning. Although they could hardly arrest me—or even evict me from the store—for that. At least my clothes were expensive. No, I was taking on the team paranoia. Act like a super-heroine, I told myself, throwing my shoulders back. I could hardly be the first person in the world to browse Tiffany's an hour after having sex at Neiman Marcus.

A moment later, Sharon hung up. "Your friend, Mr. Seriodkin, is having tea with our head of security." She smiled. "He apologizes for alarming you and will be with you shortly. Is there something I could show you in the meantime?"

I shook my head, relieved, then remembered Donatella's ring. "My God, I can't believe I forgot this. It's the whole reason we're here." I handed Sharon the receipt.

"Oh, I love this ring! I sold this to Mrs. Milos." She picked up the phone again and called the repair department. She was positively twinkling at me now; it seemed that any friend—or servant—of Donatella's was persona grata at Tiffany's. "And we got a fax from Kimberly, the other Mrs. Milos, saying you'd be in today. Could I trouble you for a look at your driver's license?"

"No problem." I reached into my purse. "Do you remember all your sales?"

"Well, this one's memorable. So is Mrs. Milos. All the Mrs. Miloses. The ring's an antique, a pear-shaped blue diamond, graded fancy intense blue, in a bezel setting. Loads of tiny pavé diamonds surrounding it. One of them got loose," she said, reading the repair order.

"What's it worth?" I asked. "Do you remember?"

"Somewhere in the neighborhood of four hundred, I think."

I gulped. "Four hundred—"

"—thousand, yes." Sharon laughed at my reaction. "Crazy, isn't it? But it was a trade. Right after her divorce, she brought back her engagement ring, which she'd also gotten here, and walked away with this one. I'm not being indiscreet, just so you know. *Town and Country* did a feature article on Mrs. Milos, everything I just told you. Oh, this must be your friend."

Felix was getting off the elevator alongside a man in a suit, who introduced himself to me as the head of security, then bid Felix a friendly farewell. Minutes later we took possession of Donatella's blindingly expensive ring.

"It's like being entrusted with the Hope Diamond," I said to Sharon.

"You know what I'd do?" she said, leaning over the counter, winking. "I'd wear it. Until you hand it over to Mrs. Milos."

This seemed crazy, like asking to be mugged, until it occurred to me that carrying a small Tiffany's shopping bag was also an invitation to assault, perhaps more than wearing a diamond ring that looked too big to be real. I decided to go for it, but turned the stone around, to the inside.

Once outside the store, I questioned Felix about the lost half hour in our lives.

"Oh, this was nothing," he said with a wave of the hand. "I get lost with ease. I ask this nice man where am I, and we talk of Jesus and he gives me tea."

"Okay," I said. "I wonder if I'm supposed to write that in my report to Yuri."

"What?" Felix came to a sudden stop, causing a pedestrian behind him to bump into him with a Michael Kors shopping bag. "So sorry," he said, turning to her, and then back to me. "No, please. Yuri will not want to know this."

"Sure he will," I said. "Making friends is what public relations is all about, isn't it?"

"No, really, Wollie, I would like not to mention this, please."

"Okay," I said, pulling him along. It's not like I didn't understand the desire for secrecy. I wasn't going to put my own afternoon activities into my report either.

I led Felix up Rodeo Drive, on the lookout for potential muggers until I realized half the people we passed probably wore far more than $400,000 on their bodies.

We'd just reached the Suburban when I remembered that I was to take Felix on a lunch date. I fed the meter and dragged him off to the nearest restaurant. Provençale.

Felix's table manners were just fine. In fact, his knowledge of salad forks versus dessert forks surpassed mine, which made sense once he reminded me that he'd been a devoted eater before Jesus made him skinny.

"I didn't realize you'd been a foodie, though," I said. "Here in America, we're more likely to binge on Hostess cupcakes than tiramisu."

Not Felix. "For me, say czar," he told the waitress. "No bread balls, cheese, and fish, and a bowl of oil." I reinterpreted this for the befuddled server as a Caesar salad with oil and vinegar on the side, minus croutons, Parmesan, and anchovies, also known as a bowl of romaine lettuce. In the interest of solidarity, I ordered the same. I then explained to Felix the concept of Ladies First, a polite, if not feminist, policy in many social situations. Felix was an enthusiastic learner, confiding to me that he hoped that one day God would deliver unto him a mate. Especially now that he was to be, as he put it, a stud. This led to a discussion of what Dr. Rosen would be doing to Felix's excess skin, the offspring of his twenty-year relationship with desserts. Felix pulled out of his back pocket a wad of notepaper and set it on the table. Dr. Rosen, not content with the before-and-after shots in the brochure, had also drawn maps and diagrams of Felix's body. As a graphic artist, I found these interesting. As a diner, I did not. When Felix excused himself to go to the bathroom, the artist in me won out and I flipped idly through the pages until I came across one that was not like the others.

It was a hand-drawn diagram of Tiffany's.

In particular, the security system. Notations of hidden cameras, emergency exits, uniformed guards and the positions they occupied.

Dear God.

Did he plan a robbery, a jewel heist? At Tiffany's, of all places? Felix, of all people?

"Miss Shelley?" A voice, practically a purr, interrupted this train wreck of thought.

I looked up and gasped. Standing over me was a woman with ice-blond hair, wickedly beautiful, both underfed and overdressed. I knew her by name only, and the place she occupied in my imagination.

Lucrezia.

THIRTY-ONE

"Hello," I said.

"May I sit?" she asked.

I nodded, and she took the chair Felix had been occupying.

"You know me?" she asked.

"Yes." I'd met her once, six months earlier. She'd been with Simon, draped on his arm, if memory served. Of course, memory didn't always serve. Sometimes memory tyrannized, making one miserable. "You are Lucrezia."

"And you are Simon's lover." She was the kind of woman who said the word "lover" with perfect ease. She probably said "darling" a lot too, which would befit a woman at home in fur coats and French twists. But why didn't she call him Daniel Lavosh?

"Is there something I can do for you?" I asked, trying to mask my surprise.

"I've followed you this afternoon."

"How—peculiar of you." My face was heating up. Had she been on the Neiman Marcus roof? "Any particular reason?"

"I want you to stop seeing him. There are things you don't know about Simon."

The audacity of the statement stopped me in my verbal tracks. "Like?"

"He's an FBI agent," she said. "I presume you know this."

Should I admit to that? He was undercover, for God's sake. Maybe she was here fishing, hoping to verify that. "Go on."

"He's on the take."

The room began swimming. My stomach turned. Had I eaten something bad? No, I hadn't eaten, period. I heard myself say, "I don't believe you."

"I was right, then. You didn't know."

I swallowed. "About what?"

"My brother was of the opinion that you knew. But I can tell when a woman understands something about men and when she doesn't. Simon would never expose this part of himself to you."

"Could you be more specific?" I asked. "And maybe less offensive?"

Lucrezia sat back and crossed her legs. She wore a white wraparound jersey dress, tight and unforgiving. On her, there was nothing to forgive. "He works for the government. But he also takes money from the people he investigates. Not always, but sometimes. He's now investigating my company. My brother gives him money and he takes it. Quite a lot of money. In cash. Simon was specific about that."

"Why would I believe any of this?"

"Have you seen his penthouse? His clothes?"

Yes, and yes. The belt I'd unbuckled earlier in the afternoon had been Prada. I didn't even want to think about how much it had cost. "Family money," I said. Simon had never said it in so many words, but I'd assumed it.

"Yes, that's the story he's given the FBI too. Amazingly, they are as credulous as you. There *was* family money, in fact. He went through it rather quickly."

"Have you any proof of this?"

"Ask yourself. Does a good agent let someone know they are being investigated? Or reveal his real name when he has an alias, like 'Daniel Lavosh'?"

Yes, my thoughts exactly. I took a sip of water, stalling for time until my brain could come up with a rebuttal. "He told you this?"

"He told me. And my brother. None of Simon's colleagues knows that we know."

"Why on earth are you telling me this?"

"Because I don't like to share the men I sleep with."

I felt the blood drain out of my face. I stared at her. Even when Felix came up behind her, I couldn't stop looking at her.

She turned, sensing Felix. "Hello," she said, standing.

"Hello, I'm Felix," he said, beaming. "Please, sit."

"Only for a moment." She sat back down as Felix went to find an extra chair.

I leaned in and whispered, "What makes you think I won't ask Simon about this?"

She leaned in too. "I expect you will. He will deny it. And you will ask yourself—" She looked up at Felix and stretched her lips into a smile. "Have you room to squeeze in? Good." She turned back to me. "You will ask, Is this the truth? Is this a man I trust? Have I known him years and years? Have I met his family? His friends?"

"Length of friendship is not the only criterion for trust," I said with a glance at Felix, who was preoccupied with his chair.

"No, that is evident." Lucrezia smiled. She too glanced at Felix, but apparently decided he was of no consequence. "I'm sure your 'friendship' has been marked by many hours together, perhaps days and weeks in one another's company, long vacations, endless conversation, all the things that make for strong relationships."

I was blushing again. Damn it. How did she know that the one thing Simon and I lacked was time? Opportunity for endless conversation. We'd never had it in the six months we'd known each other. Not talking was the central feature of our affair.

"Of course," Lucrezia added, "you could go to his employer and share your concerns, but with nothing to show them, would you get past the gatekeepers?" Lucrezia picked up Felix's glass of water and turned to him with raised eyebrows, speaking the international language of "May I?"

"Please," Felix said, obviously delighted to be of service.

"Or," Lucrezia said, "would you speak with some lackey who would pretend to listen but perhaps look upon you as a scorned . . . *friend* . . . and give you little respect or credence? But perhaps you have no problem looking spiteful. And foolish." Here she looked me up and down, as much as possible, given the fact that I was seated.

I pictured myself telling Bennett Graham that Simon was crooked. Ha. It would never happen. Of course, I didn't at all believe that Simon was crooked, but if Lucrezia thought he was, then it was because he wanted her to think he was. So how could I best encourage her in that belief?

"Maybe I don't go to the employer," I said. "Maybe I decide that it doesn't matter, that there are certain advantages to my . . . alliance . . . that outweigh this liability. Nobody's perfect. You don't seem repelled by this. Maybe I'm not either. What if I just don't care?"

A slow smile came over her face. "Oh, you care. Women like you have 'conventional morality' written all over them. Even if it were not the case, you are risk averse. There is danger in this game that you haven't the stomach for. I have." She let that sink in, then gathered her purse. Prada too, I now saw. Like Simon's belt. "Well, thank you for your time," she said, standing. Felix stood too, once more showing himself to have excellent manners. "And thank you, Felipe, for your water."

"It's Felix," I snapped. "And Lucrezia? What if I ignore the report? What if the outcome of this conversation does not live up to your expectation, what if you and I continue to share the same interest?"

"Then it's likely another report will surface, perhaps concerning you, to be given to the other party. I believe the other party would see the wisdom of severing the connection, given certain information. Good day."

And off she slithered. Felix watched her go. So did I. That kind of walk was in the genes, along with small bones and a twenty-three-inch waist. I would never achieve it, even if I began life over as a European royal and studied at the Sorbonne.

And what, exactly, did Lucrezia have on me that would appall Simon?

Felix returned to his own chair, picked up the water that Lucrezia had just sipped, and set it on another table. "So," he said, "what does this bitch blackmail you about?"

THIRTY-TWO

By the time we were halfway to Calabasas, Felix had worn me down with sympathy and a willingness to listen. I talked non-stop while he turned from client into romantic adviser, pulling out of me the salient facts of my affair with Simon, which I managed to divulge without spilling government secrets or blowing anyone's cover, including my own.

"The question is," Felix said, "this Simon, does he have honor?"

"Well, that's the thing. An hour ago, I'd have said yes, absolutely. Now I don't know. I mean, yes. Professionally. Yes. But . . ."

"This woman makes you to doubt him."

"She's doing her best. But that's because she wants him herself."

"You should pray to God. Is this God's plan for you? Do you belong with this man?"

"If it's between me and Lucrezia, no question. She's too short for him. She wears fur."

"And also, she is a bitch. Wollie, if God does not plan him for you, then you cannot make this happen. But if it is God's will, then no earthly power will keep you from him."

No earthly power. How about superpowers? If I could construct a superheroine who could plant bugs in chandeliers, why not one who could out-seduce Lucrezia? "Felix, how about asking for divine intervention to make me sexier?"

"No, you miss the point."

"Oh." Why was I seeking spiritual advice anyway from a man planning to rip off Tiffany & Co.? "And you, Felix. Do you have secrets?"

"My secret is this," he said. "I work for God. God is the boss of me."

"That's not a big secret for anyone who's spent five minutes with you. But tell me, would God ever ask you to—I don't know, rob a bank? Or something?"

"Wollie, this is the question you have already said. You are obsessed with this."

"No, I—" He was right. I was growing too transparent. The nosey parker factor.

"Human laws," Felix said, "they are not divine laws. In my country, the law can change each month, or each week. Shall I obey it then? Which one? Last month? This month? I follow Jesus. In His church, I am a sheep. In the streets, I am a lion. The laws of the state, if they do not follow divine laws, then I break them, yes."

Uh-oh. This was not reassuring. "And what about trade laws?" I asked. "Like, I don't know, the laws that govern . . . exports."

"This I don't know," Felix said. "Economics, they don't interest me."

We came to a stop at the light halfway up Topanga Canyon. "Intellectual property, customs regulations, film piracy—?" I said, watching him closely.

He looked at me pleasantly. "Yes? Sorry? What is these?"

I believed Felix was too much like me—open face, open book—to be faking it. I was willing to bet anything he'd never heard of piracy, let alone dabbled in it. This both relieved and confused me. Felix was up to something and it was something that I imagined that the State of California, if not the entire United States government, might not like. But I was sure it wasn't stolen DVDs.

So what was it?

Back at Palomino Hills, someone was having a party. Felix and I waited while the guard dealt with the cars in front of us, doing painstaking security checks, phoning residents, issuing hand-lettered guest passes before letting them through the gates. The Residents lane was closed, blocked by a sawhorse. Behind the sawhorse, the electronic arm was severed and splintered, suggesting some marauding partygoer had hacked his way through with an axe. I inched forward, wondering if this felt to Felix like a police state, having to get through checkpoints just to drive into your own driveway. Felix, however, after studying his cosmetic surgery brochures, opened a Bible and settled in to read.

I took out my purse sketchbook and began a Happy Rhinoplasty! greeting card, then remembered I was to hand into Yuri a written report about my date with Felix. As I wrote a highly expurgated account of the afternoon, depression overtook me. Probably a combination of stress and sleep deprivation, followed by sex, sadness, outrage, and dismay. And now nausea, because while I was fairly confident about Simon's professional integrity, I was suddenly convinced that he *had* been sleeping with Lucrezia.

The nausea grew more insistent. "Felix," I said, "I need some air." I hopped out of the Suburban and leaned against it, leaving the door open. There was only one car in front of us now, but if I had to throw up, I sure didn't want to do it out the Suburban's window. Or in front of Felix and Mr. Crabby, the security guard.

But it wasn't Mr. Crabby, I now saw; it was a new guard, and he was giving grief to the driver ahead of me. "I don't care what your previous arrangement was," he said loudly. "I only know the rules I was given. You're not on the list, so I can't let you in."

"I don't wanna go in," the driver yelled. "I wanna leave the package with you. I do this all the time. I leave it here, Alik Milos comes and gets it here."

"I'm not taking that responsibility," the guard said. "No one's answering at the Milos residence, and I can't accept packages for them."

I walked up to the guard. "I'll take it," I said. "I'm Wollie Shelley, I live at the Milos compound, and I'll make sure it gets to Alik."

"Uh—you sure?" the driver of the car asked. He was just a kid, I now saw. No older than Crispin had been. "I'm just supposed to give it to the guard, nobody else."

"I'm the guard," the guard said, in case anyone was in the dark on that point. "And I'm not taking anything without authorization from the home owner."

"It's okay," I told the kid. "You can give it to me. I'm fairly trustworthy."

The kid handed over a small padded manila envelope. "Make sure he gets it, okay? Because I'll get canned if he doesn't."

"Really?" I asked. "That's pretty harsh."

"That's showbiz."

"What kind of work do you do?" I asked.

"Editing. But I'm just an assistant." He looked over his shoulder.

"Where do you work?"

He mumbled something that sounded like "mouse house," but I couldn't be sure because he was already doing a U-turn, making his escape.

Why was Alik Milos receiving packages from some paranoid editor-in-training? There was at least one obvious explanation. There was no return address or label on the package, just the handwritten "Alik Milos," and that seemed irregular. I kneaded the package, trying to feel what was inside. Bubble-wrapped DVD was my guess. I was heading back to the Suburban when the guard came hurrying after me, clipboard in hand.

"Would you just sign this, say that you took that package?" he asked. "Sorry, I'm just trying to cover my ass. I'm new."

"I figured," I said, signing my name. "What's going on today?"

"Wedding reception at the Brophy residence."

"And what's up with the gate?"

"Someone got drunk last night at the bachelor party, rammed through it."

"Good grief," I said.

"Yeah. So I have to sign in residents by hand, and I don't know people yet and have to check ID, which of course every single resident grouses about. But I don't wanna get fired my first day."

"Heck no. Where's the guy who's usually here?"

"Fired."

"For what?" I asked.

He looked over his shoulder, then turned back to me. "You hear about the kid got murdered up on the ridge? Cops showed his photo around, some residents said they'd seen him lurking here. So everyone figures he sneaked in on foot. Maybe the murderer sneaked in too. So everyone's all uptight and management's cracking down."

"Unless the murderer was a resident," I said, handing back the clipboard. "A resident wouldn't have to sneak in."

"Good point," he said. "I'll be sure to tell that theory to everybody."

Back in my room in House of Blue, I stared at the package. Could I get a peek inside without committing mail fraud? It was smothered in clear plastic tape, impossible to simply steam open. And once open, would it say "Pirated Property"? No. I'd probably have to play it. And how could I, with a broken computer and no TV in sight? My superheroine, I decided, would have X-ray vision, or laser vision, some kind of vision that could see the contents of DVDs. Meanwhile, there was no way around it: if I gave the package to Alik, I had to give it to him unopened. If I opened it, I had to keep it. Keeping it would get me in trouble if Alik was expecting it and traced the delivery to me. And opening it would be a federal offense, of course. But I was working for the feds, so couldn't I commit a federal offense on their behalf? I tried to imagine Bennett Graham or Lendall Mains springing me from prison. I could maybe see that happening. I could also see Bennett Graham saying, "Wollie who?" And my job was to plant bugs, not steal from Alik Milos, who'd never been anything but charming to me. Maybe this was a movie trailer that he'd been hired to render a psychological evaluation of. Maybe it was on the level. What did I know? Handing it to him would be the safe thing to do, and I could assess his reaction, see if he expressed any guilt or paranoia. That was something, right?

I changed out of my wrinkled, sweaty, dirt-encrusted designer clothes and into black pants, black camisole, black silk blouse, and flat ballet shoes in preparation for dinner. I felt much better and looked like a cat burglar. I stuck the last bugging device in my pocket and, package in hand, went down the dark hallway, with no idea of what I was about to do.

Alik Milos's quarters, Parashie had told me my first day, comprised a whole wing of House of Blue one level above the rest of the bedrooms. I tiptoed past Nadja's room, and Zeffie's, and another that I assumed to be Nell's, featuring, visible through the open door, a bookcase filled with endless foreign-language dictionaries alongside a Save the Earth Wetlands poster. I tiptoed onward, then backed up and, with another look around, walked into Nell's room.

The room was neat, but a desk showed evidence of a work in progress. I looked through piles of papers, then noticed a file box. I rifled through it and saw a file marked "Idioms, Belarus." I took it out.

Bingo. On a piece of notebook paper were handwritten notes. The alphabet was Cyrillic, but the writing was neat and the slant was unmistakable.

It was Nell who'd written on my mirror. But what had she written? And why in Russian?

She'd been surprised to hear I'd been given Chai's room. Could she have written on the mirror intending the message for someone else?

I stood still, listening.

House of Blue was quiet. It was cocktail hour over at the Big House, which would carry through into dinner, and these people took their dining rituals seriously. I was probably okay, but figured I better move on in case. If caught, I would say I was looking for Alik, to deliver the unopened package. The package might be worth more to me, in fact, unopened. But not if I got caught in Nell's room. I left.

What was I looking for, though?

I felt like a ping-pong ball, mentally hopping back and forth between film piracy and—something else. The secret room, for instance. I could understand people wanting to shoot, but why underground, in secret? This was America, land of the Second Amendment, so why not just shoot in the open? Unless they were concerned about the neighbors. I hadn't met the neighbors in Palomino Hills, but perhaps they'd have problems with bullets bouncing off the barbecue, their propensity for gate-crashing notwithstanding.

I knocked on the open door, then stepped into Alik's suite. It was gorgeous. The idea of grown kids living at home evoked images of bunk beds with cowboy sheets, but this bedroom was all gray, black, and mauve, very *il modo Italiano.*

Beyond the bedroom was a walk-in closet. After another peek out into the empty hallway, I went to the closet and walked in. Along two walls were paneled doors. With locks. Who locked up their closets? Happily, not Alik. The doors slid right open.

Inside sat a computer, with a printer, fax, and other office equipment. Why this setup here? The office in Big House was roomier and more comprehensive, so this one would seem unnecessary. Except that this one could be locked. And hidden.

Hidden from whom?

I didn't even try to deal with the computer, focusing instead on drawers and cabinets. I found paper products and a good quantity of blank DVDs and labels and cases. Was that significant?

Maybe.

Several of the drawers were locked. This denoted paranoia, but not necessarily guilt.

I moved back to the bedroom and saw, next to the bed, a phone. At last, a phone in House of Blue. I dialed the yogurt shop and left a message that I needed a quart of Very Vanilla within twenty-four hours. I hung up and stared at the king-sized bed. There was no reason that someone with built-in locks everywhere would hide things under the mattress, but I checked anyhow.

Under the mattress was a gun.

The phone rang. I jumped.

Should I answer? Might it be Bennett Graham? Lendall Mains? Simon? I grabbed it. "Hello?"

"Yogurt shop. Can you explain the urgency of your need for Very Vanilla?"

"Yes. I've come into possession of a small, square—I mean round, the item is round, but the case is square. I assume, because it's in a sealed envelope. Oh, hell, it's a DVD. It's not mine, it belongs to someone here, but it might interest you. Only I wonder if I should hand it over to the person it belongs to."

"No. Negative. Hold on to the item until you hear from us."

"Okay."

"Wollie?" The sound of my name being called in the distance stopped my heart. The voice was Parashie's. I hung up the phone.

I stuffed the envelope under my shirt and ran out of the room.

THIRTY-THREE

Dinner was in progress. Parashie escorted me to my chair, then took her place near Yuri, where she was obscured by a large tureen of cold soup in the middle of the table.

"Ah, here is Wollie, our new beauty!" cried Vlad. The beefy man rose and raised a glass of wine in my direction. "I ask about you all afternoon. Playing hard to get, eh?"

"Okroshka, Wollie," Zbiggo cried with equal enthusiasm, which I took to mean either "live long and prosper" or "try the soup."

I summoned a smile and pulled my napkin into my lap, unnerved at being the center of attention. It wasn't just shyness. I was actually "wearing" the DVD, inside its padded manila envelope. It was beneath my spandex camisole, held tight against my abdomen. Thank God the camisole fit snugly. Over the camisole, my black silk blouse effectively hid my stomach, certainly while sitting. Probably I was safe, unless someone touched me, or heard the envelope making faint crunchy noises when I moved. It had been the best I could do, in terms of hiding places, when Parashie had found me in the hallway outside Alik's room. "My father gave me six minutes to find you and return," she'd said. "You are so late to dinner, and Vlad is here. It makes Yuri crazy when someone is late. Especially if there is company."

"Let me just stop in my bathroom and—"

"No," she'd said. "First you sit down to dinner and then you get up and go if you have to go. We have thirty seconds only."

So now I stared at the bowl of soup in front of me, cold and cream-based, with little flecks of what I took to be ham. I tasted it, but was unenthused. Put off, even. What else had I eaten that day? Some bread in Beverly Hills, before Lucrezia had killed my appetite.

Everyone else was eating the soup with gusto—Vlad was slurping his—and listening to Bronwen expound on Maria Callas, whom she considered overrated and shrill.

"Maria Callas, however," Yuri said, "appeared at the Met. In 1956."

Bronwen put down her spoon and pursed her lips.

"The fat Callas?" Vlad asked. "Or the foxy one? She lost fifty kilos, the size of our Nadja here." He put an arm around the triathlete, seated at his right. Nadja, chomping on a breadstick, ignored him.

"Not fifty kilos," Yuri said. "Maybe thirty, thirty-five. Eighty pounds. Her voice, shrill or not, was her message, but in today's marketplace, Aristotle Onassis and her extreme makeover would be her hook."

"What does this mean, 'hook'?" Felix asked.

"You missed the lunch lecture," Yuri said. "The hook is that which you pitch to *Entertainment Weekly* or the producer of the talk show that will catapult you to fame. In your case, the hook is in your book title. Jesus made you skinny."

"Jesus gave me my life," Felix said, eyes shining. "He is the way, the truth, and the life. John, chapter fourteen, verse six."

"Nobody cares for that," Vlad said. "Religion will not book you on *Larry King.*"

"Sure it will," Kimberly said. "He had Tammy Faye Bakker on, and she was already dead."

"Felix, your faith is your message," Yuri said. "You can quote the Bible once the cameras roll, but what gets you on the show is Jesus removing a high percentage of your body fat. That's your hook. You are our Maria Callas." He turned to Bronwen. "How much do you want to sing at the Met?"

"More than anything," Bronwen said.

"More than dessert?" Yuri asked. "Or baguettes? More than fifteen hundred calories a day?"

Bronwen had no answer. I pitied her, having her diet discussed over dinner. Or at all.

"Pass me the bread," Vlad said. "Yuri, fat people sing at the Met every night."

"Musicality is not the only criterion," Yuri said. "Stardom is component parts. Talent, beauty, sexuality—you overlook any of these, let alone several of these, at your peril."

"Beauty?" Bronwen asked. "It is beauty to be a twig?"

"Nobody's endorsing twigs," Kimberly said. "A healthy body mass index is the cultural standard, Bronwen. I don't mean to be rude, but deal with it."

"BMI," Zeffie said, "is not so important as cholesterol and blood pressure. LDL. I prefer LDL below one hundred, everyone."

I saw Zeffie in a new light. Now she sounded like a physician.

Grusha entered and tapped Vlad on the shoulder. "Line one," she said. "Bratislava."

"Soccer team," Vlad said, rising. He made a gesture with his finger to his nostril, which I took to mean "drug problems," and followed Grusha out of the room.

Plunk!

Something had fallen into the soup tureen.

Parashie stopped talking.

It seemed we all looked at the soup, and then, collectively, looked up. At the chandelier.

THIRTY-FOUR

Bronwen and Felix, seated closest to the tureen, brought their napkins to their faces, wiping away spots of soup that had landed on them.

"What is that?" Parashie asked.

The bug. My bug. It couldn't be anything else. My bug was swimming in that tureen.

The soup was more milky than creamy; if it had been thicker, the bug would've sunk more slowly, maybe taken a moment to float on the surface. This was buying me some time. *Think, Wollie!* I screamed to myself.

"Was it a bug?" Bronwen asked, standing to peer into the tureen.

She knows! I thought. *They know!*

"A scorpion?" Zbiggo asked. "This is a scorpion, I think."

Okay, they don't know.

"We don't have scorpions in L.A.," Kimberly said. "The eastern part of the state, yes. Here, no. Tarantulas, maybe."

The thought of a tarantula throwing itself into Grusha's soup, even though I knew it wasn't the case, made me ill all over again. *Don't throw up, Wollie,* I thought. *Whatever else you do, don't throw up. Look at something besides the soup.*

Except that I had to look at the soup. A normal person would be looking at the soup, or at least at Yuri, who was now standing, ladle in hand. He fished around in the gigantic tureen. I could hardly keep staring at my bread plate. Someone would notice. Okay, I would focus on the tureen itself. Ceramic and overly painted, maybe something Grusha brought over from the old country.

Grusha! Did I hear those shuffling footsteps? Grusha mustn't know about this. If she saw the bug, she'd know in a second where it had come from and who was responsible—

"Grusha's going to be very unhappy," I blurted out, "if something's ruined her soup."

Yuri's eyes met mine. "True enough." He let go of the ladle as she walked in. "Grusha, have we any more of the red that Vlad brought over for us last year?"

"The pinot noir? The Russian?"

"No, the Pauillac."

Grusha looked affronted. "The Pichon-Baron? In the cellar?"

"Yes. Shall I go?"

"I go," she said, and stomped out.

Yuri went back to fishing. The ladle made a scraping sound and then up it came. I couldn't see the ladleful, but then Yuri reached in and plucked out the bug.

"What is it?" Bronwen asked.

Yuri said nothing. He replaced the soup ladle and set about cleaning the bug in his napkin in a methodical manner. Then he held out the napkin. "Not a scorpion at all." He looked at Kimberly. "Although I would not rule out the possibility of something poisonous in our midst."

"Yes, but what is it?" Bronwen asked again.

"A metal disk, I'd say," Stasik answered. "Bloody hell."

"Did the light break?" Parashie asked, staring at the chandelier.

"Was an earthquake?" Zbiggo asked.

Yuri directed his attention to Stasik, his face stern with no hint of the good humor that characterized him. I took a sip of water, my hand shaking. I glanced at Stasik, who returned Yuri's look steadily. Then Yuri shifted his focus to Felix. He was going around the table. Next would come Zeffie. And then it would be my turn.

I had progressed from shaking to sweating. I would simply meet his eyes and make my face go limp. No, not limp. Limpid. Yes, that was the ticket. Neutral, noncommittal, even stupid. Yes, stupid. *Stop sweating,* I told myself.

He looked at me. His eyes were blue. No, green. Keep looking at his blue or green eyes, I told myself.

And then, unexpectedly, I felt my face break into a smile. Nerves. Hysteria, maybe.

But what was more strange, he smiled back.

Then he moved on to Nadja, continuing his visual inquisition.

Safe. I had passed the test, whatever it was. Was Yuri trying to determine which one of us had placed the bug there? By our facial expressions? And why was everyone so quiet?

Zbiggo said, "Can I eat more soup?"

Grusha looked at Yuri. "Line two. For Nell. The woman she goes with to meeting?"

Yuri frowned. "What woman?"

Kimberly put down her fork. "Her sponsor, are you talking about? The one she carpools with?"

Grusha nodded. "Nell is not come to drive her. She says, where she is? The meeting is already at seven."

I looked around the table and realized with a start that Nell wasn't there. That's right—it was Thursday night, her Agoraphobics Anonymous meeting.

"But what does this mean?" Parashie asked, her face alarmed. "Did something happen to Nell?"

"I check garage, if car is there," Grusha said and left the room.

Parashie spoke to her father urgently in Russian, but he answered quietly in English that she was not to worry. Grusha came back and announced that the car was still in the garage. Again, Parashie broke into Russian. Again, in English, Yuri calmed her down. "I will look into this," he said, standing. "Kimberly, I'll be at Green House."

Everyone else continued with dessert, lime sorbet and tiny crunchy cookies that Bronwen was attempting to eat by the handful. I was too anxious to eat, feeling that Nell's disappearance was significant. Sinister. Kimberly looked pensive, I thought, and sad.

Grusha appeared at my side. "You," she said. "Phone call."

"Uh—really?"

She handed me the phone. "Line one."

I took the phone from her and left the room.

"What are you doing?" Simon's voice was soft, deep, and resonant with sexual innuendo. It was so evocative of—

The feds are listening.

"Eating sorbet," I snapped. I was in the library with the door closed.

"Look, Wollie—"

"I'm working."

"You're angry."

Treason. Infidelity. Angry? I was outraged. I was confused. I was indignant, offended, uncertain, and miserable. I couldn't say any of this. I said, "I'm busy."

"I love you," he said.

"On an unsecured line?"

"This one's secure."

"This one isn't."

Simon hung up. I'd realized my mistake the second the words were out of my mouth, even before the click.

My anger had made me careless. *Damn.* But why did he have to take me literally? I mean, almost every phone line was insecure, right? Or unsecured. It was just a figure of speech. I could've been being flippant, right? It didn't necessarily mean "the FBI has a wiretap on this phone," right?

And the FBI was listening, hearing me say it wasn't a secure line. Great. Now they'd probably arrest me for treason. Or stupidity. I scratched my stomach underneath the manila envelope that was driving me batty but I dared not dislodge.

Something occurred to me: keeping this package didn't constitute mail fraud. It hadn't gone through the mail. There was no address on it, let alone a postmark—just Alik's name. So I wasn't committing a federal offense if I didn't hand it over, I was just a garden-variety thief. But I was also lying to that poor kid at the guard gate. This bothered me. I'd given him my word, and now he would get fired and would the FBI care? My guess was no.

On impulse, I picked up the phone and again called the emergency number for Yogi Yogurt. "Listen, this is Wollie," I said. "I need that quart of Very Vanilla, and I need it tonight. I know I said twenty-four hours, but I changed my mind. I'm carrying around a lot of money that I'm not comfortable with, if you know what I mean, so I need to offload it. Got it?"

"Yeah, I guess."

Wonderful, I thought, hanging up. *That is so reassuring.*

I looked at the package and thought that if someone other than Alik was going to open Alik's package, why not me?

I grabbed scissors from the desk and cut through the taped-up envelope and withdrew a square plastic case holding a DVD. It bore a label, but the label was blank except for the small Disney logo near the bottom.

Out in the library, I heard the door open. Panicked, I switched off the light in the office and squatted near the floor.

It was a knee-jerk reaction, but a stupid one. I had a perfect reason to be in the office, so why was I acting so utterly suspicious? Good luck now explaining myself if I was caught.

It was Kimberly, walking through the library. When I heard her voice, I peeked out. She was alone, so clearly she was on the phone. "Jesus Christ, when were you planning to tell me?" she asked. ". . . And who's going to be assigned *that* little detail? Because I have a million things to do and that's going to slow me down if I've got to get us all—" She picked up a bunch of Parashie's school books from the table and walked back toward the doorway. ". . . Okay, I'll call a meeting." And she was gone. I counted to ten, then left the library myself.

There was no one in sight. I fit the Disney DVD inside my camisole and scrunched up the envelope as tightly as I could, looking for somewhere to stash it. No garbage can, but the umbrella rack in the corner of the foyer would do. It hadn't rained in months, so no one had any reason to be poking around in there. I'd collect it later, after I'd finished the mission at hand. Bug number three.

It was the last thing I wanted to do, but now was my best shot at doing it. Neither Kimberly nor Yuri was in the master bedroom right now. If I pulled this off, my assignment was over.

Except that if Yuri knew the chandelier bug to be a bug, as he obviously did, then tomorrow someone could be at the house sweeping for bugs. For all I knew, he had a bug sweeper on retainer.

I paused, my hand on the banister. Was this my problem?

No. I wanted the bug out of my pocket, I wanted it gone, I wanted to do my civic duty, fulfill my assignment, and then get out of Dodge. Whether the bugs stayed in place wasn't my business. Whether the bugs picked up conversations or got swept away or flew into cream of ham soup, that wasn't my department. I started up the stairs.

And if I needed an alibi, there was always Donatella's ring on my finger. I was going to return the massively pricey ring right to Kimberly's dresser, since Donatella was out of town. I was now wearing so many alibis, I was covered for every eventuality.

"Wollie? Where are you going?"

I froze.

THIRTY-FIVE

"Hello, Vlad," I said, my mouth going dry. I stuck the bug in my pants pocket.

"Where are you going?" the big man said again, frowning. Puzzled. "Yuri's room?"

"Oh, heavens no. I mean, not on purpose. I thought that was—never mind. I have a very poor sense of direction, did you know that?"

"No."

"Well, we've just met. I'm sure it showed up on my Myers-Briggs test. Anyhow, I was on my way back to my own room to lie down, and—lay down? Lie down. I always—"

"Perhaps," he said, coming toward me, "you and Yuri have made yourselves a little rendezous, eh? To lay down or lie down?" He wiggled his eyebrows suggestively.

"God, no. He's married. To Kimberly. As you know. Absolutely not. Not my type."

Vlad slid an arm around me, exhaling wine fumes into my hair. "What is your type?"

Okay, this was bad. He would feel the DVD on my abdomen if his hand went lower, and there was a good chance it would. "Well, younger." I tried to wiggle out of his one-armed hug. "Not to sound ageist, because some of my best friends are—"

"I am younger than Yuri." He tightened his hold. "And strong. You feel? The arms?"

"Wow. Absolutely." The DVD was slipping. I grabbed it and held it in place.

"I need your opinion on something," Vlad said. "Will you help me?"

"Of course. What is it?"

"Come," he said, herding me down the hallway. "This way."

"Where to?"

"The meeting."

"What meeting?"

"You missed the pronouncement. At dinner. Already we are late. Kimberly waits."

"Oh." My stomach turned over. Maybe I had an ulcer. Stress could do that, right? If so, I wondered if MediasRex or the FBI would put me on their health plan, because dollars to doughnuts my insurance rates would jump if I had an ulcer. "What kind of meeting?"

"With Kimberly, always a surprise."

And on we went, out of Big House, around to the back of the property. Vlad kept his arm firmly around me. I couldn't think of how to gracefully extricate myself. He was like Zbiggo's older, beefier, creepier brother. I didn't want to Just Say No, in case it had the opposite effect and caused Vlad to become more physical. My DVD could pop out. That would be bad. But were we really headed to the meeting? Maybe. But what if we weren't? Then I was out in the dark with a large lech, with no one knowing my whereabouts. Outside. I remembered how Crispin had come to a bad end outside. In the dark.

And Chai.

"Vlad," I said. "I'm freezing cold, so let me just run back and get a sweater—"

I pulled away, but he grabbed my arm and pulled me back. "Ah, but we are almost there. And it will be warm, I promise you. Patience, my cabbage."

Which was when I saw that we were taking the same path I'd taken with Olive Oyl.

Vlad was taking me to the gun room.

THIRTY-SIX

Vlad hit the lights and the room came to life.

We were alone.

My body was quivering. I couldn't help it. He was going to shoot me here. Or worse. With Vlad, it would be much worse.

He'd let go of my hand in order to open up the room, but now he had his arm around me again. "Little fox," he said. "You're shaking."

"I—I—am I?" I squeaked, and hugged myself, protecting my hidden DVD. "Where's everyone? What about the meeting?"

"We must be early."

"What is it you wanted my opinion on?"

"This," he said, and kissed me.

I turned my head away and pushed my elbow into his considerable stomach. "You're kidding," I said.

"I'm not. I want you."

"Okay, here's my opinion: No."

He laughed. "My opinion counts more than yours. I say yes."

Clearly there would be no Kimberly, no meeting. Vlad stood between me and the door and showed no signs of letting me out of there unmolested. This wasn't Zbiggo. Zbiggo was a puppy. Vlad was a full-grown rottweiler from a bad gene pool. *Wollie,* I thought. *Use your head.* Could

I fight him if I had to? I could try. But I wasn't a fistfight kind of person and Vlad almost certainly was. With a personality like his, he must've been in a lot of fistfights. And he was big. On the plus side, he'd drunk wine at dinner. He didn't seem drunk, but he wasn't totally sober. There must be a way to use this.

"Vlad," I said, taking a deep breath. "'No' in this case doesn't mean 'no, I don't want you.' It means 'no, not so fast.' Baby. Don't they have foreplay in Belarus?"

His eyes lit up. "Foreplay? What foreplay do you like?"

"Guns."

"Shooting guns?"

"This is a shooting range, isn't it?"

"Is it?"

I gave a shaky laugh. "I think I know a shooting range when I see one."

"And this excites you?"

"What thinking person doesn't love an indoor gun range? I've always wanted one."

Vlad leered at me. "Maybe I buy you one."

"Handsome, by the time we're done, you'll buy me a gun range, a bowling alley, and a yoga garden. But first, show me the artillery." Where were these words coming from?

Vlad went behind me and, with a hand on each shoulder blade, propelled me forward, across the room to the locked cupboards. There was a box on the wall, with a keypad. He punched in a code, opened the box, and withdrew a key. He opened the first of the cupboard doors and revealed a bunch of guns. Little ones. Not rifles, the other kind. Handguns. Enough handguns for the entire FBI, from the looks of it. This was chilling. What was behind door number two? And three?

"You like the Ruger?" Vlad said, showing me the gun.

"What's not to like?"

"You are familiar with it?"

"Not really." I calculated the distance across the room. Could I outrun him?

"A .22 semiautomatic. It is a good gun to begin with, to get to know one another, but perhaps, for my little soldier, we go straight to the nine-millimeter."

"Sure, bring on the nine-millimeter," I said, as if I had a clue what that was.

"Unless," he said, reaching over to touch my hair, "you like a Glock?"

"I *love* a Glock," I cried and stepped out of his reach. "My friend Joey has a Glock."

"Who doesn't? Here we go, beauty. One for you, one for me." He handed me a box of bullets. "Load them. I love to see a woman load a gun. It excites me."

"Calm yourself. Vlad, I didn't make myself clear. I'm a beginner."

"What do you mean?" He frowned.

"A gun virgin. I can't load one. I can't even shoot one. You have to teach me."

A slow smile came over his face. "A gun virgin."

"Yes. But lucky me, learning from a master—you are a master, aren't you?"

"I am. Many years in the military." He reached to touch my hair. I stepped back.

"I love a military man. So tell me about this Glock."

"Well, the Glock has no true safety. This is not a problem for you, Gun Virgin?"

"Safeties are overrated," I said, as if my personal motto were not, in fact, Safety First. "But—wait. How come it doesn't have a safety?"

"In fact, it does have one," Vlad said, loading the gun with bullets from the little box. "But when the finger is on the trigger, the safety is off. This is something to think about."

I thought about it. "When the safety's off, how do you get it back on?"

"You take the finger off the trigger." Vlad closed the gun with a snap. I jumped.

"What's the point of that? Isn't that like having car brakes that don't work?"

"I don't see the—what is the word?"

"Analogy? Sure you do," I said, taking a step back. "It's like telling someone that if they want their car to stop, they should just turn off the engine."

"At any rate," Vlad said. "Let us begin. Do you know the safety rules?"

Use a gun that has a safety would be a good one, for starters. "No, what are they?"

"I will whisper them to you," he said, moving in.

"Wait!" I yelled right into his ear.

"What?" he yelled, backing off.

"Do you have—a flak jacket or something? A Kevlar vest?"

"Why?"

"Aren't we playing soldier? I want the costume."

"So playful, you American girls." But he turned to the gun cupboards and worked the key on the second one. I threw a look once more across the room to the door, but Vlad turned to me too soon. "I love American girls," he said and made a little wiggling move with his tongue. I didn't want to think about what it signified.

"Was Chai 'playful' too?" I asked.

"Very playful. But we didn't play soldier. She made me spend money. The clubs. The dinner. Not like you."

"No, I'm a cheap date." So Vlad and Chai had been an item. If Crispin had discovered that and threatened Vlad, then Vlad would make a good suspect for Crispin's murder. Except that it was hard to imagine Crispin threatening Vlad in any meaningful way, so probably not. "Oh, my," I said as he opened the cupboard.

There, hanging in neat rows, were dozens, maybe a hundred or two, vests. Vlad reached up and brought one down and held it up to my chest. It was similar to one I'd seen in Simon's closet.

"Beautiful," I said. "I've worn black Kevlar, but not camouflage."

"Not Kevlar," Vlad said, smiling. "Spectra."

"Ooooh. Spectra!"

I put it on, slapping Vlad's hand away. He was desperate to help me zip it up, but he also seemed to enjoy being slapped.

The vest was not as heavy as I expected, and now the DVD was safe from his hands brushing against my stomach. Also, the vest covered my prominent breasts, a big plus.

"Now, my beauty," he said. "You have your costume. I want my kiss."

I fought back revulsion. "Hold on, Vlad. Are these the biggest guns you have?"

"What do you mean?"

It now hit me that I wasn't just a distressed damsel, I was a spy. I had a job to do. Playing this fearless, libidinous gun nut was inspiring me. I batted my eyes. "I listen to rap. Uzis, AK-47s, all those sexy names—I'm dying to touch one. Got any?"

"Wollie Shelley," he said. "You surprise me. Many women see the beauty of a machine gun, but I did not spot you as one of them."

I gave a modest shrug. "I'm a graphic artist, after all."

He pulled the key out of his pocket once more and dangled it in front of me, the way you'd tempt a kitten with a catnip mouse. "So you want my big guns?" he asked.

"Is the Pope Catholic?" I reached for the key and he pulled it back.

"Uh-uh," he said and wagged a finger. "Kiss first."

"Gun first."

"I say kiss." He pulled me to him. I resisted, which only tightened his grip.

"Fine," I said between my teeth. "But no gun, no tongue."

Vlad put his fleshy mouth on mine. I kept mine clamped closed, but that didn't stop him from running his tongue all over my lips. I was now breathing through my nose, inhaling the considerable odor of alcohol, along with some strong cologne, emanating from him. His tongue was wandering up my cheek heading toward my ear, like a cat cleaning its kitten, when I felt I could shut him down. "Guns," I reminded him, turning my head fast so that my nose hit his. It hurt, but it was worth it.

"Ouch. Watch it." He gave me a playful slap on the cheek.

"Ouch," I said back to him. "Let's see some firearms."

He was breathing heavily as he turned a third time to the cupboards, fumbling with the key. Was this my chance?

I didn't ask myself twice. I took off across the room.

Maybe if the door hadn't been closed, or if I'd remembered that it opened outward, I'd have made it. But I wasted seconds pulling on it, and then Vlad was on top of me.

Being tackled is no picnic. By the time I recovered my wits and reflexes, Vlad's body was crushing the breath out of me. We were both facedown, and my arms were pinned to my sides and one of my legs was free to kick upward but met nothing but air. When I felt his breath in my ear, I used the one weapon I could think of. I lowered my head, then threw it back fast, making contact with something hard. I winced. He yelled.

My head was buzzing with pain, but the impact must've been worse for him, because his hold on me loosened and I wiggled to the right as he rolled to the left.

"Bitch! What are you doing? Bitch!" Vlad sat up as I scrambled away from him. He had a hand over his mouth and when he removed his hand and stared at it, there was blood on it. He looked at me, horrified. "What are you doing?" He reached inside his mouth and pulled out something, too small and/or bloody for me to identify. "My veneer!" he cried. "It is only six months old. Bitch!"

He pulled himself to his feet and I did too, moving backward toward the guns. The DVD had fallen out of my camisole, and I wedged it back in. Vlad was too occupied with his teeth to notice. Had I killed his amorous mood or simply inspired him to kill me?

Vlad pocketed his tooth fragment and started toward me, an ugly look in his eye.

Dread washed over me. I backed up.

Could I reach the guns? Yes. I kept on moving, in reverse, toward the table.

But were any of them loaded? Could I bring myself to shoot him?

Vlad was advancing.

I continued to back up until the table stopped me, and then I put my hand down and there was the Glock.

No safety! There's no safety!

I had to use both hands to pick it up because I was shaking and I was scared it was going to go off all by itself. It was aimed at the floor. Could

I bring it up any higher? Vlad's chest, for instance? Or maybe—his balls? If I couldn't shoot him, maybe I could scare him.

Vlad stopped, seeing the Glock. Then he snorted. "It's not loaded, stupid girl." He walked toward me confidently.

"Vlad."

The voice cut through the air and Vlad froze. Then he turned.

Yuri stood in the doorway. He said a few words in Russian to Vlad, then glanced at me. "Wollie, put down the gun." He waited until I did, then walked to Vlad.

"Yuri," Vlad said, "you see what this bitch—"

Yuri punched him in the face.

THIRTY-SEVEN

Vlad didn't go down, but he reeled and twirled and listed dangerously. And yowled. His hands held his jaw. Blood flowed from his mouth.

"Go," Yuri said. "Get out, Vlad. Grusha will see to you. She's in the kitchen, baking."

To my surprise, Vlad slunk off. Yuri closed the door behind him and turned to me.

"You're okay?"

I nodded. I was more than okay, I was giddy with relief. Happy, even. I wanted to throw myself into Yuri's arms. Maybe I was in shock.

"Vlad has some fine qualities," Yuri said, studying me. "They are overshadowed by his unfortunate tendency to view half the human race as—"

"Meat?"

"Only the pretty ones. The rest he merely underestimates. Did I see blood on his face before I hit him?"

"A head butt, I think it's called. I knocked out one of his veneers."

"Well done."

I nodded. "Thank you. And—well, thank you. Your timing was phenomenal. How did you know we were here?"

Yuri pointed to the ceiling. "Surveillance cameras. Audio as well as video."

I looked up. They were in every corner, black cameras, not even attempting to hide.

Yuri walked to one of them. He grabbed a chair, stood on it, and adjusted the lens. "I watched the footage last night as well, when you came in here alone."

Uh-oh.

"You were here a good while," he said. "You seemed quite taken with the room. In fact, you sketched it."

I gulped. "Occupational hazard. I sketch everything."

"Why?"

"Well, you never know when there'll be a greeting card in it, and—"

"In a gun range?" He turned to me.

"Yes. Honestly, it was very exciting, finding this room." I tried for a cheery smile. Since I was shaking again, or still shaking, it probably looked a little manic. "Anyhow, I didn't mean to come in here at all. It was Olive Oyl. She was scratching at the door."

"Wollie, you disappoint me. Blaming the dog." He smiled and crossed the room. "I see that Vlad gave you the tour." He opened wide the last of the storage cupboard doors and stepped back.

Inside the cupboard were too many guns to count. Big guns. The kind that soldiers carry. Dozens of them, maybe a hundred, mostly alike. Yuri was either a gunrunner or a survivalist or planning to outfit an army. Or all of the above.

"Yuri, that's—quite a collection."

"It is, isn't it? Are you going to tell me what you were doing here last night?"

"I'm incurably curious." In fact, I couldn't stop staring at the cabinet full of guns. "So what are they all for? The little guns, those big ones, this Kevlar vest I'm wearing, the—"

"Spectra, not Kevlar. What's intriguing," Yuri said, selecting a big gun, "is that I wouldn't have guessed that about you. Excessive curiosity. My assessment is that you take things at face value. You have a trusting nature. I would have said that you have no great urge to delve into life's subterranean depths, the secrets of others."

"In general, you're right. In this instance—honestly, I couldn't tell you why I came in here." This was literally true: I *couldn't* tell him why. I'd promised Bennett Graham not to.

"Or why you're now so interested in my collection. Shall I offer one theory?"

Oh dear. "Oh-kay."

He closed the cupboard and brought the big gun over to me, along with a box of bullets. He set them on the table. "You are fascinated by me."

"Am I?"

"Yes." He walked back to the first cupboard and took out some paper targets, then carried them to the far end of the room and clipped them to the conveyor belt apparatus. He positioned one surveillance camera so that it focused on the target. "I captivate you," he said. "So what is mine—this room—captivates you. Why would that be so, if it is in fact so?"

"I don't know," I said. "Why?"

"Because my outstanding characteristic is a paternalistic nature. I love my children."

"True." I'd noticed that, the way he looked at Parashie and Alik. The way he paid attention when they spoke.

"Also, I am father to the entire team. Even to Vlad, not so many years my junior. I am a true patriarch." He walked back to me, smiling. "To a woman with father issues, this is exceedingly attractive. It is most likely the reason you came to work for me."

I blinked. "You think I have father issues?"

Yuri picked up the Glock from the table and a rectangular object. "This is a clip. It holds ten rounds." He loaded it with bullets from his box. "Your father left when you were five. Abandonment, whether by absence or death, has a profound effect on children. They respond to it in myriad ways, but your way is dogged loyalty—not to say slavish devotion—to those you love, and a vulnerability—not to say slavish devotion—to a certain male energy." He'd loaded the bullets into the clip and popped the clip into the gun. "But now I think that is not the whole picture. Now I think we have underestimated you."

"In what way?" I wrapped my arms around my Kevlar vest. Had Yuri seen the DVD pop out? No, he would've been outside when it happened, coming to rescue me.

"This attraction of yours. Is it to just me? Or have you a yearning to explore your own shadow? To use psychological terms. Does my extensive cache of guns and toys, my state-of-the-art playroom attract you? Do you have a desire to play here?"

"Well . . ."

One eyebrow went up. "Or is it something else altogether?"

"No, that's it," I said. "Shooting, I mean. Is that what you mean? Yes. Shooting. I have a fascination with it." A horrified fascination. "This is a seminal moment for me."

He looked at me appraisingly. Was he buying it, or was he about to say, "Oh, horse pucky"?

After a long moment, he said, "Fair enough." I exhaled slowly.

Yuri turned to the big gun and and loaded it. "Vlad gave you a visceral demonstration of the need for self-defense skills. Did he also teach you the four rules of gun safety?"

"We didn't get that far."

"So I surmised. Pay attention. Number one, all guns are always loaded. Even if you are certain they are not, you treat them as though they are."

"Okay."

"Number two, never point your gun at what you are not willing to kill. Number—"

"Whoa," I said. "Back up. Number two. What about bluffing?"

"No bluffing. This isn't poker. Number three, keep your finger off the trigger until you have the target in your sights. Number four, you are responsible for the terminal resting place of all projectiles fired. Any questions?"

"Yes. That last one in English, please."

He smiled. "I have taught it in six languages. Blood and bone and skin are not enough to stop a bullet. Who is standing behind the person you're aiming at? Because you're responsible for him too. Who is behind the wall? Are you willing to kill her too?"

If I'd ever wanted to fire a gun, I was having second and third and fourth thoughts now. *The only way out is through,* said the voice in my head. "Okay, let's shoot!" I said.

He held up a hand. "In good time. Repeat the four rules, please."

"All guns are loaded, don't pick it up unless you're willing to kill, see your target before your finger's on the trigger, pay attention to what's behind the door—target, I mean."

"Well done." He walked over to the second gun cupboard and pulled out two headset things. "So. You like the big guns? Then we will start with the big guns. Not the way I'd ordinarily train a shooter, but you are an unusual girl, aren't you?"

"I've been told so, yes."

"This," he said, picking up the big gun, "is an H & K MP5 sub-machine gun, utilizing a thirty-round magazine."

"Thirty rounds. Huh."

"Used by Navy SEALs in close-quarter combat and by special reaction teams all over."

"How wonderful." I was having a special reaction myself to all this, and reminded myself to focus on the details, for Bennett Graham. "How many of these do you have?"

"Down here? One hundred and fifty. Feel it. Nice and lightweight."

What did anyone need with a hundred and fifty of these things? And did this mean he had more stashed elsewhere? Before I could frame the question, Yuri was putting on a headset. He handed the other one to me, calling it a pair of earmuffs. The big spongy protective bagel-shaped things were unexpectedly disturbing, implying that now my hearing was at stake too. The earmuffs had an isolating effect, but this was offset by Yuri's hands on my arms and shoulders, adjusting my posture and grip. The gun was lighter than it looked, given the scary parts of it jutting out all over the place.

Yuri's touch was businesslike rather than sexual, but it was still intimate and I was still carrying the DVD. Thank God for the camouflage vest. I thought of the men whose hands had touched me in the last twelve hours, starting with Simon's that afternoon. Not to mention his other body parts. Did I still carry his scent? All I could smell was guns.

And then, after Yuri yammered on about thirty or forty more things I couldn't focus on, I closed my eyes and fired my first shot.

I had no idea where it landed, nor did I care. What I noticed was that even with the earmuffs on, it was excruciatingly loud. It made me think of being at the dentist with the drill going full blast in your mouth. Not painful—assuming there's Novocain involved—but not a lot of fun either. And with the whole posture-and-grip thing, trying to remember to breathe, relax, and not scrunch up one's face, it was as tedious as a golf lesson, which some former boyfriend had once talked me into. I could imagine that if one were the type of person who loves firecrackers, this might be a good time. I wasn't, and this wasn't.

But Yuri was patient and, in spite of myself, I was pleased to see my aim improve. Yuri took pride in my progress, and that too was strangely gratifying.

I kept shooting until the gun was empty, which seemed to take half my life, then handed it to Yuri and removed my earmuffs before he could reload. "What an amazing experience!" I said. "Got anything else?"

"Yes, I think you'll enjoy the Beretta Cx4 Storm, which, like the MP5, uses nine-millimeter rounds, like the handguns, giving us an ammunition compatibility factor."

"How handy," I said. "How many of those do you have?"

"Seventy-five. Next time on the MP5, I'll teach you the double-tap. Two shots to the center mass and, if your target's still upright, another one to the head. After a few sessions of that, you'll be ready to burst-fire the weapon."

"Something to live for!" I said brightly and made mental notes of everything he'd just said, for Bennett Graham's edification. "What's the story with compatibility factor? Are certain people more compatible with certain bullets? Kind of like astrological signs?"

Yuri smiled. "Not bullets: cartridges. Or loads. Or ammunition. In case of warfare," he said, reloading the gun, "one often fights alongside other factions. Allies. Allies may not share a common language, or even a reason for fighting, but in a gunfight what matters is that they can share ammunition. Also vital for you when you're carrying multiple weapons."

"How many wars have you fought in, Yuri?" I asked.

"That is not an easy question to answer," he said. "In a sense it is all one war, whatever the battleground."

"And what's that one called?"

"Come," he said. "Put your earmuffs back on. I want your body to have some muscle memory of tonight's work."

Eventually I got used to the little orange explosion and a certain Raggedy Ann feeling for just a second afterward as the gun threw me off balance. After that, we shot the Cx4 and the Glock, the names and numbers of which I kept repeating to myself, for Bennett Graham. A teeth-gritting half hour later, Yuri looked at his watch. "My friends across the ocean are waking now," he said. "I must make telephone calls. We will do this again, very soon."

Over my dead body, I thought. Aloud, I said, "Fabulous. It's a date."

He smiled and removed the earmuffs from my ears, at which point I realized I'd been screaming my enthusiasm for firearms.

"Yes, it is an addictive hobby." He took the gun from me, then pressed a button that made the targets return to us on the conveyor belt apparatus. "Look," he said, showing me my Target Guy, full of holes in his chest. "You have more talent for this hobby than you know. And more courage than I suspected."

"It didn't take much courage." If I had real courage, I'd press the issue and discover what was going on here. Instead of calling it a day and feeling lucky that I'd survived it.

"This time, I saved you from Vlad," Yuri said, checking the gun chambers. "Next time there is a Vlad, you will save yourself. I have just taught you how."

It was true. And against my will, I had learned. Did I want this knowledge? I pressed my fingers against my temples and rubbed, closing my eyes. When I opened my eyes, Yuri was looking at me.

"What is the secret you're keeping, Wollie?" he asked softly.

Which one? The bug in my pocket, the stolen DVD under my flak jacket? The knowledge I had of the corpse found rotting in the canyon? "I don't know what you're—"

"Candor," he said softly, "ends paranoia."

I blinked. "Allen Ginsberg?"

"'Cosmopolitan Greetings.'"

"I love Allen Ginsberg."

"I stood with one hundred thousand Czechs and cheered him." His eyes grew dreamlike. "As he challenged the dictatorship. Prague, 1965. Kral Majales. 'Stand up against governments, against God—'"

"'—Stay irresponsible.'" I was shaken. If a guy knew Allen Ginsberg by heart, how bad could he be? "Yuri," I said, taking the plunge. "You don't have to trust me with the knowledge of why you have several hundred machine guns or assault rifles or whatever they call themselves, not to mention the matching costumes, but you have to know I'm not stupid enough to think you're stupid enough to think that I'm too stupid to notice." I stopped. The look on his face stopped me.

Okay, maybe I was a little stupid.

Yuri's eyes had lost their dreamlike quality. They flickered up to the surveillance camera, then back to me. "Take off the vest," he said. "We're going for a walk."

THIRTY-EIGHT

"I don't consider you stupid," Yuri said, walking ahead of me in the dark. "I consider Vlad careless. He should never have shown you the guns. I thought I could distract you with a shooting lesson, but your interest isn't mere curiosity, it's something more dangerous. You have a conscience." He led me up a path that led to the canyon, illuminating the way with a flashlight he'd taken from the gun room.

"It's not that well developed a conscience," I said quickly. "And it's possible I'll forget it all by morning, everything I just saw. It could happen. I'm absentminded." In fact, I was scared. "Anyway, guns. Big deal. Some of my best friends are gun nuts. Second Amendment. Free country."

"Don't second-guess yourself. You asked me a serious question, deserving of an answer."

"Yes, but if this is one of those 'I'll tell you but then I'll have to kill you' situations, I'd rather not know." My nose was running now too. First my mouth, then my nose. I stumbled, and then I stopped. "Yuri? I'm at the end of the road. I'm done. It's been a long and frankly dreadful day, enlivened by only a few bright moments, and I can't walk anymore. I'm cold, it's dark, I'm tired, I'm scared."

Yuri had stopped too and turned, and now he walked back to me.

"Take my jacket. No one is killing anyone, certainly not you. Just a bit farther. Come."

I let myself be persuaded, I let him hand me his jacket, some thin Gore-Tex thing still warm from his body that raised my own temperature instantly. My fear subsided, but not my misgivings. So he gave me his jacket. That didn't mean he wasn't a murderer. This guy was full of paradoxes. However, since my chances of outrunning him were slim— he had twenty years on me, but he was also twice the athlete I was—I figured I'd trust him. I wanted to trust him. Was wanting to trust the same as trusting? Was trust like lust, something that just came over you, or was trust a matter of choice? This was a question for Uncle Theo.

We reached a stone bench in a clearing that looked out over the canyon. Lights dotted the darkness below us like stars in an upside-down sky.

"Sit," Yuri said, and waited until I did. "I am creating an intelligence agency."

I blinked. "You're kidding. Like the FBI?"

"A combination FBI, CIA, Secret Service, and Homeland Security is more accurate."

"That sounds—large. Do we need another agency?"

"It's not for the United States."

"Who's it for?"

"A very small country."

"Which one?"

He hesitated. "We'll save that for another day. I'm doing nothing anti-American, believe me—quite the contrary. I am a patriot when it comes to my adopted country."

"So this is legal, what you're doing?"

He smiled. The moonlight looked good on him. "Technically."

"How technical?"

"California Penal Code 11460 prohibits the training of paramilitary groups, but we are not, by definition, a paramilitary group. Although our equipment and training would suggest that we are. The difference has to do with our intention."

"Which is what?"

"To provide support for a new government, which will come about through legal, nonviolent means."

"In this small unnamed country."

"Yes."

"Yuri, I gotta say, when you talk about a nonparamilitary paramilitary group training on American soil, I start thinking—"

"Terrorist." He looked at me. "Wollie, my money is invested in the American stock market, I made sure my son was born here, I sent him to American schools, I own land and businesses here, I can recite to you forty-four American presidents and their vice presidents. Would you like me to?"

"No, I feel ignorant enough."

"I am a Slav. I do not embrace every Western value, but your democratic ideal is my own. My life's work is the creation of open societies in former Communist countries."

"Wow."

"Yes, wow. And so I do business with men like Vlad, and worse than Vlad, as does everyone operating in that part of Europe. But here I respect the letter of the law. I love the judicial system. Why do you suppose I went to court rather than settle with Miss Lemon? My insurance would have paid. I am the farthest thing from a terrorist that you could imagine. I am a believer."

And I believed him. Which made ridiculous the idea that this guy was involved in film piracy; whatever DVD scam was going on at the compound didn't include Yuri. I was now sure of it. "If this spy training program isn't illegal," I said, "why all the secrecy?"

"I'm going to have a cigar. Do you mind?"

"No."

He reached into the pocket of the Gore-Tex jacket I wore and removed a cigar and lighter. "Don't tell Kimberly. Or Nell. Or Donatella, or Grusha, or Parashie." He removed the cigar wrapper. "Why the secrecy? Proving our legal right to exist would create unwanted publicity. Staying under the radar of local law enforcement protects our friends."

"What friends?"

"Don't worry, they're your friends too. Your country gives aid to people like me who promote democracy. Quietly. The aid might be in the form of money, or arms, or a spirit of cooperation, but there is always an outcry when the relationships come to light. Think of Nicaragua, Angola, the Iraqi exiles, the financial scandal in Little Havana over the Cuban exiles and some misspent funds. I like to take care of my friends, not cause them trouble."

"And I imagine you need to stay off the international radar. Did Chai threaten to give up your secrets? When you took her to Kyiv last year?"

He stuck the cigar in his mouth and lit it, squinting at me. "Chai knew nothing of this operation. She worked strictly with MediasRex, which is a legitimate media training group."

"Really, Yuri?" I asked.

The lighter flicked off. "Really, Wollie. Yes, MediasRex makes for good cover, an international business requiring travel to and from southeastern Europe, where most of our operatives-in-training come from. But I promise you, Bronwen Bjöeling is not a spy."

I believed him. "Who are the spies, then?"

"You've seen some of them. The workers supposedly building a pool behind House of Blue. That's one contingent. The landscapers. There are more, in various stages of training. We have a second facility in Slovakia and a third in Moldova."

"Where Zbiggo comes from."

"A coincidence. Zbiggo is not nearly intelligent enough for intelligence work." He puffed on his cigar, watching me.

"But—my God, this is wild. So you teach people to spy. To shoot, and fight, and decode stuff, and . . . surveillance techniques?"

"We teach many things. Most of it more tedious than you might imagine, but occasionally entertaining. Tonight, for instance. What fell into the soup."

I froze. "What about it?"

"It was a bugging device. That would be one of the novices, working on their counterintelligence merit badges, as Kimberly calls them. Spying on the spymaster."

"It couldn't have been actual counterintelligence? Like, another faction in this small, unnamed country?"

"No."

"How can you tell?"

"Because it was so poorly done."

I tried not to feel offended. "Why were you grilling us, then? That's what you were doing, wasn't it, going around the table, staring at everyone?"

He smiled. "I wanted to see if someone on my media team was being used by my novices. An enterprising recruit will do that, befriend someone on the inside, persuade them to lend a hand during a training op. Intelligence is about seduction. And the recruits become extremely competitive. They are, of course, competitive to begin with. It's a necessary characteristic for spies. The gunshot that interrupted our lunch, the day you came? One of the advanced trainees, aiming at a target from down in the canyon. A stunt, nothing more. He missed and hit the house."

"Where's Nell?"

Yuri rubbed his eyes. "Frankly, I am not certain. I'm working on that."

What on earth did all this mean? I believed what Yuri was saying, and it made sense of so many things I'd seen and not understood. But not everything.

Bzzz. Something buzzed against my hip bone.

"This jacket's vibrating," I said.

"My cell phone." He stuck his cigar between his teeth and reached into the pocket of the jacket I wore, brushing my waist. I held my breath, worried about the DVD until he withdrew his hand. The camaraderie of moonlight and secret cigars and shared clothing was unexpected. And hard to describe. It wasn't sexual. It was something safer.

"Hello," Yuri said into his phone, then, "She's with me . . . can you patch him through? . . . Yes, hello? With whom am I speaking? . . . I'm Yuri Milos. She's here with me now. Would you like to speak with her?"

"Who is it?" I asked, startled. I reached for the phone, but Yuri kept talking.

"Entirely my fault," he said. "I've been working her hard . . . Is that so? How would tomorrow be for you? . . . And if she brings a date? Is that all right? . . . Then it's done. . . . My pleasure." He hung up. "Your brother wants you to bring him a book called *Superstrings and the Search for the Theory of Everything.*" He reached over and stuck the phone back into the jacket I wore.

"But I'm working tomorrow—or is that the 'date' you referred to?"

"Yes. This work/family conflict Americans find so distressing is easily solved: either recruit your family into your business or adopt your colleagues and bring your work home. I do both. So will you." He looked at his watch and stood. "Come. I need to make phone calls." He took my hand and we started down the mountain path. "Tomorrow morning, go to Santa Barbara, see your brother, and take Stasik. You are not to let Stasik drive the car, which he will try to do, and you will not let him out of your sight, which will be a challenge."

"And what *am* I supposed to do with him?" I tried to see Stasik and P.B. conversing.

"Your job. Help him acquire social skills, to alienate people a bit less."

"I'm not sure my brother's the guy to hang with for that exercise," I said. "He's a little . . . atypical, socially speaking. Not a good role model."

"Stasik needs to see the country beyond the 310 and 818 area codes. And your brother counts too. Take care of your own, Wollie. That is the first rule."

I stumbled a little in the dark. "Is there a second rule?"

"Us versus Them."

I wasn't crazy about these rules. What constituted one's own? Blood? Citizenship? Shared ammunition? Here I was being paid by both Yuri and Bennett Graham, and while Bennett Graham was a more obvious "us," he hadn't killed any snakes on my behalf or dislocated an assailant's jaw. I wanted to make a case to the feds that Yuri Milos, while arguably eccentric, wasn't doing anything wrong. Of course, there was still the piracy problem and a few dead bodies to explain, so I'd have to give it some more thought.

As if he'd read my mind, Yuri said, "Oh, Grusha says a call came in for you, before your brother's. The yogurt store is closed tonight and can't fill your order until tomorrow and asks you to be patient."

"Oh. Okay."

"Just as well. I think you are not getting enough sleep." We'd come to the entrance to House of Blue. "Go right to bed, please. Will you do that?"

"Yes." I'd considered searching out a computer or TV, to view the pilfered DVD, but I'd had enough covert operations for one day. Besides, I was feeling distinctly under par, either because I'd barely touched dinner or from the stress of the day.

"You know," Yuri continued, "that anything you need, food, sundry items, you have only to tell Grusha about it and she will put it on the shopping list? Including yogurt."

"Yes, I know."

"My jacket, please," he said, smiling.

"Oh," I said, blushing. "Of course."

He helped me out of it and I was struck by how like a date this was, where a person who began the evening in one relationship to you now had a different relationship. And the negotiations went on and on. Did one kiss? Hug? Shake hands?

Yuri put on his jacket and then took me by both shoulders, looking at me with deliberation. "Wollie, you now possess information that I would prefer not to have shared. But my gut tells me that I can trust you. Am I right? I haven't made a mistake, have I?"

My heart beat loudly. His eyes peered into mine, in the moonlight, requiring a response. I felt as though I were about to be inducted into some secret society, that my answer had the significance of a pledge.

"No," I whispered. "You haven't made a mistake. You can trust me."

And to my dismay, I realized I meant it.

THIRTY-NINE

'd told Yuri I'd go to sleep, but here I was, an hour later, making my way through Big House by way of little night-lights that glowed near the baseboards. In the library, I stumbled over an ottoman and found the phone. The lines weren't lit up; Yuri must have finished his own calls and gone to bed. Thank God. I sat and dialed Uncle Theo's number.

The overhead light went on. "Who is here? Somebody?"

I launched myself off the sofa, clutching my heart, suppressing a scream. I turned to see Donatella in the doorway of the library.

"You scared me," I said, stating the obvious. "I thought you were in—"

"Mogilev. For forty-seven minutes, yes. Thousands of hours in the sky for forty-seven minutes on the ground."

"I didn't know that was even possible, flying to Europe and flying right back."

"You need proof? I am wearing the same clothes for thirty-eight hours. Unless I am dead, this will never happen again. The shoes are a disaster. I have blisters. I send them back to Jimmy Choo. What are you doing here awake at this hour? I thought you were Yuri."

"No, I'm me. I just—was it a business trip you just took?"

"Would I fly there for a one-hour vacation? Tell me, has Nell been found?"

I shook my head. "Maybe she flew to Mogilev too."

"Nell has no passport. It took sedatives to get her to the DMV for the driver's license. To fly in a plane? Never. Not even for Yuri." Donatella perched on the arm of a chair and closed her eyes for a moment.

I thought of Crispin, found dead while Donatella was on a very long round-trip flight. She could easily have killed him and then flown to Mogilev to avoid the police interview. Drastic, but possible. "Donatella, you do think Nell's still . . . alive?"

"One can hope." She removed a high heel and massaged her foot. I wondered if it would fall to her to give away Nell's clothes, as she had Chai's, in the event of a bad outcome. "Did you ever wonder," she said, "why Fidel Castro was never seen in a suit? I have figured this out. It is so difficult to be a revolutionary and also dress well. I must be the pioneer." She stood. "*Va bene.* I am too tired to sleep. I shall pack."

"Do you mean unpack?"

"Pack. I go to Bratislava, you see. Tomorrow. I could have gone there from Mogilev. A lesser woman would have. Yuri begged me. He said Grusha will box up my clothes and ship them. Grusha? No. I don't leave couture in her hands. A Russian could. A Pole, yes. The Irish, would they come back? No. For what? The fisherman sweater? The clogs? *Però, sono Italiana, io.* My path is not for everyone. Get sleep, please. Your skin looks like dead leaves. I go."

I watched her leave, disturbed by her rambling. Donatella, it seemed, was leaving America. Perhaps for good.

Why?

"It's a hotbed of activity over there," Uncle Theo told me over the phone, three minutes later. "What country in particular are you curious about?"

Leave it to my uncle to not ask why I needed to know about Eastern Europe late at night. Uncle Theo assumed the thirst for arcane knowledge was universal and self-justifying. "Which country is Mogilev in?" I asked.

"Belarus."

"Belarus. Yes." I moved from the office into the library and turned on a table lamp. Thousands of books came to life, their spines calling "Pick me!" I moved to a section of wall devoted to oversized shelves and pulled out an atlas.

"The politics of Belarus," Uncle Theo said, "are summed up in one word: Lukashenko."

"What's that?" I lugged the atlas to a worktable.

"A president, dear, but between us, more of a dictator. Changes the constitution when it suits him. Alexander Lukashenko. His supporters call him Bat'ka."

"What's that mean?"

"'Father.'"

An entire country with father issues, I thought. "Is anyone trying to overthrow him?" I found the page in the atlas that I needed, Belarus and its many neighbors.

"Oh, wherever there's a government, there's someone trying to overthrow it. Belarus is well armed against a coup d'état, however, since the old KGB is active there."

"I thought the KBG went out with the Cold War."

"No, they're alive and well in Minsk, ready to whisk away opponents of the regime. Lukashenko struggled to take control of the country when the Soviet Union collapsed, fighting corruption and privatization. He probably made a deal with the Russian Mafia to do it, according to Mykola, my Ukranian barber. People that bent on claiming power generally like to keep it."

"Do you like him?"

"My barber?"

"Lukashenko."

"Oh. Well, even an old Socialist like me prefers free elections to fixed ones, so no, I have to say that he's not a favorite. But he's kept the developers away from the Pripet River and the surrounding wetlands—so far—so from the ecological point of view, things could be worse. That's sacred ground to all Greenies."

Wetlands. That rang a bell. "Wait—this guy's ecologically progressive?"

"It's more that he's anti capitalism and Westernization and free markets, all those things that can wreak havoc on the environment in developing countries."

I was trying to get a clear picture of Yuri's political agenda, but this wasn't helping. The Milos family was aggressively green, but if Lukashenko wasn't a big environmental threat . . . "Uncle Theo," I said, studying the map, "I see Chernobyl right here across the border. That must've had an impact on Belarus, the nuclear reactor disaster."

"Oh, dreadful. Belarusians suffered right along with the Ukrainians."

"I guess there was a big international aid effort when that happened?" I thought of Donatella. "Italy, for instance?"

"Everyone. The whole world helped. From China to Cuba. And Italy? Why, did you know that radiocesium was found in Italy, not so long ago, as a result of Chernobyl?"

I did not know, since I'd never heard of radiocesium, but a picture was coming into view of the MediasRex team coming together around the time of Chernobyl—Donatella, Yuri, Alik's mother, and Zeffie, too, a physician from Cuba, helping with the relief effort. What it had to do with secret intelligence organizations, I didn't know. Or DVD piracy. I was on my own search for the theory of everything, but the words on the atlas were swimming under my bleary eyes now, so I thanked Uncle Theo, put back the atlas, and took off for House of Blue, exhausted beyond belief.

I walked by Nell's room, but it was still empty. And in my dreams I heard footsteps outside my bedroom door while Nell was locked in a cupboard in the gun room, crying out to me for help.

FORTY

The next morning I did not watch the DVD or plant the bug. Nor did I call the frozen yogurt store. I couldn't risk getting a return message that Grusha would pick up and Yuri might hear about, because that could look suspicious, that all my social calls involved yogurt.

I thought about Chai, as I dressed in her clothes. Her "accident," it now occurred to me, could've been expertly staged to fool the cops. In a school for professional spies, wouldn't "corpse removal" be part of the curriculum? A cleanup course, to ensure that civilians didn't stumble over the carnage left in the wake of some black op? Grusha probably taught it.

I knew I would never be reconciled to Chai's death now. Crispin had begged me to look into it, and that had turned into a sort of last request, assuming a certain weight. Not to mention Crispin's own death, which more than weighed on me, it gnawed at me.

Yuri's spy operation was another story.

I'd already reported what I'd seen to the FBI, all the strange little clues that turned out to be about espionage training. If the feds chose to ignore what didn't fit into their specific crime scenario, it wasn't my problem. I wasn't going to now hand them the answer to a riddle they'd shown no interest in, endangering a mission I might well believe in, if I knew the particulars. I didn't want to break the promise I'd made to Yuri.

Of course, neither was I telling Yuri about the film piracy operation that someone—Alik, probably—was about to get busted for. It would be a big headache for Yuri, and a public relations nightmare, but he could deal with it if anyone could. And Alik could handle a big fine and even a few years in federal prison. Those were the nice prisons, right? As opposed to the chain-gang prisons? And he'd be in the white-collar wing, surely.

It was tricky business, making à la carte decisions about loyalties, and my plan still left out Chai and Crispin, and that's what I couldn't reconcile. Was Yuri capable of murder? Or condoning murder?

Wasn't anyone who was in the business of espionage?

Except me. I couldn't kill anyone, and I was in the espionage business. Sort of.

I knew at the very least that Yuri hadn't killed those two kids. Why would he? If he'd been frightened of Chai blabbing about his paramilitary stuff, he wouldn't then tell me all about it, as he'd done last night. No. He'd said Chai knew nothing about the spy training, and I believed him. Besides, if Yuri had killed Crispin, he'd have done a better job of body disposal, dumped him farther from the compound, not gone hiking there the next day.

Someone at MediasRex had done a double murder, or two single murders, but it wasn't Yuri. I didn't want it to be Yuri. Father issues, apparently. Of course, I was still left with the problem of who had done the murders, but as long as it wasn't Stasik, my date du jour, I was going to put it aside for a few hours.

I stuck the unplanted bug in my pocket and the DVD in my purse. I'd call Yogi Yogurt on the way to Santa Barbara, meet with Bennett Graham, hand over the DVD, turn in my resignation, keep the feds' secret from Yuri, keep his secret from them—my God, this was complicated. Did it make me a double agent, not ratting out Yuri to the feds? Or was I a double agent only if Yuri thought I wouldn't rat him out and then I did rat him out? Or was I a double agent if I told Yuri about the feds? I asked myself these questions in the mirror as I flossed my teeth, but I had no answers. I needed a spy dictionary.

Stasik gave me a hard time before we were out of the garage. For starters, he was dressed in a black T-shirt with cargo pants and hiking boots, while I wore Armani silk shantung pants and a satin shirt of the same color, eggshell. I'd thought I made a good choice, as it reeked of class—even Lucrezia would say so—and there was no chance I'd be having parking-lot sex today. Plus, it wouldn't hurt to impress Mrs. Winterbottom when I went to pick up P.B. But my elegance was wasted on Stasik, and next to him I felt all wrong, like crêpe suzette alongside a roast beef sandwich. And, as Yuri had predicted, Stasik was in high dudgeon over not being allowed to drive. I only got him to wear a seat belt by threatening to use the slow lane all the way to Santa Barbara.

"Do you even like to drive?" he asked, buckling up with bad grace. "They couldn't find someone for this bloody job who likes doing it?"

"This bloody job requires a little bit more than chauffeuring," I snapped. "Like a talent for—excuse me." My phone, hitting cell signal range, came to life. "Hello?"

"Wollie? Kimberly. What's your AO?"

"Excuse me?"

"Sorry. Where are you? I need you to pick up Zbiggo on Old Topanga, just east of Mulholland Highway. We're on the hiking trail and he's falling apart on me."

"No problem," I said. "Should I take him home, then? Or—"

"No, I need you to look after him today. If he's on his own, he gets into trouble. If it's not booze, it's food. Or worse. You don't want to know."

"The thing is, I've got Stasik, it's our big date, we're heading to Santa Barbara—"

"Take Zbiggo too. He'll like Santa Barbara. I'll square it with Yuri now."

I did an awkward U-turn, to Stasik's amused contempt, and six minutes later saw Kimberly, cell to her ear, flagging me down. Zbiggo sat under a nearby tree, head between his knees. Felix sat next to him, cross-legged, reading. I pulled over onto the dirt shoulder.

"Hey, guys," Kimberly said, then into her cell, "Sweetheart, what the hell do you expect me to do? I can't clone her . . . Okay, but take it easy. You're doing forty thousand things and you're not twenty anymore."

She hung up. "Yuri made reservations for all of you at Via Vai, in Santa Barbara. Felix is now joining you. I know, it's not optimal dating circumstances, but do what you can. Write up a full report. Yuri loved yesterday's, by the way, especially the illustrations, but next time use the computer. Gotta be typed. Didn't anyone go over that in the orientation? Okay, I gotta run. Good luck."

"Okay, but wait—shouldn't I take the guys back to the compound to change clothes?"

"No time. Friday traffic to Santa Barbara sucks, even at ten a.m. Also . . ." She pulled me aside and whispered into my ear. "Zbiggo's doing drugs. Grusha keeps finding pills squirreled away in his room. Not a good day for him to be on the loose, because sheriff's deputies are starting to show up again, out on the trail, investigating that poor kid's death. There was a thing in the paper, that they're waiting on the autopsy report. Yuri says there are reporters at the guard gate. Anyhow, he wants the trainees gone, especially Zbiggo."

"Okay. No problem," I said.

Of course, once we were all in the Suburban and headed to the freeway, I realized there was a problem. Zbiggo, twenty minutes into the expedition, roused himself from his post-hike stupor to ask when we'd be home.

"We're not going home," I said, glancing in the rearview mirror. "Didn't Kimberly tell you? We're all going to Santa Barbara for the day."

When comprehension set in, Zbiggo started bellowing in Russian.

Stasik bellowed right back at him, also in Russian, and then all hell broke loose.

Zbiggo was way in the back, but he unbuckled his seat belt, apparently to come up front and hijack the Suburban. He made his move, which I saw in the mirror as I negotiated the traffic on the 101 North. I'd let out no more than an aghast "Ackk!" when Stasik, next to me, had his seat belt unbuckled and was diving over the front console into the back. Felix, just behind me, moved at the same time to intercept Zbiggo.

I was sure that Felix and Stasik were no match for a professional heavyweight boxer, but I was wrong. After more Russian—including a lot of *tvoyu mats*—Zbiggo was out cold. Or else meditating.

I squinted into the mirror. "He's—he's not dead, is he?" I asked, seeing Zbiggo on the floor at Felix's feet.

"He's not dead, and he's damned lucky he's not," Stasik said. "Bloody idiot."

"Don't worry," Felix said. "Zbiggo is just suddenly tired. This happens in life."

"Can you get him to wear a seat belt?" I asked. "Zbiggo? Are you awake? Zbiggo! You need to buckle up." No answer from Zbiggo. "Guys, he needs to be buckled up, honestly. They give tickets for that. Shall I get off at the next exit or pull over?"

"No need," Felix said cheerfully, and he and Stasik got Zbiggo up into a seat and trussed him in. Zbiggo's head flopped over. He really did look dead. Again. Great. Half my job seemed to be driving an unconscious or dead world heavyweight contender around Southern California.

I turned my attention back to the road. He had to be unconscious. There was no way to spin this in a report to Yuri, that one team member had been killed by the other two in some sort of Vulcan death grip.

My phone rang. It was Fredreeq. "Where are you?" she asked.

"Halfway to Santa Barbara," I said.

"No way! I'm in Oxnard. Meet me."

"I can't meet you," I said. "I've got a carload of men that I'm supposed to be dating, one of whom may be—never mind that. What are you doing in Oxnard?"

"My cousin Ramone's gallbladder operation—never mind that. I've got something that is going to blow your mind. I'll get back to you." She hung up.

I wasn't sure I wanted my mind blown, especially if it had anything to with gallbladders. I drove on.

My phone rang again. Joey this time. "Where in Santa Barbara are you going to be?"

"Haven Lane to see P.B., and then Via Vai," I said. "Are you in Oxnard too?"

"Yes," Joey said. "Can you stop on the way up? Fredreeq scored something big."

"Oxnard?" Stasik's head whipped around. "I want to see Oxnard."

"No, you don't," I said. "There's nothing happening in Oxnard."

"That's not true," Felix said. "I believe there is—"

"What?" Stasik asked, glancing back at him.

"Nothing. Only I have always wanted to see Oxnard."

"Joey," I said back into the phone, "Oxnard seems to be very popular all of a sudden. But I'm supposed to get everyone to Santa Barbara and the traffic's bad and—"

"Oxnard's two minutes out of your way. Take the Vineyard exit and we'll be at the IHOP. You won't regret it."

I had just hung up when the phone rang again. "What?" I yelled into it.

"Wollie? Bennett Graham."

"Oh. Hello."

"I understand you have a package to deliver. Where are you?"

"Uh—101 North, heading to Santa Barbara."

"You have the package with you now?"

"Yes," I said, glancing at my purse.

"The nature of the package?"

"And I haven't had a chance to, uh, view the contents, lacking the, uh, necessary device and an opportunity, but I think you'll find it—"

"Good enough. When will you return to your base of operations?"

"No idea. Late afternoon, maybe."

"Keep your cell phone on. I'd like to accept delivery today, so I may have someone come and find you."

"May I ask something? If certain people in Calabasas are unaware—innocent—as far as this—thingy—goes, would you leave them alone? Would you single out just the key player?"

"Why is this relevant?"

"I'm just curious."

"This is something best discussed in person. Santa Barbara, you say?"

"If you hurry, you could find me in Oxnard," I said. "I might be stopping there. Through no fault of my own."

I lost the cell signal, and lost the vote, as everyone but Zbiggo seemed smitten with the city of Oxnard. Or, as none of us really knew Oxnard, the concept of Oxnard. Bowing to the collective consciousness, I got off the 101 North four exits later.

The International House of Pancakes, despite its cosmopolitan name, had a tired, small-town feel to it, at odds with the "Come Hungry, Leave Happy" motto emblazoned on everything in sight. The host, gathering up oversized menus, seemed put out by the number in our party—Zbiggo, praise God, was now conscious and even walking—although it seemed to me that four new customers wasn't cause for alarm in a restaurant with a maximum occupancy of 164 and only two tables filled.

Fredreeq and Joey waved to us from a booth in the back. Zbiggo was not so groggy that he couldn't maneuver a spot next to Fredreeq, even before I could make introductions, but then he lapsed back into a state of stupor. Stasik sat next to Joey. The host resisted the request for an extra chair, so Felix and I squeezed ourselves in on each end. Then I squeezed myself out again so that Stasik could use the men's room. This put me next to Joey. Or, rather, next to Joey's purse.

"Look," she said, pulling from it a worn book with a faded cover illustrated with daisies. "Pay dirt."

"What is it?" I asked.

She leaned to whisper in my ear. "Chai's diary."

I gasped. "You're kidding. Where'd you get this?"

"Her mom," Joey said, sotto voce. "Chai visited her mom shortly before she died and left it there. And we've read it all." Joey pointed out the bits of IHOP napkin stuck in the entries they felt were pertinent.

"Um, Felix?" I said, unable to contain myself. "Zbiggo should walk around. Would you like to show him that machine over there? The one with those little balls of gum in it?"

"The gumball machine?"

"Yes. Exactly. In fact, I'd like to take some gumballs to Santa Barbara." I began searching through my purse for coins.

"Why?"

"In America, it's customary to take a housewarming present when you go to visit someone. Someone's house. In this case, a halfway house. Where my brother lives."

"The custom is gumballs?"

"Not gumballs, per se. Gumballs is one option."

"How many gumballs?"

"As many as you can manage." I dumped a collection of coins on the table. Fredreeq added to the stash from her own purse. "Zbiggo?" I said. "Wake up, Zbiggo. Gumball time."

We roused Zbiggo from his coma and got him to accompany Felix. I turned to Joey and Fredreeq. "So you read the whole thing? How long have you guys been sitting here?"

"Not that long," Joey said. "Chai was not a deep thinker. You won't find a lot of philosophical insights."

"What will I find?" I asked, flipping through it. It was only half-filled, stopping midentry with the words *he's so cute, he'd be perfect if he just wouldn't always be so—*

"Poison."

"What do you mean, like negativity?" I asked.

"No, poison. Chai was being poisoned."

I looked up, a sick feeling sweeping over me. "What were the symptoms?"

Joey took the book and flipped through it to a napkin-marked page near the end and handed it back. I read it.

Icky feeling again. Couldn't go out with Vlad tonight. Wasted. No wine even at dinner—worse than yesterday and now I'm like too sick to smoke, so that's good, and not gaining any weight, so that's super-good, but like zero energy. Crummy tummy. Everything Grusha makes looks really gross to eat. And scaly hands and feet super-creepy and Donatella gave me her Borghese tonic, the Effecto Inmediato! which I could NOT believe she would let me use, but like useless. Then! This morning clumps of hair in my hairbrush. Gross! Me! Out! I like can't stop crying cuz my HAIR!!! Plus, no clue! Mom's like, Don't tell anyone, you'll get canned! If I tell Kimberly, number one, she makes me do the carrot juice colonic. No way. And now I'm on probation,

Yuri hears this and that's it. Over. So I can't be too sick to work. Only, I'm kind of too sick to care. But it's cool to be super-skinny but no energy to even think about new shots for my book or go-sees and who'd want me with scaly skin and bald anyway? Next year flu shot <u>definitely</u>! Not going through this again.

I looked up. "Chai's mom just gave this to you? Her dead child's last words?"

"We told her we'd immortalize her dead child."

Fredreeq leaned over the table. "Joey and I are a writing team. We do celebrity biographies. Classy stuff. Nothing cheesy."

"What do you mean, you're a writing team?" I asked. "Since when?"

"Since the early seventies," Fredreeq said. "We have quite a résumé. We write under the pen name Katie Kelly. The mom was pretty sure she's heard of us."

"Oh, my God," I muttered. "I can't believe you guys. I hope you plan to return this."

"We have to," Joey said. "We gave her a two-hundred-dollar deposit."

"Treat it nicely," Fredreeq said, then looked up.

Zbiggo and Felix were approaching with a plastic takeout container full of gumballs. "Zbiggo?" Fredreeq said. "I'm getting you chocolate chip pancakes with little pats of butter and mounds of luscious whipped cream, the kind of thing you won't find in the Kremlin."

"Fredreeq," I said. "Ixnay on that. We're eating in Santa Barbara in an hour."

"He's a growing boy," Fredreeq said, making room as Zbiggo squeezed into the booth. "And look at these nice muscles. Zbiggo, you are just all man, aren't you? My husband, Francis, is a big fan of yours and I'm going to need an autographed photo of you to give him for Christmas. And ringside seats at your next fight. How many calories do you eat while you're in training?"

The waitress came and saved Zbiggo from having to actually speak. Felix did a creditable job of ordering a shrimp Caesar salad minus the shrimp, the croutons, and the dressing, just as we'd practiced in Beverly Hills, and Fredreeq ordered the promised pancakes, against my wishes. I now had poison on the brain. Not only did I feel distinctly unwell, I was

worried that Zbiggo might vomit in the Suburban. Didn't that happen
with people who'd been knocked out and were possibly suffering con-
cussions? Also, might he not be detoxing? The mere thought of semi-
digested chocolate chip pancakes was enough to make me ill too. Or
was Chai's diary entry making me ill?

"Joey," I whispered. "Isn't it possible Chai really did just have a bad
case of flu?"

Joey took a sip of water. "Nope. Poison."

I sat back in the booth and closed my eyes. I had to stop focusing on
this. I was feeling sicker by the moment.

"How's your appetite?" Joey asked. "You're looking a little peaked
yourself."

I opened my eyes and looked at her. "I'm fine. Perfect health. I'm
never sick." In general, this was true.

"You didn't order anything."

"I told you, we're having lunch in Santa Barbara." I turned to the
boys. "Zbiggo? Felix? In America, it's a cultural imperative to wash your
hands before eating. Why don't you two go to the men's room and do
that right now? And find Stasik." I waited till they were gone, then said,
"What are you guys saying? That MediasRex is poisoning me? Because
it's ridiculous. Who would do that? Why would they?"

Fredreeq reached over and touched a lock of my hair.

"What are you doing?" I asked, alarmed.

"Just checking."

"My hair? Why? It's not falling out, is it?"

"It's hard to say."

"No, it's not," I said. "Because I'd notice. If I'd lost any hair at all, even
a few strands, I'd be bald. I have bad hair. My hair's been through a lot,
and on that score alone I can't afford to be poisoned."

"Calm down," Joey said. "Just because Chai was poisoned, if she was
poisoned, doesn't mean that you're being poisoned."

"But I'd go easy on the borscht," Fredreeq said.

"Borscht? That's bush league," Joey said. "There was a Bulgarian dissident in the seventies who was jabbed with a poison umbrella tip."

"Guys," I said. "You're giving me the creeps. Because this actually does make sense and would explain why they'd stage a car crash for Chai. But wouldn't poison show up in an autopsy?"

"If there was an autopsy," Fredreeq said.

"I imagine there was," Joey said, "but they don't routinely test car-crash victims for poison. It's expensive, running tests. Unless they had reason to suspect poison. But a model being underweight doesn't ex-actly sound an alarm."

"Wouldn't her mom sound an alarm?" I asked.

"Strictly trailer park," Fredreeq said.

"Not a Rhodes scholar," Joey said, nodding. "And the diary doesn't say she was poisoned, we inferred it. Chai herself didn't suspect it."

"Tell her about the Prius," Fredreeq said.

"Yuri Milos gave the mom a Prius."

"A *car*? Holy cow," I said. "Most people send flowers."

"A white Prius," Fredreeq. "Very environmentally conscious. He told the mom it would've been Chai's Christmas bonus. The mom thinks he walks on water."

"But did Chai write anything about secret DVDs? Or Alik Milos?"

"No," Joey said, "but she alludes to 'our little secret,' so that's probably—" She stopped, and I looked over to see Zbiggo and Felix coming back to the table.

"Where's Stasik?" I asked. "Wasn't he in the bathroom?"

Zbiggo looked at me blankly. But Felix's eyes opened wide. "No! He is not here, then?" He looked around, then hurried back toward the rest-rooms.

I got out of the booth and walked around the restaurant distractedly, with Joey right behind me. "Stasik's the putative country and western singer?" she asked.

"Yes," I said, checking the ladies' room. No Stasik. "What do you mean, 'putative'?"

"Fredreeq and I listened to his CD. He can't sing for shit. I've heard vacuum cleaners with better vocal quality."

"But where is he? I'm checking the kitchen."

"I'll see if there's a back room."

I had a distinct feeling of déjà vu, thinking of Felix being lost the day before. First Tiffany's, now IHOP. I stuck my head into the kitchen. No Felix. A moment later Joey met up with me back at the hostess station. "He's not in the employees' locker room," she said.

"He is not with the syrup cans," Felix said, which I took to mean stockroom.

We headed outside.

Joey and I searched the parking lot while Felix went farther afield, to the CVS pharmacy, but we all knew it was hopeless. It wasn't as if Stasik had wandered off or been kidnapped. He was gone with the wind, and of his own volition. How was I supposed to write this up in my report to Yuri? These men didn't need a social coach, they needed ankle bracelets.

And who was Stasik anyway? Not a singer, obviously. An aggressive, knife-wielding . . . an image of Crispin, stabbed in the face, rose up before me. Was that Stasik's real talent?

I was momentarily distracted by Joey, who was standing between a pickup truck and a motorcycle, looking disoriented. "Joey?" I asked. "What is it?"

My voice seemed to break the spell. She visibly shook herself and then looked over at me. "My car's gone."

FORTY-ONE

"Call my cell phone," Joey said. "I left it on the front seat of my car."

I did. Her voice mail answered.

"Stasik," I said after the beep. "Just in case you're there and figured out how to pick up Joey's messages, let me impress upon you the need to come back. All is forgiven. I won't call the cops, I won't even write this into my report to Yuri, that you're driving a hot car. We'll just forget it. But you have to come back right now because I don't know how they do things in Belarus or Ukraine—sorry, I can't remember where you're from—but here in America, you get deported for stealing a car. It's a big deal. In California, you're better off kidnapping a person. Depending on the car. Joey's is a Mercedes, so that's serious. Call me." *Unless you're a murderer,* I added mentally. *In that case, don't call.*

Joey grabbed my phone. "I want my goddamn car back, and if you harm it in any way, I will shoot you, you motherf—"

I pried the phone from her and repeated my cell number and then added, "If this isn't Stasik, if this is some other carjacker, I'd ditch the car and run for your life. My friend's got a gun and she's always looking for an excuse to use it." I hung up.

"Except that my gun's in the car," Joey said.

"Oh," I said. "Well, maybe he won't find it."

"He won't, unless he looks in the most obvious place. The glove box." We both thought about that, standing in the empty parking place formerly occupied by Joey's aging Mercedes. Felix joined us.

"Felix," I said, assailed by a horrible thought. "Why would Stasik steal Joey's car?"

"He what?!" Felix let forth a string of phrases peppered with the ubiquitous *tvoyu mat*. This was very un-Felix-like.

"Listen," I said. "I need to know what you know about this." What I'd do with the information, I wasn't yet sure, but I wanted to confirm my guess that Stasik was a spy, on a secret spy mission.

But Felix took a deep breath and said, "How strange a thing for Stasik to do this. I have no idea why. Okay, let us go to Santa Barbara and not give him more of our brain thoughts." He moved resolutely back toward the IHOP entrance.

Joey threw me a sideways glance with raised eyebrows, clearly communicating, "What's up with this guy?" and we followed him into the restaurant.

Back at the table, Fredreeq expressed outrage, but no surprise. "Of course he has to resort to stealing cars. He's completely talent-free. If that man is a singing star in some other country, it's a country I do not want to visit."

The only person undisturbed by the turn of events was Zbiggo, now plowing through a mountain of pancakes, oblivious to the dots of melted chocolate accumulating on his face and T-shirt. I would have to buy him some new clothes to get around Santa Barbara in.

I had just called Via Vai to push our reservation back an hour when my cell rang. It was Stasik. "Something's come up, love," he said, shocking me with his sudden use of endearments. "Had to borrow your friend's Mercedes, sorry, but I'll take good care of it and have it back at the pancake place late afternoon. Go on without me. Perhaps you could swing by the IHOP on your way back to pick me up? Or not. I could hitchhike to Calabasas."

"Whoa, whoa, whoa," I said, unnerved by his conciliatory tone. "First, what in the—"

"And no hurry. I'll need a few hours here. Must run."

"But—" And then I was talking to dead air.

"Okay, we may as well go," I said. "Since we have no idea where he is. Joey, do you and Fredreeq want to come to Santa Barbara with us, or—"

"Yes," Fredreeq said. "If the alternative is Amtrak or a day at IHOP, God in heaven, yes."

"There's Greyhound," Joey said.

"I don't do buses. We'll go to Santa Barbara. Anyway, I miss P.B."

The waitress came by to pick up the cash I'd plunked down. "He didn't eat his Caesar," she said accusingly, looking at Felix. "Something else I can get you folks?"

"A ride home," Joey said.

"That's right," Fredreeq said. "How about some parking-lot security? What's that saying you have, 'Come Hungry, Leave in Someone Else's Car'?"

"We're good, thanks," I said to the downtrodden waitress. "In fact, we'll be back later."

"Lucky me," she said.

Santa Barbara is the pride of Southern California, with more class and culture and money per capita than Los Angeles. There was, naturally, an urban underbelly, but it wasn't apparent coming off the freeway at Las Positas, passing the verdant green of a golf course. It became more obvious as I got closer to my brother's residence. Haven Lane was in a middle-class neighborhood, indistinguishable from its neighbors. It needed an exterior paint job and was a little grubby around the edges, but had a thriving flower garden and a white picket fence, fighting to avoid the appearance of institutional living.

Felix, Zbiggo, Fredreeq, and Joey accompanied me into the house despite my efforts to dissuade them. Zbiggo, now fully recovered, was displaying an edgy quality that made him a less-than-ideal car companion. Even for Fredreeq, the thrill was gone. The five of us crammed into the parlor that functioned as a reception area, and I gave Mrs. Winterbottom everyone's name, which she painstakingly wrote down in a log. This took a while.

"Zbiggo," Fredreeq said, "keep your hands to yourself, or I will have to shoot you."

Mrs. Winterbottom looked up. Zbiggo stepped back.

"We have a no-firearms policy," Mrs. Winterbottom said, "that we take seriously."

"It was a figure of speech," Fredreeq said.

"We also ban knives, scissors, sharp objects, rocks, shaving cream, chalk, permanent marker, free weights, fireworks, explosives, aerosol cans, baseball bats, and adult beverages."

"You run a tight ship," Joey said.

"Does anyone wish to check any contraband with me?" Mrs. Winterbottom asked, eyeing Felix's backpack.

"We won't be staying long enough to do that," I said. "As I told you on the phone, we're just here to take P.B. out to lunch."

"Well, you're too late for that. His uncle came and checked him out."

"You couldn't have told us that before signing us all in?" Fredreeq asked. "Did you think we came here to visit *you*?"

"If you mean my Uncle Theo," I said hastily, seeing Mrs. Winterbottom's chest puff up in affront, "that can't be right. Uncle Theo doesn't drive."

"He was driven by a young man named—" Mrs. Winterbottom checked her log. "Apollo Sp—Spanikopita?"

Zbiggo moved in, as if he might help her by reading upside down.

"Stephanopoulos," I said, growing alarmed. "Okay, this isn't good. Where did they go, do you know?"

"Yes, I do, but before we get to that, we have to discuss a few things, Miss Shelley. Such as your brother's lack of cooperation with yard work and flouting of curfew, which he's missed by as much as twenty minutes on many an evening. Also—"

"Are your breasts real?" Zbiggo asked.

Mrs. Winterbottom gasped. "I beg your pardon?"

"Your breasts." He elongated the word, rolling the *r* in an exaggerated manner.

"This is Santa Barbara, Zbiggo," Joey said. "Not Hollywood. People here keep their body parts intact."

"Except for Michael Jackson," Fredreeq said.

Mrs. Winterbottom now had two bright red spots on her cheeks, as if indignation caused fever.

"Mrs. Winterbottom," I said. "Tell us where they've gone and we'll leave you in peace. I'm sorry to tell you that you have—unwittingly, of course—delivered my brother into the care of two people who are not licensed drivers. I'll overlook that, but you need to tell me where he is before it becomes a legal issue and reaches the ears of the board of directors."

The last three words were the magic ones. Mrs. Winterbottom dragged her eyes from Felix and fixed them on me. "The mission," she snapped.

"He's on a mission?"

"Santa Barbara's Old Mission. For I Madonnari. They're off to look at your square."

"My—what?"

"The square that was bought. By Mrs. Hays. City council. For your drawing."

"What are you talking about?"

"Are you deaf? The Chalk Festival, fool."

I must have looked stupid enough to warrant the insult. With a huff, Mrs. Winterbottom stood, turned her back, and exposed her considerable bottom to us as she opened a filing cabinet behind her.

"Here," she said, straightening up. She extracted from a file a piece of paper stapled to a brochure and handed it over. "And if by this dumb-bunny routine you mean you've forgotten or will not meet your obligation, exposing Haven Lane to public humiliation, leaving an empty square, paid for and donated to us by Mrs. Hays, our valued benefactress—" She took a deep breath. "Well, let me just assure you that your brother will suffer the consequences of your irresponsibility and lack of professionalism. Does he want to remain at Haven Lane?"

"Yes!" I said. "Of course he—"

"Would you care to see the waiting list ready to take his place? You better learn which side your brother's bread is buttered on. You agreed to a portrait of the Blessed Virgin that will move and inspire, and that's what you'll produce. Or else. Because I have just about had it with you and your family. Do you hear me? I have *had* it."

"You have had it," Felix said, nodding.

I was trying to absorb the contents of the paper I was reading, with Joey and Fredreeq looking over my shoulder. It was an application, approved, specifying a twelve-by-twelve-foot square bought and paid for by a Mrs. Jake Hays on behalf of Haven Lane, for the Memorial Day weekend street-painting festival of I Madonnari. A box was checked next to "We will provide our own volunteer street painter." The name of the artist was filled in, along with the address and phone number. The handwriting was my brother's.

The artist, of course, was me.

FORTY-TWO

"'Madonnari,'" Joey said, reading from the brochure, "'is an annual festival based on the Italian chalk festival of the same name. The plaza of the Old Mission will be transformed with two hundred colorful, large-scale street paintings. The artists, or madonnari'—so-called because of their obsession with the Madonna, I presume—blah, blah, blah. 'For twenty-five thousand annual visitors—'"

"Twenty-five thousand?" I screamed. I drove wildly through the streets of Santa Barbara, or as wildly as possible, given the sluggishness of traffic and the occasional dead stops. All twenty-five thousand visitors must have been behind the wheel at that moment, driving badly.

"'Artwork must be appropriate for public viewing,'" Joey went on. "'No words or symbols intended as advertising may appear within the image.'"

"Can I use acrylic?" I asked. "I'm at home with acrylic. I could toss off a decent Madonna in an hour, in acrylic."

"'Only chalk pastels in a solid form may be used for the street painting, no acrylic paints, liquid pastels, et cetera, are acceptable.' The good news is, they provide the chalk."

"I don't do chalk! Chalk's not my medium! I suck at chalk!"

"But this is opportunity," Felix said. "Maybe, after today, you don't suck at chalk."

"But the learning curve takes time," I said. "I'm slow. I'm plodding. Contemplative. I'm a plodding, contemplative, poky artist. That's how I work. I'm a dawdler."

"So change your style. Do it fast and sloppy," Fredreeq said.

"I can't," I yelled. "Twenty-five thousand people are going to be looking at it!"

"Do we know the peoples?" Zbiggo asked.

"It doesn't matter. My name is on it."

"Professional ethics," Felix said. "Yes. I understand."

"So why you don't quit?" Zbiggo asked. "Just to quit, that is best."

"I can't quit, Zbiggo. You heard Mrs. Winterbottom. If I disappoint her, she'll take it out on my brother. She's mad now, but add to that social humiliation and it's all over for P.B. If he gets kicked out of this halfway house, it's a catastrophe. There is no good ending to that scenario. And Mrs. Winterbottom can make it happen." Even with government intervention, on orders from the FBI—assuming the feds did in fact back me up—in a fight between Mrs. Winterbottom and Bennett Graham, it was probably a dead heat. "If twenty-five thousand people see a blank square where Haven Lane is supposed to have a Virgin Mary in chalk—"

"Forget the peoples," Zbiggo said. "Is the chalks. You fight the chalks, you make the chalks fear, you see only the chalks, you don't see the peoples, you don't think the peoples."

It was so unexpected, to get motivational advice from Zbiggo, that I had no response. And how did one instill fear in a stick of chalk?

"Petition the Virgin to make you draw fast," Felix suggested.

"You *can* draw fast," Joey said. "I've seen you sketch greeting cards in seconds."

"That's different," I said. "Line drawings. Black and white. Small. Impressionistic. Which I can tear up and rework until I'm satisfied." I honked at a Viper trying to cut me off. "Twelve feet by twelve feet? That's gigantic. That's bigger than my last apartment! In chalk! Chalk's not my medium! I can't do it!"

"Calm down, Frida Kahlo," Fredreeq said. "How come you didn't get the word on this till ten minutes ago?"

"Because P.B. volunteered me without telling me, obviously. And forged my signature, for all I know. Joey, where are we?"

"Couple more blocks, then left on Laguna," she said, consulting a map.

"This mission, is it a government building?" Felix asked.

"I guess," Joey said. "It's a historical landmark. They're all over California, these missions."

"Monuments to past popes," Fredreeq said, "who imposed their tacky religious values on the Native Americans, taking away their peyote and sweat lodges, and now we spend tax dollars to preserve the buildings so that bored schoolkids who would rather be working on their soccer skills are forced to take field trips and write term papers on them, in clear violation of the separation between church and state."

"Interesting perspective, Fredreeq," Joey said.

"I'm quoting my ninth grader. I typed the term paper. She broke her wrist at soccer."

"So this building is federal?" Felix asked.

There was a moment of silence. "That's a strange question," I said, looking in the rearview mirror. And a rather arcane distinction, for a guy who was still working on the English for "dressing on the side." Felix avoided my eye in the mirror.

"I think those friars still run them," Fredreeq said. "So I guess they belong to the Vatican. But why exactly do we care about this?"

"Here's what I care about," I said. "Does anyone in this car have artistic talent? Or a feel for chalk?"

This was met with a chorus of no's. I was not surprised. Drawing scares some people the way singing scares me.

There was no way out. I was the responsible party.

I took a deep breath. Everyone could go off to lunch without me. I'd collect my designated chalk, find my designated square, and somehow crank out a substandard, half-baked image of the Blessed Virgin Mary, a thought that made me crabby to the point of madness. And a little nauseous. Unless that was me being poisoned.

First, though, I had to find P.B.

The mission grounds were bustling with prefestival activity. The mission itself was refreshingly authentic-looking, humble when compared to your average cathedral. It was white adobe with a red roof, adorned with medieval-looking flags. We walked past a fountain with just a trickle of water coming out and approached the artists' sector.

The blacktop parking-lot area surrounding the church steps was measured and marked with masking tape, creating rows of squares in various sizes. Each square featured the name of its sponsor, stenciled in chalk across the bottom, everything from Tri-County Court Reporters to the Afghanistan Dental Relief Project, Inc. My own square wasn't in view, as this area was reserved for smaller spaces. I longed for a nice, manageable four-by-six rectangle. Or even a seven-by-seven. Why twelve feet? That was me times two, laid end to end.

"This is fabulous," Fredreeq said. "I wish I'd brought my kids. This is a lot more cultural than paintball or bowling."

I might have agreed, had I been here as a civilian. A number of artists were already at work. They knelt on pieces of cardboard or scraps of rug. Some wore knee pads. Many worked from sketches, in some cases lithographs of old masters. There were grids and graph paper in evidence, and a few serious types used long sticks with the chalk on the far end to get a sweeping gesture from a standing position. Great. I had no props. No tools of the trade. I had a huge square, no ideas, no preparation. I didn't belong here. I was a fraud.

I moved my group along, anxious to find my brother.

Across from the parking lot was a large grassy lawn that was being filled up with tables and tents and vendor booths. "There they are," I said.

My brother wore ill-fitting cargo shorts and a T-shirt that said "Cat Lovers Against the Bomb" and had bits of grass in his hair, as though he'd been napping. My uncle was in his usual attire of natural fabrics, unironed. "Wollie!" he called, hopping up from the ground with more alacrity than one would expect in a man of his advanced years. "Wait until you see your canvas."

"It is a primo spot," Apollo said, jumping up too. "The whole world will see it."

"Great news." I hugged them. "Apollo, tell me you didn't drive here from Glendale."

"He's quite good," Uncle Theo said. "A better driver than even you, dear."

"That's nice to hear, Uncle Theo, but he doesn't have a license."

"Yes, but he's a very smart boy."

"He could be Wolfgang Amadeus Mozart, but he's still fifteen. The DMV doesn't have a genius exemption. And speaking of geniuses, P.B., what did you sign me up for?"

My brother looked up, his blue eyes shining. "Did you bring my book?"

"What?"

P.B.'s eyes narrowed. "*Superstrings and the Search for the Theory of Everything.* You didn't bring it."

"What am I, Supergirl? Explain this pastel thing, wouldja? What kind of opus is Mrs. Winterbottom expecting?"

"I can't believe you didn't bring it," he said. "I asked you five times this week—"

"Look!" I yelled. "My plate has been just a little bit full of late, and—"

"Children, children," Uncle Theo said, putting an arm around me. "Everything in its own time. Goodness, is that Joey? And Fredreeq! What a lovely day it's turning out to be. And is that Fredreeq's husband with her? A large fellow, isn't he?"

"Where?" I turned. "No, that's Zbiggo." The trio approached, and I started to get a bad feeling. I looked around, quickly, then back at Joey and Fredreeq.

"Where's Felix?" I called. But I knew the answer as the question hung in the air.

Gone. I'd lost another one.

FORTY-THREE

"Please God, don't let him have taken the Suburban," I said.

"No, we checked," Joey said. "It was the strangest thing. There one minute, gone the next. Hi, Uncle Theo. Hey, Apollo. Howdy, P.B."

I introduced Zbiggo to everyone and explained that I'd misplaced my other date, Felix. "He expressed an unusual interest in the mission," I said. "I'll take a look inside."

"You stay. I'm on it," Joey said, and jogged toward the building.

"Wollie, we'll find him," Fredreeq said. "You need to start drawing your Virgin. See that tent over there? That's where you sign in and get your free chalk."

"Free chalk," Uncle Theo said. "What a nice, unexpected treat."

"Wollie," P.B. said, "when are we going to the bookstore?"

"P.B.," I said, "not now."

"I would take you, P.B.," Apollo said, "but I don't have a license."

"I'll take you," Fredreeq said, "but not in that Belarusian bus we drove here in. Whose car did you steal, Apollo?"

"My cousin Archimedes has given me the Kia. It is tiny, but very fun."

"Forget it. We'll take the horse we rode in on. Keys, Wollie. Zbiggo, you stick with me. I'm not having you go missing too."

Uncle Theo accompanied me to the artist sign-in tent, where I was issued a new box of forty-eight pastels, something that, even in my current state of anxiety, evoked a little *ping!* of pleasure. No one is immune to the charm of a new box of colored chalk.

"Too bad you couldn't come to the chalk party two weeks ago," the chalk woman said, checking me off her list. "A lot of the artists made their own from pure pigments, much better than the commercial stuff. As you know."

"Do I?" I asked.

"You're the Haven Lane artist, right? Eleanor Winterbottom says you're topflight."

"She is topflight," Uncle Theo assured her.

"Oh, that Eleanor," I said. "Always so kind. But the truth is, I've never—" I stopped. Should Mrs. Winterbottom be contradicted?

The woman looked up. "Painted on a parking lot? No worries. It's nicely paved, and we just put a fresh seal coat on it. We do it every two years. Chalk sticks beautifully."

"How long do I have to work on it?" I asked.

"Until the sun goes down, and then all day tomorrow."

"Gotta finish today," I said.

She glanced at her watch. "Well, I hate to say anything's impossible. At any rate, sunset's at eight-oh-five. I know this because I've been looking it up for Samantha Tzu. She's squeezed every last minute out of the daylight, all week long. If you want a treat, go look at her work. She's our featured artist this year."

I looked to where she pointed. Directly in front of the mission entrance was a chained-off area with a woman inside, working on a huge painting. They'd have to chain me too, to work on something that big, and in public, I told Uncle Theo. But as we approached, my apprehension turned to awe. The painting was glorious. Botticelli might have been airlifted out of the fifteenth century and plunked down in Santa Barbara. A Madonna frolicked in a forest with seraphim and cherubim, along with some squirrels and a couple of greyhounds. It was nearly finished. Samantha must have begun it around Christmas.

"Look!" Uncle Theo said. "Everyone's eyes have the epicanthic fold."

The artist glanced at us, then returned to her work. I looked again. Uncle Theo was right; every cherub and angel and, most interestingly, the Madonna, looked Asian.

"Amazing," I said.

"Wonderful," Uncle Theo agreed. "My dear, I've been wondering all day, so put me out of my suspense: what will you paint?"

"Uncle Theo," I said, anxiety returning, "I haven't a clue."

Apollo stood by my twelve-foot square, a vast expanse of blacktop flanked on one side by "Channel Island Surfboards by Al Merrick" and on the other by "Gabby Mesquite, CPA." Both of my neighboring artists were hard at work on their squares, both working from photographs. The Gabby Mesquite artist was doing a credible reproduction of Monet's *Water Lilies,* which did not immediately evoke certified public accounting, but that was reassuring. It meant that I didn't have to somehow tie in Haven Lane with the Blessed Virgin Mary. My hellos to the two artists were met with a grunt on one side and a curt nod on the other. I envied them their single-minded focus on the task at hand. It beat the paralysis of fear.

"I thought you were off to the bookstore with P.B.," I said to Apollo.

"No, P.B. said I should stay behind," he said. "We have a mission."

"A mission at the mission!" Uncle Theo said.

"We are stalking Joseph Polchinski," Apollo said. "We were told he would be here."

"You're still stalking him?" I asked. "I thought you found him at Pepperdine."

"No, that was bad information. Not Polchinski at all. Joseph Polonsky."

"Polchinski deserves a wider following," Uncle Theo said. "I imagine he will be honored to be stalked by you. Ask him to expound upon the positive nature of dark energy."

"First I must discuss Maldacena duality," Apollo said. "And for P.B., Heterotic-O strings. We must stalk him again to get all the questions asked. Wollie, have you questions?"

"No. Just please don't be the kind of stalker that ends up in court," I said, and focused on the blacktop in front of me.

I had no real education in art beyond high school and the odd extension courses at community colleges. I was an on-the-job trainee. What I did have was a lot of experience in greeting cards and moderate experience with murals. My twelve-by-twelve square was something in between, neither miniature nor panoramic. In fact, it was just life-sized. Okay, larger than life. Like a giant. Or yes, an angel, if your angels were more Caravaggio, all grown up and sexy, as opposed to the cute Raphael cherubs.

Or like a superheroine.

I grabbed the application from my purse, along with a pen, and started sketching.

"Wollie," Uncle Theo said, "is that big fellow Zbiggo from Ukraine? I'm trying to place his accent."

"No. Moldova."

"Imagine not being able to distinguish Ukrainian from Moldovan. By the way, Mykola, my Ukrainian barber, gave me an update on the situation over there. There are rumors of Lukashenko entertaining ideas to develop the wetlands. He's already building nuclear energy plants, unthinkable just a few years ago. The country is very poor, so it's understandable, however distressing. There was an article in the last issue of *Welt am Sonntag,* a German newspaper. I was quite upset to learn of this, old tree hugger that I am. But *tonkey zvonek zvonit gromkey,* as Mykola says."

I turned and stared at him. "Wait a minute. You speak Russian." I did a quick sketch of the Cyrillic letters I had committed to memory. "Uncle Theo, what's this say?"

"*Poprobuji 31 Aromat, tebe legko budet osmotretsya—Udachi.*" Uncle Theo looked skyward. "Let me think. Ah, yes. A loose translation would be 'Thirty-one flavors. Easy to case the joint. Good luck.' Well. What do you suppose that means?"

My phone rang.

"Wollie, it's me," he said without preamble. Simon didn't bother with an alias this time, and he didn't bother to moderate his tone of voice. "I want to see you in an hour."

"Sorry, can't," I said. "Unless you happen to be in Santa Barbara."

"What are you doing there?"

"At this moment? Communing with the Blessed Virgin Mary."

"How soon can you get back to L.A.?"

"No idea."

"God*damn*it." He was breathing heavily enough for me to hear it, a hundred miles north. Was he exercising? "Okay, I'm coming to you. Where are you specifically?"

"Not that it's any of your business—"

"My business is exactly what it is. I can't f—" Another intake of breath. "Don't give me any grief right now. Okay? Time-out. Whatever you're mad about, put it on ice. This is serious, and the clock is ticking, for both of us."

"What do you mean?"

"I mean that you're in trouble and every minute counts. We can break up later, but right now, you've got to tell me where you are."

The words made my blood run cold. Unless that was the poison taking effect. "The Santa Barbara Mission," I said, and pressed the end button on my phone.

FORTY-FOUR

Apollo had borrowed graph paper from the Channel Island Surfboards by Al Merrick artist, explaining that the most rational way to transfer my pen sketch of the Blessed Virgin Mary to the blacktop was to work it out on a grid.

"Yes, so I gather," I said. "But I just got a phone call that was stressful to the point of hysteria, so I can't really concentrate on geometry, Apollo. It's not my métier. At the moment, I'm not sure I have a métier, but—"

"This is not even geometry," he said. "It is only a simple calculation of—"

"Apollo! Are you listening? If you talk numbers or algorithms or stringy theories, I'll start screaming. Where the hell is Felix?"

"I believe I see Joey over there," Uncle Theo said. "Perhaps she found something."

My phone rang again.

"Bennett Graham," he said, halfway through my hello. "Where precisely are you?"

"The Santa Barbara Mission."

"Don't leave until we make contact."

"But—but—"

Too late. He hung up. My phone rang again instantly. I answered.

"Wollie? Yuri."

"H-hello, Yuri," I said. "What's up?"

"I want you to come home."

"N-now?"

"Is something wrong?" he asked.

"Uh—no. Everything's fine. Relatively speaking."

"You sound uncertain."

"No, no, I'm certain." No one was dead, right? That I knew of. Today, anyway.

"Fine. I'll see you in about ninety minutes," he said.

"Wait! Okay, we're right in the middle of things and the car is a little bit of a walk," I said, and looked up to see Joey walking toward me. Felix was definitely not with her. Damn.

"You didn't use valet parking?"

"Where? Oh! No, we—the boys—wanted to meander before hitting the restaurant."

"Two hours, then. Hurry before traffic gets bad."

"But the boys—it's going to take some time to round them up and also my brother is . . . a little needy. At the moment." Joey was standing in front of me now, signaling. "So P.B. may need a little transition time, since we were expecting to spend the afternoon togeth—"

"How long?" Yuri asked. "An hour?"

"An hour?" I repeated. Joey shook her head. "An hour's ambitious, Yuri. How about if I leave here around . . . sundown?"

"Sundown? What are you saying, eight o'clock tonight?"

"Eight-oh-five," I said.

"Unacceptable, Wollie. You've got sixty minutes to pack up and say your goodbyes. Call me when you're on the road. I want progress reports."

"Okay, but—" I looked at my sketch. "I'm in the middle of something that—"

"Finish it, whatever it is. You've got an hour. And Wollie?"

"What?"

"You haven't yet disappointed me. Don't begin now."

I hung up and looked at Joey.

"Felix," she said, "is inside the mission. He's being held by the Santa Barbara police."

FORTY-FIVE

was on my feet instantly. "Okay, when you say 'held' do you mean under arrest?"

"Possibly," Joey said. "It looks like pre-arrest right now, but it could turn official at any moment. By the way, that outfit is beautiful, so I hope you have a good dry cleaner."

I glanced down at my chalk-encrusted eggshell shantung pants, threw a "Be right back" to Uncle Theo and Apollo, and took off with Joey toward the mission. My heart was racing faster than my feet. What had Felix done? Cased the joint, like he'd done at Tiffany's? To what end? And how was I to spring him, having no aptitude for obfuscation and possessed by an innate fear of police, no doubt having to do with my "father issues"?

Inside the mission I paused, letting my eyes adjust to the indoors. The chapel was beautiful, in a smallish, missiony sort of way, and powerful, in an old sort of way, the air thick with the resonance of a few hundred years of prayers. I added mine to the mix, genuflecting and making the sign of the cross with holy water. "Dear God, help me get Felix out of here and not in handcuffs either, Amen." I hadn't been truly Catholic since childhood, but when in Rome . . .

"Over here," Joey whispered, and led me to the only occupied pews.

Felix sat between two cops, one of whom stood as we approached. In the pew in front of them, facing backward, was a man dressed as a friar. Unless—yes, he probably *was* a friar.

"No visitors at the moment," the standing cop said to me.

"It's okay, I'm with him. Fe—" I stopped. Felix was shaking his head in tiny, tic-like shakes. "Fee, fi, fo, fum," I finished. "Sorry, my mind's on my chalk drawing. What's my friend doing here?"

"Which square is yours?" the friar asked. "Who's your sponsor?"

"Haven Lane," I said. "It's a group living facility for—"

"We know Haven Lane," the sitting cop said. *Nut jobs,* I imagined him thinking.

Felix looked at me with chagrin. "Wollie, I tell them just now I am Brad—"

"You? Quiet," the standing cop said, then turned to me. "You? Name."

"His name?" I stared at Felix, stricken. *Brad?*

"Your name," the cop said.

"Oh, *my* name. Wollie Shelley. I'm an artist." Felix was staring at me, eyes bulging, trying to communicate the right answer. This felt like *The Newlywed Game.* "But not only an artist," I said and Felix nodded slightly. "I am also, uh—"

"What's your relationship to this guy?" the talking cop asked.

"We . . . date."

Felix's eyes were nearly popping out of his head now. Wrong answer.

"In a manner of speaking!" I said quickly. "I'm more of a transportation facilitator. And Fe—Brad—is my responsibility and I misplaced him. He doesn't know our customs, being from Ukraine." Felix was frowning, hard. "Sorry. I mean . . . Belarus?"

Felix frowned harder.

"British Columbia," Joey said. My friend had no problem lying.

"Anyhow, totally my fault that he wandered in here, and now I need to get him back."

"Is your chalk drawing finished?" the friar asked.

"No. I mean, when it's finished, I need to get him back. By the way, what did he do?"

"I'd like to see your driver's license," the talking cop said. "Your friend was snooping behind the altar."

"Oh, I can explain that," I said, looking through my purse. "Brad is very spiritual."

"Jesus freak," Joey said.

"Jesus made him skinny," I said, but Felix coughed. "Which is neither here nor there. The point is, he's intrigued by representational art—"

"Our Lady of Sorrows," Joey said, gesturing to a large painting on the wall. "All the way here, he could not shut up about it."

"Enough to help himself to it, maybe," the standing cop said.

"Good God—I mean, good grief, no," I said, handing over my license.

"Of course I would not steal," Felix said. "From a house of God, never." He turned to the friar. "Father—"

"Brother," the friar said, correcting him.

"Brother, I believe this is a government building? The city, she pays for this?"

"No. Two California missions are funded by the government. This isn't one of them."

"Like that's an excuse anyway?" the standing cop asked. "That's tax-payer money."

"The theft of sacred artifacts is a very real problem," the friar said. "We've had baskets stolen. Native American artifacts."

"Sacred baskets? Who would do this?" Felix asked, shocked.

"A thief," the cop said.

"In Monterey County," the friar said, "someone stole the statue of Saint Anthony. They walked right out with the baby Jesus, then came back for Saint Anthony."

"This is dreadful," Felix said.

"Not to mention ironic," Joey said. "Since Anthony's the patron saint of lost and stolen things."

I had to wrap this up. I had less than an hour before Yuri needed me on the road, no idea where Stasik was, a chalk masterpiece to finish, and the possibility I was being poisoned. "Well, I'm sure you tried prayer," I said suddenly. "But Brad? Maybe you have a particular Bible verse?"

"'Either what woman,'" Felix said, "'having ten pieces of silver, if she lose one piece, doth not light a candle, and sweep the house, and seek diligently till she find it?' Luke, chapter fifteen, verse eight. Father, restore to us baskets, baby Jesus, and Saint Anthony."

The cops appeared unimpressed with their praying perpetrator.

"Father—" I said.

"Brother."

"Brother, he's not a criminal. I promise you. You can see he's not."

"They come in all stripes," the standing cop said. The friar, who I thought should have a bit more faith, was not disagreeing.

"Brother, can I talk to you a second?" I asked and nodded toward the altar. The friar stood and walked with me along the nave. "I need to confess something," I told him. "Most of what I've said isn't true. But my friend really does love Jesus and really doesn't mean any harm, and he's definitely not a thief, he's a very kind person. There's no reason for you to believe me, but if you do, I promise you won't regret it. I was baptized Catholic, in case that carries any weight with you."

The friar stopped and studied me, taking his time. Making me sweat. "Will you promise to tell the truth in the future?"

I took a deep breath. "Yes. I will."

"Say ten Hail Marys. Heartfelt. Don't rattle them off."

"Now?"

"On your own." He turned back to the others and spoke loudly. "Officers, I'm inclined to give these people the benefit of the doubt. I won't be pressing charges."

We didn't need to hear that twice. Felix was on his feet and saying his goodbyes and we all said a lot of thank-yous and then Joey and I were herding him out of there, back toward my twelve-foot square.

"Okay, 'Brad,'" I said to Felix, racewalking. "What was that all about?"

"A simple misunderstanding. Not to worry."

I stopped in my tracks. "Felix. Shall I tell Yuri you were caught by the cops?"

He stopped too, fear flashing across his face. "No! Do not!"

"Then you and I have to make a deal. I'll keep it out of my report and you tell me what you were really doing in that church. And yesterday at Tiffany's."

"I—" He looked at Joey, then back at me.

"I can leave, if you like," Joey said. "But actually, I keep secrets well. I'm a cradle Catholic, just like Wollie. We're big on secrets."

"Just tell me," I said, "is this part of your training? To be a spy. Which I know about."

"You know?"

"I know. And you can tell Joey, because she just lied for you in there. Consider her a local recruit. So now I want to know what you were doing in there, because I bet it's the same thing Stasik's doing right now with Joey's car and I need to find it and him, fast."

"I cannot tell you, Wollie."

"Okay, then I'll have to tell Yuri—"

"No, no, no. I have broken the first rule. The first rule, don't get caught. No police. They don't see your face, they don't see passport. If Yuri knows, I lose hundreds of points." He looked distressed. "But if I tell you things, then I also lose points."

"Points?" I asked.

"You don't have to lose points," Joey said. "We want you to win. No one will know."

"You must swear on the blood of Christ."

"Absolutely," Joey said.

"You got it," I said.

"Okay, yes, it is the training. Do you know the scavenger hunts?"

Joey and I shook our heads.

"We have two weeks. The first day, Kimberly gives us the list. Number one, to find the dead drop in the canyon. Three of us did so, on the hike. Zeffie, no. Number two, we have each to obtain the security plan of a store. Number three, bring back a souvenir of a government building. But this church, she is not government."

"Back up," I said. "Tiffany's? You got the security layout for a scavenger hunt?"

"Yes, I am very lucky. Two days ago Nadja got the building plans for Baskin-Robbins when she is on her fifty-kilometer training run."

"Oh, for Pete's sake," I said. "Thirty-one flavors." My frightful note had been meant for Nadja all along. Nell had been giving her scavenger hunt advice.

"And," Felix continued, "Stasik tried but failed to break into Woolgreens."

"Walgreens," I said. "Wait—are you all operatives?"

"Zbiggo, no. Bronwen, no. In this group, now four. There was Vanya, but Yuri needs Vanya in Europe now, he is engineer. Something big happens there now. He will come back in seven weeks with the next group, unless we are all called to Europe. The next group is now gathered in Zurich, where they learn to shoot well and hand-to-hand fight."

"This is wild," Joey said. "So Stasik taking my car—that's part of all this?"

"Yes, he will be trying for his government building. He is angry because Nadja and I have beat him. Even Zeffie has stolen postal supplies her second day."

"Who else knows about the operation?" I started to move again toward my square.

Felix walked alongside me. "The second rule, keep your cover on. No one knows who else knows. At first. We report to Yuri and Alik and Kimberly. Then we see that Nell too and Grusha and Parashie, they all know."

"How?" I asked.

"A spy can recognize the look of a spy."

Joey was nodding enthusiastically, like this was all standard stuff. For all I knew, Joey herself was working undercover for MI6. And Fredreeq was Mossad. Nothing surprised me anymore. "But you really did write *Jesus Made Me Skinny*?" I asked.

"Of course. Jesus made me skinny to do this work. Not for vanity. This work, it is very hard and only three will go to the next level. Zeffie is very good, the best at breaking and entering. Also planting bugs. Not good at climbing ropes. She is a doctor."

"It sounds risky," I said, "to break laws for the scavenger hunt, if Yuri doesn't want you getting caught."

"Yes. But better now than later to find out if we can do it," Felix said. "So this is why, you get caught, you go home."

We were back at the Haven Lane square, where Apollo and Uncle Theo had mapped out a grid, using white chalk.

"You see what Apollo borrowed for us?" Uncle Theo asked, showing me a transparent piece of graph paper that fit neatly over my sketch of the Madonna. "Now what we do is take your delightful little sketch and blow it up—one hundred times larger than it is right now. Is that right, Apollo?"

"One hundred forty-four," Apollo said.

"In fact," Uncle Theo said, "since you have done your small sketch in color, anyone can do the enlarged version. Apollo and me, for instance. It's a simple formula."

"It is math!" Apollo said.

"But it's not art," I said. "It's paint-by-numbers. It's cheating. Isn't it?"

"Think of it as architecture," Joey said. "Or costume design. You do the picture, the seamstress executes your vision. Here, I'll help. Everyone will help."

"If you wish to work fast, this is the solution," Apollo said.

"There's a theory afloat," Uncle Theo said, "that the old masters used projection techniques themselves. And that much of their work was in fact the work of their apprentices. We shall simply walk in the footsteps of the giants."

Felix looked at my sketch over Uncle Theo's shoulder. "Is this your Madonna? To me, she is strange."

"Everyone's a critic!" I said. "You try drawing one. She's been done to death."

"But she has too many arms."

"So does Kuan Yin," Joey said, kneeling. "And you don't hear Hindus complaining."

"We might," Uncle Theo said, working alongside her, "if we spoke Hindi."

"Anyway, she needs many arms," Apollo said. "To carry all the weapons."

"Then I will help too," Felix said. "However, her clothes, these are not beautiful."

"Subjective opinion," Joey said. "Lotta men find flak jackets sexy. Poll the NRA."

"And her machine gun is pink," Uncle Theo pointed out. "I'm going to start here, Wollie, on the garland of skulls on bungee cords. Apollo has expressed interest in the earphones and the large glasses, so I'll save that part for him."

"Night-vision goggles," I said. "You really think that art by committee is okay?"

"My dear," Uncle Theo said, "trusting other people can be the scariest thing in the world. But sometimes you simply must be brave."

Which was when I turned and saw Simon.

FORTY-SIX

"Hello." My heart thumped loudly in my chest, and my head told it to pipe down.

Simon looked stressed out. He walked toward us, tall and well dressed. His face had an unguarded look about it, equal parts fatigue, anxiety, and grimness.

"Theo," he said, shaking Uncle Theo's hand, but Uncle Theo wasn't having any of that, and wrapped Simon in a hug, his serape overpowering Simon's shirt and tie. Then Joey hugged Simon, and then Apollo, which I found touching, as Apollo and Simon had only met a few times. Despite the fact that Simon was a foot taller than Apollo, he was powerless in the face of this adolescent exuberance.

I half expected Felix to follow suit, but Felix hung back. This did not escape Simon's attention. And when Uncle Theo introduced Simon as "dear Wollie's beau, from the Federal Bureau of Investigation," Felix literally choked. It was enough to distract me from my own shock at my uncle's outspokenness.

"Uncle Theo," I said, regaining my composure. "In some countries, it's considered bad form to talk about someone's job right off the bat. It's like introducing them by how much money they make. Which no doubt is what Felix is reacting to."

"In any case, I must steal her away," Simon interrupted, with an unusual lapse in manners, and took me by the hand. "I'll bring her back quickly."

I had an impulse to object to his plan, but I didn't want to create a scene, because drama takes time and I didn't have any. "Felix," I called over my shoulder, "don't wander off. I'm begging you."

"He won't," Joey said. She gave me a thumbs-up, with a nod toward Simon.

Simon walked me across the grass. I was having trouble breathing normally, probably due to the voice screaming, "Sleeping with Lucrezia! Reported to be on the take!" but Simon didn't seem to notice, so the voice must have been in my head.

Simon found us a grassy patch that was relatively secluded. "Have a seat. Please," he added in a softer tone, anticipating my recalcitrance. When I was seated, he said, "The feds are moving in on Milos."

"What? When?"

"Soon. Today, maybe. They've had some break, enough to score a search warrant."

"A warrant for what? What's the case?"

"I don't have details. I only know there's an ongoing investigation that's heating up. I don't want you anywhere close when it blows. Since this guy's an arms dealer, a number of scenarios could get played out and I don't like you being a bit player in any one of them."

"Which feds are you talking about, Simon? The FBI?"

"The particular branch of law enforcement isn't what's relevant."

"Humor me, would you? I want to know your source of information."

"What's the point of—" Simon stopped, looking over my shoulder. I turned. A child, no more than two feet tall, toddled over to us, arms outstretched like Frankenstein, a big smile on her face, displaying two teeth. She was only a foot away when she realized I was not anyone she knew. Her smile dissolved and her mouth fell open. Wailing ensued.

I felt an answering anguish and started toward her when her mother came and scooped her up, laughing. I stared after them for a moment, then turned back to Simon. "You're asking me to quit a high-paying job, with no notice, and I'm asking you, on what do you base this? Because if it's rumors, shoptalk among your friends—"

"Yes, it's the FBI. An associate of mine in the department, someone I trust, told me that an arrest is imminent, but that's all they know. What the arrest is for, I'm not privy to."

"But you assume it's for some kind of weapons violations."

"No. I assume that Milos being in the business of weapons makes him dangerous, and maybe unwilling to go down without a fight, whatever the bust is for."

"Isn't there such a thing as a legitimate arms dealer?"

"Yes."

"Then how do you know that Yuri isn't one?"

"Because my information suggests otherwise."

"Information that also comes from the FBI?"

The mask of professionalism descended. He looked as tough and impersonal as he had when we met. I suddenly saw him as he'd been back then, a stranger who'd scared me silly, not the man whose bed—when there was a bed handy, and often there wasn't—I'd been sharing for the last half year. The man I was now sharing, maybe, with Lucrezia.

"Simon." I drew a raggedy breath. "Are you concerned because you're in love with me and you can't imagine life without me? Or because you like me a lot and feel a general responsibility to keep innocent people out of harm's way?"

His face stayed immobile.

"Because if it's the latter," I said, "then you've done your best and I assume complete responsibility for my own safety and, thanks, but you're free to go. And if it's the former, then this is the time to decide if you want to let me in on things. Like your thoughts. Your feelings. Your job. Because as much as I love you, I'm not sure right now if I can trust you."

Now his face changed, growing cold. My stomach felt like I was flying through the air and my parachute wasn't opening. I kept going. "What I know for sure is that you don't trust me. And that's not right. I'm a trustworthy person. So maybe this means you're a guy who doesn't trust people. And maybe that's something I can live with, but

honestly, I'm not sure. Or else you're testing me, you have a probation-
ary period for girlfriends, and that's something I could live with, if I
knew there was an end in sight, but I'd like to know when that is. I'm so
tired of the secrecy and not knowing what page anyone's on, or even if
we're in the same book. This isn't just about your job anymore. I'm
scared it's a way of life. Your job is the perfect cover for a man who
doesn't want to give away anything."

I expected him to get up and walk off, leave me sitting on the lawn,
maybe after delivering some devastating last words, something he ex-
celled at. But instead he looked toward the mission steps, then out to Laguna Street, then back at me.

"I have a friend in the State Department," he said quietly. "Who tells
me that Yuri Milos has his own friends in the State Department. His
friends outrank my friend. That gets him a pass when it comes to rules
the rest of the population plays by. I don't know much else. There's a
'don't ask, don't tell' policy when it comes to Milos. The reasons have to
do with foreign policy. The kind of thing you've never shown any interest in."

"I've become more interested lately."

"I'm happy to explore these issues with you when we have a few
weeks free. Right now, what concerns me is a lack of communication
between agencies."

"What's that mean? That the FBI's going after him, not knowing the
State Department says to leave him alone?"

"Yes."

"Can't you ask your State Department friend to ask the FBI to call off
the investigation?"

Simon lifted an eyebrow. "That shows a naïveté about government
agencies that I would find charming if I were in the mood to be
charmed."

"Okay, but at least—"

"It also assumes that I have an interest in saving Milos, a probable
criminal, from the consequences of his actions, whatever they may be. I
haven't. And lastly, it assumes that I have an interest in throwing a
wrench in the operation of one of my colleagues at the bureau. I don't,

I'm not sure I could, and I'm damned sure the effort wouldn't be appreciated."

"What are you interested in, then?"

His eyes locked into mine, making the world fall away. "Saving your ass."

"Why?" I whispered.

"Take a guess."

My body, with no signal at all from my brain, moved toward his. I got very close, breathing in his aftershave. It had a heady effect on me. Or maybe that was his arm, snaking around me, encircling my back, drawing me in close. I was ready to clamp myself against his blue shirt, to wrinkle his tie, when the face of fur-bearing, French-twisted Lucrezia intruded. Damn. I put a hand on his chest and pushed myself away from him.

"Simon." I focused on his mouth. "I don't want a 'don't ask, don't tell' policy for us."

"Then ask."

I lifted my eyes to his. "Are you sleeping with Lucrezia?"

His own eyes shifted, looking over my shoulder, and his face changed. "Mains?" he said.

I turned to see Special Agent Lendall Mains walking toward us.

FORTY-SEVEN

scrambled to my feet, thinking I could actually hide, but the closest thing was a sausage vendor's kiosk twenty yards away. Too far.

And too late. If I recognized Lendall Mains, he'd recognized me. Of course, he was easy, wearing the same sports coat he'd had on the other night, brown with a touch of plaid. And the same prominent ears. His eyes went from me to Simon, then widened in recognition.

"Agent Alexander," Lendall said. "What are you doing here?"

"In Santa Barbara?" Simon was on his feet now too.

"On this case." Lendall glanced at me, then back to Simon, and back to me.

Damn.

Simon looked at me. I felt his stare, but didn't meet his eyes. "What," he said softly, "is he talking about?"

"Wollie?" Lendall said. "Did you bring it?"

"Um, yes," I said to Lendall distractedly. "In the car."

"What's in the car?" Simon asked.

"Nothing interesting. A DVD." My voice sounded high-pitched and unnatural. "So! You two know each other?"

"That would appear to be my line," Simon replied.

"Or mine." Lendall was now right in front of us. "Are you working with her too?"

"That's one way to put it," Simon said. He moved toward Lendall, turning his back on me. "What case are you working on, Mains?" His voice was quiet. I had to strain to hear.

Lendall turned too, and lowered his voice. "Piracy thing."

There was no one in hearing distance but me, but I had no problem eavesdropping. I had to creep up closer, though.

"Which one?" Simon asked. "The screeners for the Emmys that went missing?"

Lendall shook his head. "Features."

"Showing up in the Balkans, first-run movies? That one?"

"Bigger than the Balkans. Starting in Bulgaria and all the way to Russia. Before they even premiere over here, they're on the streets over there."

"Good quality?"

"Top. High-res DVDs. Got everything but the director's commentary. Big bucks getting siphoned off. Lot of pressure on us to plug the leak."

Even through the haze of my own paranoia, I was amazed how easily Mains gave it up to Simon, the facts of the case.

"Who's the SAC?" Simon asked. His voice was casual. "Creighton-Jones?"

"Graham," Lendall replied.

Simon's head snapped around at that, his eyes meeting mine so sharply, I jumped back. Bennett Graham, it would appear, wasn't a close friend of Simon's.

"Okay, c'mon, let's go get that DVD," I said before Simon could start asking me questions. I headed toward the parking lot, with the guys on either side of me.

So Lendall didn't know about Yuri's spy-training school. That was a relief—unless I was legally bound to inform him.

But if Simon wasn't saying anything, why should I?

Because Simon didn't know details. Simon figured there were guns on the property. I knew make, model, quantities, locations, and the reason they were there. If Bennett Graham knew that I knew what I knew and didn't let him know, I could end up in prison. Maybe.

Except that Yuri had immunity from the State Department.

But did I? No.

My stomach was doing somersaults—unless that was the poison at work—and I wanted to talk to Yuri in the worst way. Yuri wouldn't let me twist in the wind. Would he?

I walked at a good clip, but Simon had a long stride and Lendall was practically running to keep up. The men flanked me. I felt Simon's proximity, even though he was calm, probably for Lendall's benefit. I wished he would spill the beans to Lendall about his operation the way Lendall had about ours, but of course Lendall didn't have a personal interest in what Simon was up to and they were probably on different levels professionally, because Lendall seemed to be sucking up a little. Simon wasn't much of a bean-spiller or an up-sucker in any case.

"So you've had good luck getting warrants?" Simon asked Lendall.

"Very good," Lendall said. "But we got luckier last night. Had a guy on surveillance detail listening in real time, and he got an earful."

Simon moved close to me as we walked and said under his breath, "This is quite an earful I'm getting right now."

Good move, Lendall, I thought. Whatever happened to loose lips sink ships? Didn't they teach that anymore in FBI school?

We reached the parking lot and I stopped, disoriented because the Suburban wasn't where I'd left it. Then I remembered that Fredreeq had it. I called her cell phone. "Where are you guys?" I asked.

"Back from the bookstore," she said. "I'm over here staring at your twelve-foot Madonna. Do you really think camouflage and combat boots are appropriate for the Virgin Mary? Jesus Christ, she dresses worse than you do."

"Never mind that," I said. "Where's the Suburban parked?"

"Across the street from the parking lot. I sent Joey back there to keep an eye on Zbiggo. He wouldn't come with us because he's watching some movie."

"A movie?" I looked around and spotted the Suburban down the block. I started walking toward it. "Oh, right. There's a DVD player in the van. What movie?"

"Something he found in the glove box. He's got a temper, by the way. He was throwing things out the window. I nearly decked him. I can't stand litterers."

Uh-oh. I sped up. We reached the van and I threw open the back door and found Joey and Zbiggo looking up at the DVD player. Joey glanced at us, but Zbiggo kept his eyes on the screen.

It was the naked-pizza-delivery-girl movie. I recognized it even without the pizza.

"What language are they speaking?" Lendall asked.

"The international language of love," Joey said.

"Estonian," Zbiggo said. "Close the car. Too much sun."

"It's not big on dialogue, this film," Joey said. "Subtitling it will be a piece of cake." In her lap were two DVD cases. One was the pizza pornography we were now watching. The other was the plastic one I'd lugged around the night before. Both cases were empty.

Lendall Mains went around to the other side of the car and opened the door. "Where's 'eject'?" he asked, reaching over Zbiggo to the DVD player. "I'm taking possession of this."

"No!" Zbiggo yelled.

"Hold on, Lendall. That's not ours." I held up the plastic case. "Zbiggo, where's the DVD that was in here?"

He glanced at it. "That one, I throw it out the window."

"You threw it?" Lendall asked, scanning the ground outside the car. "Here?"

"Not here. On street. No good. On these machine, no good."

"I don't understand," I said.

"European DVDs," Joey said, "don't work in our DVD players and vice versa."

"But this was an American DVD—oh." I remembered that the Suburban had come from Europe. "This DVD player is European."

"PAL format, region two," Lendall said, squatting near the car, scanning the ground. "So they probably do the DVD reformatting here before sending them overseas. Sir?" he said to Zbiggo. "Where'd you throw it, the other DVD?"

"Not here!" Zbiggo yelled. "I said already. On the street."

"What street?" Lendall yelled back.

"I don't know what street," Zbiggo said. "I don't even know what is this city."

My phone rang. "Hello?" I said.

"Wollie. Yuri. Where are you?"

"Uh, the car."

"Estimated time of arrival?"

I glanced at Simon. "Uh—unclear."

"What is happening there, Wollie?"

"Small snafu," I said, moving away from the Suburban—and Simon—and heading down the street.

"How small?" he asked.

I thought about the friar, how I'd told him I wouldn't lie anymore. Not half an hour ago, and here I was already, minimizing snafus. "Yuri, it's a large snafu. I'm not sure I can get everyone back there. For one thing, I've lost Stasik. Who, frankly, scares me a little. For another, what if I lead someone—who means you harm—to your door?"

"Many people mean me harm, and they all know where I live. Wollie, I need everyone home. Don't wait for Stasik, he can find his own way if necessary. Felix and Zbiggo you must bring back. Neither drives well and on the 101, at rush hour, no."

Behind me, Lendall and Zbiggo had lost all restraint. Their voices were raised, with Zbiggo lapsing into Russian. "Yuri, I don't know if I can," I said. "I'm—"

"What? Scared?"

"You don't have time to deal with this now."

"I'll make time. Tell me what is wrong."

"What about Nell?" I asked. "And Chai, and—"

"Nell is fine. She's here. She spent yesterday in the passport office, to get an emergency passport, and then stayed last night in a hotel. To prove she could do it. She wanted to surprise me."

I closed my eyes, relieved. One less corpse to worry about.

"Come, come," he said. "What else?"

"I—" What could I say? *I'm working for the feds. I don't want to walk into a gunfight. I don't know what side I'm on. I like the bad guys more than the good guys.*

"Wollie," he said. "I won't let anyone hurt you. Whatever you're scared of, I can help. But not from sixty miles away. I'll take care of you, but you have to take care of them, Felix and Zbiggo. Stasik if you can. Bring them back. That's the job. You're the driver. Quit tomorrow, but get them home today. They would do the same for you."

They would, I realized. It was so simple, it made up my mind for me.

"I'll get them home." I shut off my phone, then turned and practically fell over Simon, who was staring at me. I brushed past him to the Suburban. "Zbiggo, stay there; I'll get Felix."

Simon was right behind me. "Mains, if you've got the DVD, are you done with her?"

"If I had the DVD," Lendall said, "I'd be done with her, but I haven't got it yet, have I? I'm sticking with her until it's in my hands."

"You are not riding with us!" Zbiggo yelled. "You I don't like."

"What do you need me for?" I asked. "The DVD's not here, it's on the street."

Fredreeq walked over to us. "What in the Sam Hill is happening here? They can hear you people yelling all the way to Montecito."

"Fredreeq," I said. "Did you see where Zbiggo threw a DVD out the window?"

"Yes, on the way back from the bookstore. I yelled at him."

"Did you stop and retrieve it?" Lendall asked.

"Risk my life in this kind of crazy traffic? For a DVD? I don't think so, honey."

"You're coming with me," Lendall said.

That was not the right tone of voice to use with Fredreeq, and while she proceeded to give Lendall a large piece of her mind, I headed to my chalk square to retrieve Felix.

"Hold up." Simon was suddenly beside me, his hand on my arm.

"I can't," I said, walking faster. "I'm in a big hurry."

"You've got to be kidding, right?" he asked, keeping pace with me.

"There's no way you're going back to Calabasas. How long has this been going on, you being a cooperating witness for Bennett Graham? Graham, of all people—"

"For as long as I've been working for Yuri Milos. And I'm absolutely going back to the compound." I moved as fast as my tight shantung pants and heels would allow. "I'm returning my dates. I don't leave people stranded. Unless you can transport us all in your Bentley, but you can't, and as you pointed out, this isn't your operation."

"You heard Mains. He's got what he needs. It's some piracy scam anyway, it's not worth risking your life over."

"As opposed to what you're doing," I said. "A textiles scam, which is naturally worth—whatever it is you're risking. Ethics, good taste—"

"Wollie—"

"Look. Mains didn't hire me, so I doubt he can fire me. Or accept my resignation. Plus, I'm a double agent, so there's Yuri to consider too. He definitely hasn't fired me. And he's my friend. He's counting on me."

"Are you mad?"

"As a matter of fact, I'm very mad. But I don't have time for a fight right now."

Simon pulled me around to face him, gripping my upper arms so tightly I winced. He shook me once, which shocked me. "You're crazy," he said, between clenched teeth. "No one cares about you. Not Milos, not the feds. You're disposable to them all. Cooperating witnesses are a dime a dozen to us, whatever Bennett Graham told you, and he's the worst. You're being used, don't you know that?"

"I should. Having been used in exactly this way by you once. How do you suppose Bennett Graham got the idea to have me work for him?"

Something flashed in his eyes that told me I'd hit home. Guilt. I pressed on. "And speaking of operations, are you playing both sides of yours? Are you on the take?"

"What gives you that idea?"

"Lucrezia."

He looked like he'd been slapped. I turned away, but he pulled me back around to face him. "That's my cover," he said, his voice low. "I'm playing an agent gone bad."

I knew that. I felt embarrassed by having asked the question, and still I couldn't stop myself. "How bad?" I whispered. "And what game are you playing with Lucrezia?"

He didn't answer, but I saw it in his face. He was sleeping with her. "Wollie—"

"Wollie?" Zbiggo was coming up behind Simon.

"Let me go." I tried again to wrest my hands from his grip.

"Let her go, you," Zbiggo echoed. "What you doing to Wollie?"

Without even looking, Simon told Zbiggo to mind his own business, in more colloquial terms.

There are some words that some guys hear as an invitation to fight, the f-word being one of them. Zbiggo put one hand on Simon's shoulder, and before I knew what was happening, Simon let go of me so suddenly I nearly fell over. I regained my balance just as Simon lost his. I didn't see Zbiggo's fist meet Simon's face, but I saw the effect.

Red sprayed across my once-white clothes and then I looked down to see Simon on the ground, looking up at me, blood pouring out of his nose.

FORTY-EIGHT

Simon was on his feet and facing off with Zbiggo, both of them impervious to me yelling at them to stop. Simon had six inches on Zbiggo, but Zbiggo had hopes for the world heavyweight title. God knows how it might have ended if not for seven chalk artists intervening. Felix was there too, and Uncle Theo. And the friar, sans cops.

It took a moment to determine that Simon's nose wasn't broken and that his ego was suffering more than his body at having been sucker punched. I didn't waste any more time on him, the way some people—Lucrezia, e.g.—might. I didn't want him dead, but I didn't mind if he lost some blood. These things happen. I grabbed Felix and Zbiggo, with Uncle Theo following, and hurried toward the Suburban.

"Must you go?" Uncle Theo asked. "Because someone's come by to watch our progress and very much wants to meet you. You'll never guess who. The mayor!"

"Whose mayor?" I was practically running now.

"Santa Barbara's. At least, I believe that's who she is. She's with a gentleman, on the Santa Barbara City Council, who wants to discuss the Jungian symbolism in our drawing. Or it may be that he's the mayor and she's on the city council. Anima and Animus!"

"That's very good news, but I still must go." I gave one last look over my shoulder at Simon, who was tucking in his shirttail while bleeding onto his shirt. There was something so Simon-like about that, I wanted to make the image into a greeting card, but for what occasion? This wasn't the time to work it out.

Lendall Mains had succeeded in drafting Fredreeq into the search for the DVD Zbiggo had tossed out the window. With a quick prayer that she would forgive me and that Lendall Mains would get her back to Los Angeles, I started up the Suburban and found my way to the 101 South, with Joey playing navigator. I'd figured out something. If I made it back to Calabasas with my three dates before the FBI showed up with their search warrants, I was home free. I'd take any available car and go, my cover intact. Leave the feds, the spies, and the DVD pirates to duke it out among themselves. To quote Mrs. Winterbottom, I had had it.

But I had to make it back before the feds arrived.

Within an hour we were in the IHOP parking lot, where we found the Mercedes, fresh from a trip to the car wash, with little vanilla fragrance squares all over the interior.

Joey gave me her jean jacket to cover up Simon's blood splattered across my eggshell silk blouse, and we headed into the pancake house. Stasik sat eating an omelette. He handed keys and cell phone to Joey. "Good wheels," he said. "I filled it with petrol. And you just got a call from a friend—Freddie?"

"Fredreeq," Joey said.

"She'd like you to come pick her up, at some mission. She says hell will freeze over before she'll drive back to L.A. with the man she's with."

"Oh, good," Joey said. "Another ride up the coast." She stole a piece of Stasik's toast and headed for the door.

"Stasik," I said, peeling off a twenty-dollar bill and setting it by his plate for the waitress. "Did Fredreeq say whether they found the DVD they were looking for?"

"She did. This bloke is heading to Calabasas with it."

"Then I want to get there first," I said. "You're driving."

This produced the first smile I'd ever seen on Stasik's face. He handed me back my twenty. "I know better than to let a girl pick up the check on a first date." He turned out his own pockets and found some bills, along with a widget he described as a souvenir from Point Mugu, a piece of surveillance equipment. "And—oh," he added, handing me something bulky, covered in IHOP napkins. "Forgot to return this to your friend. Careful of it."

I unwrapped from the napkin Joey's Glock, and rewrapped it just as quickly. "Please tell me you didn't use it," I said.

"No, but I couldn't leave it in the Mercedes. Anyone could break into that car."

I slipped it into my jacket pocket and followed him out of IHOP. We were no sooner back in the Suburban and buckled up than Stasik was hurtling down the freeway, weaving in and out of traffic like a police cruiser. We made it back to Palomino Hills in what seemed like twenty minutes. Lendall Mains would have to have a helicopter to be anywhere close behind us.

Driving through the guard gate, I realized I felt sick as a dog, queasy, even though I hadn't eaten a thing since breakfast. It had to be more than Stasik's driving. I was now sure I was being poisoned. I decided that my best course of action was, as soon as I dropped off my passengers, to drive myself to the hospital.

I did not get the chance.

The compound was eerily quiet.

There was no one in the Big House. The kitchen was spotless and empty. For the first time since I'd arrived, there was no pot boiling on the stove, nothing in the oven, no smells of onion, spices, or cooking oil, despite the fact that it was the dinner hour.

Stasik and Felix went to check out Green House. Zbiggo and I headed to House of Blue. We found suitcases lined up near the front door. I recognized them as the team's—bags that I'd loaded into the Suburban and/or dumped onto Sepulveda Boulevard.

"What's going on?" Zbiggo asked. "Peoples is leaving?"

"Looks that way," I said. "Is your stuff here?"

"No. I go to my room now."

The bags belonged to Felix, Stasik, Nadja, and Zeffie, the four spies-in-training.

I hurried off to my own room. It was as I'd left it, with my clothes and personal items occupying their normal positions. I heard voices through the window and went to look out.

A car pulled into the drive and passed out of view. I heard doors slam and the unmistakable sound of static. Radio—walkie-talkie—someone was communicating with someone else via walkie-talkie. Cops? FBI agents with search warrants? Or Yuri's people?

Behind me, a door creaked. I whipped around.

"Wollie?" The small voice came from my bathroom. The door opened wider and Parashie's head peeked out. "Are you alone?"

"Yes," I said, going to her and matching her whisper. "What's going on?"

"Vlad isn't here?" Her head peeked out farther. "Have you seen him anywhere?"

"No. What's wrong, Parashie?"

"He's looking for me. He's—"

"Where's Yuri?" I asked. "Where's your father?"

Parashie's eyes grew huge. "Do you have your cell phone?"

I checked the pocket of the jean jacket. "Yes, but—"

"Wait." The girl scurried out of the bathroom and over to the window. She looked down at the driveway, then turned back to me. "Okay. Please come. Quickly."

"Where to?"

"We need a cell signal." Parashie took my hand and led me out of the bedroom.

"Why? Why can't we use a landline?"

"Vlad will see. The phone lines, they light up. He will see we make a phone call and he will come find us."

"But what's going on?"

"Vlad," she said, pulling me toward the stairs. "He found me here alone."

I was getting a bad feeling about everything. "What happened?"

The words tumbled out. "I have never been here alone with him, ever. Kimberly always said not to. But Grusha went with Yuri because he needed her help, everyone is in a big hurry, but then Kimberly also was gone, she got a phone call and Vlad came back to the house. I didn't know, I was in the library, and he comes in. He—" Parashie began to cry.

"Parashie, it's okay. I'm here now. You're not alone." I squeezed her hand, trying to slow her, but she hurtled down the stairs, oblivious.

"And he told me," she said, between sobs, "he told me, 'Think what happens to Chai, think what happens to people who talk, who tell stories.' I want Grusha. Grusha will know what to do." She pulled me outside the house with her and then we stopped, huddling under the protection of the portico. We looked both ways. The coast was clear. "This way," she said, and she took off, sprinting across the grass.

I followed, more slowly and with difficulty. She wore a T-shirt, shorts, and hiking shoes; I did not. She crossed the drive and came to a row of trees and hid herself among them, waiting for me.

"Listen," I said when I reached her, breathing heavily. "There's no need to run. You're safe now. Stasik and Felix are here and Zbiggo, so there's no way Vlad can—"

"No! They are men. I will not talk to men, only Grusha. I want Grusha."

She knelt to tie her shoe and I saw with shock that there was blood on her leg. I gave up trying to reassure her. My other concern now was the feds. If there was a raid, if they showed up with search warrants, if Yuri wasn't here and Parashie was taken into custody, to Child Protective Services, with her fear of institutions—

"Let's drive to Gelson's," I said. "We'll get a cell signal—"

"No, Vlad would find us before we are out of the driveway, he would hear us."

And if the feds were here, they'd hear us. And in any case, my car keys were in my purse, back in my room. The distant sound of a siren made up my mind. I didn't want to face the feds or Vlad. "Okay, let's go," I said, and let her take the lead.

We focused on moving rather than talking. I tried not to imagine creepy Vlad accosting a girl who couldn't have been more than a hundred and ten pounds. I wanted to believe she had escaped before anything horrible had happened, but I was scared to ask, scared to think about the blood on her leg and where it had come from. If grim Grusha was her choice of confidante, we'd get Grusha on the phone, once we reached the top of the hill.

We stopped at the lookout point, at the bench that Yuri and I had sat on the night before. I turned on the phone, got a signal, and handed it to Parashie. She dialed with shaking hands. I didn't hear the little computer beeps of the numbers being compressed, just the word "Grusha" and then Russian. She must be leaving a message. I watched the ground, thinking of snakes. That was all we needed, a snake in the grass, to complete the day. After a minute or two, Parashie hung up and held on to the phone with both hands, as if praying. It reminded me that I hadn't said my ten Hail Marys.

"Did you tell her to come home right away?" I asked. "Was that voice mail?"

She nodded, sniffing. She was pulling herself together.

"Do you have your father's cell phone number? We should call him too."

Parashie didn't say anything. She just looked at me.

"Okay?" I asked.

She wiped her nose with her hand and wiped her eyes, methodically, first the left, then the right. Parashie was completely relaxed now, as if the phone call to Grusha had flipped off the panic button. "So, Wollie?" she said. "Why don't you tell me what you have done with my brother's DVD?"

It was such a non sequitur, it took a moment for me to understand the question. I saw the light change, the sun glinting off a piece of glass on the trail as it prepared to drop behind the mountain. Everything, it seemed, had just turned a shade darker.

Parashie's eyes, in particular.

Then she did the strangest thing. She threw my cell phone in an arc high over my head. I watched it go down the cliff, bouncing twice before it disappeared among the rocks.

"You—did you talk to Grusha?" I asked.

"No. I didn't talk to anybody."

I stood and began to back away from her.

Her hands were in her pockets and she came toward me.

I kept backing up, not knowing how an adolescent girl could be so sinister. It was the darkness in her eyes, the blood on her leg, the hands in her pockets.

After three or four steps in reverse, I stopped. The earth seemed to crumble a bit beneath my feet and I saw I had nowhere to go except down the very steep mountainside.

FORTY-NINE

"So?" Parashie asked. "Where is the DVD?"

"What DVD?"

"You know what. The new Disney movie. Alik called today to his editor friend and said where is it and they said the blond woman with big breasts took it yesterday."

"Parashie," I said, trying to control my shaky voice. "There are a hundred thousand blond women with big breasts in Calabasas, let alone the greater Los Angeles area—"

"They said they drove to the gate. The woman lived at the same house as Alik Milos. And Grusha found the envelope in the umbrella box. And Crispin told me he spoke with you. Just before he died, he told me this. So don't think I am stupid. I'm not born in America but I'm not stupid."

The mention of Crispin intensified my shaking. "God, no one thinks you're stupid," I said. Mentally unhinged, but that was a far cry from stupid. If anyone knew that, it was me. "Parashie, I know that Alik's exporting DVDs, yes, but that's not a problem for me. I don't care about it. He can break every law in America with my blessing. It's hard to overstate how little it bothers me." Suddenly, this was absolutely true. The feds were on their own. Let Alik hijack the entire Hollywood box office receipts for the year, only let me off this mountain.

"So where is the DVD?" She was six inches from me now, crossing the line into an invasion of personal space. There was something deeply threatening about her, even though she was short. It was that athleticism. That wiry thing. Why were her hands in her pockets?

"In the car." Lendall Mains's car, anyway. "Let's go get it. You can have it. I don't want it."

"Thank you," she said. "That's what I needed to know."

One hand came out of her pocket holding something that flashed briefly in the fading light. Something thin and pointed, not a gun. It was in my face and I slapped her hand away and gave her a push as hard as I could.

She went down, but so did I, losing my balance and grabbing onto her for support. And then I was on top of her, which was not where I wanted to be, and then she was on top of me, having managed to flip me over.

She clung like an enraged kitten, clawing, and I felt the stab of something in my arm and then another in my leg, something puncturing me, again and again. After the first yowl of indignation when she hit the ground, she worked in silence. Not me. I was screaming, fighting her off, unable to believe that someone not even full grown could do such damage.

I couldn't shake her. She stuck, leechlike, stabbing me with whatever it was clutched in her hand, skinny like a pencil, like a long, sharp nail. I squirmed, pulling my knees toward my chest, trying to get my legs between us, clutching her forearms to keep her weapon hand away, but I could feel some of the thrusts connect, puncturing me. Unless I could shake her off, one of those punctures would be in my heart or lung or throat, and that would be that.

Something was beneath me in the dirt, something I rolled onto repeatedly, hurting my back. And then that pain reached my brain, distinguishing itself from the other pain: it was Joey's gun under me. It had fallen out of my pocket.

In order to get it, I had to let go of Parashie.

If I let go of Parashie, she would stab me.

I couldn't believe there was no other option, no help coming, no better idea. There was just the sky above me and the dirt beneath me, neither caring about the outcome.

I gave Parashie the biggest push I had in me, let go, rolled six inches to the left, and Parashie stabbed me hard in the leg as I grabbed Joey's gun.

It went off.

Everything stopped.

FIFTY

The shot from Joey's Glock freaked me out. I hadn't actually decided to pull the trigger, and the fact that it seemed to have a life of its own had me in a panic.

But it got Parashie off me.

She leaped away from my body as if ejected, scrambling backward like a little crab, low to the ground, scanning the terrain until she found a huge boulder, across the trail, twenty or thirty feet away, to hide behind.

Silence.

I hadn't hit her. The hope that I had, that by some magical accident I'd wounded her without killing her, came and went. She'd moved too well. She wasn't even panicking, probably. She was, I guessed, just playing it safe. Thinking about her next move now that the game had changed. The gun changed the game.

I breathed heavily and tried to recover my wits along with my breath. My whole body seemed to be pulsing, my heart was beating so hard. I set down the gun, scared it would go off again. But I kept it close, knowing Parashie could cover that distance fast.

Now what? If I took off down the path, she could catch me. But would she? I wouldn't chase someone with a gun, but that's just me.

And if she knew what a novice I was—but maybe she didn't know. Maybe she thought I was a crackerjack shot. At home with a gun, even at a dead run. Maybe I could bluff, maybe—

I turned to pick up the Glock again and that's when I saw blood. Everywhere. So much blood on my eggshell shantung pants, you could no longer guess at their color from the knees up. It looked like someone had dumped a bucket of V-8 juice in my lap. Could it really be all mine? If it was, wouldn't it hurt more?

It was mine. It was still coming out of me.

My leg, up near my groin, was pulsating with it, churning it out at a steady rate.

Forget the gun. I put both hands there, as hard as I could, applying pressure. When the geyser stopped, I averted my eyes, knowing that the visuals of my own wound could send me over the edge.

In fact, I was too close to the edge. I maneuvered myself away from it, pushing with one hand and my working leg, getting myself closer to the trail. Then I reached back to grab the Glock, to bring it closer.

Okay, no running. Very little mobility at all. No cell phone. No one within shouting distance, except a girl across the trail who wasn't going to be a lot of help, because she wanted me dead.

I had to change her mind. I had to get Parashie to help me and relatively quickly or I wasn't getting off this mountain outside of a body bag.

"Parashie?" I called. "Listen. You don't have to hurt me. I'm on your side. Your father trusts me, he told me everything, I know about the training school he's running—"

"I don't care!" she yelled. "My father doesn't know about this."

"What do you mean, 'this'?" I called. No answer. "The DVDs? He doesn't know that Alik is trafficking in stolen DVDs?"

"He will kill Alik if he finds out."

She could have been any teenage girl talking about her brother flunking chemistry and being in danger of death-by-parent.

"Parashie, I won't tell him," I said.

"You would. He said you are moral. He said you are that type."

"Who said?"

"Alik. He said you would not cooperate if you knew. He said Chai would cooperate, she had no morals. But I didn't trust her."

"Okay, understandable. I wouldn't've trusted her either. But you can trust me."

"Uh-uh."

"Parashie, think!" I yelled. It wasn't a great yell, because my voice was wavering. "You—whatever you did to Chai. Poison. Car crash. Fine. And then I guess you killed Crispin. But I guarantee if you kill me too you'll get caught. It's too big a risk. People notice these things. Three bodies in Calabasas in the space of—"

"No. The only risk is to leave someone behind to tell the story."

"It's just DVDs! Home entertainment! Alik will have to pay a fine if he's caught, but it's a minor crime, a venial sin, not a mortal sin—" My arguments were getting weaker. I couldn't even convince myself.

"You don't know anything," Parashie yelled. "My father, what will he do? He will send Alik away. He will cut him off. It will be a big scandal. How is Alik to take his place in the new government, after the revolution, if there is a scandal? In Belarus, they will say he is a pawn of the West. Yuri will exile him. We will not be a family."

My left hand was cramped, and I switched to my right to stanch the flow of blood. I couldn't keep this up forever, let alone discuss politics or family dynamics while I did it. Underneath me, blood was turning the dirt to mud.

"Parashie, I'll cover for Alik," I said. "He can run for president, for all I care—"

"You care that I have killed Chai. And Crispin."

I was about to answer that I didn't care if she'd killed Jimmy Hoffa when I saw, coming up the trail, an animal. Loping wearily, tongue hanging out.

Olive Oyl.

I made a clucking sound, and she stopped, then saw me, and bounded over with renewed energy. She set about licking the blood from my face.

"Olive Oyl," I mumbled. "Tell them I'm here. Go tell someone to come find me."

Olive Oyl, instead of answering, turned her head and snapped at the air. Some annoying bug.

Bug.

I switched hands once more on my blood-soaked leg, to feel the skintight back pocket of my shantung pants. There it was.

The last bug.

FIFTY-ONE

I turned the switch to "on" and stuck it onto my skin, just below my collarbone. "I'm bleeding quite a lot. I'm no doctor, but I have to get down the trail fast or it's not good news. From the Milos house I'm straight up the trail, a ten-minute walk. I'm lying near a bench that's on a promontory that overlooks the ocean. I think that's the right word, 'promontory.'"

"Olive Oyl! Come!"

I looked over to see Parashie's head emerge from behind the rock, calling the dog. Olive Oyl abandoned me in a second and ran to the girl. Parashie hugged the dog around the waist and held her and then moved toward me in a crouch.

Olive Oyl struggled against the awkwardness of this, but Parashie held fast. I watched them make their painstaking way toward me for a full minute before I understood. The girl was using the dog as a canine shield.

I'd been holding my leg with both hands, trying to maintain pressure, but now I picked up the Glock once more. "Don't come any closer," I called.

"Don't make me laugh," Parashie said. "You won't shoot a dog."

"How do you know?"

"Americans can't shoot a dog."

"I will," I said.

"Go ahead," she said.

But I couldn't. I wasn't sure I could shoot her either, only I had to look like I could. I raised the gun.

She said nothing. Olive Oyl's big yellow body advanced toward me, walking sideways, protecting the girl. I was lying down on the uneven ground, my upper body propped up against a boulder. I had little stability. Parashie was going to come and roll me down the mountain. I knew it. I'd be found like Crispin had been found, if I was found at all.

She was close now. She stopped twelve feet away, forcing Olive Oyl up on her hind legs so that the dog's stomach was exposed. Olive Oyl whimpered, not liking the dance in the least. I held the Glock up, trying to get the girl's head in my sights. The problem was, I needed both hands to do it the way Yuri had taught me, but I was too scared to let go of my leg. My life seemed to be draining away with my blood, and my hands were both slippery. I had no confidence I could pull it off. There was one chance in a million that I'd hit the girl and not the dog. If I hit anything. The odds improved if I hit the dog first and then got a second shot off at Parashie. Or shot through the dog to the girl. Except I couldn't shoot the dog.

I felt blood flow out of me. I had to make a decision. If I waited too long, my arms wouldn't hold the gun up any longer. It would be death by indecision.

"Parashie, stop," a voice said. "Wollie? You put down the gun."

I looked over to see Grusha on the trail, in her yellow housedress in the fading light. She held an MP5, aimed at me.

"Let go of the dog, Parashie," Grusha said.

"No," Parashie said, her voice petulant. "She has to put down her gun first."

"You," Grusha said to me. "Put down your gun."

It was a funny kind of moment. If I put down the gun first, then Grusha would shoot me. Or Parashie would push me over the edge into the canyon. I wouldn't survive the fall. I knew this.

I knew something else now too. If Parashie let go of Olive Oyl, then

I would shoot her. If she rushed me, if she came at me, I would do it. I no longer had any compunction about it. If she stood still, I wasn't sure I could do it, but if she came at me, I could. Maybe I was in some primal, wounded-animal mode, close enough to death that I was willing to take someone else along.

It was a strange thing to discover about myself, that I could kill someone.

"Put down your gun," Grusha said.

"Why?" I asked.

"Trust me."

Trust her? The witch in the housedress? Who'd never said a kind word to me in all the time she'd known me? Who was pointing a submachine gun at me? The notion was so unlikely that I smiled. The smart thing to do, of course, would be to shoot Grusha first, then try for Parashie, dog or no dog. But that's not what I did. I took a different sort of chance.

I put down the gun.

Parashie let go of the dog.

Olive Oyl ran to Grusha.

Parashie came toward me, reaching for the Glock.

Grusha shot her in the heart.

FIFTY-TWO

I opened my eyes and saw a cottage cheese ceiling like they have in cheap apartments—the kind I generally live in—and in hospitals.

"She's waking up," someone said.

My ears worked, along with my eyes. That was good news. I turned my head and found there was something in my mouth. A tube. I looked down at it, my eyes crossing.

Joey was at my side suddenly. "There's an IV in your arm," she said. "So be cool."

"What's up?" I croaked out. It came out as "Mmfqueek?" but Joey and Fredreeq nodded, like they spoke the language.

"You had a hole in your femoral artery," Fredreeq said. "And they fixed it up and gave you a few gallons of someone else's blood and you've been having a lot of naps. You're going to be fine, but you should abandon your dreams of being a Rockette. And you're not looking great. If it were up to me, Simon would never see you like this. But he's been here a whole lot, throwing his weight around like he's J. Edgar Hoover."

"What about Parashie?" I asked, which came out as "Fmpruchna?"

Joey shook her head. "Parashie's dead. Justifiable homicide. The housekeeper did it, to save you. But also because she'd promised the kid that no one would ever take her away from her family. It seems that the orphanage Yuri found her in did a number on her brain."

"Yeah. She was missing a conscience," Fredreeq said.

"She was almost totally normal," Joey said, "except for a habit of killing people. By the way, none of this is common knowledge and don't ask how come we know because we can't ever tell you and, in fact, we'll deny it all, if forced to."

I closed my eyes. Then opened them. "Alik?"

Joey shook her head again. "Long gone. Halfway to Paris while we were all in Santa Barbara. The FBI is trying to extradite him, but the State Department will probably step in. On the other hand, there was an arrest this morning, an editor working at Disney was making copies of new films before the watermark went on them. So that leak's plugged and the route's closed, and that'll make the news. The trades and the *L.A. Times* at least."

"Howdjaknowthisstuff?"

"I told you, don't ask," Joey said.

"But since you did ask," Fredreeq said, "We had a long talk with your boyfriend, who realized that indiscretion was the better part of valor. That if he wanted us to plead his case with you, he had better be forthcoming."

"Whywouldja?"

"Plead his case?" Fredreeq asked. Her eyebrows went up and down twice. "You'll find out. When you can keep your eyes open for longer than four minutes."

And she said some more stuff, I think, but I was asleep by then.

My ears woke up before my eyes the next time. I heard a rhythmic breathiness and a whimper. I opened my eyes. On the hospital bed next to me was Olive Oyl.

"Hey, puppy," I said.

"Good," said a voice in the doorway. "I thought I would have to leave the country without saying goodbye."

I turned to see Yuri smiling at me. He looked at least ten years older than when I'd last seen him. He looked, finally, his age.

"Where are you flying to?" I asked. My voice was working much better. The tube in my mouth was gone.

"Bratislava. The family has a small castle in the countryside of Slovakia. We've been slowly moving our base of operations to that part of the world, preparing for the coup that will happen soon now, if all goes as planned."

"Everyone's gone now? The whole family?"

"Everyone you know, except Bronwen and Zbiggo. We placed them with excellent media consultants."

"I'm sorry," I said. "About how things turned out."

Yuri nodded. "I knew I could live in the West without succumbing to its temptations. I did not consider my children. We all have our blind spots." He walked over to my bedside. "I saw that Parashie was damaged the moment I found her, but I didn't think it was irrevocable. Alik, I knew not at all." He looked down at his hands. "I believed it was Grusha who had killed Chai. It happened when I was in Mogilev. Grusha told me not to ask, and I trusted her. She is a soldier. Grusha found Chai dead, and she recognized the signs of selenium poisoning. Parashie had put it in Chai's borscht. Parashie had tried foxglove too, earlier, but it only made Chai sick."

"And the car crash?"

"Grusha went to Alik, told him about Chai. They covered it up, with the help of two trainees—it's the kind of operation they can do. Alik wanted to protect his sister. And himself, I suppose." Yuri looked deeply tired. "He and Grusha thought they could keep her under control, that it was one aberrant incident. The death of the young man dashed that hope. Once we learned of his connection to Chai, it was clear that Parashie had stabbed him. She is—was—a talented fighter. So. Alik came to me, told me everything, and we knew it was time to go. We moved quickly, but not quickly enough. The police know nothing of what I've just told you, about Alik or Grusha, that they covered up a murder. They won't be coming back to America."

"You would have taken Parashie with you?"

He didn't blink. "She was my child."

I was tired myself, more tired than I could remember ever being before. I let my head fall back on the pillow. The world was changed. Questions of morality and loyalty and right and wrong were no longer black and white for me, if they ever had been. I was too tired to judge Yuri's choices. I looked at the sleeping form on the bed next to me. "Do they let dogs in hospitals?"

Yuri half smiled. "I am not without connections. Kimberly would like her to stay with you for a time. The quarantine procedures in Europe are quite Byzantine and my wife can't bear for the dog to be crated up. Grusha thought you would be willing to keep her until we straighten it out."

I nodded. I had no idea what the Oakwood Garden Apartments pet regulations were, but if I had to move, I had to move. It wouldn't be the first time.

Yuri must've read my mind. He came to the foot of my bed. "Your things have been returned to your apartment, and a check deposited into your account. I hope that's not intrusive."

I looked down at myself, at the thin blanket covering me. Fluids were entering and leaving my body through translucent tubes, and my hospital gown was open in the back. Intrusiveness was relative. "Yuri, I wasn't just working for you," I said. "I was working for the FBI. They hired me to spy on you."

"So I've been told." Yuri came to the head of the bed and brushed the hair from my forehead and planted there a gentle kiss. "*Vyzdoravlivajte.* Heal."

When I opened my eyes again, Yuri was gone. On the bed next to Olive Oyl, Simon was stretched out, asleep. I watched him a long while, his breath rising and falling in time with the yellow dog. After a few minutes, I turned my face to the wall and fell back asleep.

FIFTY-THREE

He stood at the foot of my bed, where Yuri had stood the day before, and looked at me. Then his face broke into a big grin. "You've been talking in your sleep."

"Really?" I said. "Did I say anything of interest?"

"You wanted to know if we wore the same size hospital gown."

"And what'd you say?"

"That I'd steal one for you when they let you out. We'll wear it every night. We'll alternate."

"Very sexy."

He pulled up a chair. "In other news, Bennett Graham retired two days ago."

"Retired?"

"Yes. It was agreed by all concerned that his use of civilians was such an egregious violation of policy that he would be happier in the private sector. And in still other news, Lucrezia Zola was indicted three days ago, along with her brother Guillermo."

"For how long?"

"If she deals, she could be out in fifteen. Or she could do twenty-five to life. I'm hoping for life."

"You going to tell me about the case?" I asked.

"In exhaustive detail. Until it puts you to sleep. I'll read to you from the transcripts. You can watch the trial. I can teach you how to smuggle pseudoephedrine hidden in bolts of raw silk."

"That could be fun. Did you sleep with her?"

His eyes didn't waver from mine. "Twice."

My heart stopped. Then started again. "Was it fun?"

"Not as fun as arresting her."

I leaned back in my bed and closed my eyes. "I think I'd like to be alone."

When I opened my eyes, he was gone.

FIFTY-FOUR

"Wollie, wake up."

My brother's voice pulled me out of a sound sleep. My eyes blinked open. "What? P.B., what's happened? Are you okay?"

"You're the one lying in a hospital bed," he pointed out. "You don't look so good. They said you're okay, but you don't look okay."

"How'd you get here?" I asked.

"Apollo and Uncle Theo. They're down in the cafeteria."

"Apollo drove?"

P.B. nodded and, apparently satisfied I wasn't at death's door, opened a book.

"What are you reading?"

He held it up. *Superstrings and the Search for the Theory of Everything.*

"So how are those superstrings?" I asked. "And did they find the theory?"

"I'm only on page one thirty-one."

"Well, how's it look? Will there be a happy ending?"

He shrugged. "They've dealt with relativistic covariance, quantization, and grand unified symmetries, so Green and Schwarz are happy. But they haven't even broached the deeper meaning of closed loops."

"Well, then." I thought for a moment. "Is Mrs. Winterbottom mad at me for ditching the Madonna?"

"I don't think so," he said without looking up. "She sent you flowers. Those yellow ones. Uncle Theo read all your cards."

"You're kidding." On a table by the window, there they were, an extravagance of yellow roses, screamingly cheerful. "So I guess she liked our chalk painting?"

"I don't know, but a bunch of other people liked it. They liked that it was a collective work. We named her SuperVirgin, and she changed a little. Apollo wanted her to have rings, like Saturn. And bright green skin."

"That's fine. So the book's good?"

"It's my new meds." He still didn't look up. "I can read on them. For the last seven years, all I could concentrate on was comic books."

I hadn't realized that. How could I not know that? "Hey—did you ever get your guy?"

"Who am I, Sergeant Preston? What guy?"

"Your physicist. Joseph—Plutonski?"

"Polchinski." He kept reading.

"Who's Sergeant Preston?"

He looked up, astonished. "You're kidding."

"About what?"

"Man, Wollie. You don't remember Sergeant Preston? The first comic book you ever bought for me?"

I shook my head.

"You read it to me for a whole year till I learned to read myself. Sergeant Preston and his dog King. They always got their man."

"Really?" I wondered in what deep recesses of my mind Sergeant Preston dwelled, exerting his subconscious influence. "So, did you ever find your man?"

My brother looked up again, a slow smile breaking over his face, the kind he graced me with every year or so. "No. But it ain't over till the fat lady sings."

FIFTY-FIVE

A man stood at the foot of my bed with a chart in hand. "Hello, there. I'm Dr. Hurwitz and I'll be your physician this evening. Would you care to hear the specials?"

"Uh . . ."

"Jell-O. Okay, moving on. The patch job we did on your artery is healing nicely. Equally important, your hair's not going to fall out."

"Well, that is good news."

"It is, isn't it? Your friends were concerned that someone might be poisoning you, so we ran some tests."

"And I'm normal?"

"No. You have highly elevated levels of hCG. I'll run another test tomorrow, to see if the hCG levels are increasing. You've been through a lot, so we'll have to see."

"What is hCG? Poison?"

He finished writing on my chart and looked up at me. "Not exactly, although it can produce nausea, starting at about five weeks. It's a hormone."

The room went blurry. "What kind of hormone?" I asked.

"The pregnancy hormone."

My heart stopped.

FIFTY-SIX

Jeanne, the nurse, wheeled me out of the hospital, with Fredreeq at my side. It was impossible not to feel chirpy, wearing street clothes and not being hooked to anything resembling a catheter.

"And here's our ride now," Fredreeq said, helping me up out of the wheelchair at the hospital entrance.

"Where?" I asked, looking around for Joey's Mercedes.

"There," Fredreeq said, pointing to a car a half block away, pulling out of a parking lot on Gracie Allen Drive.

"That's—Simon's car," I said.

"Yes. Oh, well. Suckered again. But as long as he's here, he can drive you home."

"No."

"Listen—"

"No. I'm not driving anywhere with him. I don't want to see him anymore."

"Wollie, I—okay, hold on." Fredreeq waved to Simon, then yelled, "Drive around the block." She waited until he pulled away, then turned back to me. "He's mad about you, and you're nuts about him. You can't let some crazy felonness in a fur coat ruin your life. She's up the river and you're down here in the yacht, so wake up and smell the flowers.

That man wasn't seduced by her, he was seduced by his job. These superhero guys are all alike."

"He was seduced by her too."

"Okay, so he's a pig. But you gotta realize that he was on that textiles case before he met you. He was single when he signed on for it and they moved him into that penthouse and gave him that cover story. That's what I call a mitigating circumstance. By the way, I told him not to tell you the truth about sleeping with her, but he's got integrity, so what are you going to do?"

I stared at her. "Fredreeq, don't take this wrong, but is it possible for you to mind your own business?"

"When you find me minding business that is not mine to mind, you let me know. But this is not that. Here, I want to fix your lips so you don't look so much like a corpse."

I brushed her hand away. "I'm not going to forgive—or get back with— Hey, Fredreeq, I'd have thought you'd be the first one to tell me to forget this guy."

"Well, I'm not. And here's why. Nobody's perfect. And when there's no ring on the finger and no promises made, it's understandable that men do stupid-ass things. Women too. It's that damn job. Listen, I have not even started yelling at you about letting some delinquent girl punch holes in your arteries with a meat thermometer."

"That's got nothing to do with this."

"I'm looking at the big picture here and you are looking at the microscopic view. I know you had some near-death experience up on that mountain, but it's time to come back to life now. That girl died up there, but you didn't. And you didn't kill her, either."

"But I could have." I started to cry.

"I should hope so. It means you have a life wish and not a death wish." She looked over my shoulder. "One more time around the block!" she called to Simon.

"You don't understand," I said.

"No, I'm stupid that way," she said, straightening my shirt and undoing one button. "So explain it to Simon. He'll understand. It's probably some spy thing you two have in common now. Along with everything else." She did the thing with her eyebrows, going up and down fast, signaling something very significant.

"I don't want to talk about that. You said Simon doesn't know anything about that."

"The baby? That's right, sister. Just you and me and Joey and Dr. Hurwitz and a couple of lab technicians and four of the nurses. Nobody else." She rooted around in her purse. "And I purposely haven't brought it up, because if there's one thing I know, it's that a baby's no guarantee of anything, especially happy endings for grown-ups. It's just one more damn thing to fall madly in love with."

"If it even survives," I mumbled. "After what I put it through." My resolve was crumbling, my longing for Simon growing.

"What you put it through is nothing compared to what it's gonna put you through. You just wait till middle school." She pulled a huge handkerchief out of her purse. "Hang on to this in case you throw up again. Here he comes. Simon!" she called and gave a whistle that could have hailed a cab in Manhattan, three thousand miles away. "Go get him, honey," she said and gave me a kiss on the cheek.

The Bentley pulled up to the curb. The passenger-side window went down, along with the music he'd been listening to. Opera. And there sat Olive Oyl. How despicable, using the dog as bait to lure me in. Hadn't she been through enough? And why did she look so happy?

"So," I said, pointedly not getting in. "Is this car yours? Or is it just part of the cover story for Daniel Lavosh, Agent on the Take?"

"It's mine, but only as long as I stay with the bureau."

I let the implications of that hang in the air.

"And the penthouse on Wilshire?" I asked. "Is that yours?"

He shook his head. "It belongs to the company."

"Where do you live?"

"Mandeville Canyon."

"What part?"

"Mango Way."

"Apartment?"

"House."

"Nice?"

"Small. I've been working on it. Putting in an extra room."

"For what?"

"An artist studio. For a friend of mine. She does greeting cards."

"I didn't know you could build rooms. Like, with a hammer and nails?"

"There's a lot you don't know about me," he said, snapping his fingers at Olive Oyl, who obligingly lumbered over the front seat into the back. "And probably one or two things I've yet to discover about you."

"Baby, you don't know the half of it."

"So let's take it from the top," he suggested. "Start over."

I stood on the sidewalk and looked around.

The month of May had slipped away while I'd lain in a hospital bed, and most of this day was gone as well. The morning fog had long since burned off, June gloom giving way to an afternoon suitable for surfing and picnics and kite flying. Relentless happiness. The fog would roll back in by midnight, but now people were heading home to fire up barbecues and open bottles of wine or driving to Dodger Stadium with their tops down. Olive Oyl sniffed the air through the back window, gathering information, smiling the way dogs do.

It was too much. I had no defenses against such optimism.

"Okay," I said. "But this time around I drive."

The look of fear that passed over Simon's face was gone in a second, but not before I'd seen it. I laughed for the first time in a week.

"Gotcha," I said, and climbed into the passenger seat and turned up the music. Simon put the car in gear.

And away we drove, westbound on West Third Street, off into the sunset.

Acknowledgments

My brother Joe Kozak inspired a large part of this story, with his knowledge of and passion for faraway places, and I owe him, as always, a big debt of gratitude. Nancie Hays cares deeply about getting the firearms right; William Simon is the go-to guy for things you don't even want to know about; D.P. Lyle is the last word in poison; and Dr. Barry Fisher is always good for the corpse questions. My Russian-speaking friends include Lera-in-the-Ukraine, J. Renée Stuart, and Yevgeniya Yerekskaya-Pozzessere—*spasibo*, all. Michele Martinez, Rick Steinberg, and Marcus Wynne generously shared their knowledge of government agencies but are not responsible for any inaccuracies found in my story. Agatha and Rugi Aldisert and Kathy Kouri gave me the insider's view of i Madonnari; Holly Gault helped with chalk; Karen Olson helped with something I can't remember if I can reveal or not; Rob Aldisert spoke Italian with me; Sharon Fiedler knows where all the bodies are buried at Tiffany & Co.; Hawk Koch and David Rosenbloom lent me their filmmaking expertise; and Joel Roberts really is the media trainer to the stars. Thanks to David Mize of Santa Monica Chevrolet, to Ian Tansley, and to Ash Reid, who will talk anyone into fuel-conversion, given half a chance. Thanks finally to Dr. Terence Kite of Pepperdine University.

I couldn't have written this book without my friends. That's always true, but some years it's truer than others. My seven brothers and sisters and their families, Gregg Hurwitz and Delinah Blake Hurwitz, Patty and Robert Flournoy, Brian and Elizabeth Kuelbs, Laura Hogan, Jenny Aldisert, Lisa Aldisert, Sandy and Jim Brophy, Alessandra Brophy, Leah Goodman, Carolyn Clark, David Dean, DawnMarie Moe, Beth Karish, Victoria Vanderbilt and Tom Chaney, Margaret Winter, Cynthia Tarr, Hayley Andrus, David Corbett, Bob and Pat Crais, Kim Terranova, Anja Kubertschak, Jon McCormick, Madeira James, Tara Fields, Mary Anne Cook, Janet Hamilton, Heather Graham, Alexandra Sokoloff, the Killer Thriller Band, the Slush Pile Players, Patricia Waldo, the Book Club moms, the Yoga moms, Cath Carper, Writers Group (Bob, John, JB, Linda, Sharon, and Jamie), Space 7 in Alaska, Charlaine Harris, Laurie King, my TLC Blog sisters, Nancy Martin, Sarah Strohmeyer, Elaine Viets, the aforementioned Michele Martinez, and, especially in the middle of the night, Kathy Sweeney, helped me more than I can say. Thanks to all TLC commenters; to Gavin Polone; to Laura Swerdloff; to my kind and talented editor, Stacy Creamer; and my beautiful agent, Renée Zuckerbrot. And to Audrey, Louie, and Gia, for whom words aren't enough.